Praise for **New York Times** *bestselling author*
Maya Banks

"[Maya] Banks' story has it all: wit, charm, mystery
and sparkling chemistry between the characters."
—*RT Book Reviews* on *Billionaire's Contract Engagement*

"Banks does a great job of keeping to the core
of the characters and making
The Tycoon's Secret Affair work well."
—*The Romance Reader.com*

"Banks has an extraordinarily moving romance with
wonderfully charismatic protagonists on her hands."
—*RT Book Reviews* on *The Tycoon's Secret Affair*

Praise for *USA TODAY* **bestselling author**
Carol Marinelli

"Carol Marinelli illustrates how life is full of
surprises and you never know who will end up being
your soul mate."
—*RT Book Reviews* on *Expecting His Love-Child*

"Be prepared for a sensual trip to a faraway land
enhanced by lyrical dialogue, fulfilling all fantasies
of romancing an Arabian prince."
—*RT Book Reviews* on *Heart of the Desert*

MAYA BANKS

has loved romance novels from a very (very) early age, and almost from the start, she dreamed of writing them, as well. In her teens she filled countless notebooks with overdramatic stories of love and passion. Today her stories are only slightly less dramatic, but no less romantic.

She lives in Texas with her husband and three children and wouldn't contemplate living anywhere other than the South. When she's not writing, she's usually hunting, fishing or playing poker. She loves to hear from her readers, and she can be found on Facebook, or you can follow her on Twitter (@maya_banks). Her website, www.mayabanks.com, is where you can find up-to-date information on all of Maya's current and upcoming releases.

CAROL MARINELLI

Originally from England, Carol now lives in Melbourne, Australia. She adores going back to the U.K. for a visit—actually, she adores going anywhere for a visit—and constantly (expensively) strives to overcome her fear of flying. She has three gorgeous children who are growing up so fast (too fast—they've just worked out that she lies about her age!) and keep her busy with a never-ending round of homework, sports and friends coming over.

A nurse and an author, Carol writes for the Harlequin® Presents and Medical Romance lines and is passionate about both. She loves the fast-paced, busy setting of a modern hospital, but every now and then admits it's bliss to escape to the glamorous, alluring world of her Presents heroes and heroines. A bit like her real life actually!

For more on Carol and her latest releases, visit her website, www.carolmarinelli.com.

BESTSELLING AUTHOR COLLECTION

New York Times Bestselling Author

MAYA BANKS

The Mistress

ISBN-13: 978-0-373-18061-5

THE MISTRESS
Copyright © 2012 by Harlequin Books S.A.

The publisher acknowledges the copyright holders of the individual works as follows:

THE MISTRESS
(Previously published as THE TYCOON'S PREGNANT MISTRESS)
Copyright © 2009 by Maya Banks

WANTED: MISTRESS AND MOTHER
Copyright © 2006 by The SAL Marinelli Trust Fund

This edition published by arrangement with Harlequin Books S.A.

For questions and comments about the quality of this book please contact us at CustomerService@Harlequin.com.

www.Harlequin.com

Printed in U.S.A.

CONTENTS

Dear Reader,

The Mistress (originally released as *The Tycoon's Pregnant Mistress*) marked my foray into Harlequin Desire. It was such an exciting moment for me to realize a long-held dream of writing the scrumptious, shorter contemporary stories that I loved so much. Marley and Chrysander hold a special place in my heart because they were that first couple I was able to write about, and I'm so thrilled that their story is being reissued and will be back in print.

Marley is my favorite kind of heroine—one who endures much but becomes stronger all the more for it. She's one who learns to stand up for herself and fight for her own happiness. I hope you enjoy reading *The Mistress* as much as I enjoyed writing it.

Much love,

Maya Banks

New York Times Bestselling Author

Maya Banks

THE MISTRESS

To Marty Matthews and Shara Cooper.

That bar conversation at RT 2007 was the first kick in the behind to do something about my long-standing dream of writing for Harlequin Desire. I still remember that gush-fest fondly.

Chapter 1

Pregnant.

Despite the warmth of the summer day, an uncomfortable chill settled over Marley Jameson's skin as she settled on the bench in the small garden just a few blocks from the apartment she shared with Chrysander Anetakis.

She shivered even as the sun's rays found her tightly clenched fingers, the heat not yet chasing away the goose bumps. Stavros wouldn't be happy over her brief disappearance. Neither would Chrysander when Stavros reported that she hadn't taken proper security measures. But dragging along the imposing guard to her doctor's appointment hadn't been an option. Chrysander would have known of her pregnancy before she could even return home to tell him herself.

How would he react to the news? Despite the fact they'd taken precautions, she was eight weeks pregnant. The best she could surmise, it had happened when he'd returned from an extended business trip overseas. Chrysander had been insatiable. But then so had she.

A bright blush chased the chill from her cheeks as she remembered the night in question. He had made love to her countless times, murmuring to her in Greek—warm, soft words that had made her heart twist.

She checked her watch and grimaced. He was due home in a few short hours, and yet here she sat like a coward, avoiding the confrontation. She still had to change out of the faded jeans and T-shirt, clothes she wore only when he was away.

With reluctance born of uncertainty, she forced herself to her feet and began the short walk to the luxurious building that housed Chrysander's apartment.

"You're being silly," she muttered under her breath as she neared the entry. If the doorman was surprised to see her on foot, he didn't show it, though he did hasten to usher her inside.

She stepped onto the elevator and smoothed a hand over her still-flat stomach. Nervousness scuttled through her chest as she rode higher. When it halted smoothly and the doors opened into the spacious foyer of the penthouse, Marley nibbled on her lip and left the elevator.

She walked into the living room, shedding her shoes as she made her way to the couch, where she tossed her bag down. Fatigue niggled at her muscles, and all she really wanted to do was lie down. But she had to determine how to broach the subject of their relationship with Chrysander.

A few days ago, she would have said she was perfectly content, but the results of today's blood tests had her shaken. Had her reflecting on the last six months with Chrysander.

She loved him wholeheartedly, but she wasn't entirely sure where she stood with him. He seemed devoted when

he was with her. The sex was fantastic. But now she had
a baby to think about. She needed more from the man she
loved than hot sex every few weeks as his schedule per-
mitted.

She trudged into the large master suite and started
when Chrysander walked from the bathroom, just a towel
wrapped around his waist.

A slow smile carved his handsome face. Every time she
laid eyes on him, it was like the first time all over again.
Goose bumps raced across her skin, lighting fire to her
every nerve-ending.

"Y-you're early," she managed to get out.

"I've been waiting for you, *pedhaki mou,*" he said huskily.

He let the towel drop, and she swallowed as her eyes
tracked downward to his straining erection. He paced
forward predatorily, closing rapidly in on her. His hands
curved over her shoulders, and he bent to ravage her mouth.

A soft moan escaped her as her knees buckled. He was
an addiction. One she could never get enough of. He had
only to touch her, and she went up in flames.

His mouth traveled down her jawline to her neck, his
fingers tugging impatiently at her shirt. Of their own ac-
cord, her fingers twisted in his dark hair, pulling him
closer.

Hard, lean, muscled. A gleaming predator. He moved
gracefully, masterfully playing her body like a finely tuned
instrument.

She clutched at his neck as he lowered her to the bed.

"You have entirely too many clothes on," he murmured
as he shoved her shirt up and over her head.

She knew they should stop. They needed to talk, but
she'd missed him. Ached for him. And maybe a part of her
wanted this moment before things changed irrevocably.

He released her bra, and she gasped when his fingers found her highly sensitized nipples. They were darker now, and she wondered if he'd notice.

"Did you miss me?"

"You know I did," she said breathlessly.

"I like to hear you say it."

"I missed you," she said, a smile curving her lips.

It shouldn't have surprised her that he made quick work of her clothing. He tossed her jeans across the room. Her bra went one way, her underwear the other. Then he was over her, on her, deep inside her.

She arched into him as he possessed her, clinging to him as he made love to her, their passion hot and aching. It was always like this. One step from desperation, their need for each other all consuming.

As he gathered her in his arms, he whispered to her in Greek. The words fell against her skin like a caress as they both reached their peaks. She snuggled into his body, content and sated.

She must have slept then, because when she opened her eyes, Chrysander was lying beside her, his arm thrown possessively over her hip. He regarded her lazily, his golden eyes burning with sated contentment.

Now was the time. She needed to broach the subject. There would never be a better occasion. Why did the thought of asking him about their relationship strike terror in her heart?

"Chrysander," she began softly.

"What is it?" he asked, his eyes narrowing. Had he heard the worry in her voice?

"I wanted to talk to you."

He stretched his big body and pulled slightly away so he could see her better. The sheet slid down to his hip and gathered there. She felt vulnerable and exposed and trembled when he slid his hand over the peak of one breast.

"What is it you want to talk about?"

"Us," she said simply.

His eyes grew wary and then became shuttered. His face locked into a mask of indifference, one that frightened her. She could feel him pulling away, mentally withdrawing from her.

A buzz sounded, startling her. Chrysander cursed under his breath and reached over to push the intercom.

"What," he demanded tersely.

"It's Roslyn. Can I come up?"

Marley stiffened at the sound of his personal assistant's voice. It was late in the evening and yet here she was, popping into the apartment she knew he shared with Marley.

"I'm very busy at the moment, Roslyn. Surely it can wait until I come into the office tomorrow."

"I'm sorry, sir, but it can't. I need your signature on a contract that's due by 7:00 a.m."

Again Chrysander swore. "Come then."

He swung his legs over the side of the bed and stood. He strode toward the polished mahogany wardrobe and pulled out slacks and a shirt.

"Why does she show up here so often?" Marley asked quietly.

Chrysander shot her a look of surprise. "She's my assistant. It's her job to keep up with me."

"At your personal residence?"

He shook his head as he buttoned up his shirt. "I'll return in a moment, and we can have our talk."

Marley watched him go, her chest aching all the more. She was tempted to save the discussion for another night, but she had to tell him of her pregnancy, and she couldn't tell him of the baby before she knew how he felt about her. What he thought of their future. So it had to be done tonight.

As the moments grew longer, her anxiety heightened. Not wanting the disadvantage of being nude, she rose from the bed and dragged on her jeans and shirt. So much for looking composed and beautiful. She shook her head ruefully.

Finally she heard his footsteps outside the bedroom suite. He walked in with a distracted frown on his face. His gaze flickered over her, and his lips twitched.

"I much prefer you naked, *pedhaki mou*."

She gave a shaky smile and moved back to the bed. "Is everything all right with work?"

He waved his hand dismissively. "Nothing that shouldn't have already been taken care of. A missing signature." He stalked toward the bed, a lean, hungry glint in his eyes. As he came to a stop a foot away from where she sat, he reached for the buttons on his shirt.

"Chrysander...we must talk."

Annoyance flickered across his face, but then he gave a resigned sigh. He sank down on the bed next to her. "Then speak, Marley. What is it that's bothering you?"

His closeness nearly unhinged her. She scooted down the bed in an effort to put distance between them. "I want to know how you feel about me, how you feel about us," she began nervously. "And if we have a future."

She glanced up to check his reaction. His lips came together in a firm line as he stared back at her. "So it's come to this," he said grimly.

He stood and turned his back to her before finally rotating around to face her.

"Come to w-what? I just need to know how you feel about me. If we have a future. You never speak of us in anything but the present," she finished lamely.

He leaned in close to her and cupped her chin. "We don't have a relationship. I don't do relationships, and you know this. You're my mistress."

Why did she feel as though he'd just slapped her? Her mouth fell open against his hand, and she stared up at him with wide, shocked eyes.

"Mistress?" she croaked. Live-in lover. Girlfriend. Woman he was seeing. These were all terms she might have used. But mistress? A woman he bought? A woman he paid to have sex with?

Nausea welled in her stomach.

She pushed his hand away and stumbled up, backpedaling away from him. Confusion shone on Chrysander's face.

"Is that truly all I am to you?" she choked out, still unable to comprehend his declaration. "A m-mistress?"

He sighed impatiently. "You're distraught. Sit down and let me get you something to drink. I've had a trying week, and you are obviously unwell. It benefits neither of us to have this discussion right now."

Chrysander urged her back to the bed then strode out of the suite toward the kitchen. After a long week of laying traps for the person attempting to sell his company out from under him, the last thing he wanted was a hysterical confrontation with his mistress.

He poured a glass of Marley's favorite juice then prepared himself a liberal dose of brandy. The beginnings of a headache were already plaguing him.

He smiled when he saw Marley's shoes in the middle of the floor where she'd left them as soon as she'd come off the elevator. He followed the trail of her things to the couch where her bag was thrown haphazardly.

She was a creature of comfort. Never fussy. So this emotional outburst had caught him off guard. It was completely out of character for her. She wasn't clingy, which is why their relationship had lasted so long. Relationship? He'd just denied to her that they had one. She was his mistress.

He should have softened his response. She probably wasn't feeling well and needed tenderness from him. He winced at the idea, but she'd always been there ready to soothe him after weeks of business trips or tedious meetings. It was only fair that he offer something more than sex. Though sex with her was high on his list of priorities.

He turned to go back into the bedroom and try to make amends when the piece of paper sticking out of Marley's bag caught his eye. He stopped and frowned then set the drinks down on the coffee table.

Dread tightened his chest. It couldn't be.

He reached out to snag the papers, yanked them open as anger, hot and volatile, surged in his veins. Marley, *his* Marley, was the traitor within his company?

He wanted to deny it. Wanted to crumple the evidence and throw it away. But it was there, staring him in the face. The false information he'd planted just this morning in hopes of finding the person selling his secrets to his competitor had been taken by Marley. She hadn't wasted any time.

Suddenly everything became clear. His building plans had started disappearing about the time that Marley had moved in to the penthouse. She'd worked for his company, and even after he'd convinced her to quit so that her time would be his alone, she still had unimpeded access to his offices. What a fool he'd been.

Stavros's call to him hours earlier stuck in his mind like a dagger. At the time, it had only registered a mild annoyance with him, a matter he'd planned to take up with Marley when he saw her. He'd lecture her about being careless, about being safe, when in fact, it was him who wasn't safe with her. She'd gone to his office then disappeared for several hours. And now documents from his office had appeared in her purse.

The papers fisted in his hand, he stalked back to the bedroom to see Marley still sitting on the bed. She turned her tear-stained face up to him, and all he could see was how deftly she'd manipulated him.

"I want you out in thirty minutes," he said flatly.

Marley stared at him in shock. Had she heard him correctly? "I don't understand," she choked out.

"You have thirty minutes in which to collect your things before I call security to escort you out."

She shot to her feet. How could things have gone so wrong? She hadn't even told him about her pregnancy yet. "Chrysander, what's wrong? Why are you so angry with me? Is it because I reacted so badly to you calling me your mistress? It came as a great shock to me. I thought somehow I meant more to you than that."

"You now have twenty-eight minutes," he said coldly. He held up a hand with several crumpled sheets of paper in them. "How did you think you'd get away with it, Marley? Do you honestly think I would tolerate you betraying me? I have no tolerance for cheats or liars, and you, my dear, are both."

All the blood left her face. She wavered precariously, but he made no move to aid her. "I don't know what you're talking about. What are those papers?"

His lips curled into a contemptuous sneer. "You stole from me. You're lucky that I'm not phoning the authorities. As it is, if I ever see you again, I'll do just that. Your attempts could have crippled my company. But the joke is on you. These are fakes planted by me in an attempt to ferret out the culprit."

"Stole?" Her voice rose in agitation. She reached out and

yanked the papers from his hand. The words, schematics, blurred before her eyes. An internal e-mail, printed out, obviously from his company ISP address, stared back at her. Sensitive information. Detailed building plans for an upcoming bid in a major international city. Photocopies of the drawings. None of it made sense.

She raised her head and stared him in the eye as her world crumbled and shattered around her. "You think I stole these?"

"They were in your bag. Don't insult us both by denying it now. I want you out of here." He made a show of checking his watch. "You now have twenty-five minutes remaining."

The knot in her throat swelled and stuck, rendering her incapable of drawing a breath. She couldn't think, couldn't react. Numbly, she headed for the door with no thought of collecting her things. She only wanted to be away. She paused and put her hand on the frame to steady herself before turning around to look back at Chrysander. His face remained implacable. The lines around his mouth and eyes were hard and unforgiving.

"How could you think I'd do something like that?" she whispered before she turned and walked away.

She stumbled blindly into the elevator, quiet sobs ripping from her throat as she rode it down to the lobby level. The doorman looked at her in concern and offered to get her into a cab. She waved him off and walked unsteadily down the sidewalk and into the night.

The warm evening air blew over her face. The tears on her cheeks chilled her skin, but she paid them no heed. He would listen to her. She would make him. She'd give him the night to calm down, but she would be heard. It was all such a dreadful mistake. There had to be some way to make him see reason.

In her distress, she took no notice of the man following her. When she reached the curb, a hand shot out and grasped her arm. Her cry of alarm was muffled as a cloth sack was yanked over her head.

She struggled wildly, but just as quickly, she found herself stuffed into the backseat of a vehicle. She heard the door slam and the rumble of low voices, and then the vehicle drove away.

Chapter 2

Three months later

Chrysander sat in his apartment brooding in silence. He should have some peace of mind now that there was no longer any danger to his company, but the knowledge of why was hardly comforting. He stared at the pile of documents in front of him as the evening news droned in the background.

His stopover in New York was going to be short. Tomorrow he'd fly to London to meet with his brother Theron and have the groundbreaking ceremony for their luxury hotel—a hotel that wouldn't have happened if Marley had gotten her way. A derisive snort nearly rolled from his throat. He, the CEO of Anetakis International, had been manipulated and stolen from by a woman. Because of her, he and his brothers had lost two of their designs to their closest competitor before he'd discovered her betrayal. He should have turned her over to the authorities, but he'd been too stunned, too *weak* to do such a thing.

He hadn't even ridded his apartment of her belongings. He'd assumed she'd return to collect them, and maybe a small part of him had hoped she would so he could confront her again and ask her why. On his next trip back, he'd see to the task. It was time to have her out of his mind completely.

When he heard her name amidst the jumble of his thoughts, he thought he'd merely conjured it from his dark musings, but when he heard Marley Jameson's name yet again, he focused his angry attention on the television.

A news reporter stood outside a local hospital, and it took a few moments for the buzzing in Chrysander's ears to stop long enough for him to comprehend what was being said. The scene changed as they rolled footage taken earlier of a woman being taken out of a rundown apartment building on a stretcher. He leaned forward, his face twisted in disbelief. It was Marley.

He bolted from his desk and fumbled for the remote to turn the volume up. So stunned was he that he only comprehended every fourth word or so, but he heard enough.

Marley had been abducted and now rescued. The details on the who and why were still sketchy, but she'd endured a long period of captivity. He tensed in expectation that somehow his name would be linked to hers, but then why should it? Their relationship had been a highly guarded secret, a necessary one in his world. His wish for privacy was one born of desire and necessity. Only after her betrayal had he been even more relieved by the circumspection he utilized in all his relationships. She'd made a fool of him, and only the knowledge that the rest of the world didn't know soothed him.

As the camera zoomed in on her pale, frightened face,

he felt something inside him twist painfully. She looked the same as she had the night he'd confronted her with her deception. Pale, shocked and vulnerable.

But what the reporter said next stopped him cold, even as an uneasy sensation rippled up his spine. He reported mother *and* child being listed in stable condition and that Marley's apparent captivity had not harmed her pregnancy. The reporter offered only the guess that she appeared to be four or five months along. Other details were sketchy. No arrests had been made, as her captors had escaped.

"Theos mou," he murmured even as he struggled to grasp the implications.

He stood and reached for his cellular phone as he strode from his apartment. When he broke from the entrance of the well-secured apartment high-rise, his driver had just pulled around.

Once inside the vehicle, he again flipped open his phone and called the hospital where Marley had been taken.

"Her physical condition is satisfactory," the doctor informed Chrysander. "However, it is her emotional state that concerns me."

He simmered impatiently as he waited for the physician to complete his report. Chrysander had burst into the hospital, demanding answers as soon as he'd walked onto the floor where Marley was being treated. Only the statement that he was her fiancé had finally netted him any results. Then he'd immediately had her transferred to a private room and had insisted that a specialist be called in to see her. Now he had to wade through the doctor's assessment of her condition before he could see her.

"But she hasn't been harmed," Chrysander said.

"I didn't say that," the doctor murmured. "I merely said her physical condition is not serious."

"Then quit beating around the bush and tell me what I need to know."

The doctor studied him for a moment before laying the clipboard down on his desk. "Miss Jameson has endured a great trauma. I cannot know exactly how great, because she cannot remember anything of her captivity."

"What?" Chrysander stared at the doctor in stunned disbelief.

"Worse, she remembers nothing before. She knows her name and little else, I'm afraid. Even her pregnancy has come as a shock to her."

Chrysander ran a hand through his hair and swore in three languages. "She remembers nothing? Nothing at all?"

The doctor shook his head. "I'm afraid not. She's extremely vulnerable. Fragile. Which is why it's so important that you do not upset her. She has a baby to carry for four more months and an ordeal from which to recover."

Chrysander made a sound of impatience. "Of course I would do nothing to upset her. I just find it hard to believe that she remembers nothing."

The doctor shook his head. "The experience has obviously been very traumatic for her. I suspect it's her mind's way of protecting her. It's merely shut down until she can better cope with all that has happened."

"Did they…" Chrysander couldn't even bring himself to complete the question, and yet he had to know. "Did they hurt her?"

The doctor's expression softened. "I found no evidence that she had been mistreated in any way. Physically. There is no way to find out all she has endured until she is able to tell us. And we must be patient and not press her before she is ready. As I said, she is extremely fragile, and if pressed too hard, too fast, the results could be devastating."

Chrysander cursed softly. "I understand. I will see to it that she has the best possible care. Now can I see her?"

The doctor hesitated. "You can see her. However, I would caution you not to be too forthcoming with the details of her abduction."

A frown creased Chrysander's brow as he stared darkly at the physician. "You want me to lie to her?"

"I merely don't want you to upset her. You can give her details of her life. Her day-to-day activities. How you met. The mundane things. It is my suggestion, however, and I've conferred with the hospital psychiatrist on this matter, that you not rush to give her the details of her captivity and how she came to lose her memory. In fact, we know very little, so it would be unwise to speculate or offer her information that could be untrue. She must be kept calm. I don't like to think of what another upset could cause her in her current state."

Chrysander nodded reluctantly. What the doctor said made sense, but his own need to know what had happened to Marley was pressing. But he wouldn't push her if it would cause her or the baby any harm. He checked his watch. He still had to meet with the authorities, but first he wanted to see Marley and said as much to the doctor.

The physician nodded. "I'll have the nurse take you up now."

Marley struggled underneath the layers of fog surrounding her head. She murmured a low protest when she opened her eyes. Awareness was not what she sought. The blanket of dark, of oblivion, was what she wanted.

There was nothing for her in wakefulness. Her life was one black hole of nothingness. Her name was all that lingered in the confusing layers of her mind. Marley.

She searched for more. Answers she needed to questions that swarmed her every time she wakened. Her past lay like a great barren landscape before her. The answers dangled beyond her, taunting her and escaping before she could reach out and take hold.

She turned her head on the thin pillow, fully intending to slip back into the void of sleep when a firm hand grasped hers. Fear scurried up her spine until she remembered that she was safe and in a hospital. Still, she yanked her hand away as her chest rose and fell with her quick breaths.

"You must not go back to sleep, *pedhaki mou.* Not yet."

The man's voice slid across her skin, leaving warmth in its wake. Carefully, she turned to face this stranger— or was he? Was he someone she knew? Who knew her? Could he be the father of the child nestled below her heart?

Her hand automatically felt for her rounded belly as her gaze lighted on the man who'd spoken to her.

He was a dominating presence. Tall, lithe, dangerously intent as his amber eyes stared back at her. He wasn't American. She nearly laughed at the absurdity of her thoughts. She should be demanding to know who he was and why he was here, and yet all she could muster was the knowledge that he wasn't American?

"Our baby is fine," he said as his gaze dropped to the hand she had cupped protectively over her abdomen.

She tensed as she realized that he was indeed staking a claim. Shouldn't she know him? She reached for something, some semblance of recognition, but unease and fear were all she found.

"Who are you?" she finally managed to whisper.

Something flickered in those golden eyes, but he kept his expression neutral. Had she hurt him with the knowledge she didn't know him? She tried to put herself in his position. Tried to imagine how she'd feel if the father of her baby suddenly couldn't remember her.

He pulled a chair to the side of the bed and settled his large frame into it. He reached for her hand, and this time, despite her instinct to do so, she didn't retract it.

"I am Chrysander Anetakis. Your fiancé."

She searched his face for the truth of his words, but he looked back at her calmly, with no hint of emotion.

"I'm sorry," she said and swallowed when her voice cracked. "I don't remember...."

"I know. I've spoken to the doctor. What you remember isn't important right now. What is important is that you rest and recover so that I can take you home."

She licked her lips, panic threatening to overtake her. "Home?"

He nodded. "Yes, home."

"Where is that?" She hated having to ask. Hated that she was lying here conversing with a complete stranger. Only apparently he wasn't. He was someone she had been intimate with. Obviously in love with. They were engaged, and she was pregnant with his child. Shouldn't that stir something inside her?

"You're trying too hard, *pedhaki mou*," he said softly. "I can see the strain on your face. You mustn't rush things. The doctor said that it will all come back in time."

She clutched his hand then looked down at their linked fingers. "Will it? What if it doesn't?" Fear rose in her chest, tightening her throat uncomfortably. She struggled to breathe.

Chrysander reached out a hand to touch her face. "Calm yourself, Marley. Your distress does you and the baby no good."

Hearing her name on his lips did odd things. It felt as though he was speaking of a stranger even though she did remember her name. But maybe in the madness of her memory loss, she'd been afraid that she'd gotten that part wrong, and that along with everything else, her name was a forgotten piece of her life.

"Can you tell me something about me? Anything?"

She was precariously close to begging, and tears knotted her throat and stung her eyes.

"There will be plenty of time for us to talk later," Chrysander soothed. He stroked her forehead, pushing back her hair. "For now, rest. I'm making preparations to take you home."

It was the second time he'd mentioned home, and she realized that he still hadn't told her where that was.

"Where is home?" she asked again.

His lips thinned for just a moment, and then his expression eased. "Home for us has been here in the city. My business takes me away often, but we had an apartment together here. My plan is to take you to my island as soon as you are well enough to travel."

Her brows furrowed as she sought to comprehend the oddity of his statement. It sounded so…impersonal. There was no emotion, no hint of joy, just a sterile recitation of fact.

As if sensing she was about to ask more questions, he bent over and pressed his lips to her forehead. "Rest, *pedhaki mou*. I have arrangements to make. The doctor says you can be released in a few days' time if all goes well."

She closed her eyes wearily and nodded. He stood there a moment, and then she heard his footsteps retreating. When her door closed, she opened her eyes again, only to feel the damp trail of tears against her cheeks.

She should feel relief that she wasn't alone. Somehow, though, Chrysander Anetakis's presence hadn't reassured her as it should. She felt more apprehensive than ever, and she couldn't say why.

She pulled the thin sheet higher around her body and

closed her eyes, willing the peaceful numbness of sleep to take over once more.

When she woke again, a nurse was standing by her bedside placing a cuff around her arm to take her blood pressure.

"Oh, good, you're awake," she said cheerfully as she removed the cuff. "I have your dinner tray. Do you feel up to eating?"

Marley shook her head. The thought of food made her faintly nauseous.

"Leave the tray. I'll see to it she eats."

Marley looked up in surprise to see Chrysander looming behind the nurse, a determined look on his face. The nurse turned and smiled at him then reached back and patted Marley's arm.

"You're very lucky to have such a devoted fiancé," she said as she turned to go.

"Yes, lucky," Marley murmured, and she wondered why she suddenly felt the urge to weep.

When the door shut behind the nurse, Chrysander pulled the chair closer to her bed again. Then he settled the tray in front of her.

"You should eat."

She eyed him nervously. "I don't feel much like eating."

"Do you find my presence unsettling?" he queried as his gaze slid over her rumpled form.

"I—" She opened her mouth to say no, but found she couldn't entirely deny it. How to tell this man she found him intimidating? This was supposed to be someone she loved. Had made love with. Just the thought sent a blush up her neck and over her cheeks.

"What are you thinking?" His fingers found her hand and stroked absently.

She turned her face away, hoping to find relief from his scrutiny. "N-nothing."

"You are frightened. That's understandable."

She turned back to look at him. "It doesn't make you angry that I'm frightened of you? Quite frankly, I'm terrified. I don't remember you or anything else in my life. I'm pregnant with your child and cannot for the life of me remember how I got this way!" Her fists gripped the sheet and held it protectively against her.

His lips pressed to a firm line. *Was* he angry? Was he putting on a front so as not to upset her further?

"It is as you said. You don't remember me, therefore I am a stranger to you. It will be up to me to earn your... trust." He said the last word as if he found it distasteful, and yet his expression remained controlled.

"Chrysander..." She said his name experimentally, letting it roll off her tongue. It didn't feel foreign, but neither did it spark any remembrance. Frustration took firm hold when her mind remained frightfully blank.

"Yes, *pedhaki mou?*"

She blinked as she realized he was waiting for her to continue.

"What happened to me?" she asked. "How did I get here? How did I lose my memory?"

Once again he took her hand in his, and she found the gesture comforting. He leaned forward and touched his other hand to her cheek. "You shouldn't rush things. The doctor is quite adamant in this. Right now the most important thing for you and our child is to take things slowly. Everything will come back in its own time."

She sighed, realizing he wasn't going to budge.

"Get some rest." He stood and leaned over to brush his lips across her forehead. "Soon we will leave this place."

Marley wished the words gave her more reassurance

than they did. Instead of comfort, confusion and uncertainty rose sharply in her chest until she feared smothering with the anxiety.

Sweat broke out on her forehead, and the food she'd picked at just moments ago rolled in her stomach. Chrysander looked sharply at her, and without saying a word, he rang for the nurse.

Moments later, the nurse bustled in. At the sight of her, sympathy crowded her features. She placed a cool hand on Marley's forehead even as she administered an injection with the other.

"You mustn't panic," the nurse soothed. "You're safe now."

But her words failed to ease the tightness in Marley's chest. How could they when soon she was going to be thrust into an unknown world with a man who was a complete stranger to her?

Chrysander stood by her bed, staring down at her, his hand covering hers. The medication dulled her senses, and she could feel herself floating away, the fear evaporating like mist. His words were the last thing she heard.

"Sleep, *pedhaki mou.* I will watch over you."

Oddly, she did find comfort in the quiet vow.

Chrysander stood in the darkened room and watched as Marley slept. The strain of the frown he was wearing inserted a dull ache in his temples.

Her chest rose and fell with her slight breaths, and even in sleep, tension furrowed her brow. He moved closer and touched his fingers to her forehead, smoothing them across the pale skin.

She was as lovely as ever, even in her weakened state. Raven curls lay haphazardly against the pillow. He took one between his fingers and moved it from her forehead.

It was longer now, no longer the shorter cap of curls that had flown about her head as she laughed or smiled.

Her skin had lost its previous glow, but he knew restoring her health would bring it back. Her eyes had been dull, frightened, but he remembered well the brilliant blue sparkle, how enchanting she looked when she was happy.

He cursed and moved away from the bed. It had all been a ruse. She hadn't ever been happy. Truly happy. It seemed he'd been incapable of making her so. All the time they were together, she'd plotted against him, stolen from him and his brothers.

Though he'd considered her his mistress, he'd never placed her in the same category as his others. What he'd shared with her hadn't been mercenary, or so he'd thought. In the end, it had boiled down to money and betrayal. Something he was well used to with women.

Yet he still wanted her. She still burned in his veins, an addiction he wasn't equipped to fight. He shook his head grimly. She was pregnant with his child, and that must take precedence above all else. They would be forced together by the child, their futures irrevocably intertwined. But he didn't have to like it, and he didn't have to surrender anything more than his protection and his body.

If she would once again be placed under his protection, then he'd do all he could to ensure she had the best care, her and their baby, but he'd never trust her. She would warm his bed, and he wouldn't lie and say that prospect wasn't appealing. But she would get nothing more from him.

Chapter 3

Two days later, Marley sat nervously in a wheelchair, her fingers clutched tightly around the blanket the nurse had draped over her lap. Chrysander stood to the side, listening intently as the nurse gave him the aftercare instructions. Marley fingered the maternity top that one of the nurses had kindly provided for her and smoothed the wrinkles over the bump of her abdomen. They'd all been exceedingly kind to her, and she feared leaving their kindness to venture into the unknown.

When the nurse was finished, Chrysander grasped the handles of the wheelchair and began pushing Marley down the hallway toward the entrance. She blinked as the bright sunshine speared her vision. A sleek limousine was parked a few feet away, and Chrysander walked briskly toward it. The driver stepped around to open the door just as Chrysander effortlessly plucked her from the wheelchair and ushered her inside the heated interior. In a matter of seconds, they were gliding away from the hospital.

Marley stared out the window as they navigated the busy New York streets. The city itself was familiar. She could remember certain shops and landmarks. She possessed a knowledge of the city, but what was missing was the idea that this was home, that she belonged here. Hadn't Chrysander said they'd lived here? She felt like an artist staring at an empty canvas without the skills to paint the portrait.

When they pulled to a stop in front of a stylish, modern building, Chrysander bolted from the limousine while the doorman opened the door on her side. Chrysander reached inside and carefully drew her from the vehicle. She stepped to the sidewalk on shaky feet, and he tucked her to his side, a strong arm around her waist as they walked through the entrance.

A wave of déjà vu swept over her as the elevator opened and he helped her inside. For the briefest of moments, her memory stirred, and she struggled to part the veils of darkness.

"What is it?" Chrysander demanded.

"I've done this before," she murmured.

"You remember?"

She shook her head. "No. It just feels…familiar. I know I've been here."

His fingers curled tighter around her arm. "This is where we lived…for many months. It's only natural that it should register something."

The elevator opened, and she cocked her head as he started forward. His phrasing had been odd. Had they not lived here just a short time ago? Before whatever accident had befallen her?

He stopped and held out his hand to her. "Come, Marley. We're home."

She slid her fingers into his as he pulled her forward

into the lavish foyer. To her surprise, a woman met them as they started for the large living room. Marley faltered as the tall blond young woman put a hand on Chrysander's arm and smiled.

"Welcome home, Mr. Anetakis. I've laid out all contracts requiring your signature on your desk as well as ordered your phone messages by priority. I also took the liberty of having dinner delivered." She swept an assessing look over Marley, one that had Marley feeling obscure and insignificant. "I didn't imagine you'd be up for going out after a trying few days."

Marley frowned as she realized the woman was implying that Chrysander had been through the ordeal and not Marley.

"Thank you, Roslyn," Chrysander said. "You shouldn't have gone to the trouble." He turned to Marley and pulled her closer to him. "Marley, this is Roslyn Chambers, my personal assistant."

Marley gave a faltering smile.

"Delighted to see you again, Miss Jameson," Roslyn said sweetly. "It's been ages since I last saw you. Months, I believe."

"Roslyn," Chrysander said in a warning voice. Her smile never slipped as she looked innocently at Chrysander.

Marley glanced warily between them, her confusion mounting. The ease with which the woman moved around the apartment that Chrysander called home to both of them was clear, and yet Roslyn hadn't seen Marley in months? The proprietary way his assistant looked at him was the only thing currently clear to Marley.

"I'll leave you two," Roslyn said with a gracious smile. "I'm sure you have a lot of catching up to do." She turned to Chrysander and put a delicate hand on his arm once more. "Call me if you need anything. I'll come straight over."

"Thank you," Chrysander murmured.

The tall blonde clicked across the polished Italian marble in her elegant heels and entered the elevator. She smiled at Chrysander as the doors closed.

Marley licked her suddenly dry lips and looked away. Chrysander was stiff at her side as though he expected Marley to react in some way. She wasn't stupid enough to do so now. Not when he was so on guard. Later, she would ask him the million questions whirling around her tired mind.

"Come, you should be in bed," Chrysander said as he curled an arm around her.

"I've had quite enough of bed," she said firmly.

"Then you should at least get comfortable on the sofa. I'll bring you a tray so you can eat."

Eat. Rest. Eat some more. Those dictates seemed to compose Chrysander's sole aim when it came to her. She sighed and allowed him to lead her into the living area. He settled her on the soft leather couch and retrieved a blanket to cover her with.

There was a stiffness about him that puzzled her, but then she supposed if the roles were reversed and he'd forgotten her, she wouldn't be very sure of herself, either. He left the room, and several minutes later returned with a tray that he set before her on the coffee table. Steam rose from the bowl of soup, but she wasn't tempted by the offering. She was too unsettled.

He sat in a chair diagonally to her, but after a few moments, he rose and paced the room like a restless predator. His fingers tugged at his tie as he loosened it and then unbuttoned the cuffs of his silk shirt.

"Your assistant…Roslyn…said she left work for you?"

He turned to face her, his eyebrows wrinkling as he frowned. "Work can wait."

She sighed. "Do you plan to watch me nap then? I'll be fine, Chrysander. You can't hover over me every moment of the day. If there are things that require your attention, then by all means see to them."

Indecision flickered across his handsome face. "I do have things to do before we leave New York."

A surge of panic hit her unaware. She swallowed and worked to keep her expression bland. "We'll be leaving soon then?"

He nodded. "I thought to give you a few days to rest and more fully recover before we go. I've arranged for my jet to fly us to Greece, and then we'll take a helicopter out to the island. My staff is preparing for our arrival as we speak."

She stared uneasily at him. "Just how wealthy are you?"

He looked surprised by the question. "My family owns a chain of hotels."

The Anetakis name floated in her memory, what little of it there was. Images of the opulent hotel in the heart of the city came to mind. Celebrities, royalty, some of the world's wealthiest people stayed at Imperial Park. But he couldn't be *that* Anetakis, could he?

She paled and clenched her fingers to control the shaking. They were only the richest hotel family in the world. "How… how on earth did you and I…" She couldn't even bring herself to complete the thought. Then she frowned. Had she come from such a family?

Fatigue swamped her, and she dug her fingers into her temples as she fought the tiredness. Chrysander was beside her in an instant. He picked her up as though she weighed nothing and carried her into the bedroom. He carefully laid her on the bed, his eyes bright with concern. "Rest now, *pedhaki mou.*"

She nodded and curled into the comfortable bed, her eyes already closing with exhaustion. Thinking hurt. Trying to remember sapped every ounce of her strength.

Chrysander slumped in his chair and ran a hand through his hair. He fingered the list of phone messages as his gaze lighted on the one from his brother Theron. There was a message from his other brother, Piers, as well.

He shifted uncomfortably and knew he wouldn't be able to put them off for long. They would have gotten his messages by now and be curious. How he was going to explain this mess to them and also explain why he was taking the woman who had tried to damage their business home to Greece was beyond him.

With a grimace, he picked up the phone and dialed Theron's number.

He spoke rapidly in Greek when his brother answered. "How did the groundbreaking go?"

"Chrysander, finally," Theron said dryly. "I wondered if I was going to have to fly over to beat answers from you."

Chrysander sighed and grunted in response.

"Do hold while I get Piers on the phone. It'll save you another call. I know he's as interested in your explanation as I am."

"Since when do I answer to my *younger* brothers?" Chrysander growled.

Theron chuckled and a moment later Piers's voice bled through the line. He didn't bandy words.

"Chrysander, what the hell is going on? I got your message, and judging by the fact you never showed up in London, I can only assume that you're otherwise occupied in New York."

Chrysander pinched the bridge of his nose between his

fingers and closed his eyes. "It would appear that the two of you are going to be uncles."

Silence greeted his statement.

"You're sure it's yours?" Theron finally asked.

Chrysander grimaced. "She's five months pregnant, and five months ago, I was the only man in her bed. This I know."

"Like you knew she was stealing from us?" Piers retorted.

"Shut up, Piers," Theron said mildly. "The important question is, what are you going to do? She obviously can't be trusted. What does she have to say for herself?"

Chrysander's head pounded a bit harder. "There is a complication," he muttered. "She doesn't remember anything."

Both brothers made a sound of disbelief. "Quite convenient, wouldn't you say?" Piers interjected.

"She's leading you around by the balls," Theron said in disgust.

"I found it hard to believe myself," Chrysander admitted. "But I've seen her. She's here…in our—my apartment. Her memory loss is real." There was no way she could fake the abject vulnerability, the confusion and pain that clouded her once-vibrant blue eyes. The knowledge of her pain bothered him when it shouldn't. She deserved to suffer as she'd made him suffer.

Piers made a rude noise.

"What do you plan to do?" Theron asked.

Chrysander braced himself for their objections. "We're flying out to the island as soon as I feel she's well enough. It's a more suitable place for her recovery, and it's out of the public eye."

"Can't you install her somewhere until the baby comes and then get rid of her?" Piers demanded. "We lost two multimillion dollar deals because of her, and now our designs are going up under our competitor's name."

What he didn't say but Chrysander heard as loudly as if his brother had spoken the words was that they had lost those deals because Chrysander had been blinded by a woman he was sleeping with. It was as much his fault as it was Marley's. He'd let his brothers down in the worst way. Risked what they'd spent years working to achieve.

"I cannot leave her right now," Chrysander said carefully. "She has no family. No one who could care for her. She carries my child, and to that end, I will do whatever it takes to ensure the baby's health and safety. The doctor feels her memory loss is only temporary, merely a coping mechanism for the trauma she has endured."

"What do the authorities have to say about her abduction?" Piers asked. "Do you know why yet, and who was responsible?"

"I spoke briefly with them at the hospital, and I have a meeting with the detective in charge of the investigation tomorrow," Chrysander said grimly. "I hope to find out more then. I'll also tell them of my plans to take her out of the country. I have to think of her safety, and that of the baby."

"I can see you're already decided in this," Theron said quietly.

"Yes."

Piers made a sound as though he'd protest but was cut off when Theron spoke once more. "Do what you have to do, Chrysander. Piers and I can handle things. And for what it's worth, congratulations on becoming a father."

"Thanks," Chrysander murmured as he pressed the button to end the call.

He set the phone aside. Instead of making him feel any better about the situation, his discussion with his brothers had only reinforced how impossible things were. He didn't doubt that Marley didn't remember him or the fact that she'd stolen from him. Her confusion couldn't possibly be that feigned.

Which left him with the only choice he had, one he'd made the instant he'd known she was pregnant with his child. He would keep her close to him, take care of her, ensure she had the best care possible. He'd hire someone to stay with her when he couldn't be there and to provide the more intimate details of her care. It would enable him to keep her at arm's length while still keeping a close watch on her progress. And he would set aside, for now, the anger over her betrayal.

Chapter 4

The next morning, Marley sat across from Chrysander as he watched her eat breakfast. He nodded approvingly when she managed to finish the omelet he'd prepared, and he urged her to drink the glass of juice in front of her.

Despite her anxiety and uncertainty, it felt good to be taken care of by this man. Even if she wasn't entirely sure of her place in his world. He was solicitous of her, but at the same time he seemed distant. She wasn't sure if it was out of deference to her memory loss, and he had no wish to frighten her, or if this was simply the normal course of their relationship.

She caught her bottom lip between her teeth and nibbled absently. The idea that this could be ordinary bothered her. Surely she hadn't desired marriage with someone who treated her so politely, as though she were a stranger.

And yet, for all intents and purposes, they were strangers. At least he was to her. A flood of sympathy rolled through her. How awful it had to be for him to have his fiancée, a woman he loved and planned to marry, just forget him, as though he never existed. She couldn't imagine being in his shoes.

He'd watched her closely through breakfast, and she knew she must be broadcasting her unease, but he said nothing until he'd cleared their dishes away and taken her into the living room. He settled her on the couch and then sat next to her, his stare probing.

"What is concerning you this morning, Marley?" Chrysander asked.

His gaze passed over her face, and his expression left her faintly breathless.

"I was just thinking how perfectly rotten this whole thing must be for you."

One eyebrow rose, and he tilted his head questioningly. He looked surprised, as though it were the last thing he'd expected her to say.

"What do you mean?"

She looked down, suddenly shy and even more uncertain. He reached over and touched his fingers to her chin. He slid them further underneath and tugged until she met his gaze.

"Tell me why things are so horrible for me."

When put like that, it sounded ridiculous. Here was a man who could have, and probably did have, anything he wanted. Power, wealth, respect. And yet she presumed to think it was so terrible that his mousy fiancée couldn't remember him. It would have been enough to make her laugh if she hadn't felt so forlorn.

"I was trying to imagine myself in your place," she said sadly. "What it feels like when someone you love forgets you." His thumb rubbed over her lips, and a pecu-

liar tingling raced down her spine. "I think I would feel...
rejected."

"You're worried that I feel rejected?" Faint amusement
flickered in his eyes, and a smile hovered near the corners of his mouth.

"You don't?" she asked. And did it matter? She hated
this lack of confidence. Not only was her memory of
this man stolen, but any faith she had in who she was
to him had been erased, as well. She hated the idea that
she couldn't speak of their relationship frankly because
she worried that she might make errant assumptions and
look a fool.

Embarrassment crept over her cheeks, leaving them
tight and heated as he continued to stare at her.

"You cannot help what happened to you, Marley. I don't
blame you, and neither do I harbor resentment. It would
be petty of me."

No, she couldn't see him as petty. Dangerous. A little
frightening. But not petty. Was she afraid of him? She
shivered lightly. No, it wasn't him she was afraid of. It was
the idea that she could have been so intimate with a man
such as him and not remember it. She couldn't imagine
ever forgetting such an experience.

"What happened to me, Chrysander?" A note of pleading crept into her voice. Her hands shook, and she clenched
them together to disguise her unease.

He sighed. "You had...an accident, *pedhaki mou*. The
doctor assures me your memory loss is only temporary
and that it's imperative for you not to overtax yourself."

"Was I in a car accident?" Even as she asked, she
glanced down, searching for signs of injury, bruising. But
she had no muscle soreness, no stiffness. Just an overwhelming fatigue and a wariness she couldn't explain.

His eyes flickered away for the briefest of moments. "Yes."

"Oh. Was it very serious?" She raised a hand to her head, feeling for a wound.

He gently took her hand and lowered it to her lap, but he didn't relinquish his hold. "No. Not serious."

"Then why...how did I lose my memory? Did I suffer a concussion? My head doesn't hurt that way."

"I'm very glad your head doesn't pain you, but a head injury isn't what causes memory loss."

She cocked her head to the side and stared at him in puzzlement. "Then how?"

"The physician explained that this is your way of coping with the trauma of your accident. It's a protective instinct. One meant to shield you from harmful memories."

Her forehead wrinkled as her eyebrows came together. She pressed, trying to struggle through the thick cloak of black in her mind. Surely there had to be something, some spark of a memory.

"Yet I wasn't harmed," she said in disbelief.

"A fact I'm very grateful for," Chrysander said. "Still, it must have been very frightening."

A sudden thought came to her, and her hand flew from his in alarm. "Was anyone else hurt?"

Again his gaze flickered away from her for just a second. He reached up and recaptured her hand then brought it to his lips. A soft gasp escaped her when he pressed a kiss to her palm. "No."

She sagged in relief. "I wish I could remember. I keep thinking if I just try a little harder, it will come, but when I try to focus on the past, my head starts to pound."

Chrysander frowned. "This is precisely why I do not like to discuss the accident with you. The doctor warned against causing you any upset or stress. You must put the incident from your mind and focus on regaining your strength." He placed his other hand over her abdomen and cupped the bulge there protectively. "Such upset cannot be good for our baby. You've already gone through too much for my liking."

She tugged her hand free and placed both of hers lightly over his hand that was still cupping her belly. Beneath his fingers, the baby rolled. He snatched his hand back, a stunned expression lighting his face.

Her brows furrowed as she gazed curiously at him. His hand shook slightly as he returned it to her stomach. His fingers splayed out, and once again her belly rippled underneath his palm.

"That's amazing," he whispered.

He looked so completely befuddled that she had to smile. But on the heels of that smile came confusion. He acted as though he'd never experienced their baby kicking.

She licked her lips and cursed the fact that she couldn't remember. "Surely you've felt it before, Chrysander."

He continued his gentle exploration of her stomach. It was a long moment before he spoke. "I was often away on business," he said with a note of discomfort. "I had only just returned when I learned of your accident. It had been…a while since we'd been together."

She let her breath out, relief sliding over her and lightening her worry. If they had been separated for a time, it would explain a lot.

"I don't suppose it was the homecoming you expected," she said ruefully. "You left a woman who knew you, who was pregnant with your child and planned to marry you. When you came back, you faced a woman who treats you like a stranger."

She glanced down at her finger automatically as she spoke. No ring adorned it. She frowned at it before she quickly looked back up, trying to make the uneasiness disappear once more.

"I was only happy that you and our baby were unharmed," he said simply. He eased away from her, shifting his body until more space separated them. His gaze still drifted back to her belly as though he was fascinated with the tiny life making itself known there.

A buzz sounded, and Chrysander stood and strode to the call box on the wall. Marley strained to hear who he was speaking to, but she only heard his command to come up.

He returned to her and sat down, collecting her hands in his. "That was the nurse I hired to look after you. I have a meeting that I can't miss in an hour's time."

Her eyes widened. "But Chrysander, I don't need a nurse. I'm perfectly capable of remaining here while you attend to your business."

His grip on her hands tightened. "Humor me, *pedhaki mou*. It makes me feel better knowing I'm leaving you in capable hands. I don't like to think of you having need of anything in my absence."

A smile curved her lips at his insistence. "How long will you be gone?" She hated the hopeful, almost mournful quality to her voice. She sounded pathetic.

He stood as the sound of the elevator opening filtered into the living room. "Stay here. I'll return with the nurse."

Marley relaxed against the back of the couch and waited for Chrysander to return. His attentiveness was endearing, even if unnecessary.

A moment later, he walked back in with a smiling woman dressed in slacks and a sweater. She beamed at Marley as she stopped a few feet away from the sofa.

"You must be Marley. I'm so pleased to meet you. I'm Mrs. Cahill, but please do call me Patrice."

Marley couldn't help but return the older woman's smile.

"Mr. Anetakis has discussed his wishes with me, and I'll do my utmost to make sure you're taken care of."

Marley pinned Chrysander with a stare. "Oh, he did, did he? May I ask what his instructions were?"

Chrysander made a show of checking his watch. "Her instructions are to make sure you rest. Now, I'm sorry, but I must go out for a while. I'll return in time for us to have lunch together."

"I'd like that," she softly returned.

He leaned down and stiffly brushed a kiss across her forehead before turning to walk away. Her gaze followed him across the room, and she realized how clingy she must look.

With effort, she dragged her stare from his retreating back and looked up at Patrice. "I'm really quite fit," she explained. "Chrysander makes it sound like I'm a complete invalid."

Patrice smiled and winked. "He's a man. They're famous for that sort of thing. Still, there's no harm in a little rest, now is there? I'll see you to bed, and then I'll see about making us a nice cup of tea for when you wake."

Before Marley even realized what was happening, the other woman was effectively shuttling her toward the bedroom. She blinked when Patrice tucked her solidly into bed and arranged the covers around her.

"You're quite good at this," Marley said faintly.

Patrice chuckled. "Getting my patients to do what they don't want to is part of my job. Now get some rest so that man of yours is happy with me and with you when he returns."

Marley heard the light sounds of Patrice's shoes as she walked from the bedroom. When the sound faded away,

Marley glanced to the fireplace on the wall opposing the foot of her bed. Chrysander had started the flame the evening before, more for coziness than actual warmth, because the apartment suffered no chill. Even the floors were heated, which she loved, because she hated to wear shoes indoors.

The thought hit her even as a burst of excitement swept over her. What else could she remember about herself? She concentrated hard, but the effort caused her head to ache again.

The baby moved, and she slid her hand down to rest over her swollen abdomen. The movement eased the discomfort in her head, and she smiled. Despite the temporary loss of her past, she had a future to look forward to. Marriage and a child. She just wished she could remember how she'd gotten to this point.

With a sigh, she resigned herself to living in the moment. Hopefully her memories would return and fill in the gaps.

She dozed, and when she awoke, she looked at the clock by her bed and saw that an hour had elapsed. She felt refreshed and drew away the covers, wanting to get up and move around. The constant rest was starting to make her restless.

Though she was dressed in soft pajamas, she nevertheless reached for the silk dressing robe lying at the foot of her bed. Tying it around her body, she walked out of the bedroom and into the living room, where she found Patrice.

She smiled at the other woman and assured her she was feeling well when Patrice prompted her. Patrice nodded approvingly, and as if sensing Marley's need to be alone, excused herself.

Marley took the opportunity to explore the spacious penthouse. She walked from room to room, acquainting herself with her home. Only it didn't *feel* like home. She could see Chrysander in the style and makeup of the decorations and furnishings, but she couldn't see anything that made her feel as though she'd made any mark on the apartment. For some reason, that discomfited her. She felt like a guest intruding where she didn't belong.

When she entered the master suite, her frown grew. Chrysander had placed her in what apparently was one of the guest rooms. She hadn't given any thought when he'd put her to bed and seen to her comfort in the extra bedroom. She'd been too overwhelmed, too focused on trying to process everything.

She retreated, unable to shake the thought that she was somehow trespassing. Next to the master suite was a large office. It was obviously Chrysander's work space. The furnishings were dark and masculine. Bookcases adorned the back wall, and a large mahogany desk sat a few feet in front of them. Her feet brushed across a plush rug as she walked farther into the middle of the room.

A laptop rested on the desk, and she sat down in the leather executive chair in anticipation of browsing the Internet. She only hoped he had a wireless connection since she could see no evidence of a cable line connected to the computer.

She touched the keypad, and the monitor lit up. At least she wasn't a useless vegetable and had retained knowledge of the basics. As frustrating as her memory loss was, she was relieved to know it was confined to her personal history and not to the world around her.

She shook her head, plagued by the sheer absurdity of it all.

For the first half hour, she did countless searches on memory loss, but wading through the mass of conflicting opinions only gave her a vile headache. So she turned her attention to looking up information on Chrysander.

It was a bit frightening to see just how powerful and wealthy Chrysander was. He and his two brothers were a formidable presence in the hotel industry. There wasn't much personal information, though, and that was what she craved.

She sat back, irritated with her cowardice. What she needed was to ask Chrysander for the information she wanted. For goodness' sake, he was her fiancé, her *lover*. They'd created a child together, and he'd asked her to marry him. If only she could remember those events, she would feel more sure of herself.

"What are you doing?"

Chrysander's whiplike voice lashed over her, and she jerked in surprise and fright. She stared up to see him standing in the doorway, anger and suspicion glittering in his eyes. His mouth was drawn into a tight line. He strode toward her before she could even formulate a response.

"Chrysander, you scared me." Her hand went to her chest to try and calm the erratic jumping of her pulse.

"I asked you what you were doing," he said coldly as he walked around the desk to stand beside her.

Hurt and confusion settled over her. "I was just surfing the Internet. I didn't think you'd object to me using your laptop."

"I prefer if you leave the things in my office alone," he said curtly, even as he reached out and closed the computer.

She slid out of the chair and stood staring at him in shock. Tears burned the corners of her eyes. He looked at her with such…loathing. A shiver took over her body, and she desired nothing more than to be as far away from him as possible.

"I'm sorry," she managed to choke out. "I was just trying to discover something about me…you…this horrid memory loss. I won't bother you or your things again."

She turned and fled the room before she embarrassed herself and broke into sobs.

Chrysander watched her go and cursed under his breath. He dragged a hand through his hair before he sat down and reopened the laptop. A quick check of the browsing history showed she'd done nothing more than research memory loss and a few articles about his company. Another check of his files indicated none of his business documents had been accessed.

He cursed again. He'd reacted badly, but seeing her using his computer had immediately put him on guard. In that moment, he'd wondered if her memory loss was all a ruse and she was plotting again to betray him.

He propped his elbows on the desk and held his head in his hands. His meeting with the detective in charge of the investigation into Marley's abduction had been an exercise in frustration. They had little to no information to go on, and the one person who could supply it couldn't remember.

Marley hadn't been rescued as the news had led viewers to believe; rather, she'd been abandoned by her kidnappers, and an anonymous caller had alerted police to her presence in the rundown apartment building. When they'd arrived, they'd found a frightened pregnant woman obviously in shock. When she'd awoken in the hospital, she'd remembered nothing. Her life, in essence, began on that day.

So many questions, so much unknown.

What had been made clear to him, though, was that he couldn't take chances with her safety. Whatever threat there was to her was still out there, and he'd be damned if he let anyone get close enough to hurt Marley or his child again. He'd expected the authorities to balk when he said he was taking Marley out of the country, not that he cared, because her well-being was his top priority and he would do whatever it took to ensure it.

Instead, they'd agreed that it was the best choice and advised him to step up his security. They wanted to be notified the moment her memory returned, so they could question her. Chrysander supplied them with his contact information and told them he would be leaving with her the next day.

There was much to do to prepare for their departure. He'd already alerted his security team both here and on the island. Preparations were under way, but he still had many phone calls to make. Yet the sight of Marley's tears and the hurt in her voice gave him pause. He should shove it aside and continue with his plans. Her safety was important. Whether she was upset was not.

Even as he thought it, he was on his feet and going after her.

Marley stood in the closet of the bedroom Chrysander had given her, staring blindly at the row of clothing hanging in front of her. She wiped the tears with the back of her hand and concentrated on what to wear.

She rummaged through the many outfits, but none of them felt like her. With an unhappy frown she turned to the row of shelves that lined the right side of her closet and saw a stack of faded jeans next to several neatly folded T-shirts.

She reached for the jeans, knowing that this was what she felt comfortable in. But when she unfolded the first pair, she saw that they weren't maternity pants. A quick search of the rest yielded the same results.

She turned back around and flipped through outfit after outfit on the hangers and saw that they, too, were not suitable clothing for a woman in the more advanced stages of pregnancy. Why did she have nothing to wear? She glanced down at the bulge of her stomach. While she wasn't huge, the waistlines of the clothing in her closet were too confining for a woman five months along.

She felt his presence before he ever made a sound. Slowly, she turned to see Chrysander standing in the doorway of her closet. His expression softened when she swiped at her face and turned quickly away.

He stepped forward and captured her wrist in his hand. "Marley, I'm sorry."

She stiffened and raised her chin until she met his gaze. "I shouldn't have meddled in *your* belongings." She raised her hand to gesture at the closet full of clothes. "We obviously keep a very separate lifestyle. You'll pardon me while I relearn the ropes."

He frowned darkly and stared at her in confusion. "What are you talking about? There will be no separation of our lifestyles."

She shrugged indifferently. "The evidence is here. It doesn't take an idiot to figure it out. You've put me in my own room. My clothes are separate. Our things are separate. Our beds are separate. It's a wonder I ever got pregnant," she added wryly. She swallowed and then pressed on with the question burning uppermost in her mind. "Why are you marrying me, Chrysander? Was my pregnancy an accident? Was I some lascivious bitch who trapped you into a relationship?"

She knew she sounded hysterical even as the words tumbled out, but the hurt was eating away at her insides. She needed reassurance, some sign that the life he claimed was hers was a happy place and not one filled with dark gaps like the holes in her memory.

"*Theos!* Come with me."

Before she could protest, he was dragging her from the

closet. He ushered her over to the bed and sat her down before settling beside her.

She glanced uncomfortably around. "Where is Patrice?" She had no wish to have a disagreement in front of anyone else.

"I dismissed her when I arrived," he said impatiently. "She is only here when I cannot be until we leave for Greece. She'll remain on the island with us for as long as you have need of her."

Marley couldn't keep the disappointment from her expression. "But Chrysander, I don't need her at all, and I thought we would be alone once we reached the island."

His look told her that he wanted anything but, and hurt crashed in again at his seeming rejection.

"You may think she isn't needed, but I won't take chances with your recovery. Your health is too important to me." His voice became softer, and his eyes lost some of their hardness. "You're pregnant, and you've undergone a great deal of stress. It's only natural that I would want the best care possible for you."

She swallowed and slowly nodded.

He stared intently at her. "Now, as for my earlier rudeness…I apologize. I had no right to speak to you that way."

She snorted, which caused his eyebrows to rise. "I don't think rude adequately covers it. You were a first-class jerk."

Color rose in his cheeks, and he swallowed. "Yes, I was, and for that I apologize. I have no excuse. I've been busy making arrangements for our travel, and I took my frustrations out on you. It's unforgivable, but I ask for your forgiveness nonetheless."

"I accept your apology," she said coolly.

"And as for your other assertions." He took one of his hands away from hers and dragged it carelessly through his dark hair. "We do not lead separate lives. Nor will we. You did not trap me into a proposal, and I won't have you say it again." He paused and sighed. "I put you in this room out of deference to your condition. I didn't think it fair of me to expect you to share a room and a bed with a man who is a stranger to you. I had no wish to put such pressure on you."

In that light, her worry seemed silly. What she'd perceived as a slight had in fact been an act of caring on his part. Her shoulders sagged as her breath escaped in a sigh.

"I thought…"

"What did you think, *pedhaki mou?*"

"I thought you didn't want me," she said lamely.

He let out a curse and cupped her face in his palm. For a long moment, he stared at her. Light blazed in his golden eyes, and then he lowered his head to hers. Her breath caught in her throat and hung there as his lips hovered over hers.

A fierce longing ignited within her, and suddenly she wanted nothing more than his mouth on hers. When their lips met, a bolt of electricity shot down her spine and rebounded, spreading through her body like wildfire.

Instinctively, she arched into him, working her body into the shelter of his as his fingers fanned across her cheek and he deepened the kiss. Her breasts tightened as desire hummed through her belly. His chest brushed across her taut nipples, and she flinched in reaction.

Her arms snaked around him, and her fingers dug into the hair at his nape. Peace enveloped her. A sense of rightness she hadn't experienced since waking in the hospital bed lodged in her mind.

A low groan worked its way from his throat as he pulled away. His breath came in ragged spurts, and his eyes shimmered with liquid heat.

"Your body remembers me, *pedhaki mou,* even if your mind does not." Pure male satisfaction accentuated his statement. It sounded arrogant, self-assured, but it gave her flagging confidence a much-needed boost. He sounded very pleased at the idea that she recognized him, if only on a physical level.

"I don't have any suitable clothing," she blurted, then blushed at the absurdity of her statement. Her brain had gone to mush as soon as he'd kissed her, and now she scrambled to cover the awkwardness.

One brow went up again.

"Why don't I have any maternity clothes?" she asked. "Did I not buy any?" She reached for any plausible explanation as to why she wouldn't have appropriate clothing among the closetful of outfits she owned.

Chrysander frowned. "I am sorry, *pedhaki mou.* I did not think of this. Of course you cannot go around in your jeans." He smiled a slow, sensual smile. "Even if I do love to see you in them."

She cocked her head to one side.

He chuckled, and the sound, sexy and low, vibrated over her hypersensitive body. "You do not like to wear them around me. Something about looking nice when we are together, but I assure you, you would look beautiful in a sackcloth if you chose to wear one."

Heat bloomed in her cheeks, and she smiled at the compliment.

He shook his head ruefully. "I am not doing a good job of taking care of you since your release from the hospital. I've upset you and not seen to your needs. This is something I must remedy at once. I admit, though, that your safety and well-being, not your clothing, was uppermost on my mind."

"Don't say that," she protested. "You've been wonder-

ful. Well, except the brief stint as a big jerk." She smiled
teasingly at him as she spoke. "This can't have been easy
for you, and yet you've been incredibly patient. I'm sorry
for being such a shrew."

He touched her face again, and for a moment, she
thought he'd kiss her once more. "I won't let you apologize, Marley. You keep worrying about how hard this is for
me, when you are the one who has suffered." He took his
hand away and stood. "Now I must make some phone calls
so I can have more appropriate clothing arranged for you."

She blinked in surprise. "Couldn't we just go shopping?"

He frowned. "You are not up for a shopping trip. I want
you to rest. We're leaving for the island tomorrow morning, as soon as you have seen the doctor and he gives his
approval for you to travel."

"Tomorrow?" she parroted. "So soon?"

He nodded. "Now you know why I must hurry if I am
to have your clothing delivered on time."

She put her hands up helplessly. He said it as though he
had much experience in making things happen in accor-
dance with his wishes. If he could have clothes delivered
to her on such short notice, then who was she to argue?

"Now—"

She held up a hand to silence him. She knew enough
about the look on his face and the tone of his voice to know
that an order to rest was about to follow.

"If you tell me to rest again, I may well scream."

His gaze narrowed, and he was about to protest.

"Please, Chrysander. I feel well. I napped while you
were gone. Now, you promised me lunch when you returned from your meeting, and I find myself starving.
Can we go eat?"

He cursed again and clenched his fingers into fists.

"Of course. Apparently, I strive to be thoughtless in all things. Come and sit down at our table. I'll get us something to eat."

Chapter 5

The next morning, Marley dressed in one of the chic outfits that had been delivered straight to their penthouse by a local boutique specializing in maternity wear. Chrysander had insisted she see an obstetrician before they departed for his island, and so, accompanied by Chrysander and flanked by several members of his security team, they entered the medical building where the doctor's offices were housed.

She felt conspicuous and faintly embarrassed, but she also glowed under Chrysander's constant attention and his apparent concern for her well-being.

To her surprise, there was no waiting once Chrysander announced their arrival to the receptionist. His security detail remained in the lobby, and Marley smiled at the image of the big, burly men standing amidst a dozen pregnant women.

She and Chrysander were ushered to an exam room by

a young nurse who assured them that the doctor would attend them shortly.

When the nurse retreated, Chrysander lifted Marley and settled her on the exam table. Instead of sitting in the chair to the side, he stood in front of her and rubbed his hands up and down her arms in a comforting manner.

She leaned into his arms, unable to resist the pull between them. She rested her cheek on his broad chest and closed her eyes as his hands slipped around to caress her back.

The door opened, and Marley quickly pulled away. But Chrysander seemed in no hurry to relinquish her. He slipped an arm around her shoulders and pulled her against him as the doctor introduced himself.

After a few preliminaries and a discussion of her condition, the doctor looked over his clipboard and said, "I'd like to perform an ultrasound just to make sure everything is as it should be."

Chrysander frowned. "Do you have cause for concern?"

The doctor shook his head. "It's purely precautionary. Given the fact that you're traveling out of the country, and that Miss Jameson has recently suffered a trauma, I'd just like to take a look at the baby and make sure everything is well."

Chrysander nodded and took Marley's hand. As the doctor left the room, he turned to her. "I will be with you, *pedhaki mou*. There is nothing to fear."

She smiled and squeezed his hand. "I'm not worried. I wasn't even injured in the accident, so there's no reason anything should be wrong with the baby."

His expression became unreadable, but his hand remained tight around hers.

A few moments later, the doctor returned and instructed Marley to recline on the table. When he asked her to tug her pants below her waistline and to raise her shirt, Chrysander frowned fiercely.

"Her belly must be exposed in order to perform the scan," the doctor said, amusement twinkling in his eyes.

Chrysander himself arranged her clothing, only baring the minimal amount of flesh, and he hovered close, his hand resting above the swell of her stomach.

When the probe slid over her belly and the screen lit up with a blurry image that resembled a blob, Marley reached a shaking hand for Chrysander's. Chrysander bent over her, his face close to her ear as he strained to see the monitor.

"Would you like to know what you're having?" the doctor asked with a broad smile.

Chrysander looked at Marley, and she held her breath for a moment, excitement making her pulse race. "I do," she whispered to Chrysander. "Do you?"

He smiled and brought her hand to his lips. "If that is what you wish, *pedhaki mou*. I, too, would like to know whether we're having a son or a daughter."

Marley turned her head to look at the doctor. "Yes, please. Tell us."

She watched as the screen changed, blurring in and out as the probe moved over her belly. A few seconds later, the image slowed and then became clearer.

"Congratulations, you're having a boy."

Marley's breath caught in her throat. "Is that him?" she whispered as she viewed what appeared to be two legs and round buttocks.

"Indeed it is. Handsome devil, isn't he?"

"He's beautiful," Chrysander said huskily. He bent and brushed his lips across Marley's cheek. "Thank you, *pedhaki mou*."

She twisted to look up at him. "Why are you thanking me?"

"For my son." His gaze was riveted to the screen, and delight shone deeply in his eyes. He was clearly enthralled with the tiny baby, and her heart squeezed with emotion.

"We're finished here," the doctor said.

Chrysander gently arranged Marley's clothing and then put an arm behind her back to help her sit forward again.

"Was everything all right?" Chrysander asked the doctor.

"Quite so. Make sure she checks in with an obstetrician when you arrive in Greece. I don't anticipate any problems. She and the baby appear perfectly healthy, but it's a good idea if she has regular care during her pregnancy."

"I've arranged for a private physician as well as a nurse to remain on the island as long as we do," Chrysander said. "She will be well looked after."

The doctor nodded his approval and then smiled at Marley. "Take care, young lady, and best wishes on your pregnancy."

Marley returned his smile then took Chrysander's hand as he helped her from the table. He ushered her out moments later and helped her into the waiting limousine.

"Are you feeling all right?" Chrysander asked as they pulled away. "The plane is waiting at the airport, but if you're tired from your appointment we can take the flight after you've rested."

"Are our bags already there?" she asked in surprise.

He nodded. "I had them brought over while you were at your appointment."

"We can leave now. I can rest on the plane."

He leaned forward to tell the driver to take them to the airport, and then he closed the privacy glass between them.

She gazed at him, suddenly a little shy. "Are you happy about our son, Chrysander?"

He looked startled by her question. Then he pulled her closer to him, until she was nearly in his lap. He cupped his hand to her belly and rubbed tenderly over the swell.

"Have I given you reason to think I am not happy about our child?"

She shook her head. "No, I just wondered. I mean, now that I know what I'm having, it suddenly seems so *real.*"

"I couldn't be happier about our son. I would have loved a daughter just as well. As long as our child is healthy and safe, I am very content."

"Yes, me, too." She sighed. "Now if only I could remember, things would be so perfect. It's been such a good day."

He put a finger over her lips. "Don't spoil it by lamenting over things that are out of your control. It will come. Don't rush it."

She grimaced. "You're right. I just wish…"

"What do you wish, *pedhaki mou?*"

"I wish I could remember loving you," she said quietly.

His eyes darkened, and for a moment, what she saw sent a shiver down her spine. There was such conflicted emotion in the golden orbs.

"Maybe you can learn to love me again," he finally said.

She smiled. "You're making it easy." She settled against him, content. But then an uneasy thought assailed her. She'd spoken of loving him, something she couldn't remember, but felt that she had, but there had been nothing said of his love for her. Not once had he voiced words of love, and shouldn't they have come? When she was in the hospital. Weren't reaffirmations of love common after a scare? Wouldn't he seek to reassure her that he loved her when she couldn't remember their life together?

She raised her head to ask him, to seek confirmation

of that fact, but the question died on her lips when she saw his attention was already focused on the small television screen in the corner of the large compartment of the limousine.

She let the question die and contented herself with remaining snuggled into his body. The next thing she knew, they were arriving at the airport.

"We are here," Chrysander said.

She nodded, and Chrysander stepped from the limousine. He reached in and helped her out, and she blinked as the bright sunshine hit her eyes. The wind blew, and she shivered against the slight chill.

Chrysander wrapped an arm around her and hurried her toward the waiting plane. The inside was warm and looked extremely comfortable.

As he guided her toward a seat, he said, "There is a bed in the back. Once we've taken off, you can go lie down."

"That sounds lovely," she said with a smile as he settled into the seat next to her. She turned and looked out the window and then glanced toward the front of the plane as she saw several of Chrysander's security detail file into the cabin.

"Chrysander, why do you have so many security people?"

He stiffened beside her. "I am a very wealthy man. There are those who might seek to harm me…or those important to me."

"Oh. Is the danger very high?" she asked as she turned her gaze on him.

"It is the job of my men to ensure there is no danger. Do not worry, Marley. I will see to the safety of you and our child."

She frowned. "I didn't mean to imply that you wouldn't. I'm merely trying to understand your world."

"Our world." He stared pointedly at her. "It's our world, Marley. One that you are very much a part of."

A blush colored her cheeks. "I'm trying, Chrysander. I'm trying very hard. It's difficult when I'm in a place but can't remember any part of it. Please be patient with me."

"If I spoke too harshly, then I apologize," he said soothingly. He reached across her lap to pull her seat belt over her waist. With a click, he secured it then pulled it snug. "We'll be taking off soon."

A few minutes later, the plane began to move, and she settled back in her seat, trying not to think too hard about the uncertainty that lay ahead.

They landed at a small airstrip in Corinth several long hours later, and Chrysander helped her down the few steps onto the concrete runway. He urged her toward a waiting helicopter several feet away. When she looked questioningly at him, he leaned in close and said, "The island is a fifteen-minute ride by helicopter."

She glanced appreciatively out the window of the helicopter as it rose over Corinth and headed out to sea. In the distance, she saw ancient ruins and turned to question Chrysander about them. When she had no luck making him hear over the noise of the rotors, he slid a pair of earphones with an attached microphone over her head and suddenly she could hear him clearly.

"The Temple of Apollo," he explained. "If you like, we can fly back and tour the ruins when you've recovered from your journey."

"I'd like that."

She turned her attention to the brilliant blue expanse of sparkling water, but already in the distance she could make out a small dot of land. "Is that it?" she asked, pointing.

He nodded.

"Does it have a name?"

"Anetakis," he responded.

She laughed. "I should have known." She shook her head. It seemed unreal that he'd own an entire island. But his naming the island Anetakis didn't surprise her in the least. He wore arrogance like most people wore clothing.

As the island loomed larger on the horizon, she curled her fingers into tight balls. Her anxiety must have been evident to Chrysander, because he reached over and took one of her hands in his. "There's nothing to worry over, *pedhaki mou*. You'll like it on the island, and it will be good for you to have time to relax and concentrate on regaining your strength."

She didn't argue with him over her condition, knowing full well it was a useless expenditure of energy. But she had no intention of spending her time on the island "resting."

They landed on a small concrete helipad situated at the rear of a palatial house. Chrysander curled a protective arm around her as they ducked and walked away from the helicopter.

He touched her shoulder and indicated that she wait while he spoke to the pilot. She stood, staring up at the sprawling house, waiting for some flicker of recognition. A cool breeze blew off the water, and a chill raced up her arms. Still, she remained, staring, hoping, but she was convinced she'd never been here.

"Come," Chrysander said as he took her hand. "You're getting cold."

As the helicopter droned away, she took a step to follow Chrysander and then paused again. He turned and looked inquisitively at her. "What is wrong?"

She swallowed as she continued to gaze over the grounds. There was a sense of wonder, as though she'd stepped into some wild paradise, but no feeling of home, that this was a place she had any knowledge of. It terrified her.

Chrysander closed the distance between them and touched her face in concern. He cursed when she trembled.

"I've never been here," she said in a low voice. She looked to him for confirmation.

He nodded. "This is so. This is your first visit to the island."

"I don't understand," she said faintly. "We're engaged, and I've never been to the place you call home?"

His lips pressed together. "We made our home in New York, Marley. I told you this."

The cloud of confusion grew around her. Would they not have visited? Even once? She allowed him to take her hand, and they walked up the long, winding path toward the house. As they neared the gate, Marley could see the sparkling waters of a swimming pool.

A large patio extended from the back of the house, and the pool was carved in the middle. To her surprise, the pool entered the house under an elaborate archway.

"It's heated," Chrysander explained as he drew her inside the house. "It's too cool this time of year for outdoor swimming, but you can enjoy a light swim indoors if the doctor gives his permission."

She rolled her eyes and allowed him to tug her along with him. They entered a huge room that looked to be in actuality three separate areas. They stood in the living room but the floor plan into the kitchen and dining area was open, and they flowed seamlessly into one another.

Marley's gaze wandered to the glass doors leading onto a patio where yet another pool was situated with a view of the ocean in the distance. To her shock, a woman in a skimpy bikini appeared at the entrance and stepped inside the house.

She recognized her as Chrysander's personal assistant,

but why would she be here? And it was certainly too cold to be out sunbathing in such a suit.

Roslyn looked up, and it was apparent to Marley that she feigned surprise at seeing them. Though she had a wrap draped over one arm, she made no move to put it on as she hurriedly crossed the floor toward Chrysander.

"Mr. Anetakis, I didn't expect you until tomorrow!"

Her long blond hair trailed seductively down her back, and Marley gaped as she saw the bottom of Roslyn's bikini was actually a thong.

"I hope you don't mind that I took advantage of the facilities," Roslyn rushed to say as she put well-manicured fingers to Chrysander's arm.

"Of course not," Chrysander said smoothly. "I did tell you to avail yourself of whatever you liked. Did you set up my office as I requested?"

"Of course. I do hope it won't be a problem for me to remain one more night? I didn't arrange for the helicopter to fetch me until tomorrow morning."

Roslyn's wide, innocent eyes didn't fool Marley, and she felt the beginnings of a headache drumming in her temples. She pulled her hand from Chrysander's and merely walked away, having no desire to listen to the mewings of his assistant any longer.

"You are welcome to stay, Roslyn. I do hope you'll have dinner with us tonight," Chrysander said politely as Marley mounted the stairs.

She really had no idea where she was going, but upstairs seemed as good a place as any, and it would put her solidly away from the source of her irritation. She was nearly to the top when Chrysander overtook her.

"You should have waited for me," he reproached. "I don't like you navigating the stairs by yourself. What if you were to fall? In the future, someone will escort you up or down."

Her mouth fell open. "You're not serious!"

He frowned, clearly not liking her tone of disbelief. "I'm very serious when it comes to your well-being and that of our child."

She blew out her breath in frustration as Chrysander escorted her from the landing of the stairs down the hall to a spacious bedroom. Clearly this was the master suite. She set aside the protests forming on her tongue and stared at Chrysander in question.

"Is this to be my room?"

"It is *our* room."

Heat rose in her cheeks. Her throat suddenly went dry as she imagined sharing the big bed with Chrysander. Satisfaction gleamed in his eyes as he observed her reaction.

"Do you have any objections?" he asked softly.

She shook her head. "N-no. None."

A slow smiled curved his sensual mouth. A predatory gleam entered his eyes. "That is good. We are in agreement then."

"I—w-well, not exactly," she stammered.

He cocked one imperious brow. "We are not?"

She shook herself from the intimate spell he was weaving over her. The one that had her reduced to a mass of writhing stupidity. She lifted her chin and stared challengingly at him. "I don't need an escort to get up and down the stairs, Chrysander. I'm not an invalid, and I don't wish to be treated like one."

"And I would prefer you had someone with you." His voice became steely and determination creased his brow.

"I will not spend our time here as a prisoner, only allowed out whenever someone can make the time to fetch me back and forth." She crossed her arms over her chest and glared mutinously at him.

To her surprise, his shoulders relaxed and laughter escaped him.

"What's so funny?" she demanded.

"You are, *pedhaki mou.* You sound just like you always have. Always arguing with me. You've always accused me of being too set on having things my way." He gave a shrug that said he accepted as much.

"Well, since we're arguing, what is that woman doing here parading around in next to nothing?"

She hadn't meant it to come out quite like that. She'd wanted to sound more casual and less like a jealous shrew, but she'd failed miserably.

Chrysander's expression hardened. "You never liked her, but I would appreciate it if you weren't rude."

Marley raised a brow. "Never? And you don't wonder why?" She turned her back to Chrysander and walked to the window that overlooked the pool and the garden to the left that separated the two swimming areas. "Why is it she is here and seems so comfortable, and yet this is my first visit?"

She tensed when Chrysander's hands cupped her shoulders. "Roslyn often travels with me. This time I arranged for her to stay in Corinth so she is available if I need her, but her presence won't be an issue for you." His lips brushed across her temple. "As to why you've never been here, I can only say that it has never come up. When I would return to New York after being away for weeks at a time, I was more interested in spending that time with you, not wasting it traveling."

Marley turned around and without thinking wrapped her arms around Chrysander and buried her face in his chest. "I'm just so frustrated. I won't apologize, however, for not liking the fact that my fiancé's personal assistant is cavorting around with barely a string covering her assets, or that she seems perfectly at home in a place that I should, but don't."

"If it makes you feel better, I did not notice her assets." There was a tone of amusement in his voice, and it only served to irritate her further.

When she tried to wrench away from Chrysander's arms, he gripped her shoulders and held her fast. His eyes glistened with a need that made her stomach do odd flips. Nervously, she wet her lips, and he groaned just before he slanted his mouth over hers.

She felt as though someone had lit a match as she went up in flames. Oh, yes, her body recognized, craved his touch. His tongue swept over her lips, demanding she open to him. Her mouth parted on a sigh, and his tongue laved hers, hot, electrifying.

She went weak and sagged against him, but he caught her, holding her tightly against him. A low moan worked from her throat, and he swallowed it as it escaped. Her hands scraped across his shoulders, clutching and seeking his strength.

Her nipples beaded and tingled when his fingers skimmed underneath the waist of her shirt, feathering across her belly and up to where the lacy bra cupped her breasts. Before she could fully process what his intentions were, her bra fell loose, and his thumb rolled across one taut point.

Uncontrollable shudders wracked her small frame as his mouth slid down her throat and lower. He blazed a molten trail to the curve of one breast, and when he took the sensitive nipple in his mouth, she nearly shattered in his arms.

"Please," she begged.

His head came up at her plea, and shock was reflected

in his golden eyes. "*Theos mou!* I would have ravaged you on the floor," he said in disgust. He quickly rearranged her bra and settled her shirt back over her body.

Her hand shook as she raised it to her swollen lips. Every nerve-ending in her body screamed in want. Her re-action to Chrysander frightened her. It was intense. Vola-tile. How easily she'd gotten carried away as soon as he'd touched her.

"Do not look at me that way," he said in a near growl.

"How?" she asked, her voice shaking.

"Like you want nothing more than for me to carry you to our bed and make love to you all night. I only have so much control."

She laughed, a hoarse and needy sound. She attempted to calm her response to his words by smoothing her hands down her sides. "And if that was what I wanted?"

He reached out to cup her chin. "The doctor will arrive in a few moments. I want him to examine you and make sure you haven't overexerted yourself with our travel. Your health is my first priority."

"I do believe I've been shot down," she murmured rue-fully.

He moved so quickly she barely had time to blink. One minute they were a foot apart, and the next she was hauled against his chest, his eyes burning into her.

"Don't mistake my hesitation for disinterest," he said in a soft, dangerous tone. "I assure you, as soon as the doc-tor has given his approval on the state of your health, you *will* be in my bed."

He slowly let go of her, and she stepped back on fal-tering feet. "I believe I hear the helicopter now. That will be the physician and Mrs. Cahill. Why don't you freshen up and make yourself comfortable. I'll send the doctor up to see you."

Marley nodded like a dolt then watched as he strode away. As soon as he disappeared, she sagged onto the bed and clenched her trembling fingers together in her lap. How could she react so strongly to a man who was, for all practical purposes, a stranger? It was as he said, though. Her body recognized him even when her mind did not. She should find comfort in that, but the intensity of her attraction to him frightened her. In just a few moments, she'd so easily lost herself to his touch.

Remembering that the doctor would be up in a few moments, and not wanting to give him any excuse to send her straight to bed, she hastened to the bathroom, where she splashed cool water on her face in an effort to rid herself of the flush that still suffused her cheeks.

She dragged a hand through her curls and frowned at her reflection in the mirror. Her hair didn't look right. A brief image flashed across her mind. It was her, laughing, but with shorter hair. Hair that curled riotously around her head in an unruly cap. Even with such a brief glance into her memories, she knew she preferred her hair short. So why had she let it grow long? She shook her head and vowed to get it trimmed as soon as she was able.

A knock sounded at her door, and she rushed out of the bathroom. Chrysander walked in, an older man following closely behind him. Patrice entered after them and smiled at Marley across the room.

"Marley, this is Dr. Karounis. He is a leading obstetrician in Athens, and he has graciously agreed to see to your care while we are here on the island," Chrysander said as he curled one arm around her waist.

"Miss Jameson, it is my pleasure to provide what assistance I may," the doctor said formally.

She smiled a little nervously. "Thank you. Chrysander

fusses a bit much. I'm sure it wasn't necessary for you to come all this way."

"He wants the best for you and his child," Dr. Karounis said with an easy smile. "I can hardly fault him for that."

She smiled ruefully. "No, I suppose you can't. Do whatever it is you need to do to persuade him I'm quite all right." She aimed a glare at Chrysander. "And that I'm perfectly capable of navigating the stairs by myself."

Chrysander's expression never wavered. "You will do this for me, *pedhaki mou*. It is a small thing I ask. Having someone assist you up and down the stairs will take no longer than if you were to go by yourself, and I would feel more at ease."

Oh, he knew just how to make her feel about an inch tall. She sighed. "Very well." She looked pointedly at the doctor and then made shooing gestures at Chrysander and Patrice.

Chrysander pulled her hand to his lips and kissed her palm. "After the doctor has finished, why don't you take a long bath and rest before dinner. I'll come up for you when it's time to go down."

She nodded, and Chrysander's eyes gleamed in triumph. He turned and walked out of the room, shutting the door behind him.

Chapter 6

Somehow, between the visit with the physician and a very long, relaxing bath, Marley had managed to forget all about Roslyn's presence at the house. When Chrysander walked into their bedroom to escort her down the stairs, she smiled welcomingly.

He stopped in front of her and studied her for a moment. Then he brushed his lips across hers and folded her hand in his. "You look beautiful. Your color is much better, and you look rested."

"The good doctor has proclaimed me fit as a fiddle. So there's no cause for concern."

"That is good, *pedhaki mou*. Your health is important to me."

He tucked her arm underneath his, and they headed out of the bedroom and down the stairs. As they neared the bottom, Marley looked up and saw Roslyn standing in the entrance to the formal dining room.

Marley stiffened. The woman was immaculately turned out in a designer dress that molded to every single one of her curves. She looked down self-consciously at her own very casual slacks and maternity blouse. She felt a sudden desire to race back up the stairs and change.

Not willing to allow the woman to know how much she had rattled her, Marley tightened her grip on Chrysander's arm and plastered a smile on her face.

"If I had known we wouldn't be dressing for dinner, I would have chosen different apparel," Roslyn said. She made a gesture at her outfit that drew attention to the plunging bodice. "You usually like a formal dinner." She made her last remark directly to Chrysander and cut her eyes toward Marley as if gauging her reaction to the fact that she knew more about Chrysander's likes than Marley did.

Chrysander ushered Marley forward, curling his arm around her waist in a casual manner. "Marley's comfort is what is most important, and since we intend to enjoy a great deal of privacy while we're here, it makes no sense to be so formal."

Marley relaxed and wanted to throw her arms around Chrysander. Roslyn didn't seem to be too affected by his statement, however.

"Come, *pedhaki mou*. Mrs. Cahill and Dr. Karounis are waiting on us to begin dining."

They walked past Roslyn, leaving her to follow. Marley could feel the other woman's malevolent stare boring into her back.

The food, she imagined, was delicious, but she didn't register the taste for all the attention she paid it. She smiled until her jaw ached and nodded appropriately when Patrice or Dr. Karounis spoke, but her focus was on the quiet conversation between Chrysander and Roslyn.

Chrysander's head was bent and his expression intent as the two spoke in low tones. When dessert was served and Chrysander showed no signs of turning his attention from the woman who sat a little too close, Marley scooted back in her chair, tossed her napkin down and rose.

Chrysander jerked his gaze to her. "Is everything all right?"

"Just fine," she said tightly. "Don't let me disturb you. I'm going upstairs." Before he could respond, she turned and walked away as calmly as she could.

When she reached the foot of the stairs, Patrice caught up to her. "Mr. Anetakis doesn't want you to go up the stairs alone," she said as she took Marley's elbow in her gentle grip.

Marley turned but saw no sign of Chrysander. He wasn't so worried that he'd see to the task himself. Obviously Roslyn's company was a little more important than his posturing over Marley's safety.

Fatigue beat at her as she entered the master suite and Patrice returned downstairs. The long, hot bath she'd taken before dinner had relaxed her, and she could have gone to bed then. Dinner had just brought back the tension she'd managed to rid herself of, and she knew she wouldn't sleep now.

She gazed down at the pool and gardens from the large window. The entire area shimmered under bright moonlight. It glowed with a magical quality, one that called to her. Maybe a walk in the garden would soothe her irritation.

She pulled a sweater from the closet and tugged it over her shoulders as she left the bedroom and headed for the stairs.

Not sparing one iota of guilt over the fact that her *doting* fiancé wouldn't be pleased that she was ignoring his dictate, Marley eased down the stairs. She held tightly to the banister, cursing the fact he'd made her paranoid with his concern.

She could still hear the murmur of voices filtering in from the dining room as she stepped down into the living room. She turned left and hurriedly crossed the floor to reach the French doors leading to the patio.

When she opened the door and slipped out, a chill blew over her face and raised goose bumps on her neck. Still, it was a lovely evening, and the moon shone high overhead.

She followed the stone pathway that led beside the pool and then veered right into the winding walkway of the garden. In the distance, the faint sound of the ocean soothed her ears. As she walked farther into the garden, the sound of running water overrode the distant waves. To her delight, as she rounded the corner of a thick row of hedges, she found a fountain, illuminated by spotlights angled from the ground.

Marley moved closer and inhaled the brisk night air. The salty breeze tasted tangy on her lips, and her fingers crept higher to pull the sweater more firmly around her body. She shivered with the cold but was reluctant to depart the scenic spot so soon.

"You should not be out here."

Chrysander's voice startled her even as his hands closed around her shoulders, spinning her around to face him. Anger glinted in his eyes, and displeasure tightened his jaw.

"How did you find me so quickly?" she asked, refusing to apologize for her flight.

"I've known where you were as soon as you left the house," he said calmly. At her confused expression, he said, "I have security posted all over the island. I was notified the moment you stepped onto the patio. You've been closely watched ever since."

Her mouth turned down into a frown even as she looked around, trying to ferret out the security he mentioned.

"You were not to navigate the stairs alone, and you should not come outside in the darkness unless I am with you."

"You could hardly accompany me anywhere, glued as you were to your personal assistant," she said dryly. She wanted to be flip and sound like she couldn't care less, but hurt registered in her voice, and she clenched her fingers together.

"I neglected you at dinner. For this, I am sorry. I had several things I needed to go over with Roslyn before she leaves in the morning. I will be away from my offices during our stay, and while I can work from here, I'd rather devote the time to you."

He drew her closer as he spoke, and she felt herself go weak. She hated jealousy and would like to believe she wasn't a jealous person, but how was she to know? Did she always feel such burning insecurity when it came to Chrysander? She hoped not. It had to be a miserable existence.

She leaned her forehead on his chest and closed her eyes. His spicy scent surrounded her, blocking out the salt in the air and the fragrance of the garden. Warmth enveloped her and bled into her body. "I'm sorry," she whispered.

He pulled her away and tilted her chin up with one finger. "Promise me you won't go off like this again. I cannot protect you and our child if you won't heed my precautions."

She stared up at him, watched slow desire burn its way through his eyes. Her breath caught in her throat, and all she could do was nod. She wanted him to kiss her again, touch her.

"I have spoken with Dr. Karounis," he said huskily. His finger trailed up her jaw and then over her cheek and back to her lips.

"What did he say?" she asked breathlessly.

He reached down and swept her into his arms. She let out a startled gasp as she landed against his hard chest.

"He saw no reason I could not make love to you."

"You asked him that?" she squeaked. Mortification tightened her cheeks, and she buried her face in his neck.

His low chuckle vibrated against her mouth. "I would not endanger you or our child, so I had to be sure I would not hurt you by taking you to my bed."

He strode back up the path toward the patio, bearing her weight without the slightest difficulty.

"Chrysander," she protested. "If there are all these security men around who see everything we do, then you shouldn't be carrying me off like this. They'll know what you're doing!"

He laughed but continued on. "You are cute when you're embarrassed, *pedhaki mou.* They are all men. They understand very well what it is I do."

She groaned and kept her face firmly planted, unable to bear the thought of looking up and seeing one of the security men milling about.

He nudged the French doors open with his foot then shouldered them aside as he ducked inside with her. As he climbed the stairs, Marley's nervousness grew. She wanted what was about to happen, but she also feared it. How could she retain any amount of control when he shattered it with one touch?

Her physical reaction to him made her feel vulnerable, as though she couldn't shelter any part of herself from him.

She wasn't even entirely sure she wanted to, but until she could fully remember the scope of their relationship, she needed to be able to protect her emotions.

Chrysander laid her on the bed and stared down at her with glittering eyes. He touched her cheek and then let his hand trail down her body and over the swell of her stomach.

He bent and tugged her shirt up then touched his lips to her belly. There was a tenderness to the gesture that made her heart ache. He placed his hands on either side of her head and held his body over hers.

"Is this what you want?"

"Yes, oh yes," she breathed. She twisted restlessly, wanting him to fulfill the promise in his eyes.

"In many ways this is our first time together," he said huskily. "I don't want to frighten you."

She reached for him, pulling him down to meet her kiss. Her uncertainties evaporated under the heat of his lips. He took command of her mouth, leaving her to clutch desperately at his shoulders.

"I want you," she whispered when he pulled away from her, his chest heaving.

He stood to his full height, and she stared up at him from her position on the bed. Her lips were full and trembling. Her pulse ratcheted up, and excitement raced through her veins as he reached for the buttons at his neck.

Slowly, with exacting precision, he divested himself of his shirt. It fell to the floor, and he began to undo his pants. Her breath caught in her throat at the familiarity of his actions. He'd done this for her before. Teased her. Taunted her until she was crazy for him.

"You've done this before," she murmured.

A predatory smile curved his lips as the pants fell down

his legs. "It is something you enjoy, or so you've told me. I like to please my woman."

Finally the silk boxers inched down his thighs, and she swallowed as his erection bobbed into view. He was simply beautiful. All powerful male. Strength rippled through the muscles in his body as he leaned forward once again.

"And now to rid you of your clothes, *pedhaki mou*."

She curved her arms over her chest in a moment of panic. Would he find her beautiful? Would he react to her as she'd reacted to him? She strained to remember more of their lovemaking, seeking more familiarity than the fact that he'd undressed for her before.

He gently took her wrists in his hands and pulled them away until they were over her head, pressed against the mattress.

"Don't hide from me. You're beautiful. I want to see all of you."

She licked her lips as little goose bumps raced across her skin. Her nipples tightened against the confines of her bra, and suddenly she ached to be skin to skin with him, without the impediment of her clothing or her doubts.

Chrysander lowered one hand and began to pull at her shirt. His mouth found the soft skin of her neck, and he began nibbling a path to her ear. The room went a little fuzzy around her, and she struggled to keep up with the need for oxygen. She simply couldn't breathe.

Amazingly, he'd removed every stitch of her clothing. Her mouth rounded in shock, and he smiled arrogantly at her as he tossed the last of her undergarments over his shoulder.

He lifted her and positioned her on the pillows in the middle of the bed then followed her down, pressing his hard body to hers. He cupped her belly protectively then slid his hand lower, finding her most sensitive flesh.

"Chrysander!" she gasped as she arched into him.

Hot, breathless and aching, her body tightened as his mouth closed around one hard nipple. A sob escaped her as his fingers brushed across the tiny bundle of nerves at her center.

"I want you so much," he whispered. "I've missed this. We're so good together. Give yourself to me. Give me your pleasure."

He covered her, his skin pressed to hers. He inserted one thigh between her legs and positioned himself. She wrapped her arms around him as he slowly entered her body.

Even as he possessed her, he cradled her tenderly against him, taking care not to put too much of his weight on the swell that rested below her heart.

He took her to paradise, and in that moment, for the first time, she felt like she was truly home. That she belonged and wasn't living someone else's life. Tears streamed down her cheeks, and only when she found completion in his arms did he shudder above her and slowly come to rest on her body.

When he tried to move, she uttered a weak protest.

"I'm too heavy," he murmured as he settled beside her. He drew her into his arms and tucked her head underneath his chin. He ran a hand down her side and came to a rest over the curve of her hip. His fingers tightened possessively as she snuggled further into his chest.

For a long moment, they breathed in silence. Warm lethargy stole over Marley, and sleepy contentment weighed on her eyelids.

"Chrysander?"

"Yes?"

"Was it always like this?" she asked softly.

He went still against her. "No, *pedhaki mou*. This… this was much better."

A smile curved her lips as she drifted off, the smell and feel of Chrysander surrounding her.

Chapter 7

Morning sun streamed into the bedroom and cast a warm glow on the bed where Marley lay. She opened her eyes and promptly burrowed more deeply underneath the covers. Her hand sought Chrysander, but she found only an empty spot.

She frowned and sat up, looking around the bedroom, but he was nowhere to be found. The unmistakable whir of the helicopter caught her attention, and she got out of bed and walked to the window.

Chrysander stood with Roslyn a short distance from the helicopter, his hand on her arm. She nodded and ducked down to hurry into the helicopter. A few seconds later, it lifted and headed toward the mainland. Marley couldn't help but breathe a sigh of relief.

She stood watching a moment longer before she turned and hurried toward the bathroom. After a quick shower, she pulled on her robe and walked back into the bedroom to dress. Chrysander was waiting for her.

She eyed him nervously and pulled her robe tighter around her.

"I'll leave you to dress," he said shortly. "I'll send Mrs. Cahill up to escort you down in half an hour."

Without another word, he turned and walked out of the bedroom, leaving Marley to gape after him. Hurt trickled up her spine. He'd acted as though he couldn't wait to be away from her, and after last night, his behavior certainly wasn't what she'd expected.

And sending Patrice to collect her? If he was so bent on her not navigating the stairs alone, then he could at least see to the task himself rather than foist her off on the hired help like she was some undesirable chore.

She drew her shoulders up and went to the closet to choose an outfit. There were enough concerns she had to deal with without adding a surly, moody man to the equation. Whatever the reason for his fit of temper, he could damn well get over it.

All warm and floaty feelings from the night's love-making evaporated as she walked out of the bedroom. She wasn't going to stand around like a lapdog and wait to be summoned. It was ridiculous that he insisted on having her helped up and down the stairs like a child.

She was halfway down when she saw Chrysander standing at the bottom, his jaw set and anger flashing in his eyes. She faltered for a moment but gripped the railing and continued downward. It made her feel childish and a little petty to defy him over such an insignificant matter, but at the moment she didn't mind irritating him in the least.

She met his gaze challengingly as she navigated the final step. His lips thinned, but he said nothing. He put a hand to her elbow to guide her to the breakfast table, but she firmly moved her arm forward and walked ahead of him.

They ate in silence, although she couldn't really say she ate anything. She pushed the fruit around on her plate and sipped mechanically at her tea, but the stony silence emanating from Chrysander had her wanting to flee.

Several times she opened her mouth to ask him what was the matter, but each time, something in his expression kept her silent. Finally, she gave up any pretense of eating and shoved her plate away.

Chrysander looked up and gave a disapproving frown when he noted the food still on her plate. "You need to eat."

"It's rather difficult to eat when a black cloud resides at your breakfast table," she said tightly.

His lips thinned, and his eyes flickered. He looked as though he would respond, but then she heard the sound of a helicopter approaching.

"It's a regular airport this morning," she murmured.

Chrysander stood and tossed down his napkin. "That will be the jeweler. I'll return in a moment."

Jeweler? She watched him go, confusion running circles through her head. What the devil did he need a jeweler for? She sat back with a sigh and wondered where Patrice or Dr. Karounis was. At least with them present, she wouldn't have to face Chrysander's stormy silence.

She stood and looked around for a moment before finally deciding to venture outdoors. The sun looked warm and inviting, and she had yet to see any of the island in daylight.

She stepped out onto the terrace and immediately closed her eyes in appreciation as the sea breeze blew over her face. It was cool but not uncomfortably so, and sunshine left a warm trail over her skin as she sought out the stone path leading to the beach.

The farther she walked from the house, the sandier the pathway became. She stopped on the walkway and shed her sandals, wondering how the warm sand would feel sliding over her feet.

At the end of the pathway, there was a short drop off to the beach. When she stepped down, her toes sank into the loose grains, and she smiled.

The waves beckoned, and so she ventured toward the frothy foam spreading across the damp sand at the water's edge. The sea was so blue it took her breath away. Paradise. It was simply paradise. And Chrysander owned it.

The wind picked up the curls at her neck and blew them around her face. After several attempts to tuck the wayward strands behind her ears, she laughingly gave up and let them fly.

She glanced back toward the house, but seeing no one coming, she continued to walk down the beach, paralleling the water. The sounds of the incoming waves soothed her, and soon the tension in her shoulders began to unravel. She felt at peace here, but more than that, she felt safe.

The word startled her, and she stopped where she was, her forehead wrinkling in consternation. Why wouldn't she feel safe? Chrysander had a veritable mountain of security that he insisted on taking everywhere with them. If anyone was safe, she was. And yet, until they'd landed on the island, she'd felt uneasy, panic just a heartbeat away.

"You're losing your mind," she muttered. "Well, you've already lost that. Maybe the sanity isn't far behind."

Marley spied a large piece of driftwood wedged against a mound of sand, and she walked toward it. There was a place on the end that was relatively smooth, so she dusted off the sand and settled down to sit.

She sighed contentedly. She could sit here for hours watching the waves roll in and listening to the soothing sounds of the ocean. If it was warm enough to swim, she'd be tempted to shed her clothing and wade in. But then she had no idea where all the lurking security men were, and she had no desire to give them a free show.

Movement out of the corner of her eye caught her attention, and she turned her head to see Chrysander striding down the beach.

She grumbled under her breath even as he approached. Stopping in front of her, he fixed her with a frown. He pursed his lips then shook his head before moving to sit down beside her on the log.

"I can see you're going to keep my security team very busy, *pedhaki mou*."

She shrugged but didn't say anything.

"What are you doing out here?" he asked mildly.

"Enjoying the beach. It's very beautiful."

"If I promise to bring you out again, will you come back to the house with me? The jeweler is waiting for us, and he must return to the mainland soon."

She glanced sideways at him. "Why is a jeweler here, and why must we meet with him? Doesn't one usually visit a jeweler in his shop?"

Chrysander stood and gave her an arrogant look that suggested everyone came to him, not the other way around. He held out his hand to her, and she extended hers in resignation.

"You're really no fun," she muttered as he pulled her up to stand beside him.

"I can see I will have to change your opinion of me."

She tried to pull her hand away as they started back toward the house, but he held it fast. Hot then cold. At this rate, she'd never figure out the man. Memory loss or not, she couldn't imagine not wanting to tear her hair out around him.

They walked into the library, where an older man was

arranging velvet-covered trays on Chrysander's desk. When they entered, he looked up and beamed.

"Sit, sit," he encouraged as he walked around the desk to grasp Marley's hand. He raised it to his lips and brushed a polite kiss over her skin.

When Chrysander had settled her into a chair, he took the one beside her, and the jeweler hastened around the desk.

Marley took in the stunning rings, the dazzling array of diamonds, in front of her, and gasped. She turned a questioning gaze to Chrysander.

"He is here so we can choose your ring," Chrysander said matter-of-factly. As if having a jeweler personally come out was an everyday occurrence.

"I don't understand," she began lamely.

Chrysander picked up her left hand and raised her fingers to his lips. "It is important to me that you wear my ring, *pedhaki mou*. We had not gotten around to choosing one when you had your…accident. I want to rectify that matter now."

"Oh." As responses went, hers wasn't terribly brilliant, but it was all she could manage.

Chrysander urged her to turn her attention to the rings, and she did so a little nervously. They were so huge. And expensive! She didn't even want to know how much they cost. After trying several on, she spotted one that she loved, but then wondered if he'd be offended by her choice.

Her gaze kept wandering to it even as she continued to try on the rings the jeweler pressed on her.

"That one," Chrysander said, pointing to a ring to the far right.

To her surprise, the jeweler plucked the one she'd been staring at and handed it to Chrysander. Chrysander slid it onto her finger, and it fit perfectly. It was smaller than the others, and simple, but it suited her. A single sapphire-cut solitaire sparkled on her finger, and suddenly she had no wish to take it off.

"You like it," Chrysander said.

"I love it," she whispered, then looked quickly up at Chrysander. "But if you'd prefer another, I don't mind."

"We'll take this one," Chrysander told the jeweler.

If the jeweler was disappointed, he didn't show it as he smiled broadly at the couple. He efficiently boxed the jewelry back up and stored it in a briefcase that he locked. A few minutes later, Chrysander walked the jeweler out to the waiting helicopter but not before issuing Marley a stern order not to move from her spot.

She giggled as he left. He looked so exasperated, but then he was probably used to people obeying his every command and staying where they were put. A sudden thought horrified her. Had she been one of those people? Surely not. She may have lost her memory, but she hadn't had a personality transplant.

With that in mind, she left the library and went in search of something to eat. Her nonbreakfast was now a regret as her stomach protested.

Before she could open the refrigerator, she heard Chrysander enter the kitchen.

"How did I know you would not be where I left you?" he said.

She turned around and smiled sweetly. "Because you didn't ask nicely?"

He let out a low laugh, a sexy sound that vibrated right up her spine. "I've asked the helicopter to return in an hour's time. If you are feeling well enough, I thought we could go visit the ruins you were interested in and maybe take in some of the other sights."

"Oh, I'd love to!" Forgotten was food or anything else

as she hurried across and threw herself into Chrysander's arms. She hugged him tightly in her excitement.

Chrysander chuckled again. "Am I forgiven then for being no fun?"

She pulled back and made a face. "Trust you to throw my words back at me. But yes, you are forgiven. Let me just go change."

"Bring a sweater," he cautioned. "It will grow cooler toward evening."

She started to hurry off, but he caught her hand and pulled her back to him. She landed against his chest and looked up to see his mouth just inches from her own.

"Surely I deserve a reward?" he murmured.

She licked her lips, and he groaned. "I suppose a little one wouldn't be remiss," she said huskily.

His mouth closed over hers, and she melted into his arms. She trembled as he deepened his kiss, and a small moan escaped her lips.

He pulled away, his eyes blazing. "I better take you upstairs to change, or we will not be going anywhere but to bed."

She grinned impishly then pulled away and headed for the stairs. Not that she thought she'd get far, and she didn't. He caught up with her before her foot hit the first step.

She gave him an exasperated look as they climbed the stairs. "I am perfectly capable of navigating the stairs on my own, Chrysander. I'm not completely helpless."

"I can be a reasonable man. Just not in this matter," he said arrogantly. "I'm sorry, but you'll have to live with the fact that I intend to take care of you."

She rolled her eyes, but a smile twitched at the corners of her mouth. She could tell she strained his patience, and for some reason that amused her.

He waited while she changed and handed her a sweater

when she was finished. She laid it over her arm, and once again he took her down the stairs and out to the helipad, where the helicopter waited.

Soon they were flying over the water and a while later landed in Corinth. A car was waiting, and to her surprise, Chrysander put her into the passenger seat of the Mercedes then slid into the driver's seat himself.

"I do know how to drive," he said dryly when she looked at him questioningly.

She laughed. "It's just that I've never seen you do so." She frowned as she realized what she'd said. "What I mean is, I haven't seen you drive since…"

He laid a hand over hers. "I know what you meant, Marley. True, I don't drive very often. I'm usually occupied with business matters, but I have a car both here and in New York."

She settled into the soft leather seat as he drove away from the airport.

They spent much of the morning walking among the ruins. He explained the history, but she was more focused on the fact that it was a beautiful autumn day and they were together. No annoying personal assistants, no doctors or nurses, no business calls or faxes. It was, in a word, perfect.

"You're not paying a bit of attention, *pedhaki mou*." Chrysander's amused voice filtered through her haze of contentment.

She blushed and turned to look at him. "I'm sorry. I'm enjoying it, truly."

"Are you ready to return to the island?" he asked. "I'm not overtiring you, am I?" The amusement had turned to concern, and if she didn't dissuade him of the notion that she was not well, she'd find herself bundled back on the helicopter and her perfect day would be at its end.

"Tell me about your family. You've said nothing about

them. I realize the information may be redundant, but since I can't remember any of it, perhaps you could humor me."

"What would you like to know?" he asked.

"Anything. Everything. Are your parents still living? You don't talk about them."

A flash of pain showed in his eyes, and she immediately regretted the question.

"They died some years back in a yachting accident," he said.

She slipped her hand into his and squeezed comfortingly. "I'm sorry. I didn't mean to bring up such a painful subject."

"It's been a long time," he said with a shrug. But she could tell speaking of them bothered him.

She opened her mouth to change the topic when he suddenly frowned and lowered his other hand to his pocket. He pulled out his cell phone and studied it for a moment before opening it and putting it to his ear.

"Roslyn," he said shortly, after a quick glance at Marley.

Marley stiffened and pulled her hand away from Chrysander's. Trust his assistant to know just when to call. She must have radar.

She could see the tension rise in Chrysander, and when he looked in her direction, it was as though he stared right through her.

"Everything is fine here," Chrysander said. "Find out from Piers how things are going for the Rio de Janeiro hotel and report back." There was a long pause. "No, I don't know when we'll return to New York." He glanced again at Marley, and she got the distinct impression Roslyn was talking about her. "No, of course not," he said in a soothing voice. "I appreciate your diligence, Roslyn. You'll be the first to know when I plan to leave the island."

Marley looked away in disgust, no longer able to listen

to his part of the conversation. A few moments later, he snapped the phone shut and put it into his pocket. As expected, when she turned back to him, his entire demeanor had changed for the worse. He looked at her almost suspiciously, though she couldn't imagine why. But she wasn't imagining it. There was a distinct change in his mood.

"I'm sorry for the interruption," he said almost formally. "What were we talking about?"

"Tell me about your hotels," she said impulsively, wanting to steer him away from his concerns.

His expression froze and wariness stole over his face. "What would you like to know?"

She found a place to sit that overlooked the tall pillars and tugged him down beside her.

"I don't know. Anything. Where do you have hotels? Imperial Park in New York is one of yours, isn't it?"

He nodded.

"Where else do you have hotels? Are you very international? I heard you say something about Rio de Janeiro. Do you have a hotel there?"

He'd gone completely stiff, and she puzzled over why. Did he not like to discuss his business? In truth, she craved whatever details about him she could get. He hadn't been very forthcoming about his work life, a fact she found odd.

"We have hotels in most major international cities. Our largest are in New York, Tokyo, London and Madrid. We have several others, slightly smaller, across Europe. We're currently working on plans for one in Rio de Janeiro."

"But not in Paris? I think I'd like for you to have one in Paris so we could visit." She grinned teasingly at him.

Her smile faded when his eyes went cold and hard. A shiver worked its way up her spine, and a knot formed in her stomach. He looked angry. No, he looked *furious*.

"No, we do not have one in Paris."

His clipped tone had her backing away. She slid several inches down the bench. "I'm sorry...." She didn't even know what she was apologizing for. His mood had gone black in an instant, and she had no idea why. She seemed to have a penchant for dredging up the wrong subjects. First his parents and now his business. Was there any safe topic for them to discuss?

She stood and clenched her fingers into tight balls. "Perhaps you're right. Maybe we should go back now." She turned swiftly, her intention to walk back toward the car, but she moved too fast and the world spun dizzyingly around her.

She thought briefly of her missed breakfast before her knees buckled and she blacked out.

When Marley regained consciousness, the first thing she heard was a furious voice rapidly firing in Greek. As her eyes opened and her gaze flickered around her surroundings, she realized she was on an exam table in what appeared to be a clinic.

Chrysander's back was to her, and he was interrogating the doctor standing in front of him.

"Chrysander," she murmured weakly.

He spun around immediately and hurried over to where she lay. "Are you all right?" His hands swept over her body even as his eyes bored intensely into hers. "Are you in pain?"

She tried to smile, but she felt shaky. The doctor moved in front of Chrysander and held a cup toward her.

"Drink this, Miss Jameson. Your blood sugar is too low, but I think some juice will set you to rights."

Chrysander took the juice then curled an arm underneath her neck to help her sit up. He held the cup to her lips as she cautiously sipped at the sweet liquid.

"When was the last time you ate, Miss Jameson?"

The doctor pinned her with an inquiring stare, and she felt her cheeks warm with embarrassment. She ducked her head. "I didn't eat breakfast," she admitted.

Chrysander bit out a curse. "Nor did you eat much dinner last night. *Theos,* but I should not have brought you here today. I knew you hadn't eaten properly, and yet I didn't think to remedy the situation."

She gave him a wan smile. "It isn't your fault, Chrysander. It was foolish of me. I didn't give it much thought in my excitement over our trip to the ruins."

"It is my job to take care of you and our child," he said stubbornly.

The doctor cleared his throat and smiled at them. "Yes, well, no harm was done. A proper meal, and she'll feel like a new woman. I'd suggest being off your feet for the rest of the day. No sense in chancing things."

"I'll personally see to it," Chrysander said stiffly.

Marley sighed. He was taking her fainting spell personally. He fairly bristled with guilt, and she knew there'd be no swaying him from his course. She might as well resign herself to the rest of the day in bed.

"Can I take her home now?" Chrysander asked the doctor.

The doctor nodded. "Just make sure she eats promptly and that she rests."

"You can be certain I will," Chrysander said grimly.

Marley made to slide off the exam table, but Chrysander put out a hand to prevent her movement. Then he simply plucked her up into his arms and strode out the door.

When they got outside, a dark car pulled immediately in front of them, and a man jumped out to open the door for Chrysander. He ducked in, still holding Marley close to him.

"So much for you driving," she muttered as they were whisked away toward the airport.

"I cannot drive and hold you at the same time," Chrysander said patiently.

"I wasn't aware of the need to be held."

"I *will* take care of you."

It was said with ironclad resoluteness, his voice solemn, and she knew he took his vow very seriously. Realizing she wouldn't win any arguments with him today, she relaxed against his chest and curled her arms around his body.

He stroked her head and murmured softly in Greek. She was nearly asleep when the car came to a halt. Soon after the door opened, and a shaft of sunlight speared her eyes as she looked up.

Chrysander threw his arm up to shield her then gently turned her head back into his chest. He got out of the car still holding her and walked rapidly toward the helicopter.

"Go back to sleep if you can, *pedhaki mou*," he murmured as he climbed in.

But when the whir of the blades started, the fog of sleep disappeared. She contented herself instead with snuggling into the curve of his neck as they lifted off toward the island.

He'd obviously called ahead and issued a montage of orders, because when he walked into the house with her, Patrice had a meal waiting, and Dr. Karounis stood by to monitor Marley's condition. After an initial fuss, Patrice and the doctor, once they'd assured Chrysander that Marley was well, excused themselves, leaving the two alone.

Marley dug into the bowl of soup first and sighed as it coated her empty stomach.

"You will not skip any more meals," Chrysander said reproachfully as he watched her from across the table.

"I didn't intend to skip any," she said. "I just got side-tracked."

"I'll make sure that doesn't happen again."

She raised an eyebrow then grinned mischievously. "So it's back to being no fun then?"

He glowered at her.

That glower reminded her of what had transpired right before she'd fainted. She sobered and looked pensively at him.

"What is the matter?" Chrysander asked.

She fiddled with her spoon then set it down. "Before, when we were at the ruins. Why did you become so angry?"

His expression remained neutral, but she could tell he had no liking for the question. "It was nothing. I was just thinking about work," he said dismissively.

She stared doubtfully at him but didn't pursue the matter. When she had finished eating, Chrysander once again swept her into his arms and carried her up the stairs to the bedroom.

He settled her onto the mattress and methodically removed her clothing. By the time he'd pulled away her pants, she lay in only her bra and filmy panties. She heard the catch in his breath just as he turned away.

"Chrysander," she whispered.

He turned back, the muscles rippling through his body as if he were under a great strain.

"Stay with me. Could we take a nap together? I find I'm very tired after all."

If he didn't look so tortured, she'd laugh. She worked to keep her expression neutral as he grappled with her request. Finally he began working the buttons to his shirt. In silence he undressed to his boxers then crawled onto the bed with her.

Then he cursed. She looked inquiringly at him as he stared down at her.

"Would you like something to sleep in? You cannot stay in your bra. It doesn't look comfortable."

She blushed but nodded. "A nightshirt will do."

He got up and returned with one of his shirts. He helped her sit up and unclasped her bra. His hands shook slightly as he pulled the shirt over her head and let it fall to her swollen belly.

With gentle hands, he urged her back down and knelt above her. "Better?"

"Much," she said huskily.

He settled down beside her and tucked her into his arms. She twisted about, trying to find just the right spot. When she scooted her behind into his groin, she froze, feeling his arousal there against her skin. She started to move away, when Chrysander growled in her ear.

"Be still."

He clamped his arms around her, rendering her immobile. Her cheeks flaming, she tried to relax. The moment he'd touched her, her fatigue had fled. Now she faced trying to sleep with him wrapped around every inch of her body.

His warmth bled into her. He stroked her hair and murmured in her ear. Greek words she couldn't understand, though the comfort they intended was well recognized. She sighed in contentment as his hand glided down her arm, to her hip, coming to rest on her thigh.

She felt a wave of such utter rightness, and she was stunned to realize the nameless emotion she'd been grappling with was love. Her eyes fluttered open even as she heard Chrysander's even breathing signal his slumber.

She loved him. It shouldn't surprise her, but now that she'd acknowledged it, she realized that she hadn't immediately recognized it after her memory loss. Shouldn't she have known on some level that she loved this man?

He was complicated, there was no disputing that. Complex, hard and reserved. Well, if she'd broken down his barriers once, then surely she could do so again.

She settled down to sleep, purpose beating a steady rhythm in her mind.

Chapter 8

Warm lips kissed a line from her shoulder down her arm. Marley stirred and opened her eyes to see Chrysander's dark head move sensuously down her body.

"That's a very nice way to wake up," she murmured.

His head came up, and she met the liquid gold of his eyes. "How are you feeling, *pedhaki mou?*"

She rolled onto her back and lifted her hand to thread it through his short hair. "Much better. I'm full and had a nap. What more could a pregnant woman want?"

"Our child did not sleep much," Chrysander said as he slid his hand over her rippling abdomen.

She smiled. "No, he's been very active lately. The obstetrician said they do the most moving in the second trimester."

He stared intently at her rounded belly, fascination lighting his eyes. "They don't move in the last trimester?"

"Yes, just not as much. There isn't as much room. In the

last month, they do very little as their environment gets even more cramped."

"I would think it would be easier for you to rest then."

She yawned then covered her mouth with her hand as her jaw nearly cracked with the effort.

"You're still tired," he said reproachfully.

"I'm pregnant. I expect I'll be tired for the next eighteen years. I feel much better though. Truly, Chrysander. Let's get up."

He straddled her body, putting one knee on either side of her hips. He looked down at her, his eyes gleaming with a predatory light. "You're so eager to rise. Why is this?"

She blushed and smacked his chest with her fist. He leaned down and tugged her lips into a kiss. He nipped at the fullness of her bottom lip until it was swollen and aching.

"I have half a mind to keep you in bed until tomorrow morning," he murmured.

Putty. She was complete putty in his hands. If he so much as breathed on her, she went to mush. She twined her arms around his neck and returned his kiss hungrily. She could feel his erection straining against her, knew he wanted her as badly as she wanted him.

With obvious reluctance he pulled away and climbed off the bed. She looked at him in confusion. Why was he withdrawing?

He reached down and touched her hair, smoothing the tendrils away from her cheek. "You've been through an ordeal today, *agape mou*. I don't want to tire you any more."

He seemed as surprised as she was when the endearment slipped out of his mouth. Her eyes widened, and he tensed. Then he turned around and strode to the closet.

She watched him dress and then disappear from the bedroom. He'd called her my love, and while it had given her an indescribable thrill, it was obvious that it wasn't something he meant to say.

But he had said it. She held tight to that truth as she got out of bed to dress. Not knowing how he felt about her and why he took such pains to hold himself distant had puzzled her from the beginning. Was it because of her memory loss? Did he fear that her feelings for him couldn't possibly be considered valid while he was still a stranger to her?

She'd focused so much on her own problems that arose from the gaping hole in her past, but it was obvious that he, too, had difficulties with the situation.

If only she could remember. If only she could reassure him that she loved him whether or not she could remember loving him in the past.

All she could do was show him. And hope that her memory was restored before too much longer.

Chrysander sat in his office, staring out the window that overlooked the beach. Marley stood close to the water, her feet bare and the maternity dress she wore rippling in the breeze. He kept careful watch over her and had instructed his security team to do the same. He wouldn't take any chances after her fainting spell of the day before.

Just moments earlier, he'd hung up after speaking to the lead investigator on Marley's case. There had been no arrests made yet. No leads. The men who had abducted her were still out there. Still a danger to her and their child. It was unacceptable.

The detective had promised to stay in touch and to inform him the moment there was a break in the case, but Chrysander still wasn't satisfied. He wanted results. He wanted to make the men who'd dared to touch Marley pay.

He focused his attention back on Marley, who was still staring out to sea. Every once in a while she raised her hand to shove the curls from her face, only for them to blow back. She lifted her chin and laughed, and Chrysander could feel the impact from where he sat.

She was beautiful and carefree. Unguarded in the moment. He searched his memory for the times when they had been together. Happy. He hadn't appreciated it at the time, but their relationship—he now admitted to himself that they'd had a relationship—had been open and undemanding.

So what had driven her to betray his trust? He'd almost have preferred she'd betrayed him with another man; but no, she'd gone after his family, his brothers. And that he couldn't forgive…could he?

Indecision wracked his brain. A large part of him was still conflicted and angry. But another, smaller part was ready to move on. To forget what she had done and embrace a new beginning. Maybe she'd never remember, and if he was honest, it would make things easier if she never did.

He continued to watch her, and his gaze moved beyond her to where one of his security detail stood on guard at a distance. She continued to defy him, and he pretended annoyance, but all he did was make sure his men shadowed her at every turn. Her determination to go against his wishes amused him because he didn't sense any real irritation on her part. She liked goading him.

And he knew he was being overprotective, but the fact that her kidnappers were still out there, that they still posed a threat to her and their child, sent dark fear through his veins. She was his. He'd failed her once. No matter that she had betrayed him. He'd sent her and his child unprotected into the hands of her kidnappers because he'd allowed emotion to cloud his judgment.

He turned in annoyance when his phone rang. Tearing his gaze from Marley, he put the phone to his ear.

"Mr. Anetakis." Roslyn's voice broke clear over the line.

"Roslyn, have you spoken to Piers about the status of the Rio de Janeiro deal?"

"Yes, sir, and he said to tell you that if you'd answer your phone he'd let you know how things were going himself."

Chrysander chuckled. "I will deal with my younger brother."

"If at all possible, you need to attend a conference call tomorrow evening, seven our time. I'll send out an e-mail with the details. Theron and Piers will both be on hand, but Mr. Diego specifically wished to speak personally with you."

"I'll make it," he said.

"And how are things with you?" Roslyn asked hesitantly.

Chrysander frowned and glanced back to the beach, where Marley stood watching the waves roll in.

"Has she regained her memory yet?" she continued.

"No," he said shortly.

There was a moment of silence, and he could hear Roslyn's soft breathing as though she battled over whether to say what was on her mind.

"If that's all," he said in an effort to end the call.

"Have you considered that she's faking her memory loss?" Roslyn said in a rush.

"What?"

"Think about it," she said impatiently. "What better way to circumvent your anger than to pretend to have forgotten it all? You can't even be sure the child is yours. She was in captivity for months. Who's to say what went on during that time?"

Ice trickled down Chrysander's spine. "That's enough," he said tersely.

"But—"

"I said enough."

"As you wish. I'll phone you if anything changes."

Chrysander hung up and yanked his gaze back to the beach, but Marley was gone. Could Roslyn be right? Could Marley be faking her amnesia? The thought had crossed his mind when they'd still been in New York and Marley was fresh from the hospital. His instincts said no, but then he'd already been so wrong about her in every way. If someone had told him six months ago that she was capable of betraying him as she had, he would have cut them down to size.

Anger and confusion took turns battering his head. He rubbed a weary hand across his face and closed his eyes. It didn't really matter what he thought at this point. She was pregnant with his child and that took precedence above all else. He could overlook a lot for his son.

A sound at the door made him look up. Marley stood just inside his office, a sparkling smile on her face. Her eyes glowed with…happiness.

He found himself relaxing, the turmoil of a few minutes ago dissipating.

"You grew tired of your walk on the beach?"

Her lips twisted ruefully as she walked forward. "I should have known you knew exactly where I was."

He gestured toward the window. "I had a prime view. You looked to have enjoyed yourself. Are you feeling well today? You haven't overdone it?"

She stopped at his desk, and he nearly gestured her around to settle on his lap, but he refrained, needing to maintain a distance while he felt so volatile, so uncertain.

He didn't want to think of her as a deceiver, nothing more than a practiced actress bent on escaping retribution.

"I'm fine, Chrysander. You worry far too much. I don't need to be coddled. You would think I was the first woman to ever be pregnant."

"You are the first woman to bear my child," he pointed out.

She laughed. "And so I am. I'll make allowances for your overbearing ways because this is your first child. When we have our next, I expect you to act sanely."

Every muscle in his body stiffened, and he fought the darkness that spread across his face. Another child. It suggested permanence. A lasting relationship. Yes, he planned to ask—no, insist—she marry him, but he hadn't given thought to what it would mean. A permanent place in his life for her. More children.

Were his brothers right? Should he have installed her in an apartment, hired suitable staff to look after her until the baby was born and then removed her from his life?

"Chrysander? Is something wrong?"

He glanced up to see her staring at him with worried eyes. There, again, as it had so many times before when she looked at him, was a flash of uncertainty. Of fear almost. He cursed under his breath. He had not intended to frighten her, nor did he want to upset her.

He reached for her. "No, *pedhaki mou*. Nothing is wrong."

She hesitated the briefest of seconds before she finally walked around and into his arms. She settled on his knee, and he watched as she worked her lower lip between her teeth.

"Don't you want more children?" she asked.

He cocked his head to the side, trying to adopt a casual

air. "I don't suppose I'd considered it yet. Our first son is still to be born."

She nodded. "I know. I suppose I just assumed since you have brothers that you'd want more than one child. Have we discussed it before? Did I want more than one? I look ahead now and feel like I'd love several more. Maybe four total. But I don't know if I've always wanted that many."

Unable to resist her worried brow, he pressed a kiss to her forehead. "Let's not worry about it now. We have plenty of time. First you have to marry me," he said teasingly. "Let's wait until our son is born to think about adding more to our family."

A beautiful, captivating smile lit up her face and knocked the breath from him all in one moment.

"That sounds so lovely when you say it," she breathed.

"What's that?"

"Family. I don't have family, or so I was told. To know that you and I will have a family of our own means so much. Sometimes I feel so lonely, like I've been lonely forever."

She shivered lightly against his chest as the haunting words left her lips.

"You aren't alone," he said softly. "You have me, and we have our son."

It was a vow. One that he felt only passing discomfort over making. Part of him wondered at the ease with which he committed himself to a woman who'd done so much damage, but the other part could no sooner turn away than he could cut off his arm.

"You should go rest," he said firmly, more because of his need to distance himself from her before he totally succumbed to the pull between them than a real concern over her health. The doctor had assured him she was fit and well, that her fainting spell had been nothing more than a product of missed meals. "I'll summon Mrs. Cahill to help you up the stairs."

Her lips turned down into a frown. She struggled up from his lap even as he put a hand to her arm. "I'm perfectly rested, Chrysander. The walk on the beach was very refreshing."

"Still, a short repose wouldn't be unreasonable," he said. "I have some work to finish. I'll come for you when I'm done, and we can have dinner together."

Disappointment dulled her eyes before she looked away. She nodded but said nothing as she left the room.

Marley closed Chrysander's door quietly and glanced up as Patrice approached. She tried to look welcoming, because after all she did like Patrice. She was just doing her job.

"Are you ready to go up?" Patrice asked with a smile.

Marley sighed. "Honestly? I'd like to smother Chrysander with the pillow he insists I rest on."

Patrice tried to stifle her laughter, but a chuckle escaped. "Could I interest you in a cup of tea on the terrace instead?"

Marley immediately brightened. "That sounds wonderful."

She fell into step beside Patrice as the two headed toward the glass doors. A cool breeze, scented by the ocean, blew over Marley's face when she stepped outside.

"I hope you don't mind if Dr. Karounis joins us." Marley noticed the way Patrice's cheeks turned pink as she spoke. "He and I take tea here every afternoon."

"Of course not," Marley replied as she settled into one of the chairs surrounding the small table overlooking the gardens.

When Patrice ducked back inside to prepare the tea, Marley was left alone. She leaned back and stared out over the grounds. Even with the constant company that Patrice and Dr. Karounis afforded, loneliness surrounded her like a cloak. That and frustration.

Every time Chrysander relaxed around her and they shared any sort of intimacy, he immediately backed away, as if he became aware of what was happening and rushed to correct it.

She was convinced that Patrice and Dr. Karounis were here more as a barrier between her and Chrysander than they were here over any worry he had of her health. Not that he didn't care. She wasn't petty enough to think he wasn't genuinely concerned for her and their child. But at the same time, she couldn't discount the convenience of him pawning her off on Patrice whenever things got too personal.

It seemed that when she actually started to relax, he only grew more uptight. Nothing about her supposed relationship with this man made any sense to her. If only she could remember. If only she knew someone she could ask. Had she truly been so closed off from the rest of the world during her relationship with Chrysander?

"Surely things aren't that bad," Patrice said as she set a tray down on the table in front of Marley. "You look as though you have the weight of the world on your shoulders."

Marley managed a faltering smile. "Oh, nothing so serious. Just thinking."

Dr. Karounis walked up behind Patrice and nodded a greeting to Marley. Patrice smiled broadly and urged the doctor to sit down while she poured tea.

Despite her own inner turmoil, Marley couldn't help but smile at the older couple. They were obviously enjoying a mild flirtation. It was good to see someone happy and content. She'd give anything to enjoy a moment's peace.

With another sigh, she collected her cup and brought it to her lips as she looked out again over the beautiful garden. Maybe she was expecting too much in too short a time. Maybe she was pushing too hard, which precipitated Chrysander pushing her away. So much would be solved if she could only remember.

At any rate, she couldn't expect an overnight miracle. There had to be a way to break through Chrysander's defenses. She just had to find it.

Chapter 9

The heir days slowly began to settle into a routine much as their nights did. Once he was assured of her health, Chrysander made love to Marley every night, possessing her with passion that left her breathless. But in the mornings, he was always gone before she woke up.

She'd made it a habit to seek him out, bothered by the fact that he left their bed so early. More often than not, she'd find him in the library, either on the phone, on his computer or poring over contracts and faxes. He'd look up when she entered, and for a brief moment, she'd see fire flare in his eyes before his expression became more controlled, and after murmuring a polite good-morning, he'd return to his work. And she was summarily dismissed.

So she spent most mornings alone or in the company of Patrice and Dr. Karounis who seemed quite content to spend their time together. At lunch, Chrysander would make his appearance as if he hadn't just spent hours sequestered in work. To his credit, he devoted the after-noons to Marley.

She'd cajoled him into taking walks with her on the beach, though he grumbled about the chill and her tiring herself. She looked forward to these times because she had Chrysander all to herself, and at least in those few short hours, he seemed to lose his cautious reserve with her.

It was during one of those walks that Chrysander pulled her down to sit on the log she often sat on to watch the ocean. He stared out over the water for a moment then turned to her, his expression serious.

"We should get married soon."

She twisted the engagement ring around her finger with her thumb and wondered why this wasn't a happier con-versation.

"I wanted to give you time to recover and regain your strength. The doctor feels you are strong and healthy now."

She relaxed a little under his intent gaze. "When were you thinking of?"

"As soon as I can arrange it. I don't want to wait any longer. I don't want our child born a bastard."

She frowned and twisted her neck to gaze up at him. It was hardly a romantic declaration of love and devotion. But then she didn't want her child to be born out of wed-lock, either. She suddenly felt selfish for wanting a more flowery reason for the hastiness of their marriage.

"Will you marry me, *pedhaki mou?* I'll take care of you and our child. You'll want for nothing, I swear it."

She worked to keep another frown from her face. The more he talked, the less desirous she was for marriage. He made it sound like a bargain. She didn't want their mar-riage to be cold and clinical.

He tipped her chin up with his finger and stared down into her eyes. "What are you thinking about so hard?"

She didn't want to tell him the truth. So instead, she slowly nodded.

One of his eyebrows lifted in question. "Is that a yes?"

"Yes," she whispered. "I'll marry you as soon as you can arrange it."

Satisfaction glinted in his eyes. He leaned down to brush his lips across hers. "You won't regret this, *pedhaki mou.*"

Such an odd choice of words. Why would she have reason to believe she'd regret marrying the man she loved, the father of her child? She wondered if he'd always been so cryptic and that she'd learned to love him in spite of it. Obviously she had.

As they walked back to the house, she slid her hand into his. There was a need for comfort in her action. After only a slight hesitation, he curled his fingers around hers and squeezed. Bolstered by the small gesture, she shrugged away the doubts tugging at her.

That night, Marley was dressing for bed when Chrysander came up behind her and curled his arms around her waist. His hands rested over the swell of her stomach as he nuzzled a line from the top of her shoulder to the sensitive region just below her ear. Goose bumps danced and scattered along her skin, and she trembled against his chest.

"I much prefer you naked, *pedhaki mou,*" he said as he slid one hand up to pluck at the string of the gown she'd just slipped on.

His words speared through her mind, sparking a distant remembrance. For a moment, she had an image of him standing before her, staring at her with glowing eyes, saying those exact words. She struggled to remember more, but it slipped away as fast as it had slipped in.

She closed her eyes in frustration even as she gave way to the pleasure of his touch.

He slid the strap over her shoulder, following it with his lips until it tumbled down her arm. Then he turned his attention to the other side, giving it the same thorough attention. He thumbed the thin string down her arm until the satin material spilled from her body and landed in a pool on the floor.

Uncertainty and vulnerability washed over her as she stood naked save for the lacy panties she wore. She jumped when he placed his hands over her belly again and then did a slow walk up and over her curves. His palms smoothed up her sides and then curved around to her breasts, where he cupped both soft mounds. His lips found her neck again, and she shivered uncontrollably as his thumbs caressed her taut nipples while he landed light nips with his teeth.

"I want you," he said in a guttural voice. "You're so beautiful, *agape mou*. Come to bed with me."

It was so easy to forget her doubts and insecurities in the shelter of his arms. When they made love, they truly connected. There were no barriers, no stiffness and no reluctance. She lived for these moments, when he made her his, when he showed her far better than words what she meant to him.

She turned, allowing his hands to slide over her skin. When she was facing him, she leaned up on tip toe and linked her arms around his neck. "Kiss me," she whispered.

With a low growl, he swooped in and captured her lips with barely controlled restraint. His movements were impatient tonight, as though he couldn't get enough of her, as if he couldn't wait to possess her.

She allowed him to urge her toward the bed, his body pressed tightly to hers. He eased her onto the mattress, his lips never leaving hers. He lifted himself off her, his eyes blazing in the dim light. With jerky motions, he stripped out of his clothing before lowering himself once more.

"Make love to me, Chrysander," she said as she reached up to touch his face.

He bent, and his lips moved heatedly down her jaw to her neck and then lower to her breasts. He tugged one taut nipple with his mouth before going to the other. Lightly, his tongue rolled over the crest, sending shock waves to her throbbing center.

His dark head bobbed as he continued a path downward to the rise of her belly. Scooting his body down, he framed the mound between his hands with a reverence that brought tears to her eyes. Then he pressed his mouth to her stomach in a gentle kiss.

Emotion knotted in her throat until it became hard to breathe around it. If only they could stay this way. Here, where there were no words, no defenses, she felt loved and cherished. No walls, no barriers, no secrets.

His mouth moved lower, and she gasped when he nudged her thighs apart and touched his mouth to her pulsing core.

"Chrysander!" she cried out as he licked over her sensitive bundle of nerves.

"You taste so sweet, *agape mou*," he said as he moved up her body again.

He fit himself against her damp heat and then slowly slid inside her body. She closed her eyes and reached for him with a sigh of pleasure. Her hand threaded through the short hair at the back of his head and down to his nape where she caressed as he moved back and forth with exquisite gentleness.

Then his lips found hers again, and he swallowed her abrupt cry as he sank deeper than before.

"Give me your pleasure," he said against her mouth. "Only to me."

She arched against him, her body tightening as the first stirrings of her release began deep and rushed in a thousand different directions. Her soft cry split the night, and he gathered her tightly to him. His hand smoothed down her side to her hip and then to the curve of her belly.

"I can never get enough of you," he admitted in a voice that sounded strangely vulnerable.

She opened her eyes to see him staring down at her, his expression fierce and haunted. And then he began to move harder, more demanding. Wordlessly he took her to indescribable heights. She floated freely, her body cocooned in bliss.

So began the night. She'd barely come down from the peaks he'd driven her to when he began making love to her all over again. He possessed her tirelessly, commanding her body with a practiced ease that left her gasping. Throughout the night he was insatiable, and just before dawn, they both fell into an exhausted sleep.

Even as Marley hovered in the euphoric aftermath, her sleep was troubled. There was a familiarity to Chrysander's demanding lovemaking, as if for the first time he'd shown her part of her past life with him.

In her dreams, she struggled to open a firmly shut door, knowing that on the other side lay her life, her memories, everything that had happened to her in her lifetime. She pulled at it then beat on it, sobbing for it to open and show her.

She clawed at it, and finally, she managed to pry it open the barest amount. Light poured from the crack, and then, as suddenly as it had shone, brilliant and white, it was doused by an overwhelming feeling of fear and despair.

She knew without a doubt that she didn't want to see what was on the other side.

In her shock, she loosened her grip and the door slammed shut, leaving her kneeling and shaking against the cold wood. No! She needed to know. She had to know. Who was she and what had happened to her?

"Marley. Marley!" Chrysander's urgent tones intruded on her dream. "You must wake up, *pedhaki mou*. It's just a dream. You're safe. You're here with me."

She opened her eyes to see Chrysander over her, his eyes bright with concern. He'd turned the lamp on beside the bed, and for that she was grateful. She felt suffocated by the darkness of her dream.

She felt wetness on her cheeks and realized she'd been crying in her sleep. Her heart still raced with panic, and she couldn't dispel the awful feeling of foreboding that had gripped her.

She tried to speak, to tell Chrysander she was all right, but a cry wrenched from her throat. He gathered her tightly in his arms and held her close as her body shook with sobs.

"You're going to make yourself ill, Marley. You must stop."

For a long time she gripped his arms, not wanting him to pull away from her. When she finally managed to regain control of herself, he gently eased her back onto the pillows.

"What has frightened you so badly, *agape mou?*"

The images from her dream came roaring back, but she was hard-pressed to make sense of them. Thankfully, the awful panic had receded so that she could breathe normally again.

"I was at a door," she said, her speech faltering. "And I knew that on the other side of the door were my memories. But I couldn't open it no matter how hard I tried. Finally, I managed to crack it but then…"

"Then what?" he asked gently.

"Fear," she whispered. "So much fear. I was afraid. I let go of the door, and it slammed shut."

He lay back down beside her and curled his arms around her. "It was just a dream, *pedhaki mou*. Just a dream. It can't hurt you. You fear the unknown. This is natural."

She slowly began to relax against him. He stroked her back, his palm gliding up and down her spine.

"Are you all right now? Do you want me to call for Dr. Karounis?"

She shook her head against his chest. "No. I'm fine. Really. I feel so silly now."

"You're not silly. Try and go back to sleep. I fear I kept you awake far too long tonight."

His voice had deepened to a husky timbre, and her body tightened all over as she remembered the ways he'd kept her up.

With a yawn, she burrowed as tightly as she could against his hard body and let herself fall into what was this time a dreamless sleep.

Chrysander rose at dawn the next morning. He hadn't slept since Marley had awakened with her nightmare. After he'd soothed her, and she had fallen into a more peaceful rest, he'd lain awake, staring at the ceiling as he realized the impossibility of their situation.

Careful not to wake Marley, he showered and dressed. After checking to make sure she hadn't been disturbed, he went quietly down the stairs. He bypassed his office, though it was his custom to begin the day with business matters.

This morning something drove him to the beach where

Marley so often visited. The air was chilly blowing off the water, but he took no notice as he stood watching the waves break and slide into shore.

Marley's past, *their* past, threatened her in sleep. Her memories waged war at her most unguarded moments, and what would he do when it all came back?

The terrible conflict that ate at him was wearing him down. He should be angry, and at times he was. But it was also easy to forget. Here on the island, safeguarded from the rest of the world, it was easy to pretend that it was just him and Marley and their unborn child. No past betrayals, no lies, no deceit.

He shoved his hands into his pockets and bowed his head in resignation. Never before in his business or personal life had he felt so out of control, so indecisive. Could he forgive her for trying to destroy him and his brothers? That was the million-dollar question, because if he couldn't, they had no future. When she remembered, things would irrevocably change, and he could either hold on to the acid taste of betrayal, or he could forge ahead and offer his forgiveness.

Theos mou, but he didn't have the answer. He didn't know if he had it in him to be so generous. He wanted her, no question. He was drawn to her, even knowing her sins. She was pregnant with his son, but could he honestly say that if she weren't pregnant, he could so easily cast her aside?

Small arms circled his waist, and a warm body burrowed against his back. He looked down to see Marley's hands clasped around his middle, and he brought his up to cover hers automatically.

She hugged him tightly, and he could feel her cheek pressed against his spine. She felt…right.

Slowly he eased her hands away so that he could turn

in her arms. She looked up at him with warm and welcoming eyes before she dove into his arms and nuzzled
against his chest.

"Good morning," he said, unable to prevent the surge
of desire from racing through his body.

"I stopped by your office but didn't find you. I was worried," she said as she pulled away.

He cocked his head. "Worried?"

"You're never not in your office," she said lightly. "And
then I couldn't find you anywhere in the house. I thought…
I thought you might have left."

He ran his hands up to her shoulders and squeezed re-
assuringly. "I wouldn't leave without telling you, *pedhaki
mou.*" Was he so distant, so caught up in his efforts to avoid
her that this was what she thought of him? If she did think
so, he could hardly blame her. Between Mrs. Cahill and
Dr. Karounis, he'd erected a veritable arsenal of people to
put between them.

"Would you like to take a walk with me?" she asked.
"I always walk on the beach in the mornings when you're
working. That is, if you aren't too busy?"

He caught her hand and brought it to his lips. "I'm not
too busy for you and our child. But should you be resting?"

An exasperated shriek left her lips, startling him with
her ferocity. She yanked her hand from him and parked
both of her fists on her hips.

"Do I look like I need to be resting?" Anger and disappointment burned in her eyes. "Look, Chrysander, if
you don't want to spend time with me, just say so, but
stop throwing out your pat 'You need to be resting' line."

She turned and stalked farther down the beach, leaving
him there feeling like she'd punched him in the stomach.
He ran a hand through his hair as he watched her hurry

away, and then he strode after her, his feet kicking up sand as he closed the distance between them.

"Marley! Marley, wait," he called as he caught her elbow.

When he turned her around, he was gutted by the tears streaking down her cheeks. She turned her face away and swiped blindly at her eyes with her other hand.

"Please, just go away," she choked out. "Go do whatever it is you do with your time. I'll wait for my *appointment* with you in the afternoon."

It came out bitter and full of hurt, and he realized that he hadn't fooled her at all with the distance he put between them.

He reached for her chin and gently tugged until she faced him. With his thumb, he wiped at a tear that slipped over her cheekbone.

"You aren't an appointment, Marley."

"No?" She yanked away from his touch and retreated a few feet until there was a respectable distance between them. "I've tried to be patient and understanding even though I don't understand any of it. Us. You or even me. I can't figure you out, Chrysander, and I'm tired of trying. I've tried to be strong and undemanding, but I can't do it anymore. I'm scared to death. I don't know who I am. I wake up one day to find myself pregnant, and there's a stranger by my bed who says he's my fiancé and the father of my child. One would think this would tell me that at least I was loved and cherished, but nothing you've done has made me feel anything but confusion. You run hot and cold, and I never know which one to expect. I can't do this."

Coldness wrapped around Chrysander's chest, squeezing until he couldn't draw a breath. "What are you saying?" he demanded.

She looked at him tiredly. "Why are you marrying me? Is it just because of the baby?"

He frowned, not liking the corner she was backing him into. "You're tired and overwrought. We should go back in and continue this conversation where it's warm—"

She cut him off with a furious hand. "I am *not* tired. I am not overwrought, and I want you to stop with the overprotective hovering. I don't even buy that you're that concerned, only that it's a convenient barrier you can hide behind when I start asking questions."

He opened his mouth to refute her words but then paused. He couldn't very well deny it when it was true. Still, he had no desire for her to become distraught. Surely *that* couldn't be good for the baby.

"What in my past am I so afraid of?" she whispered. "Last night terrified me. I woke this morning with a feeling of such fear, and not because I can't remember, but because I'm afraid to remember."

She stared earnestly at him, her eyes pleading.

"Tell me, Chrysander. I need to know. What were we like before? How did we meet? Were we very in love?"

He turned toward the water and shoved his hands back into his pockets. "You worked for me," he said gruffly.

She moved beside him, not touching him. But she was close enough that he could feel the soft hiccups of her breaths.

"I did? At your hotel?"

He shook his head. "In the corporate offices. You were my assistant."

She looked at him in shock. "But Roslyn is your assistant, and she seems awfully comfortable in that role. Like she's been there for years."

He offered a small smile. "You weren't my assistant for long. I was too intent on having you in my bed. I convinced you to quit and move in with me. You were too much of a distraction for me at work."

She didn't look pleased by his statement. A worried frown worked over her face, and her lips turned down into a dissatisfied moue.

"So you've made it a practice to put me where it's most convenient for you," she murmured.

He cursed softly under his breath, but again, he couldn't very well deny that he'd been intent on having his way when it came to her.

"And I allowed this?" she asked. "I just quit my job and moved in with you?"

He shrugged. "You seemed as happy to be with me as I was with you."

She frowned harder and curled her hands protectively over her waist. "Was our baby planned?"

He drew in his breath. Here was an area he had to tread lightly. "I wouldn't say planned, but your pregnancy certainly wasn't unwelcome."

If possible, she looked more miserable. She hunched her shoulders forward and turned away, but not before he saw the reemergence of tears.

He sighed and reached for her, pulling her into his arms. "Why are you so sad this morning, *pedhaki mou?* What can I do or say to make you feel better?"

She glanced up at him, her eyes shining with moisture. "You can stop avoiding me. You can stop using concerns over my health and that of the baby as an excuse to treat me as an invalid. You can stop treating my past like it's something I have no right to know."

He pressed his lips tightly together. "I will try to be less conscientious of your…health, though I reserve the right to be concerned."

She smiled then, and the relief that hit him almost

caused him to stumble. He hadn't realized just how much her happiness was important to him. Was he crazy to be so concerned when she'd had no regard for his happiness in the past?

She leaned up to kiss him, and he caught her against him, holding her possessively as he devoured her lips.

"Thank you," she said as she pulled back. "I just want…" She stopped, and longing flooded her eyes before she look away.

"What do you want, *pedhaki mou?*"

Her gaze flickered back to his. "I want us to be happy," she said huskily. "I want to be sure of my place in your life. I want to remember, but more than that, I want to feel like I have more than just a small piece of you and your time."

He regarded her thoughtfully. She'd never been so direct before her memory loss. She'd been shy and hesitant about voicing her wants and desires. But had she felt like this before? Had she resented his prolonged absences? The way he fit her into his life at his convenience? Was that why she'd lashed out? Had it been a bid to gain his attention?

"I want you to be happy, too, Marley. I want this very much. And while I can't convince you of your place in my life with mere words, hopefully I can prove it to you over time."

Her smile warmed him to his toes. It was like watching the sun break over the horizon. She reached for his hands and slid her palms into his grip.

"Come walk with me," she invited.

Unable to deny her anything in that moment, he gathered her close and began walking down the beach.

Chapter 10

Marley knelt in the cool soil of the garden and plucked the few weeds from around the flowers and greenery. With Chrysander's morning ritual of working, she'd found other ways to occupy her time, much to the dismay of the gardener who flew out twice a week to tend the grounds.

Ever since her outburst on the beach, Chrysander had ceased to push Patrice and Dr. Karounis at her for every little health concern. Instead, they stayed firmly in the background on an as-needed basis, and Chrysander had relented on her traveling the stairs alone.

Despite the fact that he continued to work in the mornings, he came out to have breakfast with her before returning to his office. Then the fun began for Marley. Each day she found a new method of driving him insane. He'd come looking for her when work was finished, and invariably she tried the restraint he'd promised to exercise when it came to demanding that she rest.

When Chrysander had found her in the garden on her hands and knees, she thought he was going to burst a blood vessel. He'd promptly carried her inside and up the stairs, stripped her down and put her into the bathtub.

She'd giggled at his ferocious scowl, listened with pretended solemnity to his decree that she not endanger herself in that manner anymore and promptly plotted to return as soon as he was caught up in work again.

It began a fun game between them, although the amusement was entirely hers because Chrysander failed to see the hilarity in her continued disobedience.

So here she sat, waiting with amused delight for his arrival.

She heard his sigh behind her and grinned even as she found herself lifted into the air. She tumbled against Chrysander's hard chest and smiled serenely up at his dark expression.

He strode for the house, grumbling the entire way.

"I promised to ease up on my *overprotective tendencies*. I stopped insisting you rest and even allowed you to walk unaided up and down the stairs."

Marley rolled her eyes.

"But you would try the patience of a saint," he growled.

As he had done before, and as she was counting on, he stripped her down and deposited her into an already drawn bath. He glared balefully at her, and she giggled as she sank lower into the water. He watched intently as she slowly washed herself, hunger glittering in his eyes.

Relishing the fact that she had his full attention, she took advantage as she worked the cloth over every inch of her body. When she was finished, she glanced innocently up at him as he towered over her. She flashed him her best smile, but he continued to glower at her.

"Your cuteness is not going to get you out of trouble, *pedhaki mou*," he said.

"Well, at least I'm cute," she said pertly.

"Why do you insist on provoking me? My hair is turning gray, and it is solely your fault."

She glanced up at his dark hair, not marred by a single gray strand, and raised an eyebrow. "You poor baby. Are you too old to keep up with one little pregnant woman?"

"I'll show you old," he growled as he plucked her from the bathtub.

He barely took the time to dry her before he strode into the bedroom and deposited her on the bed. Her eyes widened appreciatively as he began stripping his clothing from his muscled body.

"Clearly I need to be bad more often," she murmured. "I could learn to live with the punishment."

"Little minx," he said as he lowered himself into her waiting arms.

He was always in control in their lovemaking, and she knew this was the way it had always been, but now she had a sudden desire to turn the tables. To make him as crazy as he made her.

She pushed at him, and he withdrew with a frown. She followed him up and placed her hands on his shoulders, forcing him to lie on his back. She straddled his legs and stared at his shocked expression, a mischievous grin working at her lips.

"I want to touch you, Chrysander," she said softly. She placed her palms on the tops of his thick legs and smoothed them slowly upward.

His eyes smoldered and sparked. "Then by all means, touch me, *agape mou*."

With a little nervousness, she touched his male flesh, and he jerked in reaction. Feeling a little bolder, she wrapped her fingers around the turgid length and stroked lightly.

A groan worked from his throat, and she could see sweat beading on his brow. He was beautiful. Hard, male, his strength rippled through his every muscle.

She leaned down and pressed a kiss to his taut abdomen and then worked her way up to his flat nipples. A thin line of hair dusted his midline, and she ran her fingers over it, liking the feel of it on her skin.

She knew what she wanted to do but was unsure of exactly how she would accomplish it. He must have sensed her uncertainty and her hesitation, because he reached down with his strong hands and grasped her hips.

He lifted her then eased her down over the length of his erection. She closed her eyes as he slid inside her.

"You're killing me, *pedhaki mou,*" he rasped. "God, it's so good. You're so sweet."

Encouraged by the satisfaction and approval in his voice, she made love to him, raining kisses over his chest as his hands helped guide the movements of her hips.

Her body trembled, and she knew she was nearing her release, but she wouldn't succumb until he went with her. He tensed beneath her, and suddenly his hands tightened around her hips. He arched into her, and with a cry, the world exploded around her.

She fell forward, but he caught her with gentle hands. He lowered her to his heaving chest and stroked her hair as they struggled to catch their breaths.

He turned so that he could position her beside him, and he eased out of her body, eliciting another soft moan from her. She cuddled against him, warm and replete.

"Was I any good?" she asked, her words muffled by his chest.

He shook with laughter then turned her face up so she

could see him. "If you were any better, you really would make me an old man before my time."

"But did you like it?" she asked softly. "Or do you think I'm a brazen hussy now?"

He tweaked her on the nose then kissed the same spot. "I liked it very much. I liked it so much that I might consider letting you go play in your garden again tomorrow."

She rolled her eyes and yawned sleepily. He drew his finger down her cheek. "Sleep now. I'll wake you for dinner."

"I don't need a nap," she grumbled, but she was already drifting off.

Not wanting to be entirely predictable, Marley forewent the garden the next day and opted instead for the heated pool. She'd been eyeing it with longing since they'd arrived, and thanks to boutiques only too willing to deliver to the island, she had a simply decadent swimsuit she was dying to try out.

As she pulled the skimpy suit on, she realized that in essence she was trying to seduce Chrysander. Not that she hadn't already, but she was attempting to make him fall in love with her.

She frowned back at herself in the mirror. Wasn't this backward? He was the one with the memory. Shouldn't he be trying to make her fall in love with him? She knew she loved him but hadn't said the words. Something had held her back, and now she pondered what it was that made her unwilling to take that jump.

There was a hesitation about him that niggled at her, as though he wanted to keep a certain amount of distance between them. She didn't want that. She wanted him to love her as she loved him.

She sighed. If only she could remember.

She wiggled a bit and readjusted the bikini until she was satisfied with the result. The top cupped her small breasts and did a remarkable job of making them seem more impressive than they actually were. The bottom... She smiled as she turned at an angle to view the back of the bikini. It wasn't a thong...exactly, but it did draw attention to her gently rounded bottom.

Straightening again, she smoothed a hand over the swell of her belly. Chrysander seemed to enjoy her pregnancy. He touched and kissed her belly frequently and seemed entranced by the mound. She hoped he'd find the suit, and her, sexy.

Recognizing that she was stalling, she reached for the silk robe and tugged it on. She wanted no chance that someone else would see her in such a scandalous suit. This was for Chrysander's eyes only.

She slipped down the stairs and made it through the living room unseen. She walked into the smaller room that housed the indoor portion of the pool and eyed the rippling water with anticipation. Chrysander or no Chrysander, she was looking forward to a swim.

Shedding the wrap, she tossed it over one of the loungers and walked to the edge of the pool to dip her toe in. It was wonderfully warm. She moved to the steps and carefully descended into the water.

Oh, it was marvelous. She swam toward the back glass enclosure that overlooked the outdoor portion of the pool. She was tempted to duck under the divider and swim outside, but the breeze would be cold on her damp skin.

She floated lazily on her back for a while then did a few laps, gliding underneath the water for as long as she could hold her breath. She came up with a gasp and grabbed on to the side of the pool. And then she saw a pair of leather loafers.

She glanced up to see Chrysander watching her, arms folded across his chest, a mock scowl on his face. Even she could see that his lips were twitching suspiciously.

With an innocent blink, she smiled and offered a hello. He squatted down and put a finger underneath her chin, nudging it upward.

"Enjoying yourself, *pedhaki mou?*"

"Very much," she returned.

"And to think I was looking forward to hauling you out of your garden today," he murmured.

Her face heated as she recalled all that had happened yesterday when he'd done just that. She extended her hand. "Help me out?"

He grasped her hand, and she reached to grip his wrist with her other hand at the same time she planted her feet against the side of the pool and pulled with all her might. He gave a shout of surprise as he toppled over and hit the water with a gigantic splash.

He came up sputtering, and for a moment, she worried that he was truly angry. He scowled ferociously at her before glancing down at his soaked clothing. Then he started laughing.

Before he could think retaliation, and since she still wanted him to see her suit, she swam over to the steps and exited the pool in slow, deliberate movements. She glanced over her shoulder to see his mouth drop open as he viewed the back of her suit.

When Marley reached the top, she turned so he could see her profile, and she heard him suck in his breath. She turned away again and began walking toward where her wrap was laying.

"Oh no you don't, you little tease," he growled.

She blinked at how quickly he got out of the pool. She gave a shriek of surprise when he closed in on her then laughed when he gathered her into his arms and headed back toward the pool.

"Chrysander, your clothes!"

"As if they matter now. You've quite ruined them."

"I'm sorry."

He laughed. "No, you're not." He bent down at the side of the pool and gently eased her back into the water. Then he stood and fixed her with a glare. "You stay right there."

She giggled. Her laughter died in her throat, though, when he began peeling his clothing off his body. First his shirt came off, revealing his muscular chest. Then he kicked off his shoes and yanked off the soaked socks. When he reached for the fly of his trousers, she blushed but couldn't look away to save her life.

The discernible bulge in his boxers as he stepped out of his pants told her that she'd certainly been successful in her quest to make him a little crazy. But now she wondered what exactly he'd do about it.

He hopped over the side, landing next to her with a minimal splash. Then he hauled her against him, kissing her hungrily.

"That suit should be illegal," he said as he worked his mouth down her neck.

"You don't like it?" she asked innocently. "I could always get rid of it."

"Oh, I like it," he murmured. "I'm going to like taking it off of you even better."

She broke loose and dove beneath the water, swimming away from him as fast as she could. She surfaced after a short distance but didn't immediately see him. She looked down, too late, to see his glimmering body. He grabbed her legs and yanked her underneath.

His lips closed over hers, and he propelled them both above the water. She wrapped her arms around his neck and smiled up at him. "I suppose I'm going to have to take back what I said about you being no fun."

"It would seem so."

"I wouldn't object to you hauling me out of the pool and taking me upstairs," she said with pretended innocence.

He kissed her again, hot, breathless. His hands slid around her waist to cup her bottom. He lifted her upward, and she latched her legs around his waist.

"Hold on to me, *pedhaki mou,*" he murmured. "I'm hauling you out of the pool right now."

He mounted the steps and carefully climbed out of the pool. As he neared one of the loungers, she noticed that he'd brought two towels with him. Apparently he had planned to come in all the while. She grinned impishly at him. He wasn't so serious all the time.

He put her down in one of the loungers then reached for a towel. He dried her hair and her body, allowing his hands to linger in some of her most sensitive areas. He touched and caressed until she was squirming in the chair.

"Now who's teasing?" she said breathlessly.

He straddled the lounger and lowered his body to hers.

"Mmmm, you're warm."

"Are you cold?" he asked huskily. "I wonder what I can do to warm you."

She pulled him closer, wrapping her arms around him. She threaded her fingers into his wet hair and kissed him. A sound of contentment purred from her throat as he returned her kiss with equal ardor.

His erection strained against her belly, hot, like steel. Warmth shot through her body, leaving her flushed and aching. She wanted him. Wanted him so badly.

"Take me upstairs," she whispered as his lips scorched down her neck and to the swell of her breasts.

The sound of a door closing startled them both. Chrysander let out an oath as he rolled away from Marley and yanked up a towel to cover her. Marley stiffened when she saw Roslyn over Chrysander's shoulder.

Her surprise turned to anger. The woman had barged in, intruded on their privacy without so much as a call to let them know she was coming out to the island. They hadn't even heard the helicopter land, but then they'd been occupied with other matters.

"What are you doing here?" Chrysander said icily.

"I'm sorry to interrupt, Mr. Anetakis," Roslyn said, though her expression said she was anything but. Her gaze skimmed Marley in triumph, but the look was gone when she turned her attention back to Chrysander. "There were several things that needed your attention, and I thought it best to see to them personally rather than rely on the phone or e-mail."

"They certainly haven't failed in the past," Chrysander said stiffly. "If you'll excuse us, I think perhaps it would be better for you to wait in my office."

"Yes, of course, Mr. Anetakis. Again, my apologies for the disturbance."

Marley shivered, this time the chill setting in deep. The woman had impeccable timing.

"I'm sorry," Chrysander said as he helped her from the lounger. He wrapped the towel around her shivering body and tucked her against his side. "I'll take you upstairs so you can change into something warmer. This shouldn't take but a moment, and then I'll return."

Marley nodded, but for her, the moment was ruined. Gone was Chrysander's fun-loving mood. The passion that had sizzled between them just minutes ago was now a cold blanket thrown by his trusty assistant.

He took her upstairs and ushered her into the shower. When she stepped out, he'd already dressed and gone back downstairs. With an unhappy sigh, she gathered the towel around her and sat down on the edge of the bed.

Chrysander entered his office, irritation replacing his earlier good mood. He stared hard at Roslyn, who stood to the side. "I do not appreciate this intrusion," he said crisply. "There was no call, no warning, no *permission* asked to come out to the island."

Roslyn paled and her eyes widened.

"This is my private living area, and as such, you do not have free rein as you do in my business settings. Are we understood?"

"Yes, sir," she said stiffly.

"Now, what was so important that it didn't warrant a phone call?" he demanded.

"I've discovered that another design was stolen," she said softly.

"What?" Curses spilled from his lips, and it took a moment for him to realize he was speaking in Greek, and Roslyn didn't understand a word of it. He shook his head and put both hands down on his desk. "What design? Tell me everything."

Roslyn's expression hardened. "It's an older one, a design you discarded. It was the original plan for the Rio de Janeiro hotel. But still, she must have sold it to Marcelli with the others, because his hotel going up in Rome bears a remarkable likeness. I saw the proofs myself just two days ago."

Rage burned like acid in Chrysander's veins. "Do my brothers know of this yet?"

Roslyn shook her head. "I thought you would want to tell them."

He nodded and closed his eyes as he turned to look out the window to the beach. Every time he thought he had come to terms with Marley's betrayal, the past came back to haunt him. As much as he wanted to forget, to move on, to put the past behind them, it always came back, insidious and unrelenting.

He struggled to remember how Marley could have gotten access to the hotel plans. He certainly hadn't guarded himself at home. As careful as he was in the office and in all other aspects of his life, he'd been relaxed and free with her, never thinking to protect his interests from her.

How could he build a life with her when he could never trust her? Was he a fool for building a temporary relationship when it would all come tumbling down the minute she remembered? When she'd have to face the sins she'd committed and reap the consequences of her betrayal?

Through it all, he could only remember one thing. The way she'd looked the night he'd confronted her in their apartment. The absolute shock and horror on her face. Could anyone fake such a reaction that well?

For the first time, he took a long, hard look at the woman she'd been during their time together before her abduction and the woman she'd been since. There was no marked difference. The only inconsistency was her betrayal.

"Chrysander." Roslyn spoke up in a soft voice.

His eyes narrowed at her use of his name. It was not something he ever tolerated from his employees, though he wasn't sure why it bothered him coming from someone he had worked closely with for some time.

"You won't allow her to do it again, will you?"

He turned around to face her. "No, it won't happen again," he said tightly, anger creeping up his spine. His anger wasn't totally at Marley. For some reason, it rankled that Roslyn would think to warn him away from Marley.

Roslyn looked uncomfortable. "I just hope she doesn't

ruin things for you with this hotel deal. Not again. It's too important."

"I don't think that's any of your concern. I will handle Marley."

She flinched at his tone. "I apologize. This company, this job, is very important to me. I've worked hard for you, sir. I worked hard on the Paris deal."

Chrysander let go of some of his anger and blew out a sigh. She had worked hard, and he could see why she would harbor some anger toward Marley even if he wouldn't tolerate it. Even if he didn't feel she was justified in that anger. That thought struck him hard, because it meant on some level he didn't believe Marley capable of her crime.

"I appreciate your concern, Roslyn. However, it is not your business. If that is all you wanted, then I'll call for the helicopter to return you to the mainland."

She looked as though she would protest, but then she nodded.

Thirty minutes later, Chrysander escorted her out to the helipad, and as soon as the helicopter lifted off, he turned and strode back into the house.

His anger and uncertainty evaporated when he entered the bedroom and found Marley sitting on the bed, wrapped only in a towel, her expression sad and distant.

He knelt in front of her and touched her cheek. "What is it, *agape mou*? Are you all right?"

She smiled, though it didn't reach her eyes. Her beautiful blue eyes that had sparkled just a short time ago with laughter. He wanted them to sparkle again. He wanted that stolen moment at the pool back. Before Roslyn had arrived and given him news that could very well change everything between him and Marley. Again.

"I'm in an impossible situation," she confessed.

His brow wrinkled in confusion. He didn't like the sadness in her tone. The resignation.

"What do you mean?" he asked softly as he trailed a finger down the silken curve of her cheek.

She looked into his eyes. "I don't like the way she has free rein in our lives. This is our home. We should be able to make love, have fun together, without fear of being caught in a compromising situation by a stranger. But if I voice this, if I say I don't like her and I don't want her here, it makes me a catty bitch. There is no way for me to come out the winner and every way for me to be the loser in this."

She looked down for a moment then stared back up at him, emotion shimmering in her eyes. "I don't like the way you back away from me every time she appears. She sweeps in on some pretext of business, then she leaves and you become distant. The last weeks have been so utterly wonderful, and now she barges in and I can already feel you pulling away from me. I don't know that I can bear it."

Tears pooled in her eyes, and he was struck speechless, for what she said, all of it, was completely true. He hadn't realized how it would look to her, had thought he'd hidden the conflicting emotions he experienced when reminded of the fact she'd stolen from him, lied to him, betrayed him.

He raised one of her hands to his mouth and pressed it firmly to his lips. "I'm sorry, *agape mou*. I'm sorry her presence has bothered you and that I've ignored it. It won't happen again. I've already informed her that under no condition is she to just arrive here without at least phoning."

"I could stand her presence. I won't lie and say I like the woman, but I could tolerate her. What I cannot bear is the way you pull away from me every time she appears. Without any memories to bolster my confidence, I have nothing to point to and say, Marley, you're being ridiculous. Of course there's nothing going on between him and his assistant."

His mouth fell open in surprise. "You think I'm having an affair with her?" He couldn't control the shudder of distaste that rolled down his spine.

She shook her head emphatically. "Oh, I've made a mess of this. I'm only trying to say that for me, this is all new. Our relationship is new. I can't remember our time together before, so in essence, we're building new, starting all over. I can't help the insecurity I feel when I look at her and know she's trying to undermine our relationship."

He gathered her in his arms, having no idea what to say to her. He couldn't very well deny that Roslyn probably did want to keep him from Marley. She knew Marley had stolen from the company, a company that Roslyn was devoted to and had put in a lot of long hours for in preparing the deal that had disappeared along with the plans for the Paris hotel. And now he'd learned that yet another of the Anetakis designs would be going up under the Marcelli name. No matter it was one he'd discarded. Marley couldn't have known that at the time.

What an impossible situation. Surprising to him was the anger that Roslyn's words had caused. His first reaction had been to defend Marley and to chastise Roslyn for speaking out against Marley. But how could he when Roslyn was right?

All he knew was that he didn't want Marley to hurt. As stupid as that sounded given the hurt she'd caused him, he wanted to wipe away the sadness in her eyes. While he couldn't do anything to erase the past, what he could do was make sure that Roslyn wasn't a source of contention between them. He would honor Marley's wishes in this, for they mirrored his own. He didn't want anything to come between them here on the island. Roslyn wouldn't return.

Chapter 11

Chrysander hung up the phone with a grimace and leaned back in his leather chair. He put his hands behind his head and stared up at the ceiling.

He had to return to New York. Piers had called him with the news just moments ago, and Chrysander greeted the fact with a discomfort that was alien to him. Worse, he'd had to inform Piers and Theron that another of their designs had been stolen. They were understandably furious. With Marley. How would they react when they learned he had every intention of marrying her as soon as possible?

He was torn between wanting Marley to go with him and wanting to keep her sheltered here on the island. Away from any chance she might remember. Away from the judgment and animosity of his brothers.

The beginnings of a headache plagued him as he considered the selfishness of that particular thought. He knew, though, that when she remembered, and the doctors had assured him she would, things would irrevocably change between them.

He should still be furious with her, and he should be working to maintain distance between them, but she'd chipped away his resistance during their time on the island. As much as it shamed him, it no longer mattered to him that she'd lied, that she'd stolen from him and his brothers. He wanted things to remain as they were, and if she remembered, then they would be forced to face the events of the past.

And he'd likely lose her.

It bothered him more than it should. She was pregnant with his child, he told himself, and that should be reason enough not to want things to sour between them.

His time here with Marley had brought him back to the times they'd spent together before the night he'd discovered her betrayal. He hadn't really appreciated her before. He'd taken her and her presence in his life for granted, but now he knew how much he'd liked having her there when he returned from business.

She was fun and carefree. Gentle and loving. All the things he'd wish for in the mother of his child.

But she'd betrayed him. It always came back to that even as he wanted to forget it.

"Chrysander?"

He looked up on hearing his softly spoken name to see Marley standing in the doorway, her hand resting on the frame as she peered in. He shook himself from his grim thoughts and hoped his expression wasn't as brooding as he felt. Things had been strained and tense between them since Roslyn had come to the island. A fact he regretted but was unable to fully remedy when he still carried his own doubts and uncertainties where Marley was concerned.

"What is it, *pedhaki mou?*"

"Are you all right?" She let her hand fall and started forward, her steps hesitant.

He guessed he did look brooding.

"Come here," he said, holding out his hand to her as she neared. He pulled her down onto his lap, suddenly wanting her close. "I have to return to New York."

A shadow crossed over her face. "When?"

"In the morning. My brother called, and a dignitary we are courting for a hotel project is going to be at a reception at our New York hotel. Piers and Theron thought to handle it, but the man wished to meet with all three of us. It's something I cannot miss, I'm afraid."

She looked disappointed, and even as the uneasiness over her going back to New York lingered in his mind, he found himself saying, "You could go with me."

Her eyes lightened. "I wouldn't be in the way?"

He frowned. "You are never in the way, *agape mou.* This would be good, I think. We could announce our wedding plans. My brothers will want to meet you," he said, warming to the subject. "We could even be married in New York with my family around us and then return here."

In his mind, the sooner they married, the better.

"I'll arrange for Dr. Karounis to return to Athens. I don't think we need him any longer."

Her smile broadened. "And Patrice? Not that I don't love her, but she and Dr. Karounis seem to have gotten along extremely well. Maybe she'd like to take a trip to Athens."

"I'll extend the offer," he said with a smile.

"Then yes, I'd love to go." She threw her arms around him and kissed him exuberantly on the lips. Before he could deepen the kiss, she scrambled off his lap. "I have to go pack!"

He chuckled and caught her hand. "You have plenty of time."

But still she hurried away, and he stared after her, long after she'd disappeared through the doorway. He should feel relieved that soon they'd be married, and she'd be bound to him, but he couldn't dispel the uneasy feeling that gripped him.

Chrysander's jet touched down in New York in the late afternoon, and a limousine was waiting for them when they stepped off the plane. A tall, formidable-looking man stood by the car, and as they drew closer, Marley could see a strong resemblance between him and Chrysander.

"Theron," Chrysander called out. "I did not expect you to meet us. This is a surprise."

Theron gave a half smile. "Can I not greet my brother?"

Chrysander put an arm around Marley's waist and drew her forward. "Theron, this is Marley. Marley, this is my younger brother Theron."

She smiled. "I'm very glad to meet you."

His gaze flickered impassively over her, and he didn't return her smile. Slowly hers faded as she read the unwelcoming look on his face. Instinctively, she shrank into Chrysander.

Then Theron's gaze dropped to the hand on which she wore the engagement ring, and he outright frowned. He stared back up at Chrysander, his jaw tight.

"You will be courteous," Chrysander said in a very low tone. Even so, she could hear the bite in his voice.

"I'm pleased to meet you," Theron said stiffly, though his body language said just the opposite. He turned on his heel and walked toward another car parked a short distance away.

Marley looked up at Chrysander in bewilderment. "What was that all about?"

"It is nothing, *pedhaki mou*. I am sorry he was rude. It won't happen again."

"But *why* was he rude?" His behavior baffled Marley. And then another thought occurred to her. "Have we met before? Of course we would have. He's your brother. Did I do something to offend him in the past? Has he always disliked me?"

Chrysander ushered her into the car and slid in beside her. "No, you haven't met before. You needn't worry that you've done anything. It's just Theron's way." He sounded a bit strangled, and her gaze narrowed at what she thought must be a lie.

When his cell phone rang, he lunged for it in his haste to answer. She put her lips together and seethed in silence. Something didn't add up. Why would his brother dislike her so intensely on sight? And for that matter, why had she never met him before? It couldn't be normal for her not to have met the family of the man she was going to marry, the father of her child.

She leaned back against the seat and blew out her breath in frustration. While in New York, she fully intended to seek answers and maybe try to dislodge the block that seemed permanently embedded in her mind. There had to be some way to break her memories free. And if there was, she was going to find it. Preferably before she got married.

Yet more was in store when they reached the penthouse. She very nearly growled her frustration when the elevator opened and she caught sight of Roslyn. Was she doomed to find this woman in her home at every turn?

Roslyn smiled warmly in greeting, and Marley did not miss that it extended only to Chrysander. She stood beside him while his assistant outlined the schedule of meetings, phone calls he needed to return and contracts that needed his attention. She wouldn't retreat this time and allow Roslyn any victory, implied or otherwise.

Roslyn spoke in low, sultry tones and touched Chrysander's arm frequently. She laughed huskily at something he said, all the while overtly ignoring Marley's presence. The woman had brass. Marley had to admit that. If she weren't pregnant, she'd give serious consideration to throwing the woman out of the penthouse on her ear.

It was good as fantasies went, but Chrysander would be horrified. She sighed even as the image of the beautifully coiffed woman banned from the apartment cheered her considerably.

Finally, Roslyn made to leave, and Marley's shoulders sagged in relief. But as the elevator opened to admit her, another man, also bearing a strong resemblance to Chrysander strode off.

She wanted to ask Chrysander just how many people had access to their private quarters but bit her lip.

"It would seem our apartment is a revolving door today," Chrysander said dryly, and Marley wondered if he'd read her mind.

While Theron's disapproval of her might have been more subtle, there was nothing left to imagine about this man's opinion of her. He scowled openly even as Chrysander introduced him to her as his brother Piers.

"A word if you don't mind, Chrysander," Piers said, his jaw clenched tight.

"Don't let me interrupt," Marley said. She turned and walked toward the bedroom, having had enough of the chilly reception she'd received.

Even as she closed the door, she could hear raised voices and Chrysander's angry tone. She hesitated a moment, wondering if she should listen to their conversation. Would she want to hear what they were saying? With a sigh, she turned to survey the room that Chrysander had given her upon her release from the hospital.

Not knowing what else to do, she slipped out of her shoes and sat down on the bed. The trip hadn't been tiring, but sliding under the covers and hiding appealed to her. Her head was beginning to ache from tension, and if she could just get away for a few minutes, she might feel better. And maybe when she woke, there wouldn't be anyone in their apartment anymore.

When she did wake, she was in a different bed. She blinked the sleep-induced fog away and realized that she was in Chrysander's bedroom. She stretched and was glad not to feel the pressure in her head any longer.

She sat up and saw Chrysander standing across the room looking at her. For some reason, she felt unsure of herself in that moment.

"I must have been more tired than I realized," she said lightly. "I didn't even wake when you moved me."

"You will sleep in our room, in our bed."

She blinked. "Well, okay. I just didn't think. That was the room I had before."

He closed the distance between them and sat down on the bed next to her. "Your place is here. With me."

She cocked her head. She had the distinct impression he wasn't just speaking to the fact that she'd gone to bed in another room. It was almost as though he was convincing himself, and others, that she belonged with him.

"Your brothers don't approve of me," she said quietly.

His face became a stone. "My brothers have no say in our relationship. I will announce our forthcoming marriage at the reception two nights from now, and we'll marry in a week."

And that was that, she thought. The law laid down by Chrysander Anetakis.

He leaned down to kiss her. "Why don't you dress? We'll go out for a nice dinner."

"Lobster?" she asked hopefully then realized what she'd said. Her eyes widened in excitement. "Lobster! Chrysander, I remember that lobster is my favorite."

He smiled tightly and kissed her again. "So it is, *pedhaki mou*. I used to have it delivered here, and we'd sit naked on the bed to eat it."

She flushed to the roots of her hair but had to admit the image was appealing. Chrysander helped her up, and she went into the bathroom to shower and change. Thirty minutes later, Chrysander escorted her down the elevator and out to the waiting car.

He took her to an elegant restaurant, and they sat in an intimate corner set away from the main dining area. The lighting was low, and it reminded her of Christmas. A warm feeling of nostalgia took hold as she recalled how very much she loved the holiday season.

In another month, decorations would be going up, and many of the shops and restaurants would twinkle with lights and holly. She smiled dreamily as she imagined spending Christmas with Chrysander.

"You look lost in thought, *agape mou*. With such a sweet smile on your face, I can only hope that I am what is occupying your thoughts."

She looked across the table to see Chrysander studying her, his bronze skin illuminated by soft candlelight. "I was imagining spending Christmas with you. I was remembering how much I love the holidays."

"Your memories seem to be coming back," he said, though there was no joy in his tone.

Her lips twisted into a rueful smile. "Not very quickly,

I'm afraid. Just a snippet here and there, and it's more of an awareness, not a true memory."

"It will come. You must be patient."

She nodded, but she could feel the frustration creeping over her. Determined not to let the evening go the way the rest of the day had, she forced herself to relax and enjoy the wonderful meal and being with Chrysander. With no interruptions from family members or personal assistants.

"Would you like to go shopping tomorrow?" Chrysander asked.

She blinked in surprise at the sudden change in topic.

"I have a meeting first thing, but then we could eat lunch together and shop for the things you will need for the reception we will be attending. You could also look for a wedding dress."

She couldn't wrap her brain around the image of Chrysander shopping, and she was sure no amount of searching her memory would find one. He simply wasn't a man to do such a thing.

"Are you sure you want me there?"

He cocked one eyebrow. "As I plan to announce our upcoming wedding, it would be strange if you weren't. Unless you have no wish to go."

"No, that isn't it at all. I'd love to go. I just wasn't sure...." She trailed off, determined not to dig her hole any deeper.

"Then it is settled. We'll go out shopping tomorrow after I've fed you properly."

She grinned. "You make me sound like a pet."

A slow, sexy smile curved his mouth. "I like the sound of you being my pet. My own personal, pampered pet," he purred.

Heat sizzled through her body like an electric current.

She swallowed and took a sip of her water in an attempt to assuage the tingling warmth.

Then he laughed, and the sound sent a flutter of awareness over her nerves. "You like the idea, too, I see."

She blushed and ducked her head. "I like the idea of being your anything," she said honestly.

He reached across the table and tugged her fingers into his hand. "You are mine, *agape mou*. That is what you are."

"Then take me home and make love to me," she whispered.

Chapter 12

The next morning, Chrysander left their bed early. He kissed her softly on the brow and told her he would come for her at noon. Marley yawned sleepily, murmured her goodbye and turned over to go back to sleep. His soft chuckle echoed in her ears as she drifted off.

When she woke again, she squinted against the sunlight and glanced over at the clock. She still had hours until her lunch date with Chrysander, and she had no desire to spend them sitting around the apartment.

With so many of Chrysander's security men milling about, surely one of them would have access to transportation. She could commandeer one of them and go out on her own a bit, though she had no idea where she'd go exactly.

And then another thought occurred to her. With Chrysander being such a stickler for tight security, she doubted she'd gone anywhere without it in the time they were together. If that was the case, then surely one of them would have an idea of the places she'd visited and the things she liked to do.

Considerably cheered by that realization, she hurried into the shower. Thirty minutes later, she rode the elevator down to the lobby and got off. She could see a burly-looking man standing by the door and recognized him as the man Chrysander called Stavros.

He snapped to attention when he saw her walking toward him.

"Miss Jameson," he said in a heavy Greek accent. "Is there something I can do for you?"

She noticed the way he subtly moved to bar the door so she could not exit and nearly laughed.

"I'm sure Chrysander has told you that I...that I've lost my memory."

He nodded, and his expression softened.

"What I was wondering is if you could tell me whether or not I had security assigned to me before my accident."

"I personally saw to your protection," Stavros said.

"Oh, good! Then maybe you can help me. I'd like to go out, but I don't really know where. I mean, I don't know what places I liked to go, and since you no doubt followed me everywhere I went, maybe you could take me to some of those places today."

He paused for a moment as if considering her request. Then he dug out a cell phone from his pocket, punched a button and stuck the phone to his ear. He spoke rapidly in Greek, nodded a few times then extended the receiver to her.

"Mr. Anetakis would like to speak to you."

"Oh, for heaven's sake," she huffed as she took it. "You didn't waste any time ratting me out, did you?" She stared accusingly at Stavros, who didn't look the least bit apologetic.

Chrysander laughed in her ear. "What sort of trouble are you causing, *agape mou?*"

She sighed a little ridiculously. After that first awkward time he'd murmured the endearment, he'd used it with increasing frequency. It turned her to mush every time it slid over her ears, warm and vibrant.

"I wanted to go out for a while. I'll be back in time for our lunch, I promise."

"Enjoy your morning, but be careful and don't overexert yourself. If you find you're running late, have Stavros call me, and I can meet you for lunch so you don't have to return to the apartment."

She smiled and murmured her agreement. They rang off, and she handed the phone back to Stavros. "You and I need to have a conversation about tattling."

He didn't bat an eyelash. "I assure you, Miss Jameson, we've had such conversations in the past."

She grinned and then watched as Stavros put a hand to the small earpiece he wore and barked out several orders in Greek.

Within moments a car rolled around the front, and yet another security man got out to open the door for her. Stavros ushered her out of the building and settled her comfortably in the vehicle before he and the other man took seats in the front.

The privacy glass between the front and backseats lowered, and Stavros turned to look at her over his shoulder.

"Where would you like to go, Miss Jameson?"

"I don't know," she said with a laugh. "Can you give me a tour of some of the places I used to go?"

He nodded, and they drove onto the busy New York streets.

Their first stop was a small coffee shop a few blocks away from the apartment. It was clear that Stavros hadn't expected her to want to get out, because when she made the intention known, his lips drew into a disapproving line. Still, he and the other man with him escorted her inside the small café.

It was cozy and brimming with conversation and laughter. It felt inviting, and she could well see herself in a place like this. But it didn't spark any memories. With a sigh, she turned and told Stavros she was ready to leave.

Next they pulled up to a small market, and she looked at Stavros in surprise.

"You liked to cook for Mr. Anetakis, particularly when he'd been out of the country for an extended period of time. We would come here to shop for the necessary ingredients. Then you'd make me carry back all the sacks," he added with a small smile.

"Was I so very trying?" she teased.

"It was my pleasure to accompany you on your outings," Stavros said.

"Why, it sounds like you like me." She grinned up at the burly man, trying to gain any sort of recognition, some flicker that maybe they'd bantered like this in the past. "Where to next?"

They visited a library and a small art shop, and while she could see herself in those places, she recalled nothing. When the car rolled to a stop in front of a park, for a moment panic quivered in her stomach.

"Are you all right?" Stavros demanded.

She looked up to see him standing at the open door, waiting for her to climb out.

"Maybe we should return now. It's nearly time for your lunch with Mr. Anetakis."

"No," she said as she hastened out of the car. No, she wanted to be here. Needed to be here. Something about this place had caused a tremor in her mind even if it was uncomfortable.

She walked down the pathway and gathered her coat tighter around her. In truth, it wasn't that cold. The afternoon sun shone warmly, but she felt a chill, one that reached far inside her.

Behind her, Stavros and his second flanked her, and she had the brief thought that she appeared far more important than she was. Her gaze locked on to a stone bench that overlooked a statue, and she moved toward it, not sure why she was so drawn by it.

Marley sat down and spread her hands over the cool stone. She stared ahead and felt a glimmer of sadness. It made no sense, but she knew she had sat here before, and she knew that she had felt fear. Uncertainty.

She raised her hands to cup her face and leaned over, huddled on the bench. It was there, just out of reach, so close she could feel the heavy weight of sadness, of indecision.

A hand touched her shoulder, and Stavros's concerned voice reached her. "Are you all right? Do I need to call Mr. Anetakis? Perhaps I should take you to the hospital."

She shook her head and looked up. "No. I'm fine. It's just that I've been here before. I can feel it."

Stavros nodded, though the concern didn't leave his eyes. "You often said this was your thinking spot."

"It would appear I had a lot to think about," she murmured.

He checked his watch. "Let me call Mr. Anetakis and tell him to meet us at the restaurant. By the time we return to the apartment, you could already be eating."

She didn't object when he gently helped her up, and instead of walking just behind her, he held her elbow as they walked back to the car.

"Stavros, please don't concern Chrysander," she said as he put her into the car. "He'll have me back at the apartment in bed."

"Which is perhaps where you should be," Stavros said.

She made a face. "You're seriously no fun. I'm supposed to go shopping. For a wedding dress no less. I can't very well do that if I'm in bed."

Stavros looked to be fighting a smile as he closed the door. A moment later, the privacy glass slid down and Stavros turned to look at her. "If Mr. Anetakis asks, I'll simply say we had a quiet day on the town."

"I knew there was a reason I liked you," she said cheekily, her good spirits restored.

When they arrived at the restaurant, Chrysander met them at the car and promptly dismissed Stavros, saying he would have his driver take him and Marley home when they were through shopping.

Over lunch, Chrysander asked how her morning had gone, and she explained about all the places Stavros had taken her. But when she asked him about his morning, he grew silent and vague.

Not wanting to cast a pall over the day, she swiftly changed the topic to their shopping.

"Exactly how fancy is this reception we're attending?" she asked as she savored another bite of the rich pasta.

He quirked one eyebrow. "That depends on your definition of fancy."

"Oh, then I can wear my blue jeans and maternity top," she said sweetly.

He laughed. "While I certainly would not object to you wearing your blue jeans, I do not want others seeing you in something that cups your bottom so lovingly."

"Am I supposed to dress up then?" she asked with a sigh.

"Don't concern yourself with it, *pedhaki mou*. I will choose the perfect dress for you."

"I won't wear high heels," she said resolutely. "There is no way I'm waddling around on toothpicks."

"Of course not," he said in a tone that suggested she was crazy for even mentioning it. "I'm certain it's not advisable for a pregnant woman to put herself through such torture. What if you fell?"

"Maybe I could go barefooted," she said mischievously.

He laughed. "And maybe I should stick to a plan of keeping you at home solidly under lock and key."

She swallowed the last bite of her pasta and reluctantly pushed the plate away. "That was so wonderful, and I ate far too much."

"You need to gain some weight. You are too slight as it is. It is good that you ate well."

"And if I eat any more, I won't fit into whatever dress you plan on buying me." She glanced down at her rounded belly. "Do they make ultra-chic wear for pregnant women?"

Chrysander gave her a patient look. "Trust me, Marley. We will find you something suitable."

"Just how do you know so darn much about buying dresses anyway?" she grumbled as he took her out to his waiting car.

"Surely you don't expect me to answer that?" he said with barely suppressed amusement.

She shot him a withering look and settled into the car.

As it turned out, he did indeed have a skill for choosing the perfect dress. He nailed it with the second one she tried on. White silk in a very simple design. It had spaghetti straps with a conservative bodice, and the material hugged her belly, drawing attention to the soft mound.

"It makes me look…well, very pregnant," she said as she turned to allow Chrysander to look.

"You look absolutely exquisite," he murmured. "I think every pregnant woman should like to look as you do right now."

The appreciation in his eyes sold her on the dress. She had no desire to look any further. It was carefully wrapped and set aside along with the low-heeled shoes that she had chosen.

"Tell me, *agape mou,* do you want a traditional wedding dress?"

She pursed her lips then shook her head. "No, I'd prefer something simpler, I think."

The saleslady set several really gorgeous selections in front of them, and Marley watched Chrysander closely for his reaction.

She fell in love with a peach-colored gown that scraped the floor and fell in soft waves from her waist. It accentuated her pregnancy in such a way that she truly felt beautiful and feminine. It was clear by the look on his face that Chrysander agreed.

To her surprise, instead of returning to the car, he walked her next door to a jeweler and proceeded to choose a stunning set of diamond earrings and a matching necklace to go with her wedding dress. Already speechless, she was reduced to a mere croak when he next selected a sapphire necklace and earrings that he suggested she wear with the white silk dress to the reception.

"They will look beautiful with your eyes, *agape mou,*" he murmured next to her ear. "And later, I'd love nothing more than to see you in these jewels and nothing else."

Her face exploded in heat, and she looked around to make sure no one could see her furious blushing.

"You spoil me, Chrysander," she said as they left the jewelry store.

"It is my right to spoil my woman," he said with a shrug.

"I find I quite like it," she said with a smile.

"That is good, because it would be a shame for you not to enjoy something I intend to be doing a lot of."

Impulsively, she scooted against him in the seat and kissed him full on the lips. A staggered breath escaped him as his hands went out to grip her arms. Her cheek slid down his until she nuzzled against his neck and she hugged him tightly.

"Thank you for today. I had so much fun."

His hand went to her hair and stroked softly as he hugged her back with his other arm. "You are quite welcome."

She raised her head and started to move away, but Chrysander held her fast against him.

"Am I a good cook?" she asked, cocking her head at him.

His face registered surprise. "I'm sorry?"

"Cook. Stavros informed me that I liked to cook for you and frequently went to the market for ingredients. I wondered if I was any good at it."

A peculiar expression lit his face. "That's right. You did. I hadn't thought about it in a while, but yes, you did often cook a meal for me on my first night home."

"Were you gone very often?" she asked.

He paused for a moment then slowly nodded. "I'm afraid I was. I was often out of the country on business. Sometimes we went weeks without seeing each other."

"I can't imagine it," she said softly. "I missed you in just the few hours we were apart this morning."

He kissed her again. "And I missed you, *pedhaki mou*."

She settled against his side as they continued the ride home. She was a bit tired, but there was no way she'd tell him that. The day had been nearly perfect, and they still had the evening together.

Chapter 13

Marley fidgeted and tugged at her dress as she surveyed her appearance in the mirror. Sapphires glinted from both ears, and the matching necklace lay against the skin of her neck.

"You look beautiful, *agape mou*."

She turned to see Chrysander behind her. She sucked in her breath as she took in his appearance. The excellently tailored black suit fit him to perfection, drawing attention to his muscular build. The white shirt contrasted with his bronze skin, dark hair and golden eyes, and quite frankly, she felt like drooling.

"So do you," she finally managed.

He chuckled and walked toward her. "Beautiful? Surely you can do better than that."

"Gorgeous? Devastatingly handsome? So good-looking that I'm tempted to fall on you and tear your clothes off?"

"I like the way you think."

"I wasn't joking," she muttered.

"Are you ready? The car is waiting for us below."

She took a deep breath and twisted her engagement ring around her finger with the pad of her thumb. "As ready as I'll ever be."

He reached for her hand and tugged her into his arms. "It won't be so bad. I will be with you the whole night."

She reached up on tiptoe to kiss him. "I'm a coward. I fully admit it."

He took his time exploring her lips, moving with a sensual thoroughness that left her weak and breathless. When they drew apart, she could see he was as affected as she was.

"I think we should leave now," he said hoarsely. "Otherwise we won't be going anywhere for a very long time."

They rode to the hotel, and Marley could see several limousines lining the circular drive outside the main entrance as they pulled up. She swallowed nervously as she saw the glitz and glamour of the people stepping from the cars and entering the hotel. She suddenly felt underdressed and unprepared.

When they reached the front entrance, the doors were opened and Chrysander stepped out, extending his hand to help her from the car. He tucked her arm securely underneath his, and they walked inside the hotel.

Butterflies performed a rendition of the River Dance in her stomach as they entered the large ballroom. A jazz band played softly from a small stage at the back of the room. Waiters circled with trays of wine and champagne while others offered a selection of hors d'oeuvres.

Chrysander murmured to one of the waiters as he took a glass of wine from the tray, and a few moments later, he returned with a glass of mineral water for Marley.

As she scanned the room, glass in hand, she mentally

groaned as she saw Theron and Piers and then Roslyn. While she knew they'd be in attendance, she'd truly hoped to avoid them as much as possible. That wasn't going to happen, she mused as she saw Theron start across the room toward Chrysander.

Her first reaction was to excuse herself to the ladies' room, but Chrysander's grip tightened on her fingers as though he knew of her impending flight.

"Chrysander," Theron said by way of greeting. His gaze skimmed quickly over Marley, and he offered the briefest of nods. At least it wasn't a full-blown snub, nor did he scowl at her.

She listened as the two exchanged pleasantries, and then Theron gestured toward Piers and a distinguished older gentleman who was standing beside him. She hung back as Chrysander started toward his brother, but he tugged her along with him, and her dread increased.

Piers frowned when she and Chrysander approached. The older gentleman smiled broadly and uttered a polite greeting to Chrysander. A woman Marley assumed was his wife also offered an enthusiastic hello from his side.

Chrysander urged her forward. "Senhor and Senhora Vasquez, I'd like you both to meet Marley Jameson. Marley, this is Senhor Vasquez and his wife. They're here from Brazil on business."

Marley smiled and exchanged pleasantries with the older couple then relaxed against Chrysander. Piers was being polite, and Theron had joined the group minus the complete indifference he'd shown in her presence a moment earlier. Maybe she could endure the evening after all.

Chrysander reached down and squeezed her hand, and then he faced the others, odd tension on his face. "Marley has agreed to be my wife. We plan to marry while we're here in New York. We'd be honored if you all could attend."

A gasp sounded behind Chrysander, and Marley whirled around to see Roslyn standing a few feet away, shock reflected on her face. She recovered quickly, but not quick enough for Marley to wonder what she could possibly have found so shocking about the announcement. As she turned and looked at the others, only the Vasquezes looked congratulatory over the news.

Piers's and Theron's expressions both mirrored Roslyn's shock. Then their surprise turned to outright distaste. Chrysander shot them warning looks, but Marley was at a complete loss. She trembled against Chrysander, and his grip tightened on her hand as if he understood her desire to flee.

How could their engagement possibly be news? They were engaged before her accident, and yet everyone acted as though it was a recent development. An unpleasant one at that.

After the obligatory well wishes from the Vasquezes and more from a few people nearby who'd overheard, the conversation switched to more mundane topics. Marley remained silent, numb to the talk around her. Chrysander loosened his hold on her hand, but he slid his arm around her waist and anchored her firmly against him. There was no escaping, no matter how much she might wish it.

The conversation turned to the possible building of a hotel in Rio de Janeiro, and while Marley remained silent, only observing the others, Chrysander's arm never strayed from around her waist.

As the evening wore on, more people offered their congratulations on the upcoming wedding, and soon the room buzzed with the news. The constant smile Marley wore was starting to wear on her. As if sensing her strain, Chrysander whirled her onto the dance floor as a slow jazz song floated melodiously in the air.

She sighed as she melted into his arms. "Thanks. I needed that."

He smiled and leaned down to nibble at the corner of her mouth. "You are the most beautiful woman in the room. The men all look at you with lust in their eyes, and it's enough to make me want to pound them into the ground."

"Mmm, as much as I like the macho act, I'd much prefer if you took me home and worked off some of that male arrogance in another way."

"You tempt me."

She smiled up at him. "I was very serious."

He sighed. "As much as I would like to do just that, I'm afraid I am stuck here for the evening. If it becomes too much for you, I can have Stavros take you back to the apartment."

As if she'd leave him here with Roslyn, Miss Super Assistant.

Despite the fact that Chrysander's brothers and Roslyn seemed determined to treat her as a pariah, there were many others who went out of their way to be gracious to Marley and include her in conversation. She actually found herself enjoying the festive atmosphere despite the evening's inauspicious start.

It was growing late when Chrysander leaned in close to her ear and murmured, "I need to speak with my brothers. Will you be all right for a few moments?"

"Of course, silly," she said with a smile. "I'm going to visit the ladies' room. You go on."

He kissed her then strode toward his brothers. Marley took her time in the bathroom. It was a nice reprieve from the endless chatter and the dark glances thrown her way by the Anetakis contingent.

"You can't hide in here forever," she said to herself. Squaring her shoulders, she exited the bathroom and walked back toward the ballroom. As she passed one of the smaller meeting rooms, she heard Chrysander's voice through the open door. She faltered and came to a stop, debating whether to continue or stay and wait for him.

The next words she heard made her decision for her.

"Damn it, Chrysander, there is no need to marry her. Put her up in an apartment somewhere until the child comes. Don't tie yourself to her and give her access to everything you own."

Her mouth rounded in shock at Piers's angry words.

"She is pregnant with my child," Chrysander said icily. "That I choose to marry her is none of your concern."

She moved closer to the door, not caring whether they saw her. What right did Piers have to talk to Chrysander so?

"You can't mean to marry her!" Roslyn's shrill voice rose. "Do you forget how she stole from you? That she tried to ruin your company? If you need any reminders, just look at the new hotels going up in Paris and Rome. Your hotels, Chrysander. Only they're going up under your competitor's name."

A haze blew through Marley's mind. Red hot. Like a swarm of angry bees, tidbits of information began buzzing in her head. And suddenly it was as if a dam broke. The locked door in her mind that she'd tried so hard to budge simply opened, and the past came roaring through with vicious velocity.

She swayed and gripped the door frame tighter. Nausea boiled in her stomach as each and every moment flashed like a movie in fast-forward.

Chrysander's angry accusation of thievery. His ordering her from their apartment, his life. Her abduction and the months she'd spent in hopeless fear, waiting for Chrysander to answer the ransom demands. Demands he'd ignored.

Oh God, she was going to be sick.

He'd left her. Discarded her like a piece of rubbish. The half million dollars, a paltry sum to a man of Chrysander's means, was an amount he'd been unwilling to part with to ensure her return.

Everything had been a lie. He'd lied to her nonstop since she'd awoken in the hospital. He didn't love her or want her. He *despised* her.

She hadn't been worth half a million dollars to him.

Pain splintered through her chest as she shattered. As everything she'd known as true suddenly turned black. Her heart withered and cracked, falling in pieces around her.

He hadn't tried to save her.

The tortured cry that ripped from her mouth echoed through the room. She clamped a hand over her lips, but it was too late. Everyone looked her way. Theron flinched, and an odd discomfort settled over Piers's face. She met Chrysander's gaze, and she could see the truth in his eyes as he realized that she remembered.

As he started across the room toward her, she backed away, stumbling as she did. Oh God, she couldn't face this. Tears blurred her vision. The image of his pale face only spurred her on.

Marley fled down the hallway toward the lobby. Chrysander called her name, but she didn't stop. Sobs bubbled from her chest and exploded outward. She stumbled but regained her footing and pushed herself forward. Behind her, Chrysander cursed and called out to her again.

She was running for the exit, no clear destination in mind. She was nearly there when she met with a mountain. Stavros stepped in front of her and held her, and she exploded in fury, kicking and shoving. Her only thought was to get away, as far away from this place as she could.

She broke free but stumbled backward and fell to the floor. Stavros was down beside her, asking her if she was all right, and she knew she was trapped.

Pain cycled through her body, an unending stream of agony. She closed her eyes as Chrysander's strong hands slid over her body. In an urgent voice, he demanded to know if she was hurt, but she was incapable of answering him. She curled into a ball, uncaring that she was in the middle of the hotel lobby.

Chrysander picked her up, and she could hear him saying her name. Curses fell from his lips, and then he barked orders for someone to summon a doctor. He strode away from the noise of the lobby, and a few moments later, he entered an empty hotel room.

As soon as he lowered her to the bed, she curled herself into a tight ball again and turned away from him. She flinched when he put his hand on her, his touch light and concerned.

"You must stop crying, *agape mou*. You're going to make yourself ill."

She was already sick, she thought dully. Utterly sick at heart. She closed her eyes, but still hot tears streamed down her cheeks, even as Chrysander wiped them away with his fingers.

She wanted to escape. Go some place where it didn't hurt so much. Through the fog, she heard Chrysander conversing with the doctor. A moment later, she felt a prick in her arm, but she didn't react. She didn't care. And then she floated away, so grateful that the pain had receded. Her mind grew fuzzy as the veil of sleep descended over her. Oblivion. She reached for it. Embraced it and wrapped it around her as she slipped away to a place where there was no hurt and no betrayal.

* * *

Chrysander paced back and forth at the foot of Marley's bed while the hotel physician administered the sedative. She was beyond distraught, and the doctor had moved immediately to prevent further upset.

As the doctor stood and backed away from the bed, he looked at Chrysander, a grim expression on his face.

Fear tightened Chrysander's chest. "Is she all right? Is the baby all right?"

The doctor motioned him across the room and away from where Marley now quietly lay. "Her injuries are not physical. If they were, perhaps I would be of use. Her distress is mental. If it is as you said, and she has regained her memory, it is that which has caused her immeasurable pain."

Chrysander stirred impatiently. "What can be done? She cannot be left as she is. There must be something we can do." The sight of her pale face and her eyes, so huge with devastation, twisted his gut painfully.

"You should return her to your home, to a place that is more familiar. She needs a doctor, not for her physical well-being, but one who can help her mentally."

"A therapist you mean?" Chrysander asked grimly.

"This is a very delicate time," the doctor warned. "She is extremely fragile, and remembering such traumatic events could cause an emotional breakdown."

His face twisted in sympathy, and he reached out to grasp Chrysander's shoulder. "This will be hard, but perhaps it is for the best. It is good that her memory returned, even if it causes her such distress."

Chrysander wasn't so sure of that. With her memory regained, she also knew that he'd tossed her out of their apartment, basically put her into the hands of her kidnappers. She would also recall the cruel words he'd thrown at her. And she would remember her own part in the whole mess.

He ran a hand wearily through his hair. Part of him wished she would have never regained those memories. They had started fresh, without past deceptions and betrayals. Something niggled at him even as those thoughts passed through his mind.

Wouldn't she have greeted her memory's return with guilt? All he'd seen in her eyes was hurt. Deep and horrific hurt. There was no guilt, no embarrassment over the fact she'd stolen from him. Just distress so keen that he still felt the knife deep in his chest from the tortured sound of her cry and the memory of her stumbling away from him.

An uneasy sensation took hold of him. He couldn't help but think that there were things buried in Marley's memories that he wasn't going to like.

Chapter 14

Marley was only vaguely aware of the things going on around her. After that first pass into oblivion, she registered being carried into a car. She heard Chrysander's worried voice as he murmured to her, but she closed herself off from him, folding inward.

When she next awoke, she knew she was in a bed. As she looked around the room, recognition sparked, and with it, a surge of fresh agony, hot and raw, seared through her body and robbed her of breath.

He wouldn't do this. Surely even he could not be so cruel as to bring her back to the place they'd shared and the place he'd brutally shoved her from.

She reached for the tears, expecting them to come, but curiously all she felt was an odd detachment, a void of nothingness coupled with the need to get out of this place.

When she sat up, her gaze flickered to a chair by the window occupied by Chrysander's sleeping form. He was slouched against the arm, his clothing rumpled and the stubble of over a day's beard shadowing his jaw.

She waited for the rush of anger, of fury, but again, she felt nothing but overwhelming numbness and a need to escape.

She got out of bed, not paying attention to her own rumpled clothing. It occurred to her that maybe she should change, but she couldn't risk waking Chrysander. No, she needed to be away. She couldn't look him in the eye knowing that he'd made such horrible accusations and then left her to the mercy of her kidnappers.

Her thumb brushed across the thin band of her engagement ring, and she wrenched it off. It felt cold in her hand. She gently laid it on the nightstand beside the bed then turned and walked away.

On bare feet, she walked out of the bedroom and to the elevator. Her stomach churned as she relived the night she'd gotten on this elevator as her world crumbled around her, Chrysander's accusation ringing in her ears. How could he? It was the only thought that played over and over in her mind until she wanted to scream at it to stop.

When she reached the lobby, she paused, realizing that not only would Chrysander's security people likely be manning the front entrance but that also the doorman would never let her walk out as she was.

She turned and hurried for the back entrance. To her dismay, one of the men she recognized from Chrysander's detail was standing at the door. She quickly ducked into a service entrance and made her way down the hallway that housed rooms for laundry and building maintenance. A few minutes later, she opened the door and walked out into the pale, predawn light.

Chrysander woke with a monster catch in his neck and shifted in the too-small chair to alleviate his discomfort.

He'd wanted to spend the night with Marley tucked into his arms, but she'd resisted his touch at every turn, becoming so distraught that he'd had no choice but to retreat.

He'd taken the doctor's advice and phoned a therapist as soon as he'd returned to the apartment with Marley. The therapist was due to arrive this morning to speak with her. Chrysander just hoped she would be able to.

His gaze moved to the bed, and when he saw it empty, he shot to his feet. He started to bolt from the room, but a glimmer of something on the nightstand caught his eye. When he saw her engagement ring lying there, dread tightened his chest. He ran from the room in search of her. As he went from room to room, his panic grew. She wasn't anywhere to be found.

Even as he hurled himself into the elevator, he dug out his cellular phone. As soon as the doors opened in the lobby, he ran out and nearly collided with Stavros.

He grasped the man's shirt in his hands and pulled him up close. "Where is she?"

Stavros blinked in surprise. "We haven't seen her, sir. No one has. She was with you."

Chrysander pushed him away with a violent curse. "She's gone. Call your men in. I want her found immediately."

He strode to the entrance to question the doorman, but he seemed as baffled as the security man. He turned around to see several of his detail gather in the lobby as they were questioned by an angry Stavros.

Theos! Where could she have gone? She was in no state to be wandering around New York, and the people who had abducted her were still at large.

Worry settled hard into his chest. He turned to go out the door in search of her himself when he saw Theron walk in.

"Chrysander," he said in greeting. "I was on my way up to see you. How is Marley?"

"She's gone," he said grimly.

Theron raised one brow. "Gone? But how?"

"I don't know," he said in frustration. "She's disappeared. I have to find her."

Theron put a firm hand on Chrysander's shoulder. "We'll find her, Chrysander."

"There is something about this situation," Chrysander said in a hollow voice. "Something that doesn't add up. I saw no guilt in her face when she remembered everything. All I saw was complete devastation, as if she were the one who was betrayed. She was so distraught that she had to be sedated, and she becomes extremely upset when I get close to her. She isn't herself right now. I fear where she may have gone. Her frame of mind is not good."

"I will help you, Chrysander," Theron said quietly. "Do not worry. We will find her."

Marley shivered as she eased down onto the cold stone bench and clutched her arms around her trembling body. She glanced down at her feet but couldn't summon any rebuke for having gone out in the chill without shoes or a coat. The only thought she'd had was to get away as quickly as possible. She couldn't face Chrysander now.

Now she knew why she'd been drawn to this place. Her thinking spot, indeed. Just hours before that last night, she'd sat here, afraid of how Chrysander would react to her pregnancy. She'd been right to be afraid. He didn't trust her. He didn't love her. And he'd left her to her fate with the kidnappers.

She refused to allow the memories to roll back in her mind. They simply hurt too much. At least now she realized why she'd chosen to forget. All those weeks of living in fear as her kidnappers waited for their demands to be met had paled next to the betrayal Chrysander had handed her when he'd refused.

How could anyone be so cold? Wouldn't he have been willing to pay such a meager amount of money to free anyone? Even a complete stranger? She'd never imagined him to be so heartless. But he'd cast her aside with little regard for her. She'd been his mistress, someone to slake his lust and nothing more. The fool was her for falling in love with him, not once, but twice.

A small moan escaped her lips, and she closed her eyes as the ache built within her once more. Never had she felt so hurt, so utterly lost.

Her hands closed around the bulge of her stomach, and the tears that she'd thought locked under the ice began to well to the surface.

How could he be capable of such a despicable deception? He had to know she'd remember eventually, and yet he'd spent weeks wooing her, making her love him all over again. Pretending affection for her. And passion. The question was, why?

Was it all an elaborate ruse to punish her? To make her suffer more than she already had? She'd never imagine Chrysander to be so cruel, but it just proved how little she'd known about the man she'd given herself to.

She sat there, rocking back and forth, her arms wrapped protectively around her abdomen. The wind picked up, chasing a chill down her spine, but she ignored the discomfort.

"Marley?"

Her name came out cautiously and sounded distant, yet when she looked up, the man was standing just a few feet away, concern lighting his eyes. She recognized him. Theron. No wonder he'd been so resistant to Chrysander marrying her. He thought her the thief that Chrysander did. It was more than she could bear.

She hugged herself tighter and looked down, determined that he not see her tears.

He squatted down in front of her and put a hand on her wrist. "I need to take you back, *pedhaki mou*. It's not safe for you to be out here," he said gently.

She flinched at the endearment. It was Chrysander's pet name for her, and she wanted no part of it. She shook her head and pulled her hand up in a protective manner.

He glanced down at her feet and swore under his breath. "It's cold, and you shouldn't be out here in your bare feet. Let me take you back home."

She recoiled violently. "No." She shook her head vehemently. "I won't go back there." She slid to the end of the bench, the rough stone scratching against her clothing.

Theron put a hand out to prevent her flight. "Marley, think of your baby. Let me take you back. You're cold."

"I won't go back to that apartment," she said desperately. She stood, prepared to bolt.

Theron look at her with regret. "I cannot allow you to run. You're clearly upset and are not dressed for the weather."

Tears filled her eyes. "Why do you care? I stole from you, remember? I'm just the harlot who snared your brother and tried to ruin his company," she said bitterly.

Theron's eyes softened. "If I promise not to return you to the apartment, will you come with me? I won't leave you like this, Marley."

She swayed, and he caught her as her knees gave out. He picked her up and began striding away.

She stiffened in his arms. "Please, just leave me alone," she begged.

"I cannot do that, little sister."

"I'm just your brother's whore," she said, allowing more of the anguish in.

His grip tightened around her. "*Theos!* Never say that again."

She turned her face into his shoulder, and hot tears flooded her eyes. "It's true," she whispered.

She closed her eyes and allowed herself to drift away once again. It was easy to flee from reality when it represented so much she wanted to escape. She cursed that she'd ever regained her memory. Doing so had destroyed her.

Chapter 15

Chrysander strode into the Imperial Park Hotel, waving off members of the staff as they hastened to greet him. The elevator was being held open for him, and he got in and rode it to the top floor.

A few moments later, he walked into the luxury suite usually reserved for VIP guests. His brother met him in the sitting area, and Chrysander scowled furiously at him.

"Why didn't you bring her back to the apartment?" he demanded.

"She became hysterical at the mere mention of it," Theron said. "She was set to run as far and as fast as she could. I had to promise I wouldn't take her back to the penthouse."

Chrysander swore and closed his eyes. He brought his hand to his face and pinched the bridge of his nose between his fingers in a weary gesture.

"She's about to break," Theron said quietly. "Bring your therapist here to talk to her. Maybe she can help."

Chrysander looked sharply at his younger brother. "You seem concerned about her."

"She carries my nephew." His lips pressed together in a grim line. "It is as you said. There is no guilt in her expression, her actions. She acts as though she has suffered the deepest of hurts. It was uncomfortable for me to see. I suddenly wanted to do all I could to shield her from such pain."

"Where is she now?" Chrysander demanded.

"Asleep," Theron replied. "She fell asleep on the way here and never stirred when I carried her up the elevator and put her into bed."

Chrysander headed for the bedroom, determined to see for himself that she was safe. He made his way through the dimly lit room and stopped at the head of the bed. Even in sleep, her brow was creased in an expression of despair.

He reached down and touched her cheek, tucking a curl behind her ear. She didn't stir. Her pale face lay against the pillow, framed by her dark curls. Deep shadows smudged her eyes, and he could tell from the redness that she had been crying. His chest twisted painfully at the signs of her distress.

As he walked back into the sitting room, he pulled out his cellular phone to call the therapist and have her come to the hotel. When he was done, he closed his phone and turned to Theron.

"Where did you find her?"

Theron handed him a drink. "She was in a garden a few blocks from your apartment." He winced as he looked at Chrysander. "She was barefoot, with no coat or sweater. She looked lost and unaware of her surroundings."

Chrysander swore. "It has been so since she regained her memory. *Theos mou,* but I don't know what to do." He'd never felt so helpless.

"Do you still believe she is guilty?" Theron asked quietly.

"I don't know," Chrysander admitted. "I think sometimes that it doesn't matter." He looked bleakly up at his brother, expecting to see condemnation. Instead, Theron looked at him with understanding.

"When I saw her on the bench, it did not matter to me, either," Theron said softly.

The therapist arrived a few minutes later, and Chrysander filled her in on everything that had happened since arriving in New York.

Despite the discomfort he felt over providing such personal details to the woman, he wanted her to know whatever she needed in order to help Marley. So he told her everything. From the confrontation he'd had with Marley so many months before, to the present.

To her credit, the woman did not react. She took the information in stride and asked to see Marley.

"She is resting, but you can go in and wait for her to awaken. I don't want her to grow upset and try to leave."

The therapist nodded and followed Chrysander to the bedroom. As they entered, Marley stirred. Chrysander automatically stepped forward, but the therapist held up her hand to halt him.

"Leave me to speak to her," she said softly.

Chrysander weighed his desire to be near her with the therapist's request. Finally, he nodded curtly and turned to leave. He didn't go far, though. He stepped from the bedroom and closed the door, but left it slightly ajar so he could hear what was being said within.

There was a long period of silence, and then the slight murmur of voices filtered from the room. The therapist did most of the talking at first as she soothed Marley. After a long while, he could hear Marley's trembling voice, and he strained closer to hear what she said.

"I went to the doctor the day Chrysander was due back from overseas. When I discovered I was pregnant, I was shocked. I worried how Chrysander would react. I wanted to ask him about our relationship…how he felt about me."

"Go on," the therapist encouraged.

Marley's questions that night now made sense to Chrysander. And then he flinched at her next words.

"He told me we had no relationship. That I was his mistress. A woman he paid to have sex with," she said hollowly.

He wanted to protest. He wanted to march into the bedroom and tell her that he'd never considered her someone he paid to have sex with.

"Then he accused me of…" Her voice trailed off, and he could hear a quiet sob rise from the room.

"It's all right, Marley," the therapist soothed.

"He said I had stolen from him. He said I took plans for one of his hotels and gave them to his competitor. He told me to get out."

"And did you steal them?"

"You're the first person to actually ask," Marley said wanly.

Chrysander flinched. She was right. He hadn't asked. He'd judged and condemned her.

"I was stunned. I still don't understand. I'd never even seen the papers he threw at me. I don't know why he thought I took them or how he could even think such a horrible thing."

The tears he heard in her voice felt like little daggers to his chest. The tension grew until he felt he would explode. Dread skated up his spine. What had he done?

"And then…" She broke off as sobs took over.

There was another long period of silence as the therapist murmured words of comfort to Marley.

"Tell me what happened next, Marley."

"I left the apartment, but I knew I had to come back
the next day after he'd calmed down so I could make him
see reason and tell him I was pregnant. I felt if I could just
have the chance to talk to him that he would see what a
mistake it was."

"And what happened?" the therapist asked gently.

Chrysander pushed against the door, his body tense
with anticipation.

"A man pulled a bag over my head and forced me into a
car. I was taken to another place in the city and told that I
was being held for ransom. I was terrified. I was pregnant
and was so scared that they would hurt me or my baby."

Chrysander's hands curled into fists as he fought the
rising rage within him.

"They sent two ransom demands," Marley whispered.
"He refused both. He left me there. Oh God, he left me
to those men. I wasn't even worth half a million dollars
to him!"

Sobs ripped from her throat as she dissolved into tears.
Chrysander stood in stunned disbelief. Mother of God.
He'd never received a ransom demand. He hadn't! His
stomach boiled as acid rose in his throat. He turned and
laid his forehead against the wall and brought his clenched
fist to rest a few inches away. He felt wetness on his cheeks
but made no move to wipe it away.

A few moments later, the therapist eased out of the bedroom and looked at Chrysander. He expected condemnation in her eyes but saw only a faint sympathy.

"I've sedated her. She was nearly hysterical. She needs
rest above all else. Her reality is very painful, so she re-
treats. That same self-preservation is what prompted her

amnesia. Now that she no longer has that protective buffer, she struggles to cope in the best way she knows how. Be gentle and understanding with her. Don't push her too hard."

She patted him on the arm as she walked past.

"Call me if you need me. I'll come at once."

"Thank you," Chrysander said hoarsely.

When she left, Chrysander turned and shuffled farther into the sitting room and sagged onto the couch.

"Dear God," he said bleakly.

"I heard," Theron said with a grimace.

"She never stole anything." Chrysander closed his eyes and dragged a hand through his hair. "*Theos.* I never got a ransom demand. She thinks…she thinks I left her to those animals, that I didn't care enough to pay half a million dollars for her return."

Theron put a comforting hand on Chrysander's shoulder. "There is much we need to investigate."

Chrysander nodded. His thoughts hardened as he turned from the anguish over Marley's revelation and forced himself to play back the events of that night.

The realization, when it came, was so startlingly clear that he cursed himself for not having pieced it together before. He'd been too angry, too wounded by what he perceived as a betrayal by Marley.

"Roslyn," he said tersely.

Theron raised a brow. "Your assistant?"

"She was there. Just before I found the papers in Marley's bag. She must have planted them."

Another thought occurred to him, one that sickened him and made him want to empty his stomach. Any ransom demand would have gone to his office. His residences were highly guarded secrets. Marley had said that he'd ignored ransom demands, but now he realized they could have been delivered and intercepted. By Roslyn.

He stood and whirled around to face his brother. "You will stay here with Marley. Make sure she goes nowhere and that she is well cared for. I'll send a physician over to monitor her condition."

Theron also stood. "Where are you going, brother?"

"I'm going to find out if what I suspect is true," he said in a dangerously low voice.

"Chrysander, wait."

Chrysander paused and stared back at his brother.

"You should call the authorities. If you confront her and gain a confession, it won't do any good. Only you will know."

Chrysander clenched his fists in frustration, but he knew his brother was right. He didn't want Roslyn to get away with what she'd done. He could make her life miserable, but she would still be free. He wanted justice.

Chrysander paced the confines of his New York office as he waited for Roslyn to arrive. He didn't want to be here. He wanted to be with Marley. Theron had stayed with her, and Chrysander simmered with impatience. Her condition hadn't changed. Even when she'd awakened, she'd been distant, unfocused, there but not there. It was as if she'd gone to a place where he couldn't hurt her anymore.

He closed his eyes and tried to focus on the task at hand. When he heard Roslyn enter, he stiffened. It was all he could do not to rage at her, not to break her skinny neck. It took everything he had to smile and act as though nothing was wrong, as though he didn't loathe the very ground she walked on.

"You wanted to see me?" Roslyn said breathlessly.

"I did," Chrysander murmured. He let his gaze run suggestively over her body even as his flesh crawled.

Her eyes brightened, and her stance immediately became suggestive.

"I've only just become aware of the lengths to which you went to try and get my attention," he said with a chuckle. "Men can be thick, so you women say, but I think maybe I was thicker than most."

Confusion rippled across her face, and she struggled to retain a look of innocence. She couldn't be sure what he was talking about yet, but it would soon be clear. He watched her body language, her eyes, the windows into the soulless bitch that she was.

"Why did you not just say you wanted me?" he purred. "It would have saved us a lot of trouble. Instead, I was trapped in a relationship I didn't want, though I appreciate the efforts you made to rid me of that problem."

Roslyn relaxed, and a cold smile flashed across her face. It was strange, but Chrysander had never realized just how ugly she was.

"How did you arrange it?" he asked silkily.

He listened in horror as she outlined what she'd done to make it appear as though Marley had stolen the plans. The kidnapping had been an added bonus, but when she'd received the ransom demand at his office, she'd seen her opportunity to be rid of Marley once and for all.

So anxious was she to prove her devotion to Chrysander, that she didn't realize she'd admitted to selling his plans to his competitor.

"So you stole the plans and gave them to Marcelli." His voice was like ice, and she flinched at his tone. Her face whitened as she realized just what she'd confessed to.

"You then framed Marley, thinking not only would you have the proceeds from selling me out to my competitor, but then you would have Marley out of the way so you could move into her place."

Her mouth opened and closed, and he could see the realization settle in that he'd duped her and was furious.

"And then when the ransom demands were delivered to my office, you destroyed them, hoping what, Roslyn, that they would kill her? Permanently remove her from the picture?"

He was shaking he was so angry. She simmered before him in a red haze. All he could see was Marley alone and frightened. Pregnant with his child and vulnerable. Thinking that not only did he hate her but that he'd simply left her to her fate. He wanted to weep.

Roslyn seemed to recover her composure, and she looked scornfully at him. "You'll never prove it."

"I don't have to," he said softly. He pressed the small intercom button on his desk. "You may come in now, Detective."

Roslyn swayed as three policemen entered the room, their expressions grim.

"You can't do this!" she shrieked. "I love you, Chrysander. I would have done anything for you."

He shook his head and turned away from her rantings as she was escorted away in handcuffs. He had no desire to listen to her. He wanted to return to Marley.

"Forgive me, *agape mou,*" he whispered.

Marley was dimly aware that she was being carried yet again. It wasn't Chrysander. She was intimately familiar with his touch. For a moment she panicked, and then she heard comforting words being spoken in Greek and then in English.

"Rest easy, little sister. You are safe."

"Where are we going?" she asked weakly.

"Someplace safe," he soothed. "Chrysander won't allow anything to happen to you."

She wanted to protest that Chrysander wouldn't do anything for her, but she couldn't muster the energy. At some point, she heard Chrysander, and she cursed the fact that she immediately felt safer and that some of the panic abated.

She felt the brush of lips against her forehead and then firm hands tucking her into bed. Fingers stroked through her hair, and warmth enveloped her.

"You are safe, *agape mou*. I'll never allow anyone to hurt you again."

"Don't call me that," she cried. "Never again." But she held to Chrysander's promise even as her heart screamed in protest. He'd lied to her. She couldn't believe anything he said. And yet she relaxed and settled into a dreamless sleep.

When Marley next awoke, there was a crispness to her mind that had been absent since the day she'd regained her memory. No longer did fog shroud her memories. She both welcomed and cursed the new awareness. Gone was any confusion, but with that new clarity came inevitable heartbreak.

She felt alert, as though she'd slept a week. And maybe she had. She had no idea how much time had passed, and while her past was no longer a mystery, the events of the last few days were hazy and fractured.

With a reluctant sigh, she pushed back the covers and eased her legs over the side of the bed. As she glanced around, she realized she had no idea where she was. The room was spacious and cheerful, with several windows to allow natural lighting.

She pushed herself up and walked into the adjoining bathroom, her eyes widening at the size and luxury. She eyed the Jacuzzi tub with longing. While she might not know how many days had passed—they'd all been a blur— she did know that she hadn't had a bath in a while, and she couldn't wait to feel clean and refreshed again.

Bracing her foot on the step to the tub, she leaned over and turned the handle to start the water. When she looked up, she saw Chrysander standing in the doorway. A startled gasp escaped her.

He started forward immediately and grasped her arm to steady her. "I'm sorry for frightening you, *pedhaki mou*. It was not my intention. I worried when I came in to check on you and you were not in bed."

"I just wanted a bath," she said in a low voice.

"I do not want you to be in here alone," he said. "I'll summon Mrs. Cahill so that if you have need of anything, you can just call out."

She closed her eyes for a moment and drew in a steadying breath. Then she met his gaze. "Please, Chrysander, let's not have any further lies between us. There's no need for you to pretend that I'm important to you…that I matter."

Bleakness entered his eyes, and his face grayed underneath the olive tone of his skin. "You matter very much to me, *agape mou*."

Before she could respond, he retreated from the bathroom, and a moment later, Patrice bustled in. In a matter of minutes, Marley found herself stripped and settled into a warm bath. Not too hot, Patrice assured, since overly hot baths were not good for a pregnant woman.

As Marley settled into the fragrant bubbles, she leaned her head back against the rim of the tub and glanced over at Patrice. "Where are we? And how did you get here? I thought you were in Athens with Dr. Karounis."

"Mr. Anetakis asked me to fly back so I could be with

you," she said soothingly. "He was quite desperate. The idea of returning to the apartment upset you so badly that he brought you here."

"And where is here?" Marley asked.

"His house," she explained patiently. "We're about an hour from the city. It's quieter here, more peaceful. He thought you'd prefer it."

Tears blurred Marley's vision. And she thought she hadn't any more tears to shed. She hadn't known he owned a house outside of the city, and like the island, it was one more place she'd never visited in all the time she'd been with Chrysander. Further proof that she'd never occupied an important place in his life.

"He's been very worried about you," Patrice said, her face softening in sympathy. "We all have been."

Marley shook her head in denial. Chrysander hated her. He'd never loved her, and she'd been too stupid to realize it.

"What am I going to do?" she whispered to no one in particular. She'd been an idiot to give up her apartment, her job, every means she had of taking care of herself when she moved in with Chrysander. She'd been too blinded by her love and convinced that she had a future with him.

"Come out of the tub," Patrice said gently. "You need to get dried off so you can go down to eat."

Marley allowed Patrice to mother her. She was dried off and pampered then clothed in comfortable slacks and a maternity shirt. She rubbed a hand over her belly and whispered an apology to her unborn son.

She couldn't afford to fall apart. Her child was depending on her.

Chrysander was waiting for her when she exited the bedroom. He said nothing, but he cupped her elbow and helped her down the stairs, and she let him, too numb to protest. Marley also remained silent, her emotions too much in turmoil to try and have a reasonable conversation.

They sat at a small table that overlooked a beautifully manicured garden. Bright morning sun shone through the glass doors, and she felt warmed by the sun's rays.

Chrysander set a plate piled high with food in front of her then settled into a seat across from her. She piddled with her fork and toyed with the food, pushing it around the plate as she avoided his gaze.

He sighed, and she looked up to see him staring at her. His expression was somber, as though he was enduring the worst sort of hell. She nearly laughed at the absurdity. To her horror, she felt the prick of tears, and his face swam in her vision.

"We must talk, Marley. There is much I need to say to you." His voice sounded oddly strangled. "But first you must eat so you can regain your strength. Your health and that of our child must come first."

She bowed her head again, refusing to meet his stare any longer. She concentrated on eating, and once she started realized she was actually quite hungry.

As she was finishing the last of her juice, she heard a door slam in the distance, and then she heard the determined stride of someone walking across the floor. She turned to see Theron enter the room, a grim look on his face.

Before he could speak, Chrysander locked his gaze onto his brother and said in a steely voice, "Whatever it is, I'm sure it can wait until Marley has finished eating."

Theron cast a concerned glance her way and nodded his understanding to Chrysander. Anger tightened her throat and made swallowing difficult. Whatever it was they wished to speak about, it was obvious they didn't want to do so in front of her. But then why would they? She was someone they believed had stolen from them.

She stood abruptly and tossed down her napkin. Without a word to either man, she stalked away.

"Marley, don't go," Chrysander protested.

She turned and pinned him with the force of her glare. "By all means, have your conversation. I'd hate to intrude. After all, someone who has stolen from you and betrayed your trust isn't someone you want around when you're talking."

"*Theos,* that is not the issue here. Marley? Wait, damn it!"

But she ignored him and continued walking.

Chrysander watched her leave and cursed. He felt strangled by helplessness. How could he ever hope to make things right between them? She hated him, and she had every right to.

He turned to Theron, who had also watched Marley go, a frown etched on his face. "What brought you here in such a hurry?" Chrysander demanded.

Theron reached into the jacket of his suit and pulled out a folded newspaper. He tossed it onto the table in front of Chrysander. "This did."

Chrysander opened it and immediately cursed in four languages. On the front page was a picture of Marley being carried by Theron on the day she'd run from the apartment. Underneath were pictures of himself and of Roslyn with a story outlining the soap-opera saga that highlighted every single facet of his relationship with Marley.

He threw the paper across the room with vicious force. "It had to be Roslyn. None of my men would have spoken to the press."

Theron nodded his agreement. "Since you had her arrested for her theft and her duplicity in keeping the ransom demands from you, she likely thought she had nothing to lose and everything to gain by giving the public her spin on your supposed relationship with her."

Chrysander sank into the chair and rested his elbows on the table. "I curse the day I ever hired that woman. Marley could have died because of my stupidity."

"You love her."

It wasn't a question, and Chrysander didn't treat is as such. It was simply a statement of fact. He did love her. But he'd managed to kill her love for him not once, but twice.

He nodded and buried his face in his hands. "I wouldn't blame her if she never forgave me. How can she when I cannot forgive myself?"

"Go to her, Chrysander. Make this right between you."

Chrysander stood. Yes, it was time to try and make things right with Marley. If he could.

Chapter 16

Marley stood in the bedroom, staring out the window with unseeing eyes. Nothing Chrysander did at this point should hurt her, but he still had that power over her, much to her dismay.

"Marley."

She swung around to see Chrysander standing in the doorway. He looked tired, his features drawn and his eyes worried. There was something else in his expression. Sadness and…fear?

He started forward, a little hesitantly. "We need to talk."

She tensed then braced herself for what she knew would come. His repudiation of her. She turned her face away but nodded. Yes, they needed to talk and get it done with.

His fingers curled around her chin, and he gently turned her to face him. "Don't look like that, *agape mou*. I do not like to see you so sad."

"Please," she begged. "Just say what it is you want to say. Don't draw it out."

He lowered his hand to capture her wrist. His thumb brushed across her pulse, which jumped and sped up at his touch.

"Come, sit down."

She let him lead her over to the bed. He eased down beside her and sat stiffly, his posture screaming discomfort. Suddenly she couldn't wait for what he would say. Her anger bubbled like an inferno within her.

"You lied to me," she seethed. "Every single thing you've said to me since that day in the hospital has been one lie after another. You don't care about me. All those things you said, everything was a *lie*. When you took me to bed, you despised me, and yet you made love to me and made me believe you cared. Who does that sort of thing?"

She shuddered in revulsion and put her hands to her face.

"You are wrong," he said softly. He pulled her hands away from her face and lifted one to his lips to kiss her upturned palm. "I care a great deal about you. I didn't despise you when I made love to you. Yes, I lied to you about details. I was told not to do or say anything to upset you and to let your memory come back on its own. I lied, Marley, but about the little things. Not the important things. Like how much I care about you. *S'agapo, pedhaki mou.*"

She bowed her head. Her nose stung, and tears burned her eyelids. How she wanted to believe him. But he'd done nothing to earn her trust.

"I have wronged you greatly, Marley."

She raised her head to stare at him in shock. Chrysander admitting that he was wrong?

Shame dragged at his eyes, and deep sorrow had pasted shadows under them.

"There are things you must know. I never received any ransom demands. I would have moved heaven and earth to free you. No price would have been too high. I did not know that you had been abducted."

Her mouth fell open. "How could you not know?"

His eyes grew stormy. "Roslyn destroyed the ransom notes. You were right to dislike her, and because I ignored your feelings about her, I placed you in terrible danger."

Marley's mind reeled with all he had told her. She raised a shaking hand to her mouth. He hadn't gotten the ransom demands? "I thought—" She broke off and shook her head, emotion overwhelming her.

"What did you think, *agape mou?*" he asked softly.

"That you hated me," she whispered. "That you wouldn't pay to free me because you thought I had stolen from you. That I wasn't even worth half a million dollars to you."

He groaned and pulled her into his arms. His hands trembled against her back as he stroked up and down. "I am a fool. I was wrong to accuse you as I did. I have no defense."

She pulled away and gazed up at him. "You don't believe I stole from you?"

He shook his head sharply. "No. It was Roslyn. She planted the papers in your bag to make me think it was you." He paused and swiped a hand through his hair. "Even though I thought you had stolen from me, it no longer seemed to matter after your abduction. All that mattered to me was that you were back where you belonged. With me." His mouth twisted. "That night when you asked me about our relationship…I was frightened."

She raised one eyebrow. The idea of anything frightening Chrysander was laughable.

"I thought you were unhappy, that you wanted more than I was giving you," he admitted. "And then I was angry because it scared me. I was determined that you not be the one to decide our relationship, so I pushed you away by telling you that we had no relationship, that you were my mistress."

Her heart sped up as she viewed the vulnerability on his face. Her chest tightened, and it became harder to breathe as her pulse raced. "What are you saying?" she whispered.

"That I love you, *pedhaki mou. S'agapo.*"

Her eyes widened as she realized what the words he'd said a few minutes ago meant. She couldn't even formulate a response, so she stared at him in shock.

Self-derision crawled across his face. "I have a terrible way of showing it. I was proud, too proud to just tell you how I felt. I didn't even know it then. I just knew I didn't want you to leave and was angry that I thought you were unhappy in our current relationship. And then when I saw those papers in your bag, I was shocked and furious. I couldn't believe that you would steal from me."

"But you did," she said painfully.

He looked away, sorrow creasing his features. "I was angry. I've never been so angry. I thought you had used me so you could help our competitor. So I sent you away."

He ran a hand around to clasp the back of his neck. "And God help me, I sent you straight into the kidnappers' hands."

She closed her eyes, not wanting to remember the fear and despair she'd experienced during her captivity. Even though her memory had returned, that part was still very much a blur. Maybe she'd forever block it out.

"You *love* me?" She was still back on those words. The rest of the conversation seemed a muddle, and she was fixated on those three words.

He gathered her in his arms again and held her as delicately as a piece of hand-blown glass. "I've not done a good job of showing you, but I do love you. I want the chance to prove it to you. I want you to marry me. Please."

She shook her head in confusion at his humble plea. "You still want me to marry you?"

He tugged her closer to him until his lips pressed against the top of her head. "I don't expect you to answer now. I know I have said much to shock you. But give me a chance, Marley. You won't regret it, I swear. I'll make you love me again. I'll never abuse your precious gift as I have done."

She'd gone mad. She'd finally lost her mind. Chrysander was holding her in his arms, declaring his love for her and wanting her to marry him. For real this time. No pretense. No lies or half-truths between them.

Gently, he pulled her away and pressed a light kiss to her lips. "Think about it, *agape mou*. I'll wait as long as it takes for your answer."

He stood as if sensing her desire to be alone. He walked to the door but turned to look at her one last time before disappearing from view.

Marley sat there for a long time simply staring at the now-empty doorway. Her hands shook and her stomach rolled. He loved her? Roslyn had planted the papers in her bag and then destroyed the ransom demands?

She shivered. Had Roslyn hated her so much? Or had she just wanted Chrysander that badly? Maybe both. Or maybe Roslyn had just been working for Chrysander's competition all along.

The events of the last few days still weighed heavily on her. She couldn't just forget everything because he apologized and offered her love and marriage, could she? She couldn't even return that declaration because he'd never believe it if it came now.

She sighed and lay on her side, curling her knees to her swollen belly. She was so tired. So very worn out, both physically and emotionally. She rubbed her stomach, smiling when her son rolled and kicked beneath her fingers.

"What should I do?" she whispered. She was so afraid to trust Chrysander with her love again. She was also afraid to be without him. As much damage as he'd done to her heart, she ached at the thought of leaving him.

She closed her eyes for just a moment. Exhaustion permeated every pore. She couldn't make such a monumental decision in a few minutes' time. Too much was at stake. She had a child to consider. She had herself to consider.

Over the next few days, Chrysander saw to her every need. He coddled her, pampered her and fussed endlessly over her. He told her often that he loved her, though he was careful to keep a respectable distance between them.

It would seem he went to great pains not to pressure her in any way. He wouldn't use the passion that sparked between them as a means to sway her, and for that she was grateful.

Two days after Chrysander had asked her to marry him again, his brothers came to visit. Marley tried to excuse herself, thinking that they'd want to discuss business with Chrysander, and to be honest, she still felt awkward and shamed in their presence even though she'd done nothing to deserve their censure.

But it was her they asked to speak to, and she stared at them in bewilderment as they looked gravely at her.

"We have acted unforgivably toward you, little sister," Theron said.

Piers nodded in agreement. "It is understandable if you never forgive us. We were harsh. There is no defense for our treating you, especially since you are pregnant with our nephew, as we have."

Guilt was etched heavily into their faces, and they looked so uncomfortable, but she had no idea what to do or say to ease the situation.

Theron moved forward and put his hands gently on her shoulders. He kissed her on both cheeks then stepped back as Piers did the same.

She glanced toward Chrysander, who watched her with solemn eyes. His face was drawn and seemed thinner as though he'd lost weight. He looked…unhappy. It wasn't guilt, though there was a lot of that floating around the room. He genuinely looked as though he'd lost the one thing that mattered most to him.

Her?

The thought nearly paralyzed her. She smiled shakily at Theron and Piers and then excused herself, nearly running from the room in her haste to get away.

She threw open the door to the patio and welcomed the chilly air. She stepped outside taking deep breaths and trying to settle her rioting emotions.

Her mind skated back over everything she'd felt for the last several days. Betrayal. She'd been lied to. She stopped there, because now she wondered if Chrysander really had lied to her about his feelings.

He looked like she felt. Lost. They were both obviously hurting. If he hated her, truly hated her, then why would he enact such an elaborate charade when she lost her memory? Why would he feel obligated to someone who had stolen from him?

"You're pregnant with his child," she murmured. And yes, she could see how a fair amount of care would be due the mother of his child, but why wouldn't he have done as Theron suggested and merely set her up in an apartment somewhere? Why would he woo her, make love to her, act as though she mattered to him?

Did he love her? The declaration couldn't have been easy for him to make. Chrysander wasn't a man prone to sharing his emotions. In all the time they were together before her kidnapping, he'd never spoken to her of his feelings. But he'd shown her in a dozen ways that she had mattered to him.

Could she trust him again? The thought frightened her, and at the same time it offered her a measure of peace. The choice was hers. Her future would be of her own making.

Even as her options rolled over and over in her mind, she knew what she would do. She knew what she wanted, even knowing it might not be the best choice for her. The heart didn't always choose wisely, she thought with a grimace.

Still, she found herself returning inside and going in search of Chrysander. Worry knotted her belly, but she knew she was making the right decision, even if it didn't feel quite right at this very moment.

She found him in the room she'd left him in, staring out the window, a drink in his hand. His brothers were gone and heavy silence lay over the room. She paused for a moment, gathering her courage. He looked as though he hadn't slept in days. His slacks were wrinkled and his shirt sleeves were unbuttoned and rolled partway up his arms. A shadow of a beard covered his jaw, and his hair was rumpled.

And still, he looked so desirable to her. She wanted to cross the room and melt into his arms. She wanted him to hold her and coax away her fears and doubts. The knot in her throat grew bigger, and she knew she had to speak now or risk being unable to.

"Chrysander," she called softly.

He whirled around. He set his drink down and hurried toward her. "Are you all right, *agape mou?* Is there anything I can get you? I'm sorry if my brothers upset you."

She tried to laugh, but it ended in a small sob. She drew in a deep breath and worked to compose herself.

"I'll marry you," she said.

A dark fire sparked in his eyes, making the amber glow more golden. He grasped her shoulders in his hands and stared down at her. "Yes?" he asked in a hoarse voice.

She nodded.

He closed his eyes and then crushed her to him. For a long moment, he just held her, and then he stepped back to stare intently at her.

"You mean it? You'll marry me?"

She licked her lips nervously. "I want a small ceremony. No fuss. As quiet as we can make it."

He nodded and cupped her chin in his hand. "Whatever you'd like."

"And I want…" She looked away and drew her bottom lip between her teeth.

"What do you want, *agape mou?* Tell me. There's nothing I won't do for you. You have only to ask."

"I don't want to stay here," she said quietly. "I'd like to go back to the island." She gripped her fingers together until the tips shone white.

His expression softened, and he dropped his hands to hers and gently uncurled her fingers until they were twined with his.

"We'll fly there as soon as we're married."

Relief surged through her veins. "You mean it? You don't mind?"

"Your happiness is everything to me. You ask such a small thing. How could I not grant it? We'll make the island our home if that is your wish."

She nodded. "I'd like that."

"Then I'll make the arrangements at once."

* * *

Chrysander wasted no time in finalizing plans for their wedding and preparing for them to travel to the island. He single-handedly rearranged his business schedule, made sure everything Marley could possibly need was purchased, though they'd already shopped for her wedding gown. She stood in awe of all he could accomplish in such a short time.

The authorities questioned her now that she'd regained her memory, and she spent several exhausting hours providing them with the few details she could remember. The kidnappers hadn't harmed her and had actually shown her consideration when her pregnancy became obvious. They had watched her, knowing she was close to Chrysander, and had struck when the opportunity arose. They'd asked for a small ransom, certain they would get it with no fuss. When no ransom had been forthcoming, they abandoned the kidnapping and arranged for Marley to be found.

It was the realization that Chrysander had ignored the ransom that had pushed Marley beyond her limits. It was that moment in the kidnapping that she blocked out her past, so devastated was she over his betrayal. Overwhelming emotion had crippled her—fear of being abandoned by the kidnappers, the terror of being left alone and having nowhere to go, no one to turn to.

Marley became distraught during the retelling, and Chrysander suffered the agony of being confronted by all she'd gone through. Because of him. He hovered protectively throughout, and finally called a halt when it was clear she was past all endurance.

The police were given their contact information so that Marley could be reached if arrests were made or there was a need for her to testify.

Two days later, they were married. Theron and Piers

both attended, and Patrice was the only other witness to the ceremony. Afterward, Piers gave her a somewhat reserved welcome to the family while Theron's was more warm and enthusiastic.

"You've made him very happy, little sister," Theron murmured as he gathered her in his arms for a hug.

She offered a small smile, but she knew Theron wasn't fooled by it.

Soon after, Piers and Theron left, Theron to return to London and Piers to fly to Rio de Janeiro to oversee plans for the new hotel. Patrice returned to Athens, where she'd be met by Dr. Karounis. While Chrysander wanted to wait a day for their own departure, Marley was adamant that they leave as soon as the ceremony was done. She wanted to return to the island, a place she'd been happy even if only for a short time. New York held too many unhappy memories, and she just wanted to be away.

Chrysander bundled her on the plane and insisted she sleep for the duration of the flight. It was late when they landed and later still by the time the helicopter touched down on the island. But Marley felt relieved that she was home.

Chrysander carried her into the house and didn't relinquish her until they were upstairs in the bedroom. He set her down on the bed and then busied himself undressing her and tucking her underneath the covers.

When he crawled in beside her and merely held her lightly against him, as though he was afraid of touching her, she frowned in the darkness. She rose up and reached across him to turn on the light he'd extinguished a moment earlier.

"Marley, what is wrong?" he asked as she stared down at him.

She studied him, the lines around his mouth, the worry in his eyes. In that moment, she understood. He was afraid.

"Make love to me," she whispered.

His eyes darkened and turned to liquid. A ragged breath tore from his mouth.

"I need you to make love to me."

"You have to be sure about this, *agape mou*. I don't want to pressure you into doing anything you aren't ready for."

"I'm sure."

With a tortured groan, he rolled her beneath him. Every kiss, every touch was so exquisitely tender. He touched and stroked her with infinite care.

Her gown was removed, and he slid out of his boxers. His body, hot and straining, covered hers. Pleasure streaked through her body in waves when he closed his mouth over her nipple. He sucked lightly, tonguing the small bud, then he turned his attention to her other breast.

His hand cupped her belly protectively, cradling her against him as he kissed his way up her neck and finally to her lips.

"*S'agapo, pedhaki mou. S'agapo,*" he murmured in a voice so husky, so emotional, that it brought tears to her eyes.

She cried out as he moved over her. "Please," she begged. "I need you."

He entered her slowly, his movements careful and measured. But she didn't want him to treat her so carefully. She wanted all of him. She arched into him and wrapped her legs around his hips.

Sobs of need, of pleasure, ripped from her throat, and for once, pain had diminished to a distant memory. There was only here and now and the man who loved her.

She raced up a mountain slope and hurtled into a free fall of ecstasy. Chrysander was there to catch her, gathering her close against him as he murmured words of love against her lips.

She snuggled into his embrace, melding herself as close to him as she could. She needed this. Needed him.

"Don't let me go," she whispered.

"Never, *agape mou*," he vowed. He stroked her hair, her back, the swollen mound of her belly as she drifted off to sleep. The last thing she was aware of was him telling her he loved her.

Marley slipped out of bed and pulled on her robe to cover her nakedness. Chrysander was still firmly asleep, his arm stretched out as though reaching for her.

He'd made love to her throughout the night, the two of them falling into an exhausted sleep just before dawn. Her body still tingled from his touch, his lips, his gentle caresses. As she stared at him, she knew that she couldn't hold off any longer. She couldn't torture them both. Her uncertainty was gone. Her fears would follow in time.

She padded down the stairs, smiling ruefully at the thought of how Chrysander would fuss that she hadn't waited for him. After a stop in the kitchen, where she nibbled at a bagel and drank a glass of juice, she ventured into the living room to enjoy the view of the ocean.

It was there that Chrysander found her. He slid his arms around her, cupping her belly with his hands as he kissed the curve of her neck.

"You're up early, *agape mou*."

"I was thinking," she murmured. She swiveled in his arms and met his worried gaze.

They both stared for a long moment, and then finally Chrysander said in a hoarse voice, "Do I ever have a chance of you loving me, Marley? Have I ruined that chance forever?"

Her gaze softened, and her heart turned over again with the love that swelled within her. Love and forgiveness.

"I already do," she said softly.

Surprise flickered across his face, and then doubt crept in.

"I've always loved you, Chrysander. From the moment I met you there has never been another man for me. There never will be."

"You love me?" he said in wonder, hope flaring in his eyes.

"I couldn't tell you before," she explained. "Not in New York when things were so messed up. You wouldn't have believed it if I had said it on the heels of your declaration. I wanted to return here, where we were happy. I wanted our life to begin here."

He gathered her in his arms and held her against his trembling body. His voice shook with emotion as he murmured to her in Greek. He switched back and forth between Greek and English as he told her how much he loved her and how sorry he was for the pain he'd caused her.

Then he swept her in his arms and carried her up the stairs and back to their bed, where he made sweet, passionate love to her again. Later he tucked her against his body and stroked a hand through her hair.

"I love you so much, *yineka mou*. I don't deserve your love, but I am so very grateful for it. I'll spend the rest of my life cherishing it, I swear."

She hugged him to her. "I love you, too, Chrysander. So much. We'll be so happy together. I'll make you happy."

And she did.

Chapter 17

Ironically enough, Marley discovered she was in labor halfway down the stairs. Alone. She gripped the banister and doubled over as a contraction rippled across her abdomen. Wasn't labor supposed to start out slow?

She wanted to laugh at the fact that fate was obviously cursing her for trying to sneak down the stairs without Chrysander knowing. While he'd relented about her taking the stairs in the earlier stages of her pregnancy, now that she was so close to her due date he'd once again insisted she not walk the stairs alone. He'd go insane now that she was nine months pregnant and, if the pain ripping out her insides was any clue, about to deliver.

She stood on the step, holding on to the railing and taking deep breaths. She'd have called out if she weren't so busy sucking air through her nose. Besides, Chrysander was busy with endless calls as he and Theron worked out Theron's relocation to the New York offices. Theron was taking over operations there so Chrysander could remain in Europe. They had been tied up for hours discussing security measures since her kidnappers were still at large.

When she heard footsteps above her, she straightened and tried her best to look as though nothing was wrong. She glanced guiltily up to see Chrysander standing at the top of the stairs, a disapproving expression marring his face.

He started down, grumbling in Greek all the way. "What am I to do with you, *agape mou?*" he asked when he got close.

"Take me to the hospital?" she asked weakly. She doubled over again as another contraction hit.

"Marley! *Pedhaki mou,* are you in labor?" He didn't even wait for a response, not that he needed one. He scooped her into his arms and hurtled down the stairs, shouting for the helicopter pilot, who had remained on the island for the last two weeks for just such an event.

"Do not worry, my darling," he said in uncharacteristic English. "We'll have you to the hospital in no time."

"Darling?" She laughed and then ended it in a moan. "It hurts, Chrysander."

He paled as he climbed into the helicopter with her.

"You aren't allowed to use English endearments," she panted. "Greek sounds so much sexier."

"*Pedhaki mou, yineka mou, agape mou,*" he whispered in her ear. My little one, my woman, my love.

"Much better," she sighed. She smiled then winced again as they lifted into the air. Chrysander was a basket case the entire way to the hospital. The pilot set down on the roof, and a medical team was waiting to usher her inside.

A mere hour later, with Chrysander hovering and holding her hand, Dimitri Anetakis squirmed his way into the world to the delight of his father and mother.

"He is beautiful, *agape mou,*" Chrysander murmured as he leaned in close to mother and child. Dimitri was nursing contentedly at Marley's breast, and Chrysander watched in fascination.

"He's perfect," she said in wonder. "Oh, Chrysander, everything's so perfect."

He kissed her tenderly, his love for her overflowing his heart. *"S'agapo, yineka mou."*

She cupped his face and smiled up at him. *"S'agapo,* Chrysander. Always."

* * * * *

Dear Reader,

The idea for this story came at the end of a family holiday to the U.S. I was supposed to not be writing, or even thinking about writing. We had had a wonderful time in Florida and later New York, and right at the end of the trip, I had been invited to stay at a friend's. I was lying in her garden, listening to the sound of summer and inhaling the scents and just really enjoying the peace and tranquillity of a summer garden when the idea for this story came to me.

My heroine, Matilda, fully understood the healing and peace a garden can bring, whereas my hero, Dante, was determined to carry on with his busy schedule and alpha ways. The attraction between these two opposites was undeniable and I loved the strength in Matilda, who refused to comply with Dante's emotionally closed rules.

Happy reading,

Carol

Carol Marinelli

WANTED:
MISTRESS AND MOTHER

Chapter 1

Inappropriate.

It was the first word that sprang to mind as dark, clearly irritated eyes swung round to face her, black eyes that stared down at Matilda, scrutinising her face unashamedly, making her acutely aware of her—for once—expertly made-up face. The vivid pink lipstick the beautician had insisted on to add a splash of colour to her newly straightened ash blonde hair and porcelain complexion seemed to suddenly render her mouth immovable, as, rather than slowing down to assist, the man she had asked for directions had instead, after a brief angry glance, picked up speed and carried on walking.

Inappropriate, because generally when you stopped someone to ask for directions, especially in a hospital, you expected to be greeted with a courteous nod or smile, for the person to actually slow down, instead of striding ahead and glaring back at you with an angry question of their own.

"Where?"

Even though he uttered just a single word, the thick, clipped accent told Matilda that English wasn't this man's first language. Matilda's annoyance at this response was doused a touch. Perhaps he was in the hospital to visit a sick relative, had just flown in to Australia from… In that split second her mind worked rapidly, trying to place him—his appearance was Mediterranean, Spanish or Greek perhaps, or maybe…

"Where is it you want to go?" he barked, finally deigning to slow down a fraction, the few extra words allowing Matilda to place his strong accent—he was Italian!

"I wanted to know how to find the function room," she said slowly, repeating the question she had already asked, berating her luck that the only person walking through the maze of the hospital administration corridors spoke little English. That the tall, imposing man she had had to resort to for directions was blatantly annoyed at the intrusion. "I'm trying to get there for the opening of the hospital garden. I'm supposed to be there in…" She glanced down at her watch and let out a sigh of exasperation. "Actually, I was supposed to be there five minutes ago."

"Merda!" As he glanced at his watch the curse that escaped his lips, though in Italian, wasn't, Matilda assumed, particularly complimentary, and abruptly stepping back she gave a wide-eyed look, before turning smartly on her heel and heading off to find her own way. He'd made it exceptionally clear that her request for assistance had been intrusive but now he was being downright rude. She certainly wasn't going to stand around and wait for the translation—she'd find the blessed function room on her own!

"I'm sorry." He caught up with her in two long strides, but Matilda marched on, this angry package of testosterone the very last thing she needed this morning.

"No, I'm sorry to have disturbed you," Matilda called back over her shoulder, pushing the button—any button—on the lift and hoping to get the hell out of there. "You're clearly busy."

"I was cursing myself, not you." He gave a tiny grimace, shrugged very wide shoulders in apology, which sweetened the explanation somewhat, and Matilda made a mental correction. His English was, in fact, excellent. It was just his accent that was incredibly strong—deep and heavy, and, Matilda reluctantly noted, incredibly sensual. "I too am supposed to be at the garden opening, I completely forgot that they'd moved the time forward. My admin assistant has decided to take maternity leave."

"How inconsiderate of her!" Matilda murmured under her breath, before stepping inside as the lift slid open.

"Pardon?"

Beating back a blush, Matilda stared fixedly ahead, unfortunately having to wait for him to press the button, as she was still none the wiser as to where the function room was.

"I didn't quite catch what you said," he persisted.

"I didn't say anything," Matilda lied, wishing the floor would open up and swallow her, or, at the very least, the blessed lift would get moving. There was something daunting about him, something incredibly confronting about his manner, his voice, his eyes, something very *inappropriate*.

There was that word again, only this time it had nothing to do with his earlier rude response and everything to do with Matilda's as she watched dark, olive-skinned hands punching in the floor number, revealing a flash of an undoubtedly expensive gold watch under heavy white cotton shirt cuffs. The scent of his bitter, tangy aftershave was wafting over towards her in the confined space and stinging into her nostrils as she reluctantly dragged in his supremely male scent. Stealing a sideways glance, for the first time Matilda looked at him properly and pieced together the features she had so far only glimpsed.

He was astonishingly good-looking.

The internal admission jolted her—since her break-up with Edward she hadn't so much as looked at a man— certainly she hadn't looked at a man in *that* way. The day she'd ended their relationship, like bandit screens shooting up at the bank counter, it had been as if her hormones had been switched off. Well, perhaps not off, but even simmering would be an exaggeration—the hormonal pot had been moved to the edge of the tiniest gas ring and was being kept in a state of tepid indifference: utterly jaded and completely immune.

Till now!

Never had she seen someone so exquisitely beautiful close up. It was as if some skilled photographer had taken his magic wand and airbrushed the man from the tip of his ebony hair right down to the soft leather of his expensively shod toes. He seemed vaguely familiar—and she tried over and over to place that swarthy, good-looking face, sure that she must have seen him on the TV screen because, if she'd witnessed him in the flesh, Matilda knew she would have remembered the occasion.

God, it was hot.

Fiddling with the neckline of her blouse, Matilda dragged her eyes away and willed the lift to move faster, only realising she'd been holding her breath when thankfully the doors slid open and she released it in a grateful sigh, as in a surprisingly gentlemanly move he stepped aside, gesturing for her to go first. But Matilda wished he'd been as rude on the fourth floor as he had been on the ground, wished, as she teetered along the carpeted floor of the administration wing in unfamiliar high heels, that she was walking behind instead of ahead of this menacing stranger, positive, absolutely positive that those black eyes were assessing her from a male perspective, excruciatingly aware of his eyes burning into her shoulders. She could almost feel the heat emanating from them as they dragged lower down to the rather too short second half of her smart, terribly new charcoal suit. And if legs could have blushed, then Matilda's were glowing as she felt his burning gaze on calves that were encased in the sheerest of stockings.

"Oh!" Staring at the notice-board, she bristled as he hovered over her shoulder, reading with growing indignation the words beneath the hastily drawn black arrow. "The opening's been moved to the rooftop."

"Which makes more sense," he drawled, raising a curious, perfectly arched eyebrow at her obvious annoyance, before following the arrow to a different set of lifts. "Given that it is the rooftop garden that's being officially opened today and not the function room."

"Yes, but..." Swallowing her words, Matilda followed him along the corridor. The fact she'd been arguing for the last month for the speeches to be held in the garden and not in some bland function room had nothing to do with this man. Admin had decided that a brief champagne reception and speeches would be held here, followed by a smooth transition to the rooftop where Hugh Keller, CEO, would cut the ribbon.

The logistics of bundling more than a hundred people, in varying degrees of health, into a couple of lifts hadn't appeared to faze anyone except Matilda—until now.

But her irritation was short-lived, replaced almost immediately by the same flutter of nerves that had assailed her only moments before, her palms moist as she clenched

her fingers into a fist, chewing nervously on her bottom
lip as the lift doors again pinged open.

She didn't want to go in.

Didn't want that disquieting, claustrophobic feeling
to assail her again. She almost turned and ran, her mind
whirring for excuses—a quick dash to the loo perhaps, a
phone call she simply had to make—but an impatient foot
was tapping, fingers pressing the hold button, and given
that she was already horribly late, Matilda had no choice.

Inadeguato.

As she stepped in hesitantly beside him, the word
taunted him.

*In a*deguato—*to be feeling like this, to be* thinking *like
this.*

Dante could almost smell the arousal in the air as the
doors closed and the lift jolted upwards. But it wasn't just
her heady, feminine fragrance that reached him as he stood
there, more the presence of her, the… He struggled for a
word to describe his feelings for this delectable stranger,
but even with two languages at his disposal, an attempt
to sum up what he felt in a single word utterly failed him.

She was divine.

That was a start at least—pale blonde hair was sleeked
back from an elfin face, vivid green eyes were surrounded
by thick eyelashes and that awful lipstick she'd been wearing only moments ago had been nibbled away now—revealing dark, full red lips, lips that were almost too plump
for her delicate face, and Dante found himself wondering
if she'd had some work done on herself, for not a single
line marred her pale features, her delicate, slightly snubbed
nose absolutely in proportion to her petite features. She
was certainly a woman who took care of herself. Her eyes
were heavily made up, her hair fragranced and glossy—

clearly the sort of woman who spent a lot of time in the beauty parlour. Perhaps a few jabs of collagen had plumped those delicious lips to kissable proportions, maybe a few units of Botox had smoothed the lines on her forehead, Dante thought as he found himself scrutinising her face more closely than he had a woman's in a long time.

A very long time.

He knew that it was wrong to be staring, in a*deguato* to be feeling this stir of lust for a woman he had never met, a woman whose name he didn't even know.

A woman who wasn't his wife.

The lift shuddered, and he saw her brow squiggle into a frown, white teeth working her lips as the lift shuddered to a halt, and Dante's Botox theory went sailing out of the absent window!

"We're stuck!" Startled eyes turned to him as the lift jolted and shuddered to a halt, nervous fingers reaching urgently for the panel of buttons, but Dante was too quick for her, his hand closing around hers, pulling her finger back from hitting the panic button.

She felt as if she'd been branded—senses that had been on high alert since she'd first seen him screeched into overdrive, her own internal panic button ringing loudly now as his flesh closed around hers, the impact of his touch sending her into a spin, the dry, hot sensation of his fingers tightening around hers alarming her way more than the jolting lift.

"We are not stuck. This lift sometimes sticks here… see!" His fingers loosened from hers and as the lift shuddered back into life, for the first time Matilda noticed the gold band around his ring finger and it both disappointed and reassured her. The simple ring told her that this raw, testosterone-laden package of masculinity was already well and truly spoken for and suddenly Matilda felt foolish, not just for her rather pathetic reaction to the lift halting but for the intense feelings he had so easily evoked. She gave an apologetic grimace.

"Sorry. I'm just anxious to get there!"

"You seem tense."

"Because I *am* tense," Matilda admitted. The knowledge that he was married allowed her to let down her guard a touch now, sure in her own mind she had completely misread things, that the explosive reaction to him hadn't been in the least bit mutual, almost convincing herself that it was nerves about the opening that had set her on such a knife edge. Realising the ambiguity of her statement, Matilda elaborated. "I hate this type of thing—" she started, but he jumped in, actually nodding in agreement.

"Me, too," he said. "There are maybe a hundred places I have to be this morning and instead I will be standing in some *stupido* garden on the top of a hospital roof, telling people how happy I am to be there…"

"Stupid?" Matilda's eyes narrowed at his response, anger bristling in her as he, albeit unwittingly, derided the months of painstaking work she had put into the garden they were heading up to. "You think the garden is stupid?" Appalled, she swung around to confront him, realising he probably didn't know that she was the designer of the garden. But that wasn't the point—he had no idea who he was talking to, had spouted his arrogant opinion with no thought to who might hear it, no thought at all. But Dante was saved from her stinging response by the lift doors opening.

"Don't worry. Hopefully it won't take too long and we can quickly be out of there." He rolled his eyes, probably expecting a sympathetic response, probably expecting a smooth departure from this meaningless, fleeting meeting, but Matilda was running behind him, tapping him smartly on the shoulder.

"Have you any idea the amount of work that goes into creating a garden like this?"

"No," he answered rudely. "But I know down to the last cent what it cost and, frankly, I can think of many more important things the hospital could have spent its money on."

They were walking quickly, too quickly really for Matilda, but rage spurred her to keep up with him. "People will get a lot of pleasure from this garden—sick people," she added for effect, but clearly unmoved he just shrugged.

"Maybe," he admitted, "but if I were ill, I'd far rather that the latest equipment was monitoring me than have the knowledge that a garden was awaiting, if I ever made it up there."

"You're missing the point…"

"I didn't realise there was one," he frowned. "I'm merely expressing an opinion and, given that it's mostly my money that paid for this 'reflective garden', I happen to think I am entitled to one."

"Your money?"

"My firm's." He nodded, revealing little but at least allowing Matilda to discount the movie-star theory! "Initially I was opposed when I heard what the hospital intended spending the donation on, but then some novice put in such a ridiculously low tender, I decided to let it go ahead. No doubt the landscape firm is now declaring bankruptcy, but at the end of the day the hospital has its garden and I appear a man of the people." All this was said in superior tones with a thick accent so that Matilda was a second or two behind the conversation, blinking angrily as each word was deciphered and finally hit its mark. "Never look a gift pony in the mouth."

"Horse," she retorted as she followed this impossible,

obnoxious man up the disabled ramp that she had had installed to replace the three concrete steps and opened the small door that led onto the rooftop. "The saying is never look a gift horse..." Her words petered out, the anger that fizzed inside, the nerves that had assailed her all morning fading as she stepped outside.

Outside into what she, Matilda Hamilton, had created.

The barren, concrete landscape of the hospital roof had become available when the helipad had been relocated to the newly built emergency department the previous year. The hospital had advertised in the newspaper, inviting tenders to transform the nondescript area into a retreat for patients, staff and relatives. A landscape designer by trade, most of her work to that point had been courtesy of her fiancé, Edward—a prominent real estate agent whose wealthy clients were only too happy to part with generous sums of money in order to bolster their properties prior to sale, or to transform Nana's neglected garden into a small oasis prior to an executor's auction. But as their relationship had steadily deteriorated, Matilda's desire to make it on her own had steadily increased. Despite Edwards's negativity and scorn, she'd registered a business name and duly made an appointment to take measurements of the rooftop and start her plans. Though she hadn't expected to make it past the first round, the second she had stepped onto the roof, excitement had taken over. It was as if she could *see* how it should be, could envision this dry, bland area transformed—endless potted trees supplying wind breaks and shade decorated with fairy lights to make it magical at night, cobbled paths where patients could meander and find their own space for reflection, mosaic tables filled with colour, messages of hope and inspiration adorning them like the stained-glass windows of a church where families could sit and share a coffee.

And water features!

Matilda's signature pieces were definitely in the plural—the gentle sound of running water audible at every turn, blocking out the hum of traffic or nearby people to enable peace or a private conversation. Hugh Keller had listened as she'd painted her vision with words, her hands flailing like windmills as she'd invited him into her mind's eye, described in minute detail the image she could so clearly see—a centre piece of water jets, shooting from the ground at various, random intervals, catching the sun and the colour from the garden—a centre piece where the elderly could sit and watch and children could play. And now that vision was finally a reality. In just a few moments' time, when Hugh cut the ribbon, the water features would be turned on and the garden declared open for all to enjoy!

"Matilda!" From all angles her name was being called and Matilda was glad for her momentary popularity—glad for the excuse to slip away from the man she'd walked in with. Not that he'd notice, Matilda thought, accepting congratulations and a welcome glass of champagne, but cross with herself that on this, perhaps the most important day of her life, a day when she should be making contacts, focusing on her achievement, instead she was recalling the brief encounter that had literally left her breathless, her mind drifting from the vitally important to the completely irrelevant.

He'd been nothing but rude, Matilda reminded herself firmly, smiling as Hugh waved through the crowd and made his way over towards her.

Very rude, Matilda reiterated to herself—good-looking he may be, impossibly sexy even, but he was obnoxious and—

"Hi, Hugh." Matilda kissed the elderly gentleman on the cheek and dragged her mind back to the important event that was taking place. She listened intently as Hugh briefed her on the order of the speeches and part she would take in the day's events, but somewhere between Hugh reminding her to thank the mayor and the various sponsors Matilda's mind wandered, along with her eyes—coming to rest on that haughty profile that had both inflamed and enraged her since the moment of impact. Watching a man who stood a foot above a dignified crowd, engaged in conversation yet somehow remaining aloof, somehow standing apart from the rest.

And maybe he sensed he was being watched, perhaps it was her longing that made him turn around, but suddenly he was looking at her, making her feel just as he had a few moments ago in the lift, plunging her back to sample again those giddy, confusing sensations he somehow triggered. Suddenly her ability to concentrate on what Hugh was saying was reduced to ADHD proportions, the chatter in the garden fading into a distant hum as he blatantly held her gaze, just stared directly back at her as with cheeks darkening she boldly did the same. Although the sensible part of her mind was telling her to terminate things, to tear her eyes away, turn her back on him, halt this here and now, somehow she switched her internal remote to mute, somehow she tuned out the warnings and focused instead on the delicious picture.

"Once things calm down, hopefully we can discuss it." Someone inadvertently knocking her elbow had Matilda snapping back to attention, but way too late to even attempt a recovery, Matilda realised as Hugh gave her a concerned look. "Are you OK?"

"I'm so sorry, Hugh." Reaching for her mental remote control, Matilda raised the volume, glanced at the gold band on the stranger's ring finger and, pointedly turning her back, flashed a genuinely apologetic smile. "I really am. I completely missed that last bit of what you said. I'm a bundle of nerves at the moment, checking out that everything's looking OK…"

"Everything's looking wonderful, Matilda," Hugh soothed, making her feel even guiltier! "You've done an amazing job. I can't believe the transformation—just a bare old helipad and rooftop and now it's this oasis. Everyone who's been up here, from porters to consultants, has raved about it. I'm just glad it's finally going to be open for the people who really deserve to enjoy it: the patients and relatives."

"Me, too." Matilda smiled. "So, what was it you wanted to discuss, Hugh?"

"A job." Hugh smiled. "Though I hear you're rather in demand these days."

"Only thanks to you," Matilda admitted. "What sort of job?"

But it was Hugh who was distracted now, smiling at the mayor who was making his way towards them. "Perhaps we could talk after the speeches—when things have calmed down a bit."

"Of course." Matilda nodded. "I'll look forward to it!" More than Hugh knew. The thought of giving a speech—of facing this crowd, no matter how friendly—had filled her with dread for weeks now. The *business* side of running a business was really not her forte, but she'd done her best to look the part: had been to the beautician's and had her hair and make-up done—her hair today was neatly put up instead of thrown into a ponytail, expensive foundation replacing the usual slick of sun block and mascara. And the shorts, T-shirts and beloved Blundstone boots, which were her usual fare, had been replaced with a snappy little suit and painfully high heels. As the dreaded speeches started, Matilda stood with mounting heart rate and a very fixed smile, listening in suicidal despair as all her carefully thought-out lines and supposedly random thoughts were one by one used by the speakers that came before her. Tossing the little cards she had so carefully prepared into her—*new*—handbag, Matilda took to the microphone, smile firmly in place as Hugh adjusted it to her rather small height and the PA system shrieked in protest. Staring back at the mixture of curious and bored faces, only one really captured her, and she awaited his reaction— wondered how he would respond when he realised who he had insulted. But he wasn't even looking—his attention held by some ravishing brunette who was blatantly flirting with him. Flicking her eyes away, Matilda embarked on the first speech in her adult life, carefully thanking the people Hugh had mentioned before taking a deep breath and dragging in the heady fragrance of springtime and, as she always did, drawing strength from it.

"When I first met Hugh to discuss the garden, it was very clear that the hospital wanted a place that would provide respite," Matilda started. "A place where people could come and find if not peace then somewhere where they could gather their thoughts or even just take a breath that didn't smell of hospitals." A few knowing nods from the crowd told her she was on the right track. "With the help of many, many people, I think we've been able to provide that. Hospitals can be stressful places, not just for the patients and relatives but for the staff also, and my aim when I took on this job was to create an area void of signs and directions and overhead loudspeakers, a place where people could forget for a little while all that was going on beneath them, and hopefully that's been achieved."

There were probably a million and one other things she could have said, no doubt someone else who needed to be thanked, but glancing out beyond the crowd, seeing the garden that had lived only in her mind's eye alive and vibrant, Matilda decided it was time to let Mother Nature speak for herself, to wrap up the speeches and let the crowd explore the haven she had tried so hard to create. She summed up with one heartfelt word.

"Enjoy!"

As Hugh cut the ribbon and the water jets danced into life, thin ribbons of water leaping into the air and catching the sunlight, Matilda felt a surge of pride at the oohs of the crowd and the excited shrieks of the children, doing just as she had intended: getting thoroughly wet and laughing as they did so. Only there was one child that didn't join in with the giggling and running, one little toddler who stood perfectly still, staring transfixed at the jets of water with huge solemn eyes, blonde curls framing her face. For some reason Matilda found herself staring, found herself almost willing the little girl to run and dance with the others, to see expression in that little frozen face.

"It's pretty, isn't it?" Crouching down beside her, Matilda held one of her hands out, breaking the stream of one of the jets, the cool water running through her fingers. "You can touch it," Matilda said, watching as slowly, almost fearfully a little fat hand joined Matilda's. A glimmer of a smile shivered on the little girl's lips, those solemn eyes glittering now as she joined in with the simple pleasure. As she saw Hugh coming over, Matilda found herself strangely reluctant to leave the child, sure that with just another few moments she could have had her running and dancing with the rest of the children.

"My granddaughter, Alex," Hugh introduced them, crouching down also, but his presence went unnoted by Alex, her attention focused on the water running through her hands. "She seems to like you."

"She's adorable." Matilda smiled, but it wavered on her lips, questions starting to form in her mind as the little girl still just stood there, not moving, not acknowledging the other children or her grandfather, just utterly, utterly lost in her own little world. "How old is she?"

"Two," Hugh said standing up, and pulling out a handkerchief, dabbing at his forehead for a moment.

"Are you OK," Matilda checked, concerned at the slightly grey tinge to his face.

"I'll be fine," Hugh replied. "I've just been a bit off colour recently. She's two," he continued, clearly wanting to change the subject. "It was actually Alex that I was hoping to talk to you about."

"I thought it was a job…" Her voice trailed off, both of their gazes drifting towards the little girl, still standing there motionless. But her face was lit up with a huge smile, utterly entranced at the sight before her though still she didn't join in, she still stood apart, and with a stab of regret Matilda almost guessed what was coming next.

"She's been having some problems," Hugh said, his voice thick with emotion. "She was involved in a car accident over a year ago and though initially she appeared unharmed, gradually she's regressed, just retreated really. She has the most appalling tantrums and outbursts followed by days of silence—the doctors are starting to say that she may be autistic. My wife Katrina and I are frantic…"

"Naturally." Matilda gave a sympathetic smile, genuinely sorry to hear all Hugh was going through. He was a kind, gentle, friendly man, and even though they'd chatted at length over the last few months, he'd never given so much of a hint as to the problems in his personal life. But, then again, Matilda thought with a sigh, neither had she.

"I told my son-in-law last night that my wife and I would like to do this for Alex as a gift. There's a small gated area at the back of his property that I'm sure would be perfect for something like this—not on such a grand scale, of course, just somewhere that doesn't have rocks and walls and a pool…"

"Somewhere safe," Matilda volunteered.

"Exactly." Hugh gave a relieved nod. "Somewhere she can't fall and hurt herself, somewhere she can run around unhindered or just sit and look at something beautiful. Look, I know you're booked up solidly for the next few months, but if one of the jobs gets cancelled could you bear me in mind? I hate to put pressure on you, Matilda, but I saw the joy in the children's faces when they saw the garden today. And if it can help Alex…" His voice trailed off and Matilda knew he wasn't attempting to gain her sympathy, Hugh would never do that. "My son-in-law thinks that it's just a waste of time, that it isn't going to help a bit, but at the very least Alex would have a garden that's safe and gives her some pleasure. I'm sure I'll be able to talk him around. At the end of the day he adores Alex—he'd do anything to help her."

Matilda didn't know what to say—her diary was fill to burst with smart mews townhouses all wanting the inevitable low-maintenance, high-impact garden—but here was the man who had given her the head start, given her this opportunity. And more importantly, Matilda thought, her eyes lingering on Alex, here was a little girl who deserved all the help she could get. Her mind was working overtime—she could almost see the lazy couple of weeks' holiday she'd had planned before plunging into her next job slipping away out of her grasp as she took a deep breath and gave a small smile.

"Hugh, I'd need to get some details and then I'd need to actually see the site before I commit, but I have a couple of weeks off before I start on my next job, and I'm on pretty good terms with a few people. If I called in a few favours maybe I could do it for you. Where does Alex live?"

"Mount Eliza." Hugh saw her give a small grimace. It had nothing to do with the location—Mount Eliza was a stunning, exclusive location overlooking Port Phillip Bay—but the distance from the city meant that it would cut down Matilda's working day considerably. "It was their holiday residence before the accident, but since then… Look, would it make it easier if you stayed there? There's plenty of room."

"I don't think I'd be able to do it otherwise," Matilda admitted. "I'll have workers arriving at the crack of dawn and I'm going to need to be there to meet them and show them what I need done."

"It won't be a problem," Hugh assured her, and after a moment of deep thought Matilda gave a small nod and then followed it up with a more definite one.

"I'd be happy to do it."

"You mean it?"

"Of course." Matilda smiled more widely now, Hugh's obvious delight making her spur-of-the-moment choice easily the right one.

"I feel awful that you won't even get a break."

"That's what being in business is all about apparently." Matilda shrugged her shoulders. "Anyway, I'm sure lean times will come—it won't stay spring for ever and anyway it mightn't be such a big job. I'd be glad to do it, Hugh, but I do need a few more details from you, and you need to get your son-in-law's permission—I can't go digging up his land and planting things if he doesn't want me there in the first place. Now, I need to know the size of the land, any existing structures…" Matilda gave in as yet another group was making its way over, and Hugh's secretary tapped him on the arm to take an important phone call.

"It's impossible to discuss it here." Hugh gave an apologetic smile. "And it's probably inappropriate. You should be enjoying the celebrations—perhaps we could do it over dinner tonight. I'll see if my son-in-law can come along— I'm sure once he hears first hand about it he'll be more enthusiastic. Actually, there he is—I'll go and run it by him now."

"Good idea," Matilda agreed, crouching down again to play with Alex, her head turning to where Hugh was waving. But the smile died on her face as again she found herself staring at the man who had taken up so much of her mental energy today—watching as he walked around the water feature, a frown on his face as he watched her interact with his daughter.

"Dante!" Clearly not picking up on the tension, Hugh called him over, but Dante didn't acknowledge either of them, his haughty expression only softening when Matilda stepped back, his features softer now as he eyed his daughter. Matilda felt a curious lump swell in her throat as, with infinite tenderness, he knelt down beside Alex, something welling within as he spoke gently to his daughter.

"I'll have a word with Dante and make a booking for tonight, then," Hugh checked hopefully—too pleased to notice Matilda's stunned expression. The most she could manage was the briefest of nods as realisation started to dawn.

She'd barely managed two minutes in the lift with him and now she was about to be his house guest!

He's a husband and father, Matilda reminded herself firmly, calming herself down a touch, almost convincing herself she'd imagined the undercurrents that had sizzled between them.

And even if she hadn't misread things, even if there was an attraction between them, he was a married man and she wouldn't forget it for a single moment!

Chapter 2

She didn't want to do this.

Walking towards the restaurant, Matilda was tempted to turn on her stiletto heels and run. She *hated* with a passion the formalities that preceded a garden make-over, looking at plans, talking figures, time-frames—and the fact she hadn't even seen the garden made this meeting a complete time-waster. But, Matilda was quickly realizing, this type of thing was becoming more and more frequent. As her business took off, gone were the days where she rolled up on a doorstep in her beloved Blundstone boots, accepted a coffee if she was lucky enough to be offered one and drew a comprehensive sketch of her plans for the owners, along with a quote for her services—only to spend the next few days chewing her nails and wondering if they'd call, worrying if perhaps she'd charged too much or, worse, seriously underquoted and would have to make up the difference herself.

Now her initial meetings took place in people's offices or restaurants, and even if she *was* lucky enough to be invited into their homes, Matilda had quickly learnt that her new clientele expected a smart, efficient professional for that first important encounter.

But it wasn't just the formalities that were causing butterflies this evening. Ducking into the shadowy retreat of a large pillar beside the restaurant, Matilda stopped for a moment, rummaged in her bag and pulled out a small mirror. She touched up her lipstick and fiddled with her hair for a second, acknowledging the *real* reason for anxiety tonight.

Facing Dante.

Even his name made her stomach ball into a knot of tension. She'd wanted him to remain nameless—for that brief, scorching but utterly one-sided encounter to be left at that—to somehow push him to the back of her mind and completely forget about him.

And now she was going to be working for him!

Maybe this dinner was *exactly* what she needed, Matilda consoled herself, peeling herself from the pillar ready to walk the short distance that remained to the restaurant. Maybe a night in his arrogant, obnoxious, pompous company would purge whatever it was that had coursed through her system since she'd laid eyes on him, and anyway, Matilda reassured herself, Hugh was going to be there, too.

An impressive silver car pulling up at the restaurant caught Matilda's attention and as the driver walked around and opened the rear door in a feat of self-preservation she found herself stepping back into the shadows, watching as the dignified figure of Dante stepped out—she had utterly no desire to enter the restaurant with him and attempt small talk until she had the reassuring company of Hugh.

He really was stunning, Matilda sighed, feeling slightly

voyeuristic as she watched him walk. Clearly she wasn't the only one who thought so. From the second he'd stepped out of the car, heads had turned, a few people halting their progress to watch as if it were some celebrity arriving on the red carpet. But just as the driver was about to close the car door, just as the doorman greeted him, a piercing shriek emanating from the car had every head turning.

Especially Dante's.

Even from here she could see the tension etched in his face as he walked back towards the car, from where an anxious young woman appeared, holding the furious, livid, rigid body of his daughter. Grateful for the shadows, Matilda watched with something akin to horror as, oblivious to the gathering crowd, he took the terrified child from the woman and attempted to soothe her, holding her angry, unyielding body against his, talking to her in low, soothing tones, capturing her tiny wrists as she attempted to gouge him, her little teeth like those of a feral animal. Matilda had never seen such anger, never witnessed such a paroxysm of rage, could scarcely comprehend that it could come from someone so small.

"That child needs a good smack, if you ask me," an elderly lady volunteered, even though no one had asked her. Matilda had to swallow down a smart reply, surprising herself at her own anger over such a thoughtless comment—tempted now to step out from the shadows and offer her support, to see if there was anything she could do to help. But almost as soon as it had started it was over. The fight that had fuelled Alex left her, her little body almost slumping in defeat, the shrieks replaced by quiet, shuddering sobs, which were so pain-filled they were almost harder to bear. After a moment more of tender comfort, with a final nod Dante handed her back to the woman, his taut, strained face taking in every detail as the duo headed for the car, before, without deigning to give the crowd a glance, he headed into the restaurant.

Pushing open the door, though shaken from what she had just witnessed, Matilda attempted assurance as her eyes worked the restaurant, her smile ready for Hugh, but as the waiter took her name and guided her towards the table, she was again tempted to turn tail and run.

It was definitely a table for two—but instead of the teddy bear proportions of Hugh, instead of his beaming red face smiling to greet her, she was met by the austere face of Dante, his tall muscular frame standing as she approached, his face expressionless as she crossed the room. If Matilda hadn't witnessed it herself, she'd never have believed what he'd just been through, for nothing in his stance indicated the hellish encounter of only moments before.

In her peripheral vision she was aware of heads turning, but definitely not towards her, could hear flickers of conversation as she walked towards him.

"Is he famous...?"

"He looks familiar..."

He looked familiar because he was perfection—a man that normally glowered from the centre of the glossiest of glossy magazines, a man who should be dressed in nothing more than a ten-thousand-dollar watch or in the driver's seat of a luxury convertible.

He certainly wasn't the type of man that Matilda was used to dining with...

And certainly not alone.

Please, Matilda silently begged, please, let a waiter appear, breathlessly dragging a table over, and preferably, another waiter, too, to hastily turn those two table settings into three. Please, please, let it not be how it looked.

"Matilda." His manners were perfect, waiting till she was seated before sitting down himself, patiently waiting as she gave her drink order to the waiter. She was patheti-cally grateful that she'd chosen to walk to the restaurant—no mean feat in her fabulous new shoes, but there was no chance of a punctual taxi this time on a Friday evening, and by the time she'd parked she could have been here anyway.

Good choice.

Good, because she could now order a gin and tonic, and hopefully douse some of the rowdier butterflies that were dancing in her stomach.

"Hugh sends his apologies." Dante gave her a very on-off smile as Matilda frowned. The Hugh she knew would be the last person to have bailed—no matter how impor-tant the diversion. After all, he'd practically begged her to do the garden.

"He had a headache after the opening. He didn't look well, so I walked him back to his office where he had…" Dante snapped his fingers, clearly trying to locate his word of choice. "He had a small turn," he said finally, as Matilda's expression changed from a frown to one of hor-ror.

"Oh, my goodness…"

"He's OK," Dante said quickly. "His blood pressure has been very high for the past few months, the doctors have had him on several different combinations of tablets to try to lower it, but it would seem the one they'd recently given him has brought it down too low—that's why he had a small collapse. Luckily we were in the hospital when it happened—all I had to do was pick up the phone."

"You're not a doctor, then."

Dante gave a slightly startled look. "Heavens, no. What on earth gave you that impression?"

"I don't know," Matilda shrugged. "You seemed to know your way around the hospital…"

"I've spent rather too much time there," Dante said, and Matilda could only assume he was talking about Alex. But he revealed absolutely nothing, promptly diverting the subject from himself back to Hugh. "He's resting at home now, but naturally he wasn't well enough to come out. Hugh feels terrible to have let you down after you were kind enough to accommodate him at such short notice. I tried many times to contact you on your mobile…"

"My phone isn't on," Matilda said, flustered. "I never thought to check."

Fool, Matilda raged to herself. He'd been frantically trying to cancel, to put her off, and because her blessed phone hadn't been turned on, Dante had been forced to show up and babysit her when he hadn't even wanted her to do the garden in the first place, when clearly he wanted to be at home with his daughter.

Taking a grateful sip of her drink, Matilda eyed the proffered menu, her face burning in uncomfortable embarrassment, utterly aware that here with her was the last place Dante either wanted or needed to be tonight.

"I've agreed to the garden." Dante broke the difficult silence. "Hugh said that I had to see you to give my consent. Do I need to sign anything?"

"It isn't a child custody battle." Matilda looked up and for the first time since she'd joined him at the table actually managed to look him in the eye. "I don't need your written consent or anything. I just wanted to be sure that you were happy for me to work on your garden."

"It's not a problem," Dante said, which was a long way from happy.

"I have brought along the plans for you to look at—I've highlighted the area Hugh discussed with you." Glancing up, Dante nodded to the waiter who had approached, giving him permission to speak.

"Are you ready to order, sir?"

The waiter hovered as Dante turned to Matilda, but she shook her head.

"Could you give us a minute?" Dante asked and the waiter melted away. Clearly assuming she was out of her depth, he proceeded to walk her through the menu. "I will be having my usual gnocchi, but I hear that the Tasmanian salmon is excellent here—it's wild—"

"I'm sure it's divine," Matilda interrupted. "I do know how to read a menu, Dante. And there's really no need to go through the charade of a meal…"

"Charade?"

Matilda resisted rolling her eyes.

"The pretence," she explained, but Dante interrupted her.

"I do know how to speak English, Matilda." He flashed her a tight smile. "Why do you call it a charade?"

"Because we both know that you don't want the garden, that you've probably only agreed because Hugh's unwell…" He opened his mouth to interrupt but Matilda spoke on. "You tried to contact me to cancel. I'm sorry, I never thought to check my phone. So why don't I save us both an uncomfortable evening? We can drink up, I'll take the plans and ring tomorrow to arrange a convenient time to come and look at your property. There's really no need to make a meal out of it—if you'll excuse the pun."

"The pun?"

"The pun." Matilda bristled then rolled her eyes. "It's a saying—let's not make a meal out of things, as in let's not make a big deal out of it, but given that we were about to *have* a meal…"

"You made a pun."

God, why was the English language so complicated at times?

"I did." Matilda smiled brightly, but it didn't reach her eyes.

"So you don't want to eat?"

"I don't want to waste your time." Matilda swallowed hard, not sure whether to broach the subject that was undoubtedly on both their minds. "I saw you arrive…" Taking a gulp of her drink, Matilda waited, waited for his face to colour a touch, for him to admit to the problem he had clearly faced by being here, but again Dante revealed nothing, just left her to stew a moment longer in a very uncomfortable silence. "Alex seemed very…upset; so I'm sure that dinner is the last thing you need tonight."

"Alex is often upset," Dante responded in a matter-of-fact voice, which did nothing to reassure her. "And given it is already after eight and I haven't stopped all day, dinner is exactly what I need now." He snapped his fingers for the waiter and barked his short order. "My usual."

"Certainly, and, madam…?"

Matilda faltered, desperate to go yet wanting to stay all the same.

"*Madam*?" Dante smiled tightly, making her feel like one.

"The salmon for me. *Please*," she added pointedly as the waiter took her menu. Then, remembering that as uncomfortable as she might feel, this was, in fact, a business dinner, Matilda attempted an apology. "I'm sorry if I was rude before," she said once the waiter had left. "It's just I got the impression from Hugh that this meeting tonight was the last thing you wanted."

"Funny, that." Dante took a long sip of his drink before continuing, "I got the same impression from Hugh, too…" He smiled at her obvious confusion.

"Why would you think that?" Matilda asked.

"Hugh gave me strict orders not to upset you." He

flashed a very bewitching grin and Matilda found herself smiling back, not so much in response to his smile, more at the mental picture of *anyone* giving this man strict orders about anything. "He told me that you were booked up months ahead, and that you'd agree to come in and do this job during your annual leave."

"Yes…" Matilda admitted, "but—"

"He also told me that you were doing this as a favour because he'd backed your tender, that you felt obliged—"

"Not all obligations are bad," Matilda broke in, rather more forcibly this time. "I *did* agree to work on your garden during my holiday and, yes, I *did* feel a certain obligation to Hugh because of the faith he showed in my proposal for the hospital garden, but I can assure you that I was more than happy to do the work."

"Happy?" Dante gave a disbelieving smile.

"Yes, happy." Matilda nodded. "I happen to like my work, Dante. I just want to make sure that you're fine with me being there."

"I'm fine with it." Dante gave a short nod.

"Because Hugh's sick?"

"Does it really matter?"

Matilda thought for a moment before answering. "It does to me," she said finally. "And whether it's ego or neurosis, I'd like to think that when I pour my heart and soul into a job at least my efforts will be appreciated. If you and your wife are only doing this to pacify Hugh, then you're doing it for the wrong reasons. To make it effective, I'm going to need a lot of input as to your daughter's likes and dislikes. It needs to be a reflection of her and I'd like to think that it's going to be a place the whole family can enjoy."

"Fair enough." Dante gave a tight shrug. "I admit I do not believe that a garden, however special, can help my daughter, but I am willing to give it a try—I've tried everything else after all…"

"I clearly explained to Hugh that this garden isn't going to be a magical cure for your daughter's problems—it might bring her some peace, some respite, a safe place that could help soothe her…"

"If that were the case…" Dante said slowly and for the first time since she had met him his voice wasn't superior or scathing but distant. Matilda felt a shiver run through her as she heard the pain behind his carefully chosen words. "It would be more than worth it."

"Look." Her voice was softer now. "Why don't I take the plans and have a look? Then maybe on Sunday I could speak with your wife about Alex…"

"My wife is dead."

He didn't elaborate, didn't soften it with anything. His voice was clipped and measured, his expression devoid of emotion as he explained his situation, the pain she had witnessed just a second before when he'd spoken about his daughter gone now, as if a safety switch had been pushed, emotion switched off, plunging his features into unreadable darkness as she faltered an apology.

"I had no idea," Matilda breathed. "I'm so very sorry."

He didn't shake his head, didn't wave his hand and say that she couldn't have known… just let her stew in her own embarrassment as their food arrived, raining salt and pepper on his gnocchi until Matilda could take it no more. Excusing herself, she fled to the loo and leaned over the basin, screwing her eyes closed as she relived the conversation.

"Damn, damn damn!" Cursing herself, she relived every insensitive word she'd uttered, then peeped her eyes open and closed them again as a loo flushed and she was forced to fiddle with her lipstick as a fellow diner gave her a curious glace as she washed her hands. Alone again,

Matilda stared at her glittering eyes and flushed reflection in the massive gilt-edged mirror and willed her heart to slow down.

She'd apologise again, Matilda decided. She'd march straight out of the bathroom and say that she was sorry. No, she'd leave well alone—after all, she'd done nothing wrong. Of course she'd assumed his wife was alive. He had a child, he wore his wedding ring. She had nothing to apologise for.

So why had she fled? Why didn't she want to go back out there?

"Everything OK?" Dante checked as she slid back into her seat.

"Everything's fine," Matilda attempted, then gave up on her false bravado and let out a long-held sigh. "I'm just not very good at this type of thing."

"What type of thing?"

"Business dinners." Matilda gave a tight smile. "Though I should be, given the number that I've been to."

"I thought that your business was new."

"It is." Matilda nodded, taking a drink of her wine before elaborating. "But my ex-fiancé was a real estate agent…"

"Ouch," Dante said, and Matilda felt a rather disloyal smile to Edward twitch on her lips.

"He was very good," Matilda said defensively. "Incredibly good, actually. He has a real eye for what's needed to make a house sell well. It's thanks to Edward that I got started. If he was selling a deceased estate often it would be neglected, the gardens especially, and I'd come in…"

"And add several zeros to the asking price!" Dante said with a very dry edge, taking the positive spin out of Matilda's speech. She gave a rather glum nod.

"But it wasn't like that at first."

Dante gave a tight smile. "It never is."

"So what do you do?" Matilda asked, chasing her rice with a fork as Dante shredded his bread and dipped it in a side dish of oil and balsamic vinegar, wishing as she always did when she was out that she'd had what he'd had!

"I'm a barrister. My specialty is criminal defence." Matilda's fork frozen over her fish spoke volumes. "Ouch!" he offered, when Matilda didn't say anything.

"Double ouch." Matilda gave a small, tight smile as reality struck. "Now you come to mention it, I think I know your name…" Matilda took another slug of wine as newspaper reports flashed into her mind, as a lazy Sunday afternoon spent reading the colour supplements a few months ago took on an entirely new meaning. "Dante Costello— you defended that guy who—"

"Probably," Dante shrugged.

"But—"

"I defend the indefensible." Dante was unmoved by her obvious discomfort. "And I usually win."

"And I suppose your donation to the hospital was an attempt to soften your rather brutal image."

"You suppose correctly." Dante nodded, only this time his arrogance didn't annoy her—in fact, his rather brutal honesty was surprisingly refreshing. "I try to give back, sometimes with good intentions." He gave another, rather elaborate, shrug. "Other times because…"

"Because?" Matilda pushed, and Dante actually laughed.

"Exactly as you put it, Matilda, I attempt to soften my rather brutal image." She liked the way he said her name. Somehow with his deep Italian voice, he made it sound beautiful, made a name that had until now always made her cringe sound somehow exotic. But more than that it was the first time she'd seen him laugh and the effect was amazing, seeing his bland, unfathomable face soften a touch, glimpsing his humour, a tiny peek at the man behind the man.

They ate in more amicable silence now, the mood more relaxed, and Matilda finally addressed the issue that they were, after all, there for.

"It would help if you could tell me a bit about Alex—her likes and dislikes."

"She loves water," Dante said without hesitation. "She also…" He broke off with a shake of his head. "It's nothing you can put in a garden."

"Tell me," Matilda said eagerly.

"Flour," Dante said. "She plays with dough and flour…"

"The textures are soothing," Matilda said and watched as Dante blinked in surprise. "I found that out when I was researching for the hospital garden. A lot of autistic children…" She winced at her insensitivity, recalled that it was only a tentative diagnosis and one that the family didn't want to hear. "I'm so—"

"Please, don't apologise again," Dante broke in with a distinct dry edge to his voice. "It's becoming rather repetitive. Anyway," he said as Matilda struggled for a suitable response, "it is I who should apologise to you: I embarrassed you earlier when I told you about my wife. You can probably gather that I'm not very good at telling people. I tend to be blunt." He gave a very taut smile and Matilda offered a rather watery one back, reluctant to say anything in the hope her silence might allow him to elaborate. For the first time since she'd met him, her instincts were right. She watched as he swallowed, watched as those dark eyes frowned over the table towards her, and she knew in that second that he was weighing her up, deciding whether or not to go on. Her hand convulsed around her knife and fork, scared to move, scared to do anything that might dissuade him, might break this fragile moment, not even blinking until Dante gave a short, almost imperceptible nod and spoke on.

"Fifteen months ago, I had a normal, healthy daughter. She was almost walking, she smiled she blew kisses, she waved, she was even starting to talk, and then she and my wife were involved in a car accident. Alex was strapped in her baby seat. It took two hours to extricate my wife and daughter from the car…" Matilda felt a shiver go through her as he delivered his speech and in that moment she understood him, understood the mask he wore, because he was speaking as he must work, discarding the pain, the brutal facts, the horrors that must surely haunt him. And stating mere facts—hellish, gut-wrenching facts that were delivered in perhaps the only way he could: the detached voice of a newsreader. "Jasmine was unconscious, pronounced dead on arrival at hospital." He took a sip of his drink, probably, Matilda guessed, to take a break from the emotive tale, rather than to moisten his lips. But other than that he appeared unmoved, and she could only hazard a guess at the torture he had been through, the sheer force of willpower and rigid self-control that enabled him to deliver this speech so dispassionately. "At first Alex, apart from a few minor injures, appeared to have miraculously escaped relatively unscathed. She was kept in hospital for a couple of nights with bruising and for observation but she seemed fine…"

Dante frowned, his eyes narrowing as he looked across to where Matilda sat, but even though he was looking directly at her, Matilda knew he couldn't see her, that instead he was surveying a painful moment in time, and she sat patient and still as Dante took a moment to continue. "But, saying that, I guess at the time I wasn't really paying much attention…" His voice trailed off again and this time Matilda did speak, took up this very fragile thread, wanting so very much to hear more, to know this man just a touch better.

"You must have had a lot on your mind," Matilda volunteered gently, and after a beat of hesitation Dante nodded.

"I often wonder if I failed to notice something. I was just so grateful that Alex seemed OK and she really did appear to be, but a couple of months later—it was the twenty-second of September—she started screaming..." He registered Matilda's frown and gave a small wistful smile. "I remember the date because it would have been Jasmine's birthday. They were all difficult days, but that one in particular was..." He didn't elaborate, he didn't need to. "I was getting ready to go to the cemetery, and it was as if Alex knew. When I say she was screaming, it wasn't a usual tantrum, she was *hysterio*, deranged. It took hours to calm her. We called a doctor, and he said she was picking up on my grief, that she would be fine, but even as he spoke, even as I tried to believe him, I knew this was not normal, that something was wrong. Unfortunately I was right."

"It carried on?"

Dante nodded.

"Worse each time, terrible, unmitigated outbursts of rage, and there's no consoling her, but worse, far worse, is the withdrawal afterwards, her utter detachment. I spoke to endless doctors, Hugh was concerned, Katrina in denial..."

"Denial?"

"She refuses to admit there is a problem. So do I too at times, but I could not pretend things were OK and Katrina was starting to get..." he stopped himself then, took a sip of his drink before continuing. "After a few months I took Alex home to Italy—I thought a change of environment might help. And, of course, it did help to have my family around me, but Hugh and Katrina were devastated," Dante continued. "They'd lost their daughter and now it seemed to them that I was taking away their granddaughter. But I had no choice and for a while Alex improved, but then suddenly, from nowhere, it all started again."

"So you came back?"

"For now." Dante shrugged. "I am back in Australia to try and sort things out and make my decision. I have a major trial coming up in a week's time so I am still working, but I am not taking on any new cases. You see now why it seemed pointless to renovate the garden when I do not know if Alex will even be here to enjoy it. But I think that Hugh and Katrina are hoping if they can do something—*anything*—to improve things, there is more chance that I will stay."

"And is there?" Matilda asked, surprised at how much his answer mattered to her. "Is there a chance you might stay?"

"My family is in Italy," Dante pointed out. "I have two brothers and three sisters, all living near Rome. Alex would have her *nona*, *nono* and endless cousins to play with, I would have more family support, instead of relying on Katrina and Hugh, but…" He halted the conversation then, leaving her wanting to know more, wanting a deeper glimpse of him. Wondering what it was that kept him here, what it was that made him stay. But the subject was clearly closed. "It cannot be about me," Dante said instead, giving a tight shrug, and there was a finality to his words as he effectively ended the discussion. But Matilda, wanting more, attempted to carry it on.

"What about your work?"

"I am lucky." He gave a dry smile. "There is always someone getting into trouble, either here or in Italy—and being bilingual is a huge advantage. I can work in either country."

"Doesn't it bother you?" Matilda asked, knowing that she was crossing a line, knowing the polite thing to do would be to leave well alone, but her curiosity was piqued, her delectable salmon forgotten, barely registering as the waiter filled her wine glass. "Defending those sorts of people, I mean."

"I believe in innocent until proven guilty."

"So do I," Matilda said, staring into that brooding emotionless face and wondering what, if anything, moved him. She'd never met anyone so confident in their own skin, so incredibly not out to impress. He clearly didn't give a damn what people thought of him; he completely dispensed with the usual social niceties and yet somehow he managed to wear it, somehow it worked. "But you can't sit there and tell me that that guy who killed—"

"That guy," Dante broke in, "was proved innocent in a court of law."

"I know." Matilda nodded but it changed midway, her head shaking, incredulity sinking in. She certainly wasn't a legal eagle, but you'd have to live in a cupboard not to know about some of the cases Dante Costello handled. They were *Big*, in italics and with a capital B. And even *if* that man she had read about really had been innocent, surely some of the people Dante had defended really were guilty. His job was so far removed from hers as to be unfathomable, and bewildered, she stared back at him. "Do you ever regret winning?"

"No." Firmly he shook his head.

"Never?" Matilda asked, watching his lips tighten a touch, watching his eyes darken from dusk to midnight.

"Never," Dante replied, his single word unequivocal. She felt a shiver, could almost see him in his robes and wig, could almost see that inscrutable face remaining unmoved, could see that full mouth curving into a sneer as he shredded seemingly irrefutable evidence. And anyone, everyone, would have left it there, would have conceded the argument, yet Matilda didn't, green eyes crashing into his, jade waves rolling onto unmovable black granite.

"I don't believe you."

"Then you don't know what you're talking about."

"I know I don't," Matilda admitted. "Yet I still don't believe you."

And that should have been it. She should have got on with her meal, he should have resumed eating, made polite small talk to fill the appalling gap, but instead he pushed her now. As she reached for her fork he reached deep inside, his words stilling her, his hand seemingly clutching her heart. "You've been proud of everything you've done."

"Not everything," Matilda tentatively admitted. "But there's certainly nothing big league. Anyway, what's that got to do with it?"

"It has everything to do with it," Dante said assuredly. "We all have our dark secrets, we all have things that, given our time again, we would have done differently. The difference between Mr or Ms Average and my clients is that their personal lives, their most intimate regrets are up for public scrutiny. Words uttered in anger are played back to haunt them, a moment of recklessness a couple of years back suddenly relived for everyone to hear. It can be enough to cloud the most objective jury."

"But surely, if they've done nothing wrong," Matilda protested, "they have nothing to fear."

"Not if I do my job correctly," Dante said. "But not everyone's as good as me." Matilda blinked at his lack of modesty, but Dante made no apology. "I *have* to believe that my clients are innocent."

She should have left it there, Matilda knew that, knew she had no chance against him, but she refused to be a pushover and refused to be swayed from her stance. She wasn't in the witness box after all, just an adult having an interesting conversation. There was no need to be intimidated. Taking a breath, she gave him a very tight smile. "Even if they're clearly not?"

"Ah, Matilda." He flashed her an equally false smile. "You shouldn't believe all you read in the newspapers."

"I don't," Matilda flared. "I'm just saying that there's no smoke without fire…" She winced at the cliché and began to make a more eloquent argument, but Dante got there first.

"There are no moments in your life that you'd dread coming out in court?"

"Of course not!"

"None at all?"

"None," Matilda flushed. "I certainly haven't done anything illegal, well, not really."

"Not really?" Nothing in his expression changed, bar a tiny rise of one eyebrow.

"I thought we were here to talk about your garden," she flared, but Dante just smiled.

"You were the one who questioned me about my work," Dante pointed out. "It's not my fault if you don't like the answer. So, come on, tell me, what did you do?"

"I've told you," Matilda insisted. "I've done *nothing* wrong. I'm sorry if you find that disappointing or boring."

"I'm *never* disappointed," Dante said, his eyes burning into her, staring at her so directly it made her squirm. "And I know for a fact that you have your secret shame—everyone does."

"OK," Matilda breathed in indignation. "But if you're expecting some dark, sordid story then you're going to be sorely disappointed. It's just a tiny, tiny thing that happened when I was a kid."

"Clearly not that tiny," Dante said, "if you can still blush just thinking about it."

"I'm not blushing," Matilda flared, but she knew it was useless, could feel the sting of heat on her cheeks. But it wasn't the past that was making her blush, it was the present, the here and now, the presence of him, the feel of his eyes on her, the intimacy of revelation—any revelation.

"Tell me," Dante said softly, dangerously, and it sounded like a dare. "Tell me what happened."

"I stole some chocolate when I was on school camp," Matilda admitted. "Everyone did," she went on almost immediately.

"And you thought that you'd look an idiot if you didn't play along?"

"Something like that," Matilda murmured, blushing furiously now, but with the shame and fear she had felt at the time, reliving again the pressure she had felt at that tender age to just blend in. She was surprised at the emotion such a distant memory could evoke.

"So, instead of standing up for yourself, you just went right along with it, even though you knew it was wrong."

"I guess."

"And that's the sum total of your depraved past?" Dante checked.

"That's it." Matilda nodded. "Sorry if I disappointed you."

"You didn't." Dante shook his head. "I find you can learn a lot about a person if you listen to their childhood memories. Our responses don't change that much…"

"Rubbish," Matilda scoffed. "I was ten years old. If something like that happened now—"

"You'd do exactly the same," Dante broke in. "I'm not saying that you'd steal a bar of chocolate rather than draw attention to yourself, but you certainly don't like confrontation, do you?"

Shocked at his insight, all she could do was stare back at him.

"In fact," Dante continued, "you'd walk to the end of the earth to avoid it, steal a chocolate bar if it meant you could blend in, stay in a bad relationship to avoid a row..." As she opened her mouth to deny it, Dante spoke over her. "Or, let's take tonight for an example, you ran to the toilet the moment you thought you had upset me."

"Not quite that very moment." Matilda rolled her eyes and gave a watery smile, realising she was beaten. "I lasted two at least. But does anyone actually like confrontation?"

"I do," Dante said. "It's the best part of my job, making people confront their hidden truths." He gave her the benefit of a very bewitching smile, which momentarily knocked her off guard. "Though I guess if that's the worst you can come up with, you really would have no problem with being cross-examined."

"I'd have no worries at all," Matilda said confidently.

"You clearly know your own mind."

"I do." Matilda smiled back, happy things were under control.

"Then may I?"

"Excuse me?"

"Just for the sake of curiosity." His smile was still in place. "May I ask you some questions?"

"We're supposed to be talking about your garden."

He handed her a rolled-up wad of paper. "There are the plans, you can do whatever you wish—so that takes care of that."

"But why?" Matilda asked.

"I enjoy convincing people." Dante shrugged. "And I

believe you are far from convinced. All you have to do is answer some questions honestly."

The dessert menu was being offered to her and Matilda hesitated before taking it. She had the plans, and clearly Dante was in no mood to discuss foliage or water features, so the sensible thing would be to decline. She'd eaten her main course, she'd stayed to be polite, there was absolutely no reason to prolong things, no reason at all—except for the fact that she wanted to stay.

Wanted to prolong this evening.

With a tiny shiver Matilda accepted the truth.

She wanted to play his dangerous game.

"They do a divine white chocolate and macadamia nut mousse," Dante prompted, "with hot raspberry sauce."

"Sounds wonderful," Matilda said, and as the waiter slipped silently away, her glittering eyes met Dante's. A frisson of excitement ran down her spine as she faced him, as this encounter moved onto another level, and not for the first time today she wondered what it was about Dante Costello that moved her so.

Chapter 3

"You will answer me honestly?"

His smile had gone now, his deep, liquid voice low, and despite the full restaurant, despite the background noise of their fellow diners, it was as if they were the only two in the room.

His black eyes were working her face, appraising her, and she could almost imagine him walking towards her across the courtroom, circling her slowly, choosing the best method of attack. Fear did the strangest thing to Matilda, her lips twitching into a nervous smile as he again asked his question. "You swear to answer me honestly."

"I'm not on trial." Matilda gave a tiny nervous laugh, but he remained unmoved.

"If we're going to play, we play by the rules."

"Fine." Matilda nodded. "But I really think you're—"

"We've all got secrets," Dante broke in softly. "There's a dark side to every single one of us, and splash it on a headline, layer it with innuendo and suddenly we're all as guilty as hell. Take your ex—"

"Edward's got nothing to do—"

"Location, location, location." He flashed a malevolent smile as Matilda's hand tightened convulsively around her glass. "Just one more business dinner, just one more client to impress. Just one more garden to renovate and then, maybe then you'll get his attention. Maybe one day—"

"I don't need this," Matilda said through gritted teeth. "I've no idea what you're trying to get at, but can you please leave Edward out of this?"

"Still too raw?" He leant back in his chair, merciless eyes awaiting her response.

"No," Matilda said tersely, leaning back into her own chair, *forcing* her tense shoulders to lower, *forcing* a smile onto her face. "Absolutely not. Edward and I finished a couple of months ago. I'm completely over it."

"Who ended it?"

"I did," Matilda answered, but with renewed confidence now. She *had* been the one who had ended it, and that surely would thwart him, would rule out his image of a broken-hearted female who would go to any lengths to avoid confrontation.

"Why?" Dante asked bluntly, but Matilda gave a firm shake of her head.

"I'm not prepared to answer that," she retorted coolly. "I had my reasons. And in case you're wondering, no, there wasn't anyone else involved." Confident she'd ended this line of questioning, sure he would try another tack, Matilda felt the fluttering butterflies in her stomach still a touch and her breathing slow down as she awaited his next question, determined to answer him with cool ease.

"Did you ever wish him dead?"

"What?" Appalled, she confronted him with her eyes—

stunned that he would even ask such a thing. "Of course not."

"Are you honestly stating that you never once said that you wished that he was dead?"

"You're either mad…" Matilda let out an incredulous laugh "…or way too used to dealing with mad people! *Of course* I never said that I wished that he…" Her voice faltered for just a fraction of second, a flash of forgotten conversation pinging into consciousness, and like a cobra he struck.

"I'm calling your friend as a witness next—and I can assure you that her version of that night is completely different to yours…"

"What night?" Matilda scorned.

"*That* night," Dante answered with absolute conviction, and Matilda felt her throat tighten as he spoke on. "In fact, your friend clearly recalls a conversation where you expressed a strong wish that Edward was dead." Dante's words were so measured, so assured, so absolutely spot on that for a tiny second she almost believed him. For a flash of time she almost expected to look over her shoulder and see Judy sitting at the other table, as if she had stumbled into some macabre reality TV show, where all her secrets, all her failings were about to be exposed.

Stop it, Matilda scolded herself, reining in her overreaction. Dante knew nothing about her. He was a skilled interrogator, that was all, used to finding people's Achilles' heels, and she wasn't going to let him. She damn well wasn't going to give him the satisfaction of breaking her.

"I still don't know what night you're talking about!"

"Then let me refresh your memory. I'm referring to the night you said that you wished Edward was dead." And he didn't even make it sound like an assumption, his features so immovable it was as if he'd surely been in the room that night, as if he'd actually witnessed her raw tears, had heard every word she'd sobbed that night, as if somehow he was privy to her soul. "And you did say that, didn't you, Matilda?"

To deny it would be an outright lie. Suddenly she wasn't sitting in a restaurant any more. Instead, she was back to where it had all ended two months ago, could feel the brutal slap of Edward's words as surely as if she were hearing them for the first time.

"Maybe if you weren't so damn frigid, I wouldn't have to look at other women to get my kicks."

He'd taunted her, humiliated her, shamed her for her lack of sexual prowess, demeaned her with words so vicious, so brutal that by the time she'd run from his house, by the time she'd arrived at Judy's home, she'd believed each and every word. Believed that their relationship had been in trouble because of her failings, believed that if only she'd been prettier, sexier, funnier, he wouldn't have had to flirt so much, wouldn't have needed to humiliate her quite so badly. And somehow Dante knew it, too.

"You did say it, didn't you?" It was Dante's voice dragging her out of her own private hell.

"I just said it," Matilda breathed, she could feel the blood draining out of her face. "It was just one of those stupid things you say when you're angry."

"And you were very angry, weren't you?"

"No," Matilda refuted. "I was upset and annoyed but angry is probably overstretching things."

He swirled his wine around in the glass and Matilda's eyes darted towards it, watching the pale fluid whirl around the bottom, grateful for the distraction, grateful for something to focus on other than those dark, piercing eyes.

"So you were only upset and annoyed, yet you admit you wished him dead!"

"OK," Matilda snapped, her head spinning as the barrage continued. "I was angry, furious, in fact. So would anyone have been if they'd been told…" She choked her words down, refusing to drag up that shame and certainly not prepared to reveal it to Dante. Dragging in air, she halted her tirade, tried to remember to think before she spoke, to regain some of the control she'd so easily lost. "Yes, I said that I wished he was dead, but there's a big difference between saying something and actually seeing it through." She felt dizzy, almost sick with the emotions he'd so easily conjured up, like some wicked magician pulling out her past, her secrets, clandestine feelings exposed, and she didn't want it to continue, didn't want to partake in this a moment longer.

"Can we stop this now?" Her voice was high and slightly breathless, a trickle of moisture running between her breasts as she eyed this savage man, wondering how the hell he knew, how he had known so readily what buttons to push to reduce her to this.

"Any time you like." Dante smiled, his voice so soft it was almost a caress, but it did nothing to soothe her. "After all, it's just a game!"

The dessert was divine, the sweet sugary mousse contrasting with the sharp raspberry sauce, but Matilda was too shaken to really enjoy it, her long dessert spoon unusually lethargic as she attempted just to get through it.

"Is your dessert OK?"

"It's fine," Matilda said, then gave in, putting her spoon down. "Actually, I'm really not that hungry. I think I'll go home now…"

"I'm sorry if I destroyed your appetite."

God, he had a nerve!

"No, you're not." Matilda looked across the table at him and said it again. "No, Dante, you're not. In fact I think that was exactly what you set out to do." Reaching for her bag, Matilda stood up and picked up the roll of plans.

"I'll be at your house on Sunday afternoon. I'll look at the plans tomorrow but until I see the garden I really won't know what I'm going to do."

"We've all said it." Dante's smile bordered on the compassionate as she stood up to leave, and he didn't bother to elaborate—they both knew what he was referring to. "And as you pointed out, there's a big difference between saying it and following it through. I was just proving a point."

"Consider it proven," Matilda replied with a very tight smile. "Goodnight, Dante."

Of course it took if not for ever then a good couple of minutes for the waiter to locate her jacket, giving Dante plenty of time to catch up with her. Rather than talk to him, she took a small after-dinner mint from the bowl on the desk, concentrating on unwrapping the thin gold foil as she prayed for the waiter to hurry up, popping the bitter chocolate into her mouth and biting into the sweet peppermint centre, then flushing as she sensed Dante watching her.

She'd said she wasn't hungry just two minutes ago— well, just because he was so damned controlled, it didn't mean that she had to be. What would a calculating man like Dante know about want rather than need? The man was utterly devoid of emotion, Matilda decided angrily. He probably peeled open his chest and pulled out his batteries at night, put them on charge ready to attack his next victim. Consoling herself that she could make a quick escape while he settled the bill, almost defiantly she took another chocolate, pathetically grateful when the waiter appeared with her jacket and helped her into it. She stepped outside into the night and closed her eyes as the cool night air hit her flaming cheeks.

"How far do you have to go?"

She heard Dante's footsteps as he came along behind her, recognised his heavily accented voice as he uttered the first syllable, his scent hitting her before he drew her aside, yet she'd known he was close long before, almost sensed his approach before he'd made himself known.

"How did you…?" She didn't finish her question, didn't want to be drawn into another conversation with him. She just marched swiftly on, her stilettos making a tinny sound as she clipped along the concrete pavement.

"I eat regularly there. They send my account out once a month or so and my admin assistant deals with it."

The one who'd dared to allow herself to get pregnant, Matilda wanted to point out, but chose not to, clutching the plans tighter under her arm and walking swiftly on.

"Would you like a lift home?"

"I have an apartment over the bridge." Matilda pointed to the a high-rise block on the other side of the river. "It's just a five-minute walk."

"Then I'll join you," Dante said. "You shouldn't be walking alone across the bridge at this time of night."

"Really," Matilda flustered, "there's absolutely no need—it's just a hop and a skip."

"I'd rather *walk* if you don't mind," Dante said, his face completely deadpan, but his dry humour didn't even raise a smile from Matilda. Frankly, she'd rather take the chance of walking across the bridge alone than with the evil troll beside her.

"I have an apartment near here also," Dante said, nodding backwards from whence they'd come, but despite the proximity to hers, Matilda was quite sure any city apartment Dante owned wouldn't compare to her second-floor shoebox!

"I didn't somehow envisage you as having an apartment," Dante mused, and Matilda blinked, surprised he *en*vis*aged* her at all. "I thought, given your work you would have a home with a garden."

"That's the plan, actually," Matilda admitted. "I've just put it up for sale. I never really liked it."

"So why did you buy it?"

"It was too good an opportunity to miss. And location-wise, for work it's brilliant." She gave a low groan at the sound of her own voice. "Can you tell I spent the last couple of years dating a real estate agent?" Matilda asked, glancing over to him and surprised to see that he was actually smiling.

"At least you didn't mention the stunning views and the abundance of natural light!"

"Only because I'm on the second floor," Matilda quipped, amazed after the tension of only a few moments ago to find herself actually smiling back. "I guess the drive from Mount Eliza to the city each day would be a bit much," Matilda ventured, but again she got things wrong.

"I don't generally drive to work, I use a helicopter."

"Of course you do," Matilda sighed, rolling her eyes.

"It is not my helicopter." She could hear the teasing note in his voice. "More like a taxi service. I would rather spend that hour or two at home than in the car. When we bought the place it was meant more as weekender, or retreat, but since the accident I have tried not to move Alex too much. It is better, I think that she is near the beach with lots of space rather than the city. A luxury high rise apartment isn't exactly stimulating for a small child."

Why did he always make her feel small?

"I use the apartment a lot, though. I tend to stay there if I am involved in a difficult trial."

"I guess it would be quieter."

"A bit," Dante admitted. "I tend to get very absorbed in my cases. By the time they go to trial there is not much space left for anything else. But it is not just for that reason." They were walking quickly, too quickly for Matilda, who almost had to run to keep up with him, but she certainly wasn't going to ask him to slow down. The sooner they got to her apartment block the sooner she could breathe again. "The press can be merciless at times. I prefer to keep it away from my family."

They were safely over the bridge now, walking along the dark embankment on the other side of the river.

"This is me," Matilda said as they neared her apartment block, and she rummaged in her bag for her keys. "I'll be fine now."

"I'm sure that you would be," Dante said, "but you are my dinner guest and for that reason I will see you safely home."

Why did he have to display manners now? Matilda wondered. He'd been nothing but rude since they'd met—it was a bit late for chivalry. But she was too drained to argue, just gave a resigned shrug, let herself into the entrance hall and headed for the stairwell, glad that she lived on the second floor and therefore wouldn't have to squeeze into a lift with him again.

"Home!" Matilda said with false brightness.

"Do you always take the stairs?"

"Always," Matilda lied. "It's good exercise." They were at her front door now. "Thank you for this evening. It's been, er…pleasant."

"Really?" Dante raised a quizzical eyebrow. "I'm not sure that I believe you."

"I was actually attempting to be polite," Matilda responded, "as you were by seeing me to my door." She was standing there, staring at him, willing him to just go, reluctant somehow to turn her back on him, not scared exactly, but on heightened alert as still he just stood there. Surely he didn't expect her to ask him in for coffee?

Surely!

How the hell was she going to spend a fortnight in his company when one evening left her a gibbering wreck? She *had* to get a grip, had to bring things back to a safer footing, had to let him know that it was strictly business, pretend that he didn't intimidate her, pretend that he didn't move her so.

"Thank you for bringing the plans, Dante. I'm looking forward to working on your garden." She offered her hand. Direct, businesslike, Matilda decided, that was how she'd be—a snappy end to a business dinner. But as his hand took hers, instantly she regretted it.

It was only the second time they had made physical contact. As his hand tightened around hers she was brutally reminded of that fact, despite the hours that had passed, despite a dinner shared and the emotions he had evoked, it was only the second time they had touched. And the result was as explosive as the first time, and many times more lethal. She could feel the heat of his flesh searing into hers, as his large hand coiled around hers, the pad of his index finger resting on her slender wrist, her radial pulse hammering against it. And this time the feel of his gold wedding band did nothing to soothe her, just reminded her of the depths of him, the pain that must surely exist behind those indecipherable eyes. Never had she found a person so difficult to read, never had she revealed so much of herself to someone and found out so very little in return.

But she wanted to know more.

"You interest me, Matilda." It was such a curious thing to say, such a hazy, ambiguous statement, and her eyes involuntarily jerked to his like a reflex action, held by his gaze, stunned, startled, yet curiously reluctant to move, a heightened sexual awareness permeating her.

"I thought perhaps I bored you."

"Oh, no." Slowly he shook his head and she started back, mesmerised, his sensuous but brutal features utterly captivating. "Why would you think such a thing?"

"I just…" Matilda's voice trailed off. She didn't know what to say because she didn't know the answer, didn't know if it was her destroyed self-confidence that made her vulnerable or the man who was staring at her now, the man who was pinning her to the wall with his eyes.

"He really hurt you, didn't he?" It was as if he were staring into her very soul, not asking her but telling her how she felt. "He ground you down and down until you didn't even know who you were any more, didn't even know what it was that you wanted."

How did he know? How could he read her so easily—was she that predictable? Was her pain, her self-doubt so visible? But Dante hadn't finished with his insights, hadn't finished peeling away the layers, exposing her raw, bruised core, and she wanted again to halt him, wanted to stop him from going further—wanted that mouth that was just inches from hers be silent, to kiss her…

"And then, when he'd taken every last drop from you, he tossed you aside…"

She shook her head in denial, relieved that he'd got one thing wrong. "I was the one who ended it," Matilda reminded him, but it didn't sway him for a second.

"You just got there first." Dante delivered his knockout blow. "It was already over."

He was right, of course, it had been over. She could still feel the bleak loneliness that had filled her that night and for many nights before the final one. The indifference had been so much more painful that the rows that had preceded it. She could still feel the raw shame of Edward's intimate rejections.

"I'm fine without him."

"Better than fine," Dante said softly, and she held her breath as that cruel, sensual mouth moved in towards hers. She still didn't know what he was thinking. Lust rippled between them, yet his expression was completely unreadable. The same quiver of excitement that had gripped her in the restaurant shivered through her now, but with dangerous sexual undertones, and it was inevitable they would kiss. Matilda acknowledged it then. The foreplay she had so vehemently denied was taking place had started hours ago, long, long before they'd even reached the garden.

He gave her time to move away, ample time to halt things, to stop this now, and she should have.

Normally she would have.

Her mind flitted briefly to her recent attempts at dating where she'd dreaded this moment, had avoided it or gone along with a kiss for the sad sake of it, to prove to herself that she was desirable perhaps.

But there was no question here of merely going along with this kiss for the sake of it—logic, common sense, self-preservation told her that to end *this* night with a kiss was a foolish move, that for the sake of her sanity she should surely halt this now. But her body told her otherwise, every nerve prickling to delicious attention, drawn like a magnet to his beauty, anticipating the taste of him, the feel of him in a heady rush of need, of want.

His mouth brushed her cheek, sweeping along her cheekbone till she could feel his breath warm on the shell of her ear then moving back, back to her waiting lips, slowly, deliberately until only a whisper separated them, till his mouth was so close to hers that she was giddy with expectation, filled with want—deep, burning want that she'd never yet experienced, a want that suffused her, a want she had never, even in the most intimate moments, experienced, and he hadn't even kissed her. Her breath was coming in short, unyielding gasps, his chest so close to hers that if she breathed any deeper their bodies would touch. She was torn between want and dread, her body longing to arch towards his, her nipples stretching like buds to the sun, his hand still on the wall behind her head, and all she wanted was his touch.

As if in answer, his mouth found hers, the weight of his body pushing her down, his lips obliterating thought, reason, question, his masterful touch the only thought she could process, his tongue, stroking hers so deeply so intimately it was as if he were touching her deep inside, his skin dragging hers as his mouth moved against her, the sweet, decadent taste of him, the heady masculine scent of him stroking her awake from deep hibernation, awareness fizzing in where there had been none.

His power overwhelmed her, the strength of his arms around her slender body, the hard weight of his thighs as he pinned her to the wall and a vague peripheral awareness of a warm hand creeping along the length of her spinal column then sliding around her rib cage as his mouth worked ever on. A low needy sigh built as it slid around, his palm capturing the weight of her breast, the warmth of his skin through the sheer fabric of her dress had her curling into him, needy, wanton, desperate, swelling at his touch, her breasts engorging, shamefully reciprocating as the pad of his thumb teased her jutting nipple. So many sensations, so many responses, his tongue capturing hers in his lips, sucking on the swollen tip, his body pinning her in delicious confinement, his masculinity capturing her, overwhelming her. Yet she was hardly an unwilling participant—fingers coiling in his jet hair, pulling his face to hers as her body pressed against him, his touch unleashing her passion, her desire, flaming it to dangerous heat, a heat so intense there was no escape, and neither did she want one. His kiss was everything a kiss should be, everything she'd missed.

Till now.

And just as she dived into complete oblivion, just as she would have given anything, anything for this moment to continue, for him to douse the fire within her, he wrenched his head away, an expression she couldn't read in his eyes as he looked coolly down at her.

"I should go."

Words failing her, Matilda couldn't even nod, embarrassment creeping in now. He could have taken her there and then—with one crook of his manicured finger she would have led him inside, would have made love to him, would have let him make love to her. What was it with this man? Emotionally he troubled her, terrified her even, yet still she was drawn to him, physically couldn't resist him. She had never felt such compulsion, a macabre addiction almost, and she hadn't even know him a day.

"I will see you on Sunday." His voice was completely normal and his hands were still on her trembling body. She stared back at him, unable to fathom that he could appear so unmoved, that he was still standing after what they'd just shared. Blindly she nodded, her hair tumbling down around her face, eyes frowning as Dante reached into his suit pocket and pulled out a handful of chocolate mints, the same ones she had surreptitiously taken at the restaurant.

"I took these at the restaurant for you…" Taking her hand, he filled it with the sweet chocolate delicacies. She could feel them soft and melting through the foil as he closed her fingers around them. "I know you wanted to do the same!"

An incredulous smile broke onto her lips at the gesture, a tiny glimmer that maybe things were OK, that the attraction really was mutual, that Dante didn't think any less of her because of what had just taken place. "You stole them?" Matilda gave a tiny half-laugh, recalling their earlier conversation.

"Oh, no." He shook his head and doused any fledgling hope with one cruel sentence, cheapened and humiliated her with his strange euphemism. "Why would I steal them when, after all, they were there for the taking?"

Chapter 4

What she had been expecting, Matilda wasn't sure—an austere, formal residence, surrounded by an overgrown wilderness, or a barren landscape perhaps—but with directions on the passenger seat beside her she'd found the exclusive street fairly easily and had caught her breath as she'd turned into it, The heavenly view of Port Phillip Bay stretched out for ever before her. Chewing on her lip as she drove, the sight of the opulent, vast houses of the truly rich forced her to slow down as she marvelled at the architecture and stunning gardens, tempted to whip out her faithful notepad and jot down some notes and deciding that soon she would do just that. The thought of long evenings with nothing to do but avoid Dante was made suddenly easier. She could walk along the beach with her pad, even wander down to one of the many cafés she had passed as she'd driven through the village—there was no need to be alone with him, no need at all.

Unless she wanted to be.

Pulling into the kerb, Matilda raked a hand through her hair, tempted, even at the eleventh hour, to execute a hasty U-turn and head for the safety of home. Since she'd awoken on Saturday after a restless sleep, she'd been in a state of high anxiety, especially when she'd opened the newspaper and read with renewed interest about the sensational trial that was about to hit the Melbourne courts and realising that it wasn't just her that was captivated by Dante Costello. Apart from the salacious details of the upcoming trial, a whole article had been devoted solely to Dante, and the theatre that this apparently brilliant man created, from his scathing tongue and maverick ways in the courtroom to the chameleon existence he'd had since the premature death of his beloved wife, his abrupt departure from the social scene, his almost reclusive existence, occasionally fractured by the transient presence of a beautiful woman— anodynes, Matilda had guessed, that offered a temporary relief. And though it had hurt like hell to read it, Matilda had devoured it, gleaning little, understanding less. The face that had stared back at her from the newspaper pages had been as distant and as unapproachable as the man she had first met and nothing, *nothing* like the Dante who had held her in his arms, who had kissed her to within an inch of her life, who had so easily awoken the woman within— the real Dante she was sure she'd glimpsed.

Matilda had known that the sensible thing to do would be to ring Hugh and tell him she couldn't do the work after all—that something else had come up. Hell, she had even dialled his number a few times, but at the last minute had always hung up, torn between want and loathing, outrage and desire, telling herself that it wouldn't be fair to let Hugh down, and sometimes almost managing to believe it. As honourable as it sounded, loyalty to Hugh had nothing to do with her being there today. Dante totally captivated her—since the second she'd laid eyes on him he was *all* she thought about.

All she thought about, replaying their conversations over and over, jolting each and every time she recalled some of his sharper statements, wondering how the hell he managed to get away with it, how she hadn't slapped his arrogant cheek. And yet somehow there had been a softer side and it was that that intrigued her. Despite his brutality she'd glimpsed something else—tiny flickers of beauty, like flowers in a desert—his dry humour, the stunning effect of his occasional smile on her, the undeniable tenderness reserved exclusively for his daughter. And, yes, Matilda acknowledged that the raw, simmering passion that had been in his kiss had left her hungry for more,

"Careful." Matilda said the word out loud, repeated it over and over in her mind as she slipped the car into first gear and slowly pulled out into the street, driving a couple of kilometres further with her heart in her mouth as she braced herself to face him again, her hand shaking slightly as she turned into his driveway and pressed the intercom, watching unblinking as huge metal gates slid open and she glimpsed for the first time Dante's stunning home.

The drive was as uncompromising and as rigid as its owner, lined with cypress trees drawing the eye along its vast, straight length to the huge, Mediterranean-looking residence—vast white rendered walls that made the sky look bluer somehow, massive floor-to-ceiling windows that would drench the home in light and let in every inch of the stunning view. She inched her way along, momentarily forgetting her nerves, instead absorbing the beauty. The harsh lines of the house were softened at the entrance by climbers—wisteria, acres of it, ambled across the front of the property, heavy lilac flowers hanging like bunches of grapes, intermingled with jasmine, its creamy white petals like dotted stars, the more delicate foliage competing with the harsh wooden branches of the wisteria. The effect, quite simply, was divine.

"Welcome!" Hugh pulled open the car door for her and Matilda stepped out onto the white paved driveway, pathetically grateful to see him—not quite ready to face Dante alone. "Matilda, this is my wife Katrina." He introduced a tall, elegant woman who stepped forward and shook her hand, her greeting the antithesis of Hugh's warm one. Cool blue eyes blatantly stared Matilda up and down, taking in the pale blue cotton shift dress and casual sandals she was wearing and clearly not liking what she saw. "You're nothing like I was expecting. I expected…" she gave a shrill laugh… "I don't know. You don't look like a gardener!"

"She's a designer, Katrina," Hugh said with a slight edge.

"I'm very hands-on, though," Matilda said. "I like to see the work through from beginning to end."

"Marvellous," Katrina smiled, but somehow her face remained cold. "Come—let me introduce you to Dante…"

Matilda was about to say that she'd already met him, but decided against it, as clearly both Hugh and Dante had omitted to mention the dinner to Katrina. She wasn't sure what to make of Katrina. She was stunning-looking, her posture was straight, her long hair, though dashed with grey, was still an amazing shade of strawberry blonde, and though she had to be around fifty, there was barely a line on her smooth face. But there was a frostiness about her that unsettled Matilda.

The interior of the house was just as impressive as the exterior. Hugh held open the front door then headed off to Matilda's car to retrieve her bags and the two women stepped inside and walked along the jarrah-floored hallways, Matilda's sandals echoing on the solid wood as she took in the soft white sofas and dark wooden furnishings, huge mirrors opening up the already vast space, reflecting the ocean at every turn so that wherever you looked the waves seemed to beckon. Or Jasmine smiled down at you! An inordinate number of photos of Dante's late wife adorned the walls, her gorgeous face captured from every angle, and Matilda felt a quiet discomfort as she gazed around, her cheeks flaming as she recalled the stinging kiss of Dante.

"My daughter." Katrina's eyes followed Matilda's and they paused for a moment as they admired her tragic beauty. "I had this photo blown up and framed just last week—it's good for Alex to be able to see her and I know it gives Dante a lot of comfort."

"It must…" Matilda stumbled. "She really was very beautiful."

"And clever," Katrina added. "She had it all, brains and beauty. She was amazing, a wonderful mother and wife. None of us will ever get over her loss."

"I can't even begin to imagine…" Despite the cool breeze from the air-conditioner, despite the high ceilings and vastness of the place, Matilda felt incredibly hot and uncomfortable. Despite her earlier misgivings, she was very keen to meet Dante now—even his savage personality was preferable to the discomfort she felt with Katrina.

"Dante especially," Katrina continued, and Matilda was positive, despite her soft words and pensive smile, that there was a warning note to her voice, an icy message emanating from her cool blue eyes. "I've never seen a man so broken with grief. He just adored her, *adored* her," Katrina reiterated. "Do you know, the day she died he sent flowers to her office. It was a Saturday but she had to pop into work and get some files. She took Alex with her—that was the sort of woman she was. Anyway, Dante must have rung every florist in Melbourne. He wanted to send her some jasmine, her namesake, but it was winter, of course, so it was impossible to find, but Dante being Dante he managed to organise it—he'd have moved heaven and earth for her."

It was actually a relief to get into the kitchen. After Katrina's onslaught it was actually a relief to confront the man she'd been so nervous of meeting again. But as she stepped inside it was as if she was seeing him for the very first time. The man she remembered bore little witness to the one she saw now. Everything about him seemed less formal. Of course, she hadn't expected him to greet her in a suit—it was Sunday after all—but somehow she'd never envisaged him in jeans and a T-shirt, or, if she had, it would have been in dark, starched denim and a crisp white designer label T-shirt, not the faded, scruffy jeans that encased him, not the untucked, unironed white T-shirt that he was wearing. And she certainly hadn't pictured him at a massive wooden table, kneading bread, with his daughter, Alex's eyes staring ahead as she rhythmically worked the dough.

"Dante, Alexandra," Katrina called. "Matilda has arrived."

Only one pair of eyes looked up. Alexandra carried on kneading the dough and any thought of witnessing Dante's softer side was instantly quashed as his black eyes briefly met hers.

"Good afternoon."

His greeting was also his dismissal.

His attention turning immediately back to his daughter, picking up a large shaker and sprinkling the dough with more flour as the little girl worked on.

"Good afternoon." Matilda forced a smile to no one in particular. "You're making bread…"

"No." Dante stood up, dusted his floured hands on his jeans "We are kneading dough and playing with flour."

"Oh!"

"We've been kneading dough and playing with flour since lunchtime, actually!"

Another "oh' was on the tip of her tongue, but Matilda held it back, grateful when Katrina took over this most awkward of conversations.

"It's one of Alex's pastimes," Katrina explained as Hugh came back in. "She was upset after lunch—you know what children can be like." Dante gave a tight smile as Katrina dismissed the slightly weary note to his voice. Something told Matilda that whatever had eventuated had been rather more than the usual childhood tantrum. "Hugh, why don't you go and take Matilda around the garden?" Katrina said. "It seems a shame to break things up when Dante and Alex are having such fun."

"Hugh's supposed to be resting," Dante pointed out. "*I'll* take Matilda around."

"Fine," Katrina said, though clearly it was anything but! "Then I'll go and check that everything's in order in the summerhouse for Matilda."

"The summerhouse?" Dante frowned. "I had the guest room made up for her. Janet prepared it this morning."

"Well, it won't kill Janet to prepare the summerhouse! She's the housekeeper," Katrina explained to a completely bemused Matilda. "I can help her set it up. It will be far nicer for Matilda. She can have some privacy and it might unsettle Alex, having a stranger in the house—no offence meant, Matilda."

"None taken." Matilda thought her face might crack with the effort of smiling. "It really doesn't matter a scrap where I stay. I'm going to be working long hours, I just need somewhere to sleep and eat…"

"There's a lovely little kitchenette in the summerhouse. I'll have some bacon and eggs and bread put in, that type of thing—you'll be very comfortable."

"It's your fault." Dante broke the appalling silence as they stepped outside.

"What is?" Matilda blinked.

"That you've been banished." He gave her a glimmer of a dry smile. "You're too good-looking for Katrina."

"Oh!" A tiny nervous giggle escaped her lips, embarrassed by what he had said but relieved all the same that he had acknowledged the problem. "I don't think she likes me very much."

"She'd have been hoping for a ruddy-faced, gum-chewing, crop-haired gardener. I have the ugliest staff in the world—all hand-picked by Katrina." Startled by his coarseness, Matilda actually laughed as they walked, amazed to find herself relaxing a touch in his presence.

"Yesterday's newspapers can't have helped matters much," she ventured, referring to the string of women he'd dated since his wife's death, but Dante just shrugged.

"Ships that pass in the night even Katrina can live with."

The callousness of his words had Matilda literally stopping in her tracks for a moment, waiting for him to soften it with a smile, to tell her he was joking, but Dante strode on, forcing Matilda to catch him up, and try to continue the conversation. "Do your in-laws live here with you?"

"God, no." Dante shuddered. "They live a few kilometres away. But we're interviewing for a new nanny at the moment—preferably one over sixty with a wooden leg if Katrina has her way. That's why she's around so much. Like it or not at the moment I do need her help with Alex, but if I decide to stay here in Australia…" He stopped talking then, just simply stopped in mid-sentence with no apology or explanation, clearly deciding he had said enough. Silence descended again as they walked on the manicured lawn past a massive pool, surrounded by a clear Perspex wall. Matilda gazed at the pool longingly.

"Use it any time," Dante offered.

"Thanks," Matilda replied, knowing full well she wouldn't. The thought of undressing, of wearing nothing more than a bikini around Dante not exactly soothing.

"This is the garden," Dante said as they came to a gate. "It's in a real mess, very neglected, overgrown with blackberries and bracken, I've been meaning to get it cleared, but my gardener is getting old. It takes all his time just to keep up with the regular work, let alone this. Oh, and one other thing…" His hand paused on the gate. "The bill is to come to me."

"Hugh employed me," Matilda pointed out.

"Hugh does not need to pay for my renovations—you will send the bill to me, Matilda."

But she didn't want to send the bill to him—and it had nothing to do with money. Financially it made not a scrap of difference to Matilda who picked up the bill. Instead, it was the disturbing thought of being answerable somehow to Dante, of him employing her, that made Matilda strangely nervous.

"Do you need an advance?"

"An advance?" Instantly, she regretted her words. Her mind had been utterly elsewhere and now she sounded stupid.

"An advance of money," Dante not too patiently explained. "To pay the subcontractors. I don't know what arrangement you had with Hugh—"

"*Have* with Hugh," Matilda corrected, watching as Dante's face darkened. Clearly he was not used to being defied, but even though an advance would be wonderful now, even though she had a hundred and one people hat would need to be paid, and very soon, she damn well wasn't going to give in to him, absolutely refused to let him dictate his terms to her. "My business is with Hugh. If you want to settle up with him, that's your choice."

Surprisingly he didn't argue, but as he pushed open the gate she could tell he was far from pleased, but, refusing to back down, refusing to even look at him, she stepped into the garden and as she did all thoughts of money and who was the boss faded in an instant. Despite Dante's gloomy predictions, all she could see was beauty—the sleeping princess that lay beneath the overgrown bracken and thorns.

Dante's manicured gardens were wonderful, but, for Matilda, nothing could beat the raw natural beauty of a neglected garden, a blank canvas for her to work on. It was about the size of a suburban block of land, the centrepiece a massive willow, more than a hundred years in the making, one lifetime simply not enough to produce its full majesty. But that was part of the beauty of her work. A new garden was a mere a sketch on the canvas—the colour, the depth was added over the years, seeds sown that would flourish later, shrubs, trees that would develop, blossom and grow long, long after the cheque had been paid and her tools cleared away.

"Vistas." It was the first thing that came to mind and she said it out loud, registering his frown. "Lots of walkways all coming from the willow, lined with hedges and each one leading to a different view, a special area for Alex…"

"You can do something with it?"

She didn't answer, just gave a distracted nod as she pictured the bosky paths, a water feature at the end of one, a sand pit at the end of the other, and…

"A castle," Matilda breathed. "An enchanted castle, like a fairy-tale. I know someone who makes the most beau-

tiful cubby houses…" Her voice trailed off as she stared
down at the ground, her sandals scuffing the earth. "We'll
use turf for now, but I'll plant lots of different things so
that each path will be different—clover for one, daisies
for another, buttercups…"

"Will you be able to do it in the time-frame?"

Matilda nodded. "Less perhaps. I'll know more tomorrow once it's cleared. I've got some people coming at six.
There'll be a lot of noise, but only tomorrow…"

"That's fine. Katrina has already said she will take Alex
out or to her place during the day. You'll have the place to
yourself…" He paused and Matilda wondered if he was
going to raise the money issue again, but instead it was a
rather more difficult subject he brought up. "I'm sorry she
made you feel uncomfortable."

"She didn't," Matilda attempted, then gave in as he
raised a questioning eyebrow. "OK, she did make me feel
a bit uncomfortable, but it's fine."

"I'll take you and show you the summerhouse. But you
don't have to cook for yourself, you're very welcome to
come over for—"

"I'll be fine," Matilda interrupted. "In fact, it's probably better that I stay there…" Blowing her fringe sky-
ward, Matilda attempted the impossible but, ever direct,
Dante beat her to it.

"After what happened on Friday?" He checked and despite a deep blush Matilda gave a wry smile.

"I don't think Katrina would approve somehow if she
knew. She doesn't even know that we had dinner, let
alone…"

"It's none of Katrina's business," Dante pointed out, but
Matilda shook her head.

"Oh, but she thinks it is."

"Matilda." His black eyes were boring into her, and she

could only admire his boldness that he could actually look at her, unlike she, herself, who gave in after once glance, choosing instead to stare at her toes as he spoke. "I will tell you what I told Katrina. I have no interest in a relationship—any relationship. For now I grieve for what I have lost: a wife and the happiness of my daughter." Still she looked down, swallowing down the questions that were on the tip of her tongue. But either he could read her mind or he had used this speech many times before, because he answered each and every one of them with painful, brutal honesty, his silken, thick accent doing nothing to sweeten the bitterness of the message.

"I like women—I like beautiful women," he drawled, wrapping the knife that stabbed her in velvet as he plunged it in. "And as you would have seen in the paper yesterday, sometimes I keep their company, but there is always concurrence, always there is an understanding that it can go nowhere. If I misled you on Friday, I apologise."

"You didn't mislead me." Matilda croaked the words out then instantly regretted them. In that split second she understood what Dante was offering her, what this emotionally abstinent man was telling her—that she could have him for a short while, could share his bed, but not his heart. And all Matilda knew was that she couldn't do it, couldn't share his bed knowing she must walk away, that deadening his pain would only exacerbate hers. His hand reached out towards her, his fingers cupping her chin, lifting her face to his. Yet she still refused to look at him, knew that if her eyes met his then she'd be lost.

"You didn't mislead me, Dante, because it was just a kiss." Somehow she kept her voice even; somehow she managed to keep her cheeks from flaming as she lied through her teeth. "A kiss to end the evening. I certainly had no intention of taking things further, either then or now." She knew she hadn't convinced him and from the slight narrowing of his eyes knew that he didn't believe her. Taking a breath, she elaborated, determined to set the tone, and the boundaries in order to survive the next couple of weeks. She didn't want to be one of Dante's ships that passed in the night. "Since Edward and I broke up I've been on a few dates, had a few kisses, but…" Matilda gave a nervous shrug. "You know the saying: you have to kiss a lot of frogs…" From his slightly startled look clearly he didn't know it. "One kiss was enough for me, Dante."

"I see." He gave a tight smile. "I think."

"It won't be happening again," Matilda affirmed, hoping that if she said it enough she might even believe it herself.

"I just wanted to clear things up."

"Good." Matilda forced a bright smile, relieved this torture was almost over. "I'm glad that you did."

"And I'm sorry that you did not enjoy the kiss." His words wiped the smile from her face, his eyes boring into her. She couldn't be sure, but Matilda was positive he was teasing her, that he knew she was lying and, of course, she was. It had been the most breathtaking kiss of her life, her whole body was burning now just at the mere memory, but it was imperative Dante didn't know. He'd made it clear he wasn't interested in anything more than the most casual of casual flings, and that was the last thing she needed now—especially with a man like Dante. There was nothing casual about him, nothing casual about the feelings he evoked and if she played with this particular fire, Matilda knew she'd end up seriously burnt. "Because I thought that—"

"Could you show me where I'm staying, please?" Matilda snapped, following Dante's lead and refusing to be drawn somewhere she didn't want to go. She turned abruptly to go, but in her haste to escape she forgot about the blackberries. Her leg caught on a branch, the thorn ripping into her bare calf, a yelp of pain escaping her lips.

"Careful." Dante's reflexes were like lightning. He pulled back the branch and held her elbow as Matilda stepped back and instinctively inspected the damage, tears of pain and embarrassment filling her eyes at the vivid red gash.

"I'm fine," she breathed.

"You're bleeding."

"It's just a scratch. If you can just show me where I'm staying…" she said. She almost shouted it this time she so badly wanted out of there, wanted some privacy from his knowing eyes, but Dante was pulling out a neatly folded hanky and running it under the garden tap, before returning and dropping to his knees.

"Please." Matilda was practically begging now, near to tears, not with pain but with embarrassment and want, the thought of him touching her exquisitely unbearable. But Dante wasn't listening. One hand cupped her calf, the other pressed the cool silk into her stinging cut, and it was as soothing as it was disturbing—the ultimate pleasure-pain principle as his hands tended her, calming and arousing. Matilda bit so hard on her lip she thought she might draw blood there, too, her whole body tense, standing rigid as he pressed the handkerchief harder, her stomach a knot of nervous anticipation as she felt his breath against her thigh.

"I'll just press for a minute and stop the bleeding, then I'll take you over to the summerhouse…" Strange that his voice was completely normal, that his body was completely relaxed, while hers was spinning in wild orbit, stirred with naked lust, shameful, inappropriate thoughts filling her mind as he tended her. She couldn't believe her own thought process as she stood there, gazing down. His fingers were pushed into her calf as the cool silk pressed on her warm skin, his breath on her leg as he spoke. And how she wanted to feel that delicious mouth again, but on her thigh this time, almost willing with her eyes for his fingers to creep higher, to quell the pulse that was leaping between her legs, to calm the heat with his cool, cool hand. "I think there's a first-aid box…"

"I'll be OK." She shivered the words out.

"Of course you will, it's just a cut, but…" His voice faded as he looked up at her, his eyes fixing on hers. And she stared back, trapped like a deer in the headlights, knowing he could feel it now, could see her treacherous arousal, could smell her excitement, *knew* that she had lied when she had said she didn't want him.

The silence fizzed between them as he continued to stare, and for that moment the choice was entirely his—reason, logic, had gone the second he'd touched her. If Dante pulled her down now, they both knew that she wouldn't even attempt to resist…

"Matilda…" His voice was thick with lust, his eyes blatantly desiring her. Thank God he spoke, thank God he broke the spell, gave her that tiny moment to stab at self preservation and pull back her leg. Her face flaming she turned around, denied absolutely what was taking place, turning and heading for the gate, practically wrenching it open, just desperate for some space, some distance, a chance to think before her body betrayed her again.

There for the taking.

Those were the words he'd taunted her with on Friday night and those were the words that taunted her now as he led her over to the summerhouse and briefly showed her around.

As the door closed on Dante, not even looking at her surroundings, Matilda sank onto the bed and buried her face in her hands, cringing with shame, as sure as she could be that Dante had witnessed her arousal, had sensed her desire.

What was wrong with her? She wasn't even, according to Edward, supposed to like sex, yet here she was acting like some hormone-laden teenage girl with a king-sized crush, contemplating an affair with a man who wanted nothing more than her body.

And *how* she was contemplating! Despite her attempts at indifference, despite her brave words before, she wanted him. But unlike Dante, it wasn't just bed she wanted but the prelude to it and the postscript afterwards, the parts of him he wasn't prepared to give.

For the first time she took in her surroundings. The summerhouse was certainly comfortable—in fact, it was gorgeous. A cedar attic-shaped building, tucked away at the rear of the property, no doubt it had once been a rather impressive shed, but it had been lovingly refurbished, the attention to detail quite amazing. A small kitchenette as you entered, and to the left a small *en suite* with a shower, the rest of the floor space taken up by a large bed and a television and CDs. Janet, the rather prim housekeeper, came over with her bags and filled up the fridge with produce, explaining that the previous owners had used it as a bed and breakfast, but since the Costellos had owned it, for the most part it had remained empty.

"Mr Costello wanted to know if you'll be joining him for dinner," Janet said, once she had stocked up the fridge with enough food to feed a small army. "It's served at seven-thirty once young Alex is in bed, except for Tuesdays and Thursdays. I have my bible class on those nights…"

"No," Matilda quickly answered, then softened her rather snappy response with a smile. "I mean, tell him, no, thank you," she added.

"I'll bring your dinner over to you," Janet offered, but Matilda stood firm.

"There's really no need. I'll just have a sandwich or something, or go out to one of the cafés."

"As you wish." Janet shrugged as she headed out the door. "But if you need anything, just ring through."

Alone, Matilda changed into her working clothes—a pair of faded denim shorts that had seen better days and a flimsy T-shirt, topping the rather unflattering ensemble off with a pair of socks and her workboots. She poked her tongue out at her reflection in the mirror—at least Katrina would be pleased! Grateful for the diversion of the garden to take her mind off Dante, she turned on her mobile, winced at the rather full message bank, then promptly chose to ignore it, instead ringing the various people she would be needing, firming up a time with Declan to bring his bob-cat and confirming the large number of skips she had ordered to be delivered at Dante's in the morning. Then she headed off to the garden armed with a notebook and tape measure, ready to turn her vision into the plans that would become a reality. She lost herself for hours, as she always did when a project engrossed her, only downing tools and heading for the summerhouse when the last fingers of light had faded, hot, thirsty and exhausted, ready for a long, cool drink, followed by a long cool shower…

But not a cold one!

Yelping in alarm, Matilda fiddled with the taps, but to no avail, realising with a sinking heart that no amount of wishful thinking was going to change things: the hot-water system really wasn't working. Grabbing a towel, Matilda wrapped it around her and sat shivering on the bed, trying and failing to decide what on earth to do. If she had been here for a couple of weeks to type up notes or fix some accounts then somehow she'd have struggled through, but even if her business cards screamed the words "landscape designer," at the end of the day gardening was a dirty job—filthy at times. And a fortnight of black nails and grit in her hair wasn't a prospect Matilda relished. Of course, the obvious thing to do would be to ring Janet and explain the situation but, then, there was nothing *obvious* about this situation—the absolute last place she wanted to be was crossing Dante's manicured lawn clutching her toiletry bag! Eyeing the kettle, Matilda rolled her eyes, the irony of her situation hitting home as she filled the tiny sink and swished a bar of soap around to make bubbles—here she was in a multi-million dollar home, and washing like a pauper!

Chapter 5

God, it was hot.

Matilda filled up her water bottle from the tap and surveyed the barren scene.

The morning had been crisp—par for the course in Melbourne. Used to the elements, she'd layered her clothing—gallons of sunscreen, followed by boots and shorts, a crop top, a T-shirt, a long-sleeved top, a jumper and a hat. Up at the crack of dawn, she'd greeted the workers and given her directions. Money wasn't the problem, time was, so a small army had been hired for the messy job of clearing the site. They all worked well, the skips filling quickly. As the day warmed up the jumper was the first to go, followed an hour or so later by her cotton top, and as each layer of clothing came off Matilda, so too did the garden start to emerge—until finally, long since down to her crop top, the late afternoon sun burning into her shoulders, Matilda surveyed her exhausting day's work. The subcontractors had finally gone, the skips noisily driven away, leaving the site bare and muddy apart from the gorgeous willow. At last she had her blank canvas!

Gulping on her water bottle, Matilda walked around the site, checking the fence, pleased to see that it was in good order. All it needed was a few minor repairs and a spraypaint but there was nothing that could be done this evening—she was too tired anyway. All Matilda wanted to do now was pack up her things and head for her temporary home. Actually, all Matilda wanted to do was *leave* her things and head for home, but mindful of safety she reluctantly headed over to the pile of equipment. She splashed some water from her bottle onto her face and decided more desperate measures were needed. Taking off her hat, she filled it and sloshed it onto her head, closing her eyes in blessed relief as the water ran down her face and onto her shoulders. Feeling the sting of cold on her reddened face and catching her breath, Matilda delighted in a shiver for a moment, before the sun caught up.

"Matilda." The familiar voice made her jump. She'd been so sure she was alone, but here she was, soaked to the skin at her own doing, face smeared with mud, squinting into the low sunlight at the forebidding outline of Dante. "I startled you. I'm sorry to barge in."

"Not at all!" She shook her head and tried to look not remotely startled. "It's your garden after all—I was just packing up." Brutally aware of the mess she looked and with two nipples sticking out of her soaking top, thanks to the halflitre of water she'd just poured over herself, Matilda busied herself clearing up her tools as Dante came over.

"I thought I'd bring Alex to see the garden before she went to bed." He was carrying her, which was just as well. It was rather more a demolition site than a garden at the moment. Dante picked his way around the edge and let

Alex down on the one grassed area left—under the willow tree. It was only patchily grassed, but at least it was clean and dry—and given that the little girl was dressed in her nighty and had clearly had her bedtime bath, it was just as well. Matilda gave up in pretending to look at her tools and watched him as he came over. He was wearing shorts and runners—and no socks, which just accentuated the lean, muscular length of his brown calves. His whole body seemed incredibly toned, actually—and Matilda momentary wondered how. He didn't seem the type for a gym and he spent an immoderate time at the office.

"Hi, Alex." Matilda smiled at the little girl, not remotely fazed by the lack of her response, just enchanted by her beauty. "I know it looks a terrible mess now, but in a few days it will look wonderful."

Alex didn't even appear to be looking—her eyes stared fixedly ahead. A little rigid figure, she stood quite still as Matilda chatted happily to her, explaining what was going to happen over the next few days, pointing out where the water features would be, the sand pit and the enchanted castle.

"You've got a lot done today," Dante observed. "What happens now?"

"The boring stuff," Matilda answered. "I've got the plumber and electrician coming tomorrow and then the concreters, but once all that's out the way, hopefully it will start to take shape a bit." And though she longed to ask about his day, longed to extend the conversation just a touch longer, deliberately she held back, determined that it must be Dante who came to her now—she'd already been embarrassed enough. But the silence was excruciating as they stood there, and it was actually a relief when Dante headed over to his daughter and went to pick her up.

"Time for bed, little lady." Something twisted inside

Matilda at the tenderness in his voice, the strong gentle arms that lowered to lift his daughter. But Alex resisted, letting out a furious squeal that pierced the quiet early evening air, arching her back, her little hands curling into fists. Matilda's eyes widened at the fury that erupted in the little girl, stunned to witness the change in this silent, still, child. But clearly used to this kind of response, Dante was way too quick for Alex, gently but firmly taking her wrists and guiding her hands to her sides.

"No!" he said firmly. "No hitting."

With a mixture of tenderness and strength he picked Alex up, clasping her furious, resisting body to his chest, utterly ignoring the shrill screams, just holding her ever tighter. Finally she seemed to calm, the screams, the fury abating until finally Dante smiled wryly as he caught Matilda's shocked eyes. "Believe it or not, I think you just received a compliment. Normally I don't have to even ask to bring her in from the garden. Perhaps she is going to like it after all."

Two compliments even! Matilda thought to herself. Was Dante actually saying he liked her plans as well?

"I'll take her inside and get her to bed." Matilda gazed at the little girl, now resting in her father's arms. Not a trace of the angry outburst of only moments before remained, her dark eyes staring blankly across the wilderness of the garden. "Are you finishing up?"

"Soon." Matilda nodded. "I'm just going to pack my things."

"You're welcome to come over for dinner..."

"No, thanks!" Matilda said, and she didn't offer an explanation, didn't elaborate at all, just turned her back and started to pack up her things.

"It's no trouble," Dante pushed, but still she didn't turn around, determined not to give him the satisfaction of drawing her in just to reject her again, just to change his mind or hurt her with cruel words. "I just warm the meal up tonight. Janet has her Alcoholics Anonymous meetings on Mondays and Thursdays."

"But she said she had..." Matilda swung around then snapped her mouth closed, furious with herself for responding.

"Everyone has their secrets, remember." Dante shrugged then gave her the benefit of a very wicked smile. "Come," he offered again.

"No," Matilda countered. This time she didn't even bother to be polite, just turned her back on him and started to sort out her things, only letting out the breath she had been holding when, after the longest time, she heard the click of the gate closing. Alex didn't just have her father's eyes, Matilda realised, she had his personality, too. They shared the same dark, lonely existence, cruelly, capriciously striking out at anyone they assumed was getting too close, yet somehow drawing them in all the same, somehow managing to be forgiven.

A cold shower mightn't be so bad, Matilda attempted to convince herself as she gingerly held her fingers under the jets. All day she'd been boiling, all day she'd longed to cool down—but the trouble with her line of work was that there was absolutely no chance of a quick dart in the shower. Her hair was stiff with dust, her fingers black from the soil, her skin almost as dark as Dante's.

Biting down on her lip, Matilda dived into the shower, yelping as the icy water hit her. Forcing herself to put her head under, she frantically rubbed in shampoo, praying that in a moment she'd acclimatise, that the freezing water might actually merely be cool after a couple of minutes' more torture. Only it wasn't. Her misery lasted long after she'd turned the beastly taps off and wrapped a towel around her, her poorly rinsed hair causing a river of stinging of water to hit her eyes. Shivering and cursing like the navvy Katrina had hoped for, Matilda groped for the door handle, wrenching it open and storming head first into a wall of flesh.

"When were you going to tell me?" Dante demanded. "I could hear you screaming…"

Matilda stood in shook. "Are you spying on me?" She felt embarrassed and enraged. Her bloodshot, stinging eyes focused on the walkie-talkie he was holding in his hand.

"It's a child monitor," he explained with infinite patience, as if she were some sort of mentally unhinged person he was talking down from the roof. But she could see the tiny twitch on his lips, knew that inside he was laughing at her, her misery, her embarrassment increasing as he carried on talking. "Janet left a note, telling me about the water. I just read it, so will you, please, collect your belongings so that I can help you bring your things over."

"There's really no need for that," Matilda insisted, feeling horribly exposed and vulnerable and also somewhat deflated that even standing before him, her body drenched, clearly naked under a towel, she didn't move him at all. "I've got a plumber coming tomorrow…"

"Matilda." He gave a weary sigh. "My daughter is asleep in the house alone so could you, please, just…?" He faltered for just a fraction of a second, telling her in that fraction of time that she had been wrong—that Dante was very aware of her near-nakedness. She clutched the towel tighter around her, scuffed the floor with her dripping foot as immediately he continued. "Get dressed, Matilda," he said gruffly. "I'll come back for your things later."

Which really didn't leave her much choice.

Chapter 6

It was a very shy, rather humble Matilda that joined Dante at the heavy wooden table that was the centrepiece of his impressive al fresco area, the beastly child monitor blinking at her on the table as she approached, her face darkening to purple as she realised she'd practically accused the man of stalking her. She braced herself for a few harsh words Dante-style but instead he poured an indecent amount of wine into her glass then pushed it across the table to her.

"Is red OK?"

"Marvellous," Matilda lied, taking a tentative sip, surprised to find that this particular red actually was OK, warming her from the inside out. Holding the massive glass in her pale hand, she stared at the dark liquid, anything rather than look at him, and started a touch when the intercom crackled loudly.

"Static," Dante explained, pressing a button. "Someone

down the road mowing their lawn or drying their hair. I just change the channel, see."

"Oh."

"You don't have any experience with children, do you?"

"None," Matilda answered. "I mean, none at all. Well apart from my friend, Sally…"

"She has a baby?"

"No." Matilda gave a pale smile. "But she's thought that she might be pregnant a couple of times."

He actually laughed, and it sounded glorious, a deep rich sound, his white teeth flashing. Matilda was amazed after her exquisite discomfort of only a moment ago to find herself actually laughing, too, her pleasure increasing as Dante gave a little bit more, actually revealed a piece of himself, only not with the impassive voice he had used before but with genuine warmth and emotion, his face softer somehow, his voice warmer as this inaccessible man let her in a touch, allowed her to glimpse another dimension to his complex nature.

"Until Alex was born, apart from on television, I don't think I'd ever seen a newborn." He frowned, as if examining that thought for the first time. "No, I'm sure I hadn't. My mother was the youngest of seven children. All my cousins were older and I, too, was the youngest—very spoiled!"

"I can imagine." Matilda rolled her eyes, but her smile remained as Dante continued.

"Then this tiny person appeared and suddenly I am supposed to know." He spread his hands expressively, but words clearly failed him.

"I'd be terrified," Matilda admitted.

"I was," Dante stated. "Still am, most of the time."

Her smile faded, seeing him now not as the man that moved her but as the single father he was, trying yet know-

ing she was failing to fathom the enormity of the task that
had been so squarely placed on his shoulders.

"It must be hard."

"It is." Dante nodded and didn't sweeten it with the
usual superlatives that generally followed such a statement, didn't smile and eagerly nod that it was more than
worth it, or the best thing he'd ever done in his life. He just
stared back at her for the longest time, before continuing,
"I have a big trial starting next week, but once that it is
out of the way, I need to make a decision."

"Whether to move back to Italy?"

Dante nodded. "Every doctor I have consulted tells me
that Alex needs a routine, that she needs a solid home
base—at the moment I am having trouble providing that.
Katrina is only too willing to help, but…" He hesitated
and took a long sip of his drink. Matilda held her breath,
willing him to continue, to glean a little more insight into
the problems he faced. "She wants to keep Jasmine alive,
doesn't want anything that might detract from her daughter's memory, which is understandable, of course, only
sometimes…"

"It's a bit much?" Matilda tentatively offered, relieved
when he didn't frown back at her, relieved that maybe she
understood just a little of what he was feeling.

"Much too much," Dante agreed, then terminated the
conversation, standing up and gesturing. "I will show you
the guest room, it's already made up—then we can eat."

"I might just grab a sandwich or something when I get
my things," Matilda started, but Dante just ignored her,
leading her through the house and upstairs, gesturing for
her to be quiet as they tiptoed past Alex's room, before
coming to a large door at the end of the hallway.

Clearly Dante's idea of a guest room differed from
Matilda's somewhat—her version was a spare room with

a bed and possibly an ironing board for good measure. But Dante's guests were clearly used to better. As he pushed open the door and she stepped inside, Matilda realised just how far she'd been relegated by Katrina. Till then the summerhouse had been more than OK, but it wasn't a patch on this! A massive king-sized bed made up with crisp white linen was the focus point of the fabulously spacious room, but rather than being pushed against the wall and sensibly facing a door, as most of the population would have done, instead it stood proudly in the middle, staring directly out of one of the massive windows Matilda had till now only glimpsed from the outside, offering a panoramic view of the bay. Matilda thought she must have died and gone to heaven—ruing every last minute she'd spent struggling on in the summerhouse when she could have been here!

"I won't sleep," Matilda sighed dreamily, wandering over to the window and pressing her face against the glass, like a child staring into a toy-shop Christmas display. "I'll spend the whole night watching the water and then I'll be too exhausted to do your garden. It's just divine…"

"And," Dante said with a teasing dramatic note to his voice that Matilda had never heard before, "it has running water."

"You're kidding." Matilda played along, liking the change in him, the funnier, more relaxed side of him she was slowly starting to witness.

"Not just that, but *hot* running water." Dante smiled, sliding open the *en suite* door as Matilda reluctantly peeled herself away from the view and padded over. "See for yourself."

The smile was wiped off her face as she stepped inside. Fabulous it might be but she couldn't possibly use it, her frantic eyes scanning the equally massive window for even a chink of a blind or curtain.

"No one can see." Dante rolled his eyes at her expression.

"Apart from every passing sailor and the nightly ferry load on its way to Tasmania!" Matilda gulped.

"The windows are treated, I mean tinted," Dante simultaneously explained and corrected himself. Even a couple of hours ago she'd have felt stupid or gauche, but his smile seemed genuine enough at least that Matilda was able to smile back. "I promise that no one will see you."

"Good."

"Now that we've taken care of that, can we eat?"

This time she didn't even bother to argue.

Wandering back along the hallway, Dante put his fingers to his lips and pushed open Alex's door to check on his daughter. Matilda stood there as he crept inside. The little girl was lying with one skinny leg sticking out of between the bars of her cot, her tiny, angelic face relaxed in sleep. Matilda felt her heart go out to this beautiful child who had been through so, so much, a lump building in her throat as Dante slowly moved her leg back in then retrieved a sheet that had fallen from the cot and with supreme tenderness tucked it around Alex, gently stroking her shoulder as she stirred slightly. But Matilda wasn't watching Alex any more. Instead, she was watching Dante, a sting of tears in her eyes as she glimpsed again his tenderness, slotted in another piece of the puzzle that enthralled her.

When he wasn't being superior or scathing he was actually incredibly nice.

Incredibly nice, Matilda thought a little later as Dante carried two steaming plates into the lounge room and they shared a casual dinner. And whether it was the wine or the mood, conversation came incredibly easily, so much so that when Matilda made a brief reference to her recent breakup, she didn't jump as if she'd been burnt when Dante asked what had gone wrong. She just gave a thoughtful shrug and pondered a moment before answering.

"I honestly don't know," Matilda finally admitted. "I don't really know when the problems started. For ages we were really happy. Edward's career was taking off, we were looking at houses and then all of a sudden we seemed to be arguing over everything. Nothing I did was ever right, from the way I dressed to the friends I had. It was as if nothing I did could make him happy."

"So everything was perfect and then out of the blue arguments started?" Dante gave her a rather disbelieving frown as she nodded. "It doesn't happen like that, Matilda," Dante said. "There is no such thing as perfect. There must have been something that irked, a warning that all was not OK—there always is."

"How do you know?" Matilda asked, "I mean how do you know all these things?"

"It's my job to know how people's minds work," Dante responded, but then softened it with a hint of personal insight. "I was in a relationship too, Matilda. I do know that they are not all perfect!"

According to everyone, *his* had been, but Matilda didn't say it, not wanting to break the moment, liking this less reticent Dante she was seeing, actually enjoying talking to him. "I supposed he always flirted when we were out and it annoyed me," Matilda admitted. "We'd go to business dinners and I didn't like the way he was with some of the women. I don't think I'm a jealous person, but if he was like that when I was there…" Her voice trailed off, embarrassed now at having said so much, but Dante just nodded, leaning back on the sofa. His stance was so incredibly nonjudgmental, inexplicably she wanted to continue, actually wanted to tell him how Edward had made her feel, wanted Dante to hear this and hoping maybe in return she'd hear about him, too. "He wasn't cheating. But I wondered in years to come…"

"Probably." Dante shrugged. "No doubt when you'd just had a baby, or your work was busy and you were too tired to focus enough on him, not quite at your goal weight." He must have registered her frown, her mouth opening then holding back a question that, despite the nature of this personal conversation, wasn't one she had any right to ask, but Dante answered it anyway. "No, Matilda, I didn't have an affair, if that's what you are thinking. I like beautiful women as much as any man and, yes, at various times in our relationship Jasmine and I faced all of the things I've outlined, but I can truthfully say it would never have entered my head to look at another woman in that way. I wanted to fix our problems, Matilda, not add to them."

And it was so refreshing to hear it, a completely different perspective, her doubts about opening up to him quashed now as she saw the last painful months through different eyes.

"In the end he spent so much time at work there really wasn't much room for anything else…"

"*Anything* else?" Dante asked, painfully direct, and Matilda took a gulp of her drink then nodded.

"You know, for months I've been going over and over it, wondering if I was just imagining things, if Edward was right, that it was my fault he couldn't…" She snapped her mouth closed. In an unguarded moment she'd revealed way, way more than she'd intended and she halted the conversation there, hoping that Dante would take the cue and do the same, but he was way too sharp.

"What was your fault?"

"Nothing." Matilda's voice was high. "Wasn't what I told you reason enough to end things?"

"Of course."

Silence hung in the air. As understanding as Dante might have been, he certainly couldn't help her with the rest. There was no way she could go there, the words that had been said agony to repeat even to herself. It was none of his damn business anyway.

"You know, people like Edward normally don't respond too well to their own failings—they'd rather make you feel like shit than even consider that they had a problem." His voice was deep and unusually gentle, and though she couldn't bring herself to look at him she could feel his eyes on her. His insight floored her. She felt transparent, as if somehow he had seen into the deepest, darkest part of her and somehow shed light on it, somehow pried open the lid on her shame. And it was madness, sheer madness that she wanted to open it up more, to let out the pain that was curled up inside there…to share it with Dante.

"He said that it was my fault…" Matilda gagged on the words, screwed her eyes closed, as somehow she told him, told him what she hadn't been able to tell even some of her closest friends. "That maybe if I was more interesting, made a bit more effort, that he wouldn't look at other women, that he wouldn't have…" She couldn't go there, couldn't tell him everything, she could feel the icy chill of perspiration between her breasts, could feel her neck and her face darkening in the shame of the harsh, cruel words that had been uttered.

"I would imagine that it's incredibly difficult to be amazing in bed when you've been ignored all evening!" Her closed eyes snapped open, her mouth gaping as Dante, as direct as ever, got straight to the point. "I would think it would be impossible, in fact, to give completely of yourself when you're wondering who he's really holding—whether it's the woman in his arms or the one you caught him chatting to at the bar earlier."

And she hadn't anticipated crying, but as his words tore through her only then did she truly acknowledge the pain, the pain that had been there for so long now, the bitter aftermath that had lingered long after she'd moved out and moved on with her life. But they were quiet tears, no sobs, no real outward display of emotion other than the salty rivers that ran down her smeared cheeks, stinging her reddened face as Dante gently spoke on, almost hitting the mark but not quite. She'd revealed so much to him, but her ultimate shame was still locked inside.

"It was him with the problem, not you." His accent was thick.

"He said the same thing—the other way around, of course." Matilda sniffed. "I guess it's a matter of opinion who's right! I spent the last few months trying to get back what we'd once had, trying to make it work, but in the end…" She shook her head, unwilling now to go on, the last painful rows still too raw for shared introspection. Thankfully Dante sensed it, offering her another drink from the bottle they'd practically finished, but Matilda declined. "What about you?"

"Me?" Dante frowned.

"What about your relationship?" Matilda ventured.

"What about it?"

"You said that it wasn't perfect…"

"No." Dante shook his head.

"You did," Matilda insisted.

"I said that I knew that they were not *all* per*fect—it doesn't mean I was referring to mine.*"

Matilda knew he was lying and she also knew that he was closing the subject, yet she refused to leave it there. She'd revealed so much of herself, had felt close to a man for the first time in ages and didn't want it to end like this, didn't want Dante to shut her out all over again.

"You said that you wanted to fix your problems, Dante," Matilda quoted softly. "What were they?"

"Does it matter now?" Dante asked, swilling the wine around his glass and refusing to look at her. "As you said, there are always two sides—is it fair to give mine when Jasmine isn't here to give hers?"

"I think so," Matilda breathed, chewing on her bottom lip. And even if her voice was tentative, she reeled at her boldness, laid her heart on the line a little bit more, bracing herself for pain as she did so. "If you want to get close to someone then you have to give a bit of yourself—even the bad bits."

"And you want to get close?"

He did look at her this time, and she stared back transfixed, a tiny nervous nod affirming her want. "Tell me about you, how you're feeling…"

"Which part of hell do you want to visit?"

She didn't flinch, didn't say anything, just stared back, watching as slowly he placed his glass on the table. His elbows on his knees, he raked a hand through his hair and so palpable was his pain Matilda was sure if she lifted her hand she'd be able to reach out and touch it. She held her breath as finally he looked up and stared at her for the longest time before speaking.

"Always there is…" He didn't get to start, let alone finish. A piercing scream from the intercom made them both jump. He picked up the intercom, which had been placed on the coffee table, and stood up. "I have to go to her and then I think I'll head to bed, I've got a pile of paperwork to read. 'Night, Matilda."

"Let me help with her…"

"She doesn't like strangers." The shutters were up, his black eyes dismissing her, the fragile closeness they had so nearly created evaporating in that instant.

"Dante…" Matilda called, but he wasn't listening, her words falling on his departing back as he closed the door behind him. "Don't make me one."

Chapter 7

Predictably, Katrina had a plumber screeching up the driveway within seconds of Dante's chopper lifting off the smooth lawn, and Matilda could almost envisage her bags being moved yet again, but quietly hoped for a miracle. And it wasn't all about Dante. Waking up to the most glorious sunrise, stretching like a lazy cat in the scrummy bed, as superficial as it might be, Matilda was terribly reluctant to leave her very nice surroundings.

"White ants!" Katrina almost choked on her Earl Grey as the plumber she had summoned popped his head around the kitchen door and Matilda smothered a smile as she loaded a tray with coffee to take out to the workers for their break. "Well, surely you can replace the water system and then we'll get the place treated once…" She managed to stop herself from saying it, but the unspoken words hung in the air and Matilda took great interest in filling up the sugar bowl as Katrina paused and then, rather more carefully, spoke on. "Just sort out the water, please. It doesn't all have to be done today."

"Can't do, I'm afraid," he said cheerfully. "The wall's not stable enough to hold a new system. The place needs to be treated and then some of the walls will have to be replaced—it's going to be a big job."

It wasn't the only big job the next couple of days unearthed.

Katrina practically moved into Dante's, appearing long before he went to work and staying well into the night when Dante finally got home—not that Matilda really noticed. All her energies were taken up with the garden—her efficient start to the job but a distant memory as problems compounded problems. The glorious willow tree had roots that weren't quite as wondrous, thwarting Matilda's carefully lain plans at each and every turn. And a rather unproductive day followed by a floodlit late night were spent with the plumber and electrician, trying to find a suitable spot to lay the pipes for the water features. Then, just when that was taken care of, Matilda awoke to the news that, despite her inspection, the white ants had migrated from the summerhouse to the rear wall of the fence, which would set things back yet another day while it was ripped out and replaced. More skips delivered, more delays ensuing, and by the time she dragged herself back to the house, all Matilda could manage was a warmed-up meal and a very weary goodnight as, drooping with exhaustion, she headed off for bed.

Still as the week drew to a close, if not order then at least a semblance of control had been restored. Finally the pipes were laid, the electricity was on and the garden that had till now merely lived in her mind could actually start to emerge.

"I think we must have a mole on steroids," Dante quipped, eyeing the mounds of earth that littered the area, and his easy humour bought the first smile in a long time to Matilda's tense face as he wandered in with Alex late one evening to check on the progress. "I hear things haven't gone exactly to plan."

"On the contrary," Matilda replied. "Things have gone exactly to plan—there's always a disaster waiting to happen with this kind of work. But I think we're finally under control."

"Will you be joining us for dinner?"

"Us?" Matilda checked, because Alex was clearly ready for bed.

"Katrina and Hugh have come over—I should give Janet the numbers."

"No, thanks." Matilda shook her head but didn't elaborate, didn't make up an excuse or reason.

"I'm sorry I haven't been over." Dante switched Alex to his other hip. "My trial preparation has taken up a lot of time, things have been busy—"

"Tell me about it," Matilda said, rolling her eyes.

"I'm sure that I'd bore you to death," Dante responded, completely missing the point. But somehow the language barrier actually worked in their favour for once, the tiny misunderstanding opening a door, pushing the stilted, polite conversation way beyond the intentions of either participant. "Are you really interested?"

"Very," Matilda responded. "Completely unqualified, of course, but terribly interested."

"But you know that I cannot discuss it with you."

"I know," Matilda answered. "I mean, at the end of

the day, the barrister mulling over his case with the gardener…"

"I cannot discuss it with *anyone*," Dante broke in, and she watched as his eyes closed in shuttered regret, felt again the weight of responsibility that rode on his broad shoulders and ached to soothe him.

"I know," Matilda said softly, then gave him a little spontaneous nudge. "Well, I don't *know* exactly, but I have got pay TV." She smiled at his frown. "I've paced the courtroom floor with the best of them, and from what I've gleaned you're allowed to talk in general terms."

"You're crazy." Dante laughed, his palpable tension momentarily lifting, but the shrill of his mobile broke the moment. Matilda watched as he juggled his daughter and flicked out his mobile, watched the vivid concentration on his face, the turn of his back telling her that this call was important. She reacted as anyone would have, held out her arms and offered to take his daughter, lifting the little girl into her arms, hardly registering the surprise on Dante's face as he barked his orders into the phone.

"She went to you!"

A full fifteen minutes had passed. Fifteen minutes of Dante talking into the phone as Matilda at first held Alex but when she got a bit heavy, Matilda put her down, gathering the few exhausted, remaining daisies from under the willow, slitting the stalks with her thumb and making if not a daisy chain then at least a few links—chatting away to an uncommunicative Alex. But the little girl did appear to be watching at least and now Dante was kneeling down with them, staring open-mouthed at what Matilda considered was really a very normal scene.

"Sorry?" Matilda was trying to wrestle a very limp stalk into a very thin one.

"Alex actually went to you." Dante's voice had a slightly incredulous note as he watched Alex take the small chain of daisies Matilda was offering.

"I'm really not that scary, Dante." Matilda smiled.

"You don't understand. Alex doesn't go to anyone. You saw what she was like the other day when it was *me* trying to pick her up."

"Maybe she's ready to start trusting a little again…" Matilda looked over at Dante and spoke over the little blonde head that was between them. Even though it was Alex she was talking about, they knew her words were meant for both. "Maybe now she's done it once, it will be easier the next time." For an age she stared at him, for an age he stared back, then his hands hovered towards his daughter, ready to pick her up and head for the house, ready to walk away yet again. But Matilda's voice halted him. "Let her play for a few minutes. She's enjoying the flowers." She was, her little fingers stroking the petals, concentration etched on her face, and for all the world she looked like any other little girl lost in a daydream. "Talk to me, Dante," Matilda said. "You might surprise yourself and find that it helps."

"I don't think so."

"I do," Matilda said firmly, watching as his gaze drifted to Alex, and finally after the longest time he spoke.

"Remember when we talked at the restaurant?" She could hear him choosing his words carefully. "You asked if I ever regret winning and I said no?" Matilda nodded. "I lied."

"I know," Matilda answered.

"Not professionally, of course." Dante pondered, his accent a little more pronounced as his mind clearly wandered elsewhere. "I always walk into a courtroom wanting to win, I wouldn't be there otherwise, but, yes, sometimes there is a feeling of…" He snapped his fingers in impatience as he tried to find the right word.

"Regret?" Matilda offered, and Dante shook his head.

"Unease," he said. "A sense of unease that I do my job so well."

"There would have to be," Matilda said carefully, knowing she couldn't push things, knowing she had to listen to the little information he was prepared to give.

"There is another side, too, though…" His eyes found and held hers and Matilda knew that what he was about to tell her was important. "There are certain cases that matter more. Matter because…" He didn't continue, couldn't perhaps, so Matilda did it for him.

"Because if you won there would be no unease?" She watched the bob of his Adam's apple as he swallowed, knew she had guessed correctly, that Dante was telling her, as best he could, that the man he was defending was innocent and that this case, perhaps, mattered more than most.

"You'll win," Matilda said assuredly, and Dante let out a tired sigh and gave a rather resigned smile, pulling himself up to go, clearly wondering why he'd bothered talking to her if that was the best she could come up with! "You will—you always do," Matilda said with absolute conviction. "Your client couldn't have better representation."

"Matilda," Dante said with dry superiority, "we're *not* talking about my client and, anyway, you have absolutely no idea what you're talking about."

"Oh, but I do." Her green eyes caught his as he reached out for his daughter.

"You know nothing about law," Dante needlessly pointed out. "You know nothing about—"

"Perhaps," Matilda interrupted. "But you've already told me what you're capable of, already told me that you can do it even if you don't believe…" She paused for a moment, remembering the rules, remembering that she had to keep it general. "If I were in trouble, I mean." She gave a cheeky grin. "Suppose I *had* been caught taking those chocolates and assuming I could afford you…" She gave a tiny roll eye as her fantasy took on even more bizarre proportions. "I'd want to walk into court with the best."

"Am I the best for him, though?" He raked a hand through his jet hair and it was Dante who forgot to keep things general.

"Absolutely," Matilda whispered. "I'd want the best I could afford, Dante, but having you believe in me would mean a thousand times more. Think of what you've already achieved then imagine what you're capable of when you actually believe in someone." A frown marred his brow, but it wasn't one of tension, more realization, and Matilda knew that she'd got through to him, knew that somehow she'd reassured him, maybe helped a little even. "You're going to be fine," Matilda said again, and this time he didn't bite back, this time he didn't shoot her down with some superior remark, just gave her a gentle nod of thanks.

"Time for bed, Alex," Matilda said, holding her arms out to the little girl, and even though Alex didn't hold out her own arms, she didn't resist when Matilda picked her up and wandered with Dante to the gate.

"She likes you," Dante said as he took a sleepy Alex from Matilda.

"I'm very easy to like," Matilda answered.

"Very easy," Dante said, only, unlike before, Matilda knew there were no double meanings or cruel euphemisms to mull over. As he walked away the echo of his words brought a warm glow to her tired, aching body.

Quite simply it was the nicest thing he'd ever said.

Chapter 8

"I'm sorry to have disturbed you."

"It's fine." Matilda attempted, struggling to sit up, slightly disorientated and extremely embarrassed that Dante had found her in the middle of the day, hot and filthy in nothing more than the skimpiest of shorts and a crop top, lying on a blanket with her eyes closed. Absolutely the *last* person she was expecting to see at this hour, he was dressed in his inevitable dark suit, but there was a slightly more relaxed stance to him. He held a brown paper bag in one hand and he didn't look in his usual rush—his usually perfectly knotted tie was loosened, the top button of his shirt undone. But his dark eyes were shielded with sunglasses making his closed expression even more unreadable if that were possible.

"You've done a lot."

"It's getting there." Matilda nodded. "And if I keep going at full speed, I could still be done by early next week."

He didn't say a word, he didn't have to. Just a tiny questioning lift of his eyebrow from behind his dark glasses was enough for Matilda.

"I am allowed to take a break," Matilda retorted.

"I didn't say anything!"

"You might not have *said* it but I certainly *heard* it. I am allowed to take a break, Dante. For your information, I've been working since first light this morning—apart from a coffee at ten I haven't stopped."

"You don't have to justify yourself to me."

"No, I don't," Matilda agreed.

"How you organise your time is entirely your business. It's just…" His voice faded for a moment, a hint of a very unusual smile dusting across his face. "I think I must be in the wrong job. 'Flat out' for me is back-to-back meetings, endless phone calls, figures, whereas the twice I've seen you work, you're either taking an impromptu shower with a water bottle or dozing under a tree." She opened her mouth to set him straight, but Dante spoke over her. "I am not criticising you, I can see for myself the hours of work you have done. For once I was not even being sarcastic— I really was thinking back there when I saw you that I am in the wrong job!"

"You are." Matilda smiled, the wind taken out of her sails by his niceness. "And for the record, I wasn't dozing."

"Matilda, don't try and tell me that you weren't asleep. You didn't even hear me come over. You were lying on your back with your eyes closed."

"I was meditating," Matilda said and seeing the disbelieving look on his face she elaborated further. "I did hear you come over, I just…" It was Matilda's voice fading now, wondering how she could explain to him that in her deeply relaxed state she had somehow discounted the information.

"Just what?"

"I didn't hold onto the thought."

"You've lost me." He shook his head as if to clear it. "You're really telling me that you weren't asleep!"

"That's right—I often meditate when I'm working, that's where I get my best ideas. You should try it," she added.

"I have enough trouble getting to sleep at one in the morning, let alone in the middle of the day."

"My point exactly," Matilda said triumphantly. "I've already told you that I wasn't asleep. You're very quick to throw scorn, but sometimes the best way to find the answer to a question is to stop looking for it."

"Perhaps." Dante gave a dismissive shrug. "But for now I'll stick with the usual methods. I actually came to see if you wanted some lunch." Before she could shake her head, before she could come up with an excuse as to why she didn't want to go over and eat with Katrina, Dante held out the paper bag he was holding. "I bought some rolls from the deli."

"The deli?"

"Why does that surprise you?"

"I don't know," Matilda admitted, her neck starting to ache from staring up, feeling at a distinct disadvantage as Dante hovered over her. Wiggling over, she patted the blanket for him to sit beside her. "It just does. How come you're home?"

"I live here," Dante quipped, but he *did* sit down beside her, pulling the rolls out of the bag and offering one to her. "I've spent the entire morning trying to read an important, complicated document relating to the case and haven't got past the second page. My new administrative assistant cannot distinguish between urgent and urgent yet."

"I don't understand."

"Invariably anyone who wants to speak with me says that it is urgent—but she puts them all through, then I get waylaid. I decided to follow your business methods, they seem to be working for you."

"What method?" Matilda gasped. "I didn't know I had one!"

"Turning the phone off and disappearing. Katrina is out with Alex today. I thought there was more chance of actually getting some work done if I just came home, but first I must have some lunch."

"I didn't hear the chopper!"

"I drove," Dante said, "and it was nice." They ate in amicable silence until Dante spoiled it, his words almost causing her to choke on her chicken and avocado roll. "I was thinking about you."

"Me?"

"And how much I enjoy talking to you." He took off his dark glasses and smiled a lazy smile, utterly comfortable in his own skin as Matilda squirmed inside hers, wriggling her bare feet in the moss and staring at her toes. "And you're right, it's nice to take a moment to relax."

Relaxed certainly wasn't how Matilda would describe herself now. He was so close that if she moved her leg an inch they'd be touching, if his face came a fraction closer she knew they'd be kissing. Desire coursed through her as it had when she'd cut herself, only this time Dante didn't seem to be pulling back, this time he was facing her head on. It was Matilda who turned abruptly away, terrified he'd read the naked lust in her eyes. She took a long drink from her water bottle then, blowing her fringe skywards and trying to keep her voice normal, determined not to make a fool of herself again, to be absolutely sure she wasn't misreading things, she said, "You should try meditating if you want to be relaxed."

"It wouldn't work," Dante dismissed.

"It won't if that's your attitude…" She could feel the atmosphere sizzling between them, knew that if she said what was on her mind then she'd be crossing a line, playing the most dangerous of dangerous games. "Try it," she breathed, her eyes daring him to join her. "Why don't you lie back and try it now?"

"Now?" Dante checked, a dangerous warning glint in his eyes, which she heeded, but it only excited her more.

"Now," Matilda affirmed. "Just lie back."

"Then what?" Dante's impatient voice demanded instruction as, impossibly tense, he lay back.

"You close your eyes and just breathe," Matilda said, her head turning to face him, her own breath catching in her throat as she gazed at his strong profile. She'd been right with her very first assessment of Dante. He was astonishingly beautiful—his eyes were closed and black, surprisingly long lashes spiked downwards onto indigo smudges of exhaustion. His nose was chiselled straight, so straight and so absolutely in proportion to the rest of his features she could almost imagine some LA cosmetic surgeon downing his tools in protest as he surveyed the landscape of Dante Costello's flawless face.

Flawless.

A perfectionist might point out that he hadn't shaved, but the stubble that ghosted his strong jaw, merely accentuated things: a shiver of masculinity stirring beneath the surface; a glimpse of what he might look like in the intimate dawn of morning. His full mouth was the only softening feature, but even that was set in grim tension as he lay there.

"You have to relax," Matilda said, her words a contradiction because her whole body lay rigid beside him, her own breath coming in short, irregular bursts. Even her

words were stilted, coming in short breathy sentences as
they struggled through her vocal cords. "Use your stomach muscles and breathe in through your nose and out
through your mouth."

"What?" One eye peeped open.

"Abdominal breathing," she explained, but from the two
vertical lines appearing over the bridge of his nose Matilda
knew she was talking to the hopelessly unconverted.

"You don't move your chest," Matilda explained. "Remember when Alex was a baby and you watched her
sleep?"

The frown faded a touch, a small smile lifting one edge
of his mouth.

"Babies know how to relax," Matilda said. "They instinctively *know* how to breathe properly."

"Like this?" Dante asked, dragging in air, and Matilda
watched as he struggled with the concept. His stomach
was moving but so too was his chest.

"Almost. Look, I'll help you. Just push against my
hand." Sitting up slightly, she instinctively moved to correct him. She'd shown this to numerous friends, knew how
to show him simply, but her movements were hesitant, her
hand tentative as it reached out towards him, hovered over
the flat plane of his stomach, knowing, *knowing* where
this could lead, wanting to pull back, to end this dangerous game, but curiously excited to start, to touch him, to
feel him...

Her hand still hovered over his stomach but it was just
too much, too intimate, and instead she placed her other
hand on his chest, feeling the warmth of his skin through
his shirt, feeing the breath still in him. Her fingers ached,
literally ached to move his loosened tie, to creep between
the buttons and feel his skin against hers. But she pushed

away that thought, concentrated instead on keeping her voice even as she delivered her instructions. "My hand shouldn't move. Breathe in through your nose, using your stomach, and then out through your mouth—here." It seemed more appropriate now to touch his stomach than when the initial contact had been made, and she gently brushed her hand along on his stomach, felt the heavy leather of his belt, the coolness of his buckle and the silk of his trousers. Her whole body rippled with a lust she had never experienced—never thought she could experience— and she herself had engineered it because she wanted to be closer to him. More than that she didn't know, just knew she couldn't take a minute more of the crazy feelings that had been going on. "Push against my hand," Matilda said, "and then hold your breath before letting out it. And just let your mind wander."

For a second, two perhaps, he did. She felt him relax a touch beneath her, but it was fleeting, resistance rushing back in, his hand pushing hers away, Dante turning now to face her.

"Show me," he said.

"I don't want to." Matilda shook her head, knew she was incapable of going back to that tranquil place with Dante so close, but he was insistent. "If it's so easy to do, prove it."

Lying on her back Matilda closed her eyes, willed herself calm, trying to force herself to relax. But she could feel the tension in her hands and she drew on her reserves, dragged in the fragrant air, holding it, holding it and slowly letting it out, could feel his eyes watching her body move. And amazingly it happened. Somehow she did wander to that place she visited so often, but it was a different journey altogether, one she had never taken before. With every breath she sank deeper and yet her desire grew, visualising, willing his hands to touch her, for him to rest his palm on her stomach, fleeting, decadent thoughts that were hers only, her limbs heavy against the damp grass, the erotic thought of him near her stomach tightening with the anticipation of a touch that might never come.

His breath on her face caught her unawares. Her mind hadn't ever been so attuned to her body. She had been so sure his eyes had been there, the shiver of his breath on her cheeks was a shock, but even as her mind processed the sensation it was experiencing a new one—his mouth, pressing lightly on hers, so soft if it hadn't have been him it would surely have been imperceptible, could almost have been put down to imagination for nowhere else did he touch her. The sun blocked out as he hovered over her, her eyes still closed as she blissfully attuned to the feel of his lips lightly on hers until it wasn't enough. He was waiting for her bidding, she instinctively knew that. She could smell the bitter orange and bergamot undertones of his cologne, his breath mingling with hers, and after seconds that seemed to drag for ever she gave him her consent with her mouth, pressed her own lips into his.

The greeting was acknowledged by the reward of his cool tongue parting her lips, slipping inside, and that delicious taste of him, the intimate feel of his mouth inside hers, his tongue languorously capturing hers, playing a slow teasing game, long strokes that made her want more, countered by a tiny feather-light stroke on the tip of her tongue and then a gentle sucking as he dragged her deeper into him. And it was the most erotic of kisses yet the most frustrating, because still nowhere else did he touch her. Only their mouths were touching only their mouths in contact, and she wanted more, her body arching, trying to convey her needs. But he misread them, just kissed her ever on, till she burnt for more, literally ached for more, and only then did he give it, but in a selfish, measured dose.

The hand that she desired, that she anticipated around her waist to pull her towards him, instead lay on the soft inner flesh of her thigh, and the impact was as acute as if he'd struck her with a branding iron. It was her thigh, for heaven's sake, Matilda mentally begged, just a few square inches of flesh, and it wasn't even moving, but it was intimate, it was so damned intimate that it was surely wrong to be lying here beneath him now. She wished his hand would move, but it didn't. Instead, it pressed harder, almost imperceptibly at first but slowly she could feel his fingers digging into the tender flesh. Her breath in his mouth was coming faster now, and just as she went to push him away, to move his hand to safer ground, Dante was the one who stopped. Propped up on his elbow, she could feel him gazing down at her and she lay there vulnerable, reluctant to open her eyes, terrified, excited at the same time, wondering what he would do next.

"How else?" His words confused her, questions inappropriate now, his touch what she needed, not the mind games he played. "How else did Edward hurt you?"

"I've told you," Matilda gulped, screwing her eyes closed tighter wishing he would just leave it, and sure he knew she was lying.

"Not all of it," Dante said, his finger trailing along her arm as she spoke, the nub of his finger lingering on her radial pulse, like some perverse lie detector as he dragged her secrets out. "Was *that* supposed to be your fault, too?"

"I didn't help," Matilda croaked, her eyes still screwed closed, unable to look at him as she revealed her shame. "Edward said that maybe if I dressed up..."

"Would he want you now?" Dante breathed, interrupting her, confusing her again. "All messed up, in your work clothes?"

"Of course not," Matilda started, but her voice trailed

off, not sure what he was getting at. Her body was still throbbing with desire, an argument starting somewhere deep within, because Dante had wanted her, hadn't he?

Doubt was starting to ping in, her eyes snapping open, terrified that he was laughing at her, dreading being humiliated again. But in one movement he grabbed her wrist, rammed her tense hand between his legs. She pulled back as if she'd been scalded, the strength of his erection shocking her, the feel of him in her hand terrifying. But Dante pulled her hand back, holding it there till the fear abated, till the arousal that had always been there stirred again.

"You make me feel like this, *mi cora*."

She could feel him growing in her palm, feel a trickle of sweat between her breasts as he swelled harder beneath her touch, a bubble of moisture between her legs as his fingers crept up her T-shirt now, tiny, delicate strokes as he inched up slowly further, and it had gone too far, way, way too far. She murmured her protest, attempted to halt things, but he kissed her harder, captured her protest with his tongue and silenced it. She could feel the fleshy pad of his index finger circling her aching nipple as he held the soft plumpness of her bosom in his palm. Only now did his lips release hers. Any sooner and she would have begged him to stop, would have halted things.

But now she was putty in his skilled hands, pliable, warm, willing to move, to let him do with her what he wanted, and, oh, how he did—kissing the pulse leaping in her throat as she wriggled out of her top. The second her breasts were free, his tongue paid them the attention they deserved, tender attention, kissing the swollen, needy tips in turn, his finger retracing his steps, working downwards now. Her stomach tightened in renewed tension as he slid down the zip of her shorts, but for the first time since contact he spoke, the liquid deep tones of his voice not break-ing the spell but somehow deepening it.

"Don't hold onto those thoughts, *bella*, just let them come and go." Repeating the words she had said to him, but with entirely different meaning this time. And she tried, really tried to just relax as his hand cupped her bottom and lifted her enough to slip off the shorts and knickers in one. But the movement erased what had been achieved, embar-rassment flooding in as her flesh was exposed, her knees lifting instinctively and her hand moving down in a futile attempt to cover herself. Wanting to hide her body from Dante's gaze. She half expected his wrist to close around her hand, as Edward's had done, to roughly demand to re-turn to where he had just been.

"Don't fight," he ordered, but unlike Edward he was soothing her with words instead of touch. "Don't think about that, just think about this." His hand hovered over her stomach until she caught her breath. She wanted the contact again and he was very gently tracing tiny endless circles around the little hill of her abdomen as his lips dusted her cheeks. He was kissing away the salty tears that were spilling from her eyes with his other hand around her neck, massaging her hairline, yet still the hungry swell of him against her told Matilda how much he desired her. A barrage of sensations that could have been confusing but instead soothed, the panic that had momentarily en-gulfed her waned until she lay outstretched and acquies-cent in his arms, thrumming with anticipation for all that he might yield.

"I'm going to touch you now."

He was already touching her, his body was pressed against her, his lips on her face, his erection jutting into her, but she knew what he meant, was grateful for the strange warning, shivering as his hand reached her damp intimate curls and gently stroked them, his lip capturing the nervous swallow in her throat as his fingers crept slowly deeper, the infinitely gentle strokes he had teased her with before almost rough in comparison to the tenderness he displayed now, gently circling, pressing. But what if she couldn't, what if she let him down? She felt herself tense but not in desire, that panic again creeping in as he slid a finger into her tight space, slid it in slowly, taking her dew and then back to where it was needed. His touch firmer, massaging away her fears and replacing them with need, as she quivered at his touch, uncurling under his masterful skill, his palm massaging her swollen mound, over and over, his fingers gliding in and out, patience in every movement. She opened her eyes once, drunk on lust, moaning at the blissful warmth that fired her, and she saw his eyes smiling down at her, not a trace of superiority in them, just desire.

"Matilda." It was Dante's voice that was breathless now, *his* body pressing harder into hers. She'd been so indulgent in her own pleasure while he'd been so unselfish, but that he could be so aroused from just touching her was all the affirmation she needed. Bold, so bold now, it was Matilda making the move, wrestling with his heavy belt, unzipping him, pushing the silk of his boxers down and staring with animal lust at him, the swollen, angry tip almost explosive. And even if it was the most wanton, outrageous thing she had ever done, even if all there could be was this moment, she needed it, needed him deep, deep inside her. She wanted his weight on top of her and it was heaven as Dante pushed her down, his clothed body squeezing the breath out of her, strong knees parting her willing thighs. She could feel him nudging at her entrance and opened her legs a fraction more to accommodate him. Even before his heated length stabbed into her, her body was convulsing, her most intimate place wrapping around his, dragging him deeper with each quivering contraction of her orgasm as he moved within her.

"More!"

Her eyes opened. Breathless, speechless, she stared at him as still he moved within her. What did he mean more? She'd achieved more than she had ever thought possible—he'd already toppled her to climax.

"Give me more, Matilda." He was pushing harder and now so was she. Now he was sliding over her, pressing her harder into the ground. But her body wanted to still, to recover from her orgasm, and she'd thought he'd been close, was sure he'd wanted her as much as she'd wanted him. For a second the doubts were back, the tiny dark voices that told her over and over she wasn't quite good enough, wasn't sexy enough, wasn't woman enough to please a man.

"Matilda," Dante gasped. "Come with me. I can't hold on—see what you do to me?"

He stared down at her and it was as if Dante was struggling to stay in control—and her body that had begged respite, mere moments before, rippled into delighted action as he ambushed her. Her legs wriggled free, wrapping themselves tightly around his hips, pulling him fiercely in, her fingers digging into the taut muscle of his buttocks. And she understood, understood then that she'd never truly let go, had merely glanced around the door of the place Dante was taking her to now.

"You're beautiful *bella*." Over and over he said it. His chin was rough against her tender face, his breathing rapid and irregular, and she felt powerful now, felt his desire, his blatant need for her irrefutable. "Dante…Dante." Over and over she said. Pulling his shirt up, her hands ran over his back as her own frenzied mouth searched for comfort, sucking, licking the salty flesh of his chest.

"What you do to me!" Dante rasped. "You sexy bitch…" His body, his words were one unguarded paroxysm now, but so, too, was Matilda. She felt sexy, he *made* her sexy, her body responding to his debauched words, shivering as he spilled his precious nectar and she dragged it from him, convulsing around his length, dragging each delicious drop as if it was her right, as if it was hers to take, her whole body in rigid spasm, clinging to him as still somehow he moved, slower now, giving her all of him until, sated, exhausted, he collapsed on top of her before rolling onto his side, pulling her into his arms and welcoming her, back to a world that was more beautiful for what had taken place.

"You are so beautiful," Dante drawled, then gave a small cough. "Matilda, what I said just then…I mean, maybe I went too far…"

"Maybe I needed to hear it." Matilda smiled. "In fact, I think it's one of the nicest things anyone's ever said to me."

He laughed—a real laugh—and it sounded so good. To see him relaxed, smiling, was like glimpsing somehow a different man, and all she knew was that she wanted more of this. He ran his hand over her warm, naked body and she squirmed with pleasure, not embarrassment, couldn't believe she was lying naked in his arms in the middle of the day and feeling only beautiful. "At least we've answered your question."

"What question?"

He kissed her very slowly, very tenderly before answering.

"It was Edward's problem, not yours." He kissed the tip of her nose as his words sank in.

"Or you're just an amazing lover!"

"Oh, that, too." Dante grinned.

"You know, sometimes people say things in an argument that they don't really mean."

Matilda gazed up at him. "Perhaps," she said softly. "Or in anger they find the courage to say what's really on their mind."

The sun must have gone behind a cloud, because suddenly his face darkened, his body that had been so yielding, so in tune with hers stiffening, and Matilda wasn't sure if it was because of what she'd said or because he'd heard it first. The sound of tyres crunching on the gravel had them both jumping like scalded cats, suddenly aware of her lack of attire and Dante's trousers around his knees. She hated the intrusion, wanted so much to see him properly, the glimpse of his tumescence as he hastily pulled his trousers up and tucked himself in nowhere near enough for Matilda.

"Dante!" Katrina's voice pierced the still afternoon. Completely flustered, somehow Matilda managed to dress in record time, zipping up her shorts and almost falling over as she pulled on her boots, until, with her heart pounding, the footsteps drew closer and the gate was pushed open. Matilda did not even look over as Katrina approached and bluntly addressed Dante. "I saw your car—what on earth are you doing home?"

"Trying to catch up on some reading," Dante said casually, but it didn't wash with Katrina and after a long pause he elaborated. "I thought I'd see how the garden was coming along before I shut myself away for the rest of the day. Where's Alex?"

Katrina didn't say anything at first, suspicious eyes swivelling from Dante to Matilda. "Asleep in the car," she finally said slowly. "I was just going to carry her in."

"I'll come and help," Dante offered, but Katrina had already gone, walking out of the garden without a backward glance. Matilda stood with her cheeks flaming, her anxious eyes swinging to Dante, hoping for reassurance.

"Do you think she knew?"

"Of course not." Dante shook his head but a muscle was pounding in his cheek, his hands balled into fists by his sides, and Matilda realised that Katrina's intrusion hadn't just wrecked the intimate moment—it was almost as if she'd erased it completely. "Why on earth would she think there was anything between us?"

She truly wasn't sure if he was trying to reassure her, or was blatantly degrading her, but Matilda did a double-take, stunned at the change in him. Gone was the man who had so recently held her and in his place was the inaccessible man she had first encountered.

"Because maybe she guessed that we just made love."

Matilda eyes glittered with tears, willing him to take it back, to perhaps realise the brutality of what he had just said, to offer some sort of apology. But Dante just stood there refusing to take it as she offered him an out from his rancid words. "Because maybe she's noticed that over the last few days we've become close…"

"No." His single word hurt her even more, if that were possible, his refusal to soften it cheapening her more than she'd thought possible.

"So what was that all about?" Matilda asked, gesturing to where they had lain, where he'd found her, held her, made love to her, forcing the confrontation, steeling herself to hear the confirmation of her worst fears. "What just happened there, Dante?"

"Sex." Black eyes stung her, a warning note in his voice telling her she'd crossed the line. His lips set in a rigid line as she shook her head, refused his take on the history they'd so recently created.

"It was more than that and you know it," Matilda rasped,

shocked by his callousness, reeling from the ferociousness of his sparse summing-up, yet refusing to buy it, because she knew there was more to him, had witnessed the real Dante only moments before, and all she knew was that she wanted him back. "Dante, please, don't do this…" Matilda attempted, her hand reaching out for his arm, but he recoiled as if she was contaminated, shook her off as if she revolted him.

"Good sex, then," came the elaboration she had foolishly hoped for, the bile at the back of her throat appropriate as he told her his poisonous truth. And it was Matilda recoiling now, Matilda putting up the shutters and swearing she'd never let this man near her again.

"No, Dante, it wasn't." This time she wasn't lying, wasn't denying what she felt. Looking into his cold, hard eyes, she told him the absolute truth. "Good sex isn't just the act, Dante, it's about how you feel afterwards, and right now, I couldn't feel worse." She knew he was about to walk off, knew that if she didn't say what was on her mind now then it would fester for ever, had learnt that much at least, so whether he was listening or not she chose to say what she felt. "I don't know what your problem is, I don't know what it is that drives you to shut out something that could have been so good. Maybe you can justify it by saying that I'm not sophisticated enough to play by your rules, or that I don't hold a candle to your wife, but that's entirely your business. Frankly, I don't care any more."

His only response was a blink, but she knew that she'd surprised him, knew that even as he shut her out further, right now a little of what she was saying was reaching him. It gave her the impetus to continue, the pain he'd inflicted more than enough to go round. "I'm more sorry than you'll ever know for having *sex* with you, Dante, but, let's get one thing clear—I might have lost a bit of my pride here, but you just lost one helluva lot more…" It was Matilda who walked off, Matilda who headed to the house and left him standing in the garden. She refused to cry, just called her parting shot over her shoulder. "You just lost me!"

Chapter 9

His callousness, his emotional distancing after the intimacy they'd shared made the most painful of decisions relatively easy, made walking away from Dante about need rather than want. Because sharing his home, glimpsing his life and being shut out over and over was a torture that couldn't be sustained and gave Matilda the momentum to pick up the phone and call on every friend and colleague she could muster with a view to rapidly finishing the task she had committed herself to, and rapidly removing herself from this impossible situation she had allowed herself to fall into.

It was the most exhausting time of her life. Hanging the expense, more than happy to bill him, more than happy to pay for it herself even, Matilda ordered floodlights to enable her to work long into the warm nights, grateful for the soothing diversion of nature, grateful that by the time her aching body fell into bed at night, all she was capable of was rest, taking the respite of a dreamless, exhausted sleep while knowing the pain would surely come later.

"I can't believe what you've achieved." Deep into a humid, oppressive Saturday evening, Hugh poured her a glass of champagne Matilda didn't want from the bottle he was holding, having wandered over from the al fresco area where the *family* had eaten a leisurely dinner. He was now staring in astonishment at the garden, which was almost complete, the sleeping beauty truly awoken, the overgrown wilderness a distant memory. In its place was a child's paradise—a maze of soft hedges, each leading to its own exciting end, soft turf underfoot and thousands of tiny fairy-lights adorning the massive willow—twinkling in the dusky light and bidding enchantment. "What do you think, Katrina?"

"It's very nice." Katrina's response wasn't exactly effusive, but Matilda couldn't have cared less. The only thing she needed to see her through was the knowledge that in less than twelve hours she'd be out of there, in less than twelve hours she could start to pick up the pieces of her life Dante had so readily shattered. "Of course," Katrina added, "it's Alex's opinion that counts."

Almost on cue, the gate opened and, as she had over the last couple of days whenever their paths had inadvertently crossed, Matilda didn't even look at Dante. Instead, she focused her attention on Alex, who walked tentatively alongside him, her tiny hand in his. She looked utterly adorable, dressed in cotton pyjamas and cute kitten slippers, newly washed blonde curls framed her pretty face. And as livid and as debased as Matilda felt, momentarily at least, it faded as she watched the little girl's reaction. Watched as her normally vacant eyes blinked in wonder as she actually surveyed the transformation, a smile breaking out on her serious face as Matilda flicked on a switch and the water features danced into life. It was like seeing the sun come out as a tiny gasp of wonder escaped Alex's lips. She moved forward, reached out and ran, *ran* as most children would have, but because it was Alex it was amazing.

"I think she likes it." She could forgive Hugh's stilted words, because tears were running down his cheeks as he watched his granddaughter run through the water jets, and for that moment in time Matilda decided that the pain she'd endured had been worth it. To see this distant, reclusive child emerge from her shell, even if only for a moment, that her vision, her concept had actually reached this troubled, fractured child caused something good and pure to well deep inside her. Matilda's usual happiness, which had been stifled since Dante's rejection, bubbled to the surface again as she witnessed her work through the eyes of a child.

A child like Alex.

"Look!" Matilda's voice was an excited whisper. She crouched to Alex's level, as she had on the first day, taking her cautious hand as she had back then and beckoning Alex to new wonders as Katrina and Hugh wandered around to explore. "Look what's here!" Parting the curtain of willow, Matilda led her inside the cool enclosure, the fairy-lights she had so carefully placed lighting the darkness and creating a cool, emerald oasis, an enchanted garden within a garden, a place for Alex to simply just be. But the innocent pleasure of the moment was broken as the leaves parted, as Dante stepped into the magical space and completely broke the spell.

"You could put engravings on the bark." Matilda's voice was a monotone now as she addressed Dante, talking like a salesperson delivering her pitch. "Or hang some mirrors and pictures, perhaps put down a blanket and have a crib for her dolls…"

"She loves it," Dante broke in, the emotion that was usually so absent in his voice rolling in the distance as he sat down on the mossy ground, watching as his daughter stared up at the twinkling lights, her hands held in the air, fingers dancing along with them. "It is the first time I have seen her happy in a long time."

"Not so bad for a *stupido* garden?" Matilda said, and if she sounded bitter, she was: bitter for the way he had treated her; bitter for all they had lost. But because Alex was present, Matilda swallowed her resentment down, instead giving Dante the information he would need if the garden she had planted was to flourish. "I've just got to clean up and attend to a few minor details tomorrow, but I'll be gone by lunchtime."

"By lunchtime?" There was a tiny start to his voice, a frown creeping across his brow, which Matilda chose to ignore. "I probably won't catch up with you tomorrow, but I'll write up some instructions for your gardener and run through a few things with you now. Know that the whole garden will improve with time." Picking at some moss on the ground, Matilda continued, "Every day you should see some changes. The paths are littered with wild seeds—buttercups, daisies, clover—so you shouldn't mow too often…"

"Matilda?"

"There are no sharp edges." Ignoring him, she continued, trying to get through her summing-up, knowing this was one job she wouldn't be following up, knowing she was seeing it for the last time. "And no plants that can hurt, no thorns that could scratch, nothing that might sting— she should be perfectly safe here. This garden is what you make of it—you could pick marigold leaves with Alex to add to your salad at night—"

"Matilda, we need to talk," he interrupted again, one hand creeping across the ground to capture hers. But she pulled away, determined to see this last bit through with whatever dignity she could muster, yet unable to stop herself from looking at him for what was surely going to be the last time. Her final instructions to him were laced with double meaning, littered with innuendo, and from Dante's tense expression she knew he felt each one.

"No, Dante, *you* need to listen. This garden may look beautiful now, but tomorrow when I've cleaned up and gone, you'll come for another look and see its apparent faults. Tomorrow, in the cold light of day, you'll wonder what the hell you paid all this money for, because the lights won't be on and the bushes will look a bit smaller and sparser than they do tonight. You'll see all the lines where the turf was laid and the sticks holding up the plants and—"

"It will still be beautiful to me," Dante interrupted. "Because it's already given me more pleasure than I ever thought possible." And, yes, he was talking about Alex, because his hands were gesturing to where his daughter sat, but his eyes were holding hers as he spoke and she knew that he was also referring to them. "Yes, it might just take a bit of getting used to, but I can understand now that in the end it would be worth it…" She stared back at him for the longest time, swallowing hard as he went on. "That if I nurture it, care for it, tend it…" With each word he tempted her, delivering his veiled apology in a low silken drawl. "Then it will reward me tenfold."

"It would have," Matilda said softly, watching his wince of regret at her refusal to accept it, actually grateful when Katrina and Hugh ducked inside the emerald canopy and broke the painful moment, because whatever Dante was trying to say it was too little, too late—even a garden full of flowers wasn't going to fix this.

"Join us for a drink," Hugh offered. "Dante's just about to put Alex to bed..."

"I've got too much to do here." Matilda smiled as she shook her head. "But thank you for the offer."

"I think we might have to stay over." Katrina pretended to grimace. "Hugh's had a couple too many champagnes to drive."

"I've had one," Hugh said, but Katrina had clearly already made up her mind. Matilda was tempted to tell her that she needn't bother, that Dante didn't need to be guarded on her final night here, but instead she offered her goodnights and headed to the mountain of tools that needed to be sorted.

"You really ought to think about finishing up," Dante called. "There's a storm brewing and with all these cables and everything it could be hazardous."

She didn't even deign a response, grateful when they left, when finally the garden gate closed and she was alone.

Despite her utter exhaustion, working a sixteen-hour day, when finally Matilda showered and fell into bed, sleep evaded her, the body Dante had awoken then tossed aside twitching with treacherous desire. Lying in the darkness, she gazed out over the bay, watching the dark clouds gathering in the distance, the ominous view matching her mood as she listened to the talking and laughter coming from the garden below. Katrina's grating voice telling tales about the wonderful Jasmine did nothing to soothe her and she wished over and over that she'd managed to avoid Dante tonight.

Reluctantly she replayed his words in her mind. With

total recall she remembered the look on his face as he had spoken to her, and she knew that she'd almost forgiven him, that had he touched her, she'd have gone to him.

A whimpering cry carried down the hallway and Matilda listened as Alex called out in her sleep. Her first instinct was to go to the little girl, but she stayed put, knowing that Dante would hear her on the intercom. She waited for the sound of his footsteps on the stairs, but they never came. Alex's cries grew louder and more anguished and Matilda screwed her eyes closed and covered her ears with her hands in an attempt to block them out, knowing that it was none of her business, while praying someone would come soon.

"Mama!"

Alex's terrified little voice had Matilda sitting bolt upright in bed, the jumbled babbles of a child's nightmare tearing at her heartstrings until she could bear it no more. The sensible thing would have been to go downstairs and alert Dante, and she had every intention of doing so, even pulling on a pair of knickers for manners' sake! But as she padded down the hallway in her flimsy, short nightdress, as the screams got louder, instinct kicked in, and pushing open the bedroom door, she called out to Alex in the darkness, gathering the hot, tear-racked body in her arms and attempting to soothe her, trying not to convey her alarm as Alex sobbed harder, her balled fists attempting to slam into Matilda's cheeks.

"Shush, honey," Matilda soothed, capturing her wrists. Instead of holding her away, she brought a hand up to her face, controlling the movement, stroking her face with Alex's hand as over and over she told her that everything was OK, relief filling her as gradually the child seemed to calm.

"It's OK, Alex." Over and over she said it, even letting

go of Alex's wrist as finally the little girl started to relax, rocking her gently in her arms.

"What happened?"

She'd been so focused on Alex, Matilda hadn't even heard him come in, but as his deep-voiced whisper reached her ears, for Alex's sake she forced herself not to tense, just carried on rocking the child as she spoke.

"She was screaming. I was going to come and get you, but…" Her voice trailed off. How could she tell him that she'd been unable to just walk past? "I thought you'd hear her on the intercom."

"It's not working—there's a storm coming so it's picking up interference." He was standing over her now and she assumed he'd take Alex from her, but she was wrong. Instead, he gazed down at his daughter, his hand stroking her forehead, pushing back the damp blonde curls from her hot, red face. "She was really upset," Dante observed, then looked over at Matilda. "And you managed to calm her."

"I just cuddled her," Matilda said, "as you do, and spoke to her."

"No one can usually calm her." Dante blinked. "No one except me and sometimes Katrina."

They stood in silence for the longest time, a deep, pensive silence broken only by the fading sobs of Alex, until finally she was quiet, finally she gave in. "I think she's asleep," Matilda whispered, gently placing Alex back in her cot, grateful she'd remembered to put on knickers as she lowered the little body.

"It's hot in here," Date said, his voice not quite steady. As he opened the window a fraction more, the sweet scent of jasmine filled the air. Matilda stepped back as Dante took over tucking the sheets around Alex, tears filling her eyes as he placed a tender kiss on his daughter's cheek until she could bear it no more, the agony of witnessing such an intimate scene more than she could take. Matilda headed out into the hall, wiping the tears with the backs of her hands, cringing as his hand closed around her shoulder, as Dante tried to stop her.

"Matilda…"

"Don't," Matilda begged, because she knew what was coming, knew he was going to apologise again, and she was terrified she'd relent. "Just leave me alone, Dante."

"I cannot do that." His hand was still on her shoulder but she shook it off, turned her expressive face to his, the anger that had never really abated brimming over again. Aware of Alex, she struggled to keep her voice down.

"Why me?" she whispered angrily, tears spilling down her face as she glared at him. "Why, when you could have any woman you wanted, did you have to pick on me?" Her hoarse whisper trailed off as she heard Hugh and Katrina at the foot of the stairs. Horrified, she stared at him, excruciatingly aware of her lack of attire, knowing how it would appear and not up to the confrontation.

His reflexes were like lightning. His hand closed around hers and in one movement he opened a door, practically pulling her inside, but she was plunged from desperation to hell. The mocking sight of his bedroom twisted the knife further, if that were possible, and she let him have it, her fists balling like Alex's, pushing against his chest as she choked the words out. "You knew what this would do to me. You knew how much this would hurt me in the end. So why did you even start it, why, when you could have anyone, did you have to pick on me?"

"Shh," Dante warned, the voices on the other side of the door growing nearer, but Matilda was past caring now.

"Why," she said nastily, "are you worried what Katrina will say?" She never got to finish. Both his hands were holding hers so he silenced her in the only way he could, his mouth pressing on hers, pushing her furious body against the door as she resisted with every fibre of her being, clamping her mouth closed, trying not to even breathe because she didn't want to taste him, smell him, didn't want to taste what she could never have again.

"'Night, Dante…"

A million miles away on the other side of the door Katrina called to him. Warning her with his eyes, he moved his mouth away, his breath hot on her cheeks, his mouth ready to claim hers again if she made a single move.

"'Night, Katrina."

And shame licked the edges then, shame trickling in as he stared down at her till the moment had passed, till Hugh and Katrina were safely out of earshot and Dante told her a necessary home truth.

"I do not have to answer to Katrina, but I do respect her, Matilda. She is the mother of my wife and the grandmother of my child. I will not flaunt a relationship in front of her without fair warning."

"What relationship?" Matilda sneered, but her face was scarlet, knowing that in this instance he was right. "Sex with no strings isn't enough for me, Dante." Which was such a contrary thing to say when her whole body was screaming for him, her nipples like stinging thistles against her nightdress, her body trembling with desire, awoken again by the one-sided kiss.

"It isn't enough for me either," Dante said softly. "At least not since you came along." His hands had loosened their grip but his eyes were pinning her now, and she stared back, stunned, sure she must have somehow misheard. She dropped her eyes, didn't want to look at him when surely he would break her heart again, but his hand cupped her chin, capturing her, ensuring that she remained looking at him, his fingers softly holding her, his thumb catching tears as they tumbled down her cheeks. "A lady who asks me for directions, a lady who steps into a elevator and into my life. It was I who wanted to see you again. Hugh told me to cancel that dinner, it was I was who insisted that we go ahead..." Utterly bemused, drenched in hope, she blinked back at him, struggled to focus as she shifted the murky kaleidoscope of the their brief past into glorious High Definition. "I had to kiss you. I convinced myself that when I did it would be over, but no..." It was Dante who appeared confused how, Dante shaking his head as he recalled. "Like a drug, I need more, we make love and still I tell myself that it is just need that propels me, male needs, that when the garden is finished then so too will we be. I don't want to feel this, Matilda..."

"Why?" Matilda begged. "Because of Jasmine?"

Pain flickered across his face and for a fragment of time she wished she could retract, take back what she had just said, yet somehow Matilda knew it had to be faced, that they could only glimpse the future if he let her into the past. But Dante shook his head, refuted her allegation almost instantly.

"Alex is the one who has to come first..."

"She will," Matilda breathed, sure that wasn't the entire issue, sure that, despite his denial, and his apparent openness, still he was holding back. But as he pulled her into his arms, as he obliterated the world with his masterful touch, she let it go, reassured by his words and a glimpse of the future with Dante by her side and utterly sure she had all the time in the world to source his pain.

One hand was circling the back of her neck now, tiny circular motions that were incredibly soothing but at the same time incredibly erotic. She could feel the steady hammer of his heart against her ear, inhale the unique maleness of him as his gentle words reached her, his lips shivering along the hollow of her neck, moving down to the creamy flesh of her shoulder. His teeth nibbled at the spaghetti strap of her nightdress, his tongue cool against her burning skin, eyes closing as, giddy with want, he pulled the delicate garment downwards, sliding it over her breasts. His hands lingered over her hips as, guided by him, she stepped out of it, facing him now with a mixture of nervousness and raw sexuality, naked apart from the palest of pink silk panties. And the low moan of desire that escaped his lips erased for ever the poisonous roots of self-doubt Edward had so firmly planted, her body fizzing with new hope and desire as he sank to his knees, knowing that to Dante she was beautiful.

His hands were still on her hips but he was kissing her stomach now, deep, throaty kisses that were as faint-making as they were erotic. She could feel his tongue on her skin and it was overwhelming, her tummy tightening in reflex as one hand slipped between her thighs, stroking the pale, tender skin on the inside as his lips moved down. She could feel the heat through the cool silk fabric, his tongue, his lips on her making her weak with want, desperate for him to rip at her panties, to satisfy the desire that was raging in her. She gave tiny gasps in her throat as her fingers knotted together in his hair, as still he teased her more, his teeth grazing the silk, his tongue moistening her more, and even if it was everything she wanted, it still wasn't enough. Realisation hit her that, despite what had taken place in the garden, she'd never seen him naked. Need propelling her, she pulled back a touch, saw the question in his eyes as slowly he stood up. Her fingers, nervous at first, but bolder as desire took over, wrestled with the buttons of his shirt, pushing the sleeves down over his muscular arms. Closing her eyes in giddy want, her pale breasts pressed against his chest. She felt the naked silk of his dark skin against her, skin on skin, as she opened his belt and unzipped his shorts. She held her breath in wonder as Dante now shed the garments that stood between them, and if he'd been beautiful before, he was stunning now.

Never had she seen a more delicious man, his body toned and muscular, his dark, olive skin such a contrast to hers, the ebony of the hair that fanned on his chest tapering down into a delicious, snaky black line that led to the most decadent, delicious male centre. His arousal was terrifying and exciting at the same time, jutting out of silky black hair, proud and angry and alive, and the bed that had looked so daunting was just a tiny breathless step away. As they lay face to face she held him in her hand, marvelling at the strength, the satin softness of the skin that belied the steel beneath it, nervous, tentative at first. But his tiny moans of approval told her she was doing it right. Her other hand was audacious too, cupping his heavy scrotum, holding all of him, and loving it, as his lips found her breasts, suckling on her tender flesh, a tiny gasp catching in her throat as felt him growing stronger, nearer.

"Careful." His voice was thick with lust as his hand captured her wrist, stopped her just in time, and she was greedy now for her turn, biting down on her bottom lip as he ran the tip of his erection over her panties, could see the tiny silver flash that told her he was near. She almost wept with voracious need as his finger slipped inside the fabric, gently parting her pink, intimate lips, sliding deep inside as still he teased her on the outside, sliding his heat against her till she was frenzied, her neck arching backwards, her whole body rigid, fizzing with want.

And Dante was the same, she knew it, as he tore at the delicate panties, ripped them open and plunged deep inside, her orgasm there to greet him, her intimate vise twitching around him as he entered, thrusting inside her.

And yet he made her wait for his, their heated bodies moving together, long, delicious strokes as his moist skin slid over hers, her orgasm fading then rising again as he worked deliciously on, her fingers clutching his taut buttocks, her neck rigid as his tongue, his mouth devoured it, tasting her, relishing her, arousing her all over again. She could feel the tension in him building, his movements faster now, delicious involuntary thrusts as his body dictated the rhythm for both of them, no turning back as he drove them both forward.

He spilled inside her as she came again, crying out his name as he took her higher than she had ever been then held her as she came back down. But if making love with Dante had been exquisite, nothing could rival the feeling of him holding her in his arms, his body spooning into her warm back, the bliss of being held by him, his tender, warm hand on her stomach, his breathing evening out, experiencing the beauty of a bed shared tonight.

And the promise tomorrow could bring.

Chapter 10

"Dante!"

She barely said it, more breathed the word, her eye snapping open as the bedroom door opened. A tiny rigid figure was silhouetted in the doorway, staring at the vast bed, and all Matilda knew was that Alex mustn't see her. She wriggled slightly in his arms, pulling her legs down straight, trying to remain inconspicuous yet somehow awaken him. Gently she prodded him, slipping beneath the covers as he came to, feeling like an intruder hiding, chewing on her bottom lip and cringing inside as Dante took in the scene.

"Alex, darling." She could feel him pull back the covers, groping on the floor for his boxers then stepping out of the bed and crossing the room. "Did something wake you?"

And because it was Alex, there was no answer to his question. Instead, Matilda listened to his comforting words as he scooped the little girl up and carried her back to wards her bedroom. She waited till the coast was clear before wrapping the sheet around her and heading for the *en suite,* pulling on Dante's bathrobe and, despite the oppressive heat of the night, heading back to the bed to sit and shiver on the edge till Dante returned.

"Is she OK?" Worried eyes jerked to his. "I don't think she saw me. It's so dark in here I'm sure that she couldn't have. I just heard the door open…"

"She's fine," Dante instantly reassured her. "I gave her a drink of water and she settled back down. I don't know what's wrong with her tonight…" Sitting down on the bed, he wrapped an arm around her, but she could sense his distraction, knew that he was worried about what Alex might have seen.

"I heard the door open and saw her. I honestly don't think that she saw me. The only reason I could make her out was because the hall light was on. As soon as I heard something, I slipped under the covers."

"She didn't seem worried," Dante agreed. "I think she was just thirsty…" His voice trailed off and Matilda watched as he raked his fingers through his hair, seeing him now not as a lover but as the father he was…

Would always be.

"I'll go back to my room."

"No." He shook his head, one hand reaching out and attempting to grab her wrist. But Matilda captured it, holding his strong hand in her gentler one. And as much as she didn't want to go, as much as she knew Dante wanted her to stay, she knew it was right to leave.

"Dante, it's fine. Alex might come back and neither of us is going to relax now. I'll go and sleep in my room. It's better that way. We've got away with it once…"

"You understand?"

"Completely," Matilda said softly, her free hand cap-

turing his cheek, feeling the scratch of his stubble beneath
her fingers. Although she longed to sleep with him, to
wake up with him, she knew some things were more im
portant, knew that she had to act unselfishly now. "You
need to be here for Alex," she whispered, kissing his taut
cheek, feeling the tension in his body as she held him for
a precious second, knowing he was torn between want
and duty, knowing that she could make things easier for
him by going.

And it wasn't a small comfort as she slipped into her
king-sized single bed, still wrapped in his robe, still warm
from his touch, his intimate spill still moist between her
legs. It was the most grown-up decision she'd ever made.

It was love.

"Dante!"

Brutally awoken by the piercing shout, Matilda sat up
in bed, her mind whirling as chaos broke out. She tried to
piece together the events of the night before and failed as
the urgent events of today thundered in.

"Where is she?"

Wrapping the tie of Dante's bathrobe around her,
Matilda climbed out of bed, her heart hammering at the
urgency in Katrina's voice, waiting, *waiting* for Dante to
reply. For him to tell her that Alex was in bed with him.
Her stomach turned as she opened her bedroom door and
saw Dante's pale, anguished face as he ran the length of the
hallway, desperation in his voice as he called his daugh
ter's name, terrified, frenzied eyes meeting hers as he ex
plained the appalling situation.

"Alex isn't in her bed. We can't find her."

Dashing down the hallway, she careered into Dante, his
face a mixture of fixed determination and wretched pain.

"The pool!" They both said it at the same time. His

worst nightmare eventuating, she followed him, bare feet barely touching the surface, jumping, running, taking the stairs two, three at a time as her mind reasoned. The pool was fenced and gated, Matilda attempted to reason as she ran; Dante was always so careful with his daughter's security there was no way Alex could have got in. As she dashed across the lawn, Dante was miles ahead, naked apart from his boxers, his whole body taut with dread. Finally she reached him, shared in that anguished look at the cool glittering blue surface. But there was little solace to be taken. The glimmering bay twinkled in the sunrise, a vast ocean just metres away and a tiny, fragile child missing.

"Call the police." Dante's voice was calm but his lips were tight, a muscle hammering in his cheek as his idyllic, bayside view turned again to torture. "Tell them to alert the coastguard."

"She was fine last night!" Katrina's brittle voice grated on Matilda's already shot nerves. The police had long since arrived, their radios crackling in the background as officers started the appalling process—interviewing the adults, searching the house and gardens. A frantic race against time ensued. She could hear the whir of helicopter motors as they swooped along the coastline. As she stared at Dante, who had returned at the police's bidding from a frantic race to the beach to look for his daughter, sand on his damp legs, his proud face utterly shattered, her first instinct was to reach out and hold him, to comfort him, but aware of Katrina and how it would look, she held back. "I looked in on her as I went to bed…"

"What time was that?" An incredibly young officer asked as another sat writing notes.

"Eleven, twelve perhaps," Katrina responded. "Dante had already gone up."

"So you were the last person to see her?"

"No," Dante broke in. "I was the last person to see her.
Matilda held her breath as he carried on talking, wonderin
if he would reveal what had happened and with a sinkin
heart knowing that he had to. "She was distressed when
went up, but she went back to sleep. Katrina would hav
seen her a few moment after that, but a couple of hour
later she came into my room."

"She'd climbed out of her cot?"

"She's started to do that," Dante said, raking his fin
gers through his hair, his whole body in abject pain. Sh
ached to comfort him yet sat completely still as he spok
on. "She seemed thirsty so I gave her a drink and cuddle
her for a moment."

"Was she upset?"

"No." Dante shook his head, his face contorting with ag
onized concentration as he recalled every detail of the las
time he had seen his daughter. "At least, I don't think so.

"You don't think so?" the policeman pushed, an
Matilda could have slapped him for his insensitivity. Bu
Dante was calmer, explaining Alex's problem in a mea
sured voice, but his voice was loaded with pain.

"My daughter has problems—behavioural problems.
Katrina opened her mouth to argue, but Dante stood firm
shaking his head at Katrina, clearly indicating that no
wasn't the time for futile denial. "She doesn't react in th
usual way—you never really know what she's thinking
Look, you *have* to tell your colleagues that they could b
just a metre away from her, could be calling her name, an
she won't answer them, she won't call out…" His voic
broke for a second and Matilda watched as he attempte
to recover, his eyes closing for an agonising second as h
forced himself to continue. "You have to tell them that.

The officer nodded to his partner, who left the room t

mpart the news before he continued with the interview.
'You gave her a drink—then what?"

"I opened the window a fraction more—there are locks
on it, so she could never have opened it wide enough to
get out. Her room was…" His English momentarily failed
him. Dante balled his fists in frustration as he tried to give
the police officer each and every piece of information he
could. "Confined," he attempted. "With the storm coming and everything…" As if in answer, a crack of thunder
sounded and Matilda watched the fear dart in his eyes.
The rain started to pelt on the window, each drop ramming
home the fact that his baby was out there with the elements

"Anything else?" the officer checked. "Is there anything else that happened last night that was out of the ordinary? Any strange sounds, phone calls—anything, no
matter how irrelevant it might seem, that might have upset
your daughter?"

Dante's eyes met Matilda's.

"No." He shook his head, dragged his eyes away but
his expression haunted her. The guilt in his eyes as he bypassed the truth made her know without hesitation what
was coming next, that the only person Dante wanted to
protect here, and rightly so, was his daughter.

"Officer, may I speak to you outside?"

"About what?" Katrina demanded as the two of them
walked out of the room. "What aren't you telling us, Dante?
What happened last night that you can't say in front of
me?"

Embarrassed, terrified, Matilda stood there as Katrina
answered her own question.

"You tart," Katrina snarled, and Matilda winced at the
venom behind it. "That's Dante's gown that you're wearing." Katrina eyed Matilda with utter contempt but didn't
leave it there. Her lips were white and rigid with hatred.

"You were in bed with Dante, weren't you? That's why the poor little mite ran off into the night!"

"I truly don't think that she saw me," Matilda said. "We were both asleep and she just pushed open the door…"

"And saw a woman who wasn't her mother in her father's bed! Do you realise what you have done, Matilda?" Disgust and fury were etched on Katrina's features and for an appalling moment Matilda thought that Katrina might even hit her. "Do you have any idea the damage that you've done to my grandchild?"

"Leave it, Katrina." Dante's voice was weary as he came back into the room, but it had a warning note to it that Katrina failed to heed.

"I most certainly will not leave it." Furious eyes swivelled between Dante and Matilda, her face contorted with disgust. "Did Alex see you?" Her eyes were bulging in her head. "That little girl walked in and found the pair of you—"

"It wasn't like that," Matilda said, but Katrina shot her down in a second.

"Shut up!" she screamed. "Shut the hell up. You have no say here! None at all."

"Katrina." Dante crossed the room, his face grey. "This isn't helping…"

"Of course it isn't helping. How, Dante, did you think sleeping with her was going to help your daughter? How did you think shaming my daughter's memory like that was going to help Alex? But, then, I suppose you didn't even stop to think. I warned you, Dante, warned you to be careful, to keep things well away from Alex, and then some little—"

"I said leave it!" Still he didn't shout, but there was such icy power behind his words that even in full, rage-fuelled flood Katrina's voice trailed off. It was Matilda who stepped in. Running a dry tongue over her lips, she again attempted to calm things down.

"All we can do for now is give the police all the information we have and then look for Alex. Arguing isn't going to help."

"She's right," Dante said, addressing Katrina, which momentarily Matilda found strange. But she didn't hold the thought. Her mind was already racing ahead, trying to work out how they could find Alex, where the little girl might be. But as Dante continued talking, Matilda knew that the agony that had pierced her consciousness since awakening had only just begun, because nothing Katrina had said in rage could have hurt her more than the expression on Dante's face as he turned and finally faced her, his expression cold and closed, his eyes not even meeting hers.

"I think you should leave, Matilda…"

"Leave?" She shook her head, her voice incredulous, horrified by what he was saying. "Don't shut me out now, Dante. Last night you said—"

"Last night you were his whore," Katrina shouted. "Last night he said what he had to, to get you to share his bed. Dante loved my daughter." She was screeching now, almost deranged. "Jasmine's barely cold in her grave. Did you really think you could fill her space? Did you really think he meant what he said, that he'd besmirch her memory with you?"

"No one's trying to besmirch Jasmine's memory," Dante said, his face as white as marble as he turned to Katrina.

"No one could!" Katrina yelled. "Because if you truly loved my daughter then last night can be nothing more than a fling and I know that you loved her. I know that!"

"I did." Dante halted her tirade. "I do," he insisted, his hands spreading in the air in a helpless gesture, utter panic on his face as reality started to sink in. "But right now all I can think of is Alex. All I know is that my baby is out there…"

"Let me help with the search," Matilda pleaded, but Dante's back was to her, demanding action from the officer that stood there, picking up the phone and punching in numbers. "Dante, please…"

"You want to help?" His face was unrecognisable as he finally faced her. "If you really want to help, Matilda, you will do as I ask and just go home. It will be better."

"Better for who?" Matilda whispered through chattering teeth, knowing the answer even before it came.

"Better for everyone."

It took about ten minutes to pack, ten minutes to throw her things into her suitcase and drag it down the stairs, ten minutes to remove herself from Dante's life. The scream inside was a mere breath away, her teeth grinding together with the agony of keeping it all in. She wanted to slap him, to yell at him, confront him, couldn't believe that he'd done it to her again, that she'd been stupid enough to let him fool her, to be beguiled by him over again, but somehow she choked it down, the horror of a child missing overriding everything. She placed her own pain, her utter humiliation on total hold. Wincing against the sting of the rain on her bare arms, she threw her case into the boot, imagining its impact on a little girl dressed in nothing but pyjamas.

"We need a contact number, miss." The young officer tapped on the steamed-up car window as Matilda started the engine. She scribbled her number on a piece of paper and handed it to him. "Can I help—with the search I mean?

"Hold on a second, love." The policeman halted her as his radio crackled into life and Matilda waited, her heart in her mouth at the urgent note in the officer's voice, flashes of conversation reaching her ears.

"They've found her?" Matilda begged.

"I need to tell the child's father first." He was making to go but Matilda shot out of the car and ran alongside him as he headed for the house.

"How is she?" Matilda demanded. "Is she okay?"

"I'm not sure," the officer reluctantly answered. "They found her wandering in some dunes. She seems OK but she's not talking. They're taking her to the local hospital…"

"She rarely speaks." Matilda could feel relief literally flooding her at the seemingly good news. "Oh, I have to tell Dante…"

"Miss I really think…" Something in his voice stilled her and, despite the police officer's youthful looks, Matilda saw the wisdom in his eyes as he offered some worldly advice for free. "I think that for now at least you need to leave this family alone. Emotions are already pretty high. Give it a day or two and it will calm down, but I think the best thing you can do now is take Mr Costello's advice and go home."

Chapter 11

Everything was hard—even tidying her tiny apartment required a mammoth effort, yet she felt compelled to do it. Despite her fatigue, and utter exhaustion, she needed to somehow clear the decks, to get things in order before she took on the even bigger task of getting on with the rest of her life.

A life without Dante.

Pushing the vacuum around, Matilda wished the noise from the machine could drown out her thoughts, wished she could just switch off her mind, find some peace from the endless conundrums.

Two weeks ago she hadn't even known he'd existed, he hadn't factored into even one facet of her life, and now he consumed her all—every pore, every breath every cell of her. She was drenched with him, possessed by him, yearned for him, but was furious with him, too. A molten river of anger bubbled over the edge of her grief every now and then that Dante would have let her leave without even knowing whether his daughter was alive or dead, assuming that the world ran on the same emotionless clock as he did, where feelings could be turned off like a light switch and the truth distorted enough to conjure up reasonable doubt.

She'd been home four days now. Four days when he hadn't even bothered to pick up the phone and let her know about Alex—surly she deserved that much at least?

For the first couple of nights Matilda had watched him on the nightly TV news, striding out of the courtroom without comment. She had scanned the newspapers by day for a glimpse of him, trying to read messages that weren't there in the tiny stilted statements that were quoted. But it had become unbearable, seeing him, reading about him yet knowing she couldn't have him, so instead she'd immersed herself in anything she could think of, anything that might turn her mind away from him and give her peace even for a moment. She knew it was useless, knew that she could work till she dropped, could fill her diary with engagements, could go out with friends every night, but she'd never fully escape, that all she could hope was that the agony might abate, might relent just enough to allow her to breathe a little more easily.

Kicking off the vacuum, Matilda gave in and padded towards the wardrobe, as she had done repeatedly for the last four days. She pulled out Dante's dressing-gown, which in her haste she had inadvertently packed, feeling the heavy fabric between her fingers, knowing that the sensible thing to do would be to throw it into the washing machine, to parcel it up and mail it to him. But it was the one task she was putting off, pathetically aware that apart from her bittersweet memories it was the only reminder of Dante she had. Sitting on the edge of the bed, she buried her face in the robe, dragging in his evocative aroma. And it was like feeling it all over again, every breath reinforcing the agony of his rejection, the blistering pain of his denial. A scent that had once been so beautiful was tainted now for ever. In fact, it almost made her feel nauseous now as she revisited the pain, the devastation…

"Alex!"

For the first time in days, Dante left her mind, the name of his daughter shivering out of her lips, but it wasn't a sob. Her tears turned off like a tap, thoughts, impossible, incredulous thoughts pinging in, realisation dawning. She shook her head to clear it, because surely it couldn't be so…surely the thought that had just occurred would be flawed on examination, that Alex's problems couldn't really be that simple. But instead, the more she thought about it the more sense it made, the more she had to share it.

"Hugh." Her hands were shaking so much after several fruitless attempts to reach Dante that she'd had to dial his number several times. "I need to speak to Dante. His phone's turned off, but is there any way when the court takes a break—"

"He's not here." Hugh's voice was so flat, so low, that Matilda had to strain to catch it.

"Can you give me his assistant's number?" Matilda asked, shame and embarrassment pushed aside. Right now she didn't care about Dante's response to her—this was way, way more important.

"Matilda, have you seen the newspaper, the television?" Hugh asked, as her free hand flicked on the remote, wondering what on earth Hugh was going on about. "The charges were all dropped, the trial finished two days ago…"

"Two days ago?" Matilda's mind raced for comfort but there was none to be had. She couldn't even pretend it was because of the trial, because of work that he hadn't called her. But she dragged herself to the present, forced herself to focus on the reason she needed to talk to him so badly. "Hugh, I need to speak to him urgently." Her voice was the most assertive she'd ever heard it. "Now, can you, please, tell me how I can get hold of him?"

"He's in Italy." And even though she wanted to have misheard, even though at the eleventh hour she mentally begged for a reprieve, Matilda knew from the utter devastation in Hugh's voice that there wouldn't be one.

Dante really had gone.

"He's asked me not to ring for a few weeks, Matilda. He wants some time to sort things out and I've tried to respect that—not that it matters. I know that his housekeeper won't put me through and I'm pretty sure she wouldn't put…"

He didn't say it, didn't twist the taut knife any further, but they both knew the words that filled the silence that crackled down the telephone line. If he wouldn't even speak to Hugh, what hope was there of Dante speaking to her?

"Hugh." Matilda's mind was going at a thousand miles an hour. She knew she couldn't tell Hugh what she thought she knew, couldn't build him up just to tear him down, knew she had to tread carefully now. "Could I ask you to give me his address?"

"I don't know." She could feel his hesitation, knew that she was asking him to cross a line, but she also knew that Hugh wanted Dante back in Australia more than anything in the world, and if something Matilda said could make that happen then perhaps it was worth a try. "I guess it wouldn't do any harm to write to him, then it's up to Dante whether or not he reads it."

Matilda held her breath as she scrabbled for a pen, then closed her eyes in blessed relief as finally, after the longest time, Hugh gave it to her.

"Thanks, Hugh." Matilda said, clicking off the telephone, and even though it was the biggest, possibly the most reckless decision of her life, amazingly she didn't hesitate. She flicked through the phone book before making her second call of the day, knowing that if she thought about it, tried to rationalise it, she'd never do it.

"I'd like to book a flight to Rome, please."

"When did you want to go?" Running a shaking hand through her hair, Matilda listened to the efficient voice, could hear the taps on the keyboard as the woman typed in the information. Taking a deep breath, she uttered the most terrifying words of her life.

"I'd like the next available flight, please."

Chapter 12

"**I**'m sorry the flight has been overbooked."

Matilda could barely take it in, just blinked back as the well-groomed woman tapped over and over at her computer. She was scarcely able to believe what she was hearing, that the seat she'd booked and paid for just a few short hours ago had never been available in the first place, that flights were often overbooked and that if she read the fine print on her ticket she'd realise that there was nothing she could do—that she'd just have to wait until the next flight.

"When is the next flight?" Matilda's trembling voice asked, watching the long, immaculately polished nails stroking the keyboards.

"I can get you on tomorrow at eleven a.m."

She might just as well have said the next millennium, Matilda realised, because her conviction left her then, the conviction that had forced her to pick up the telephone and book her flight, the conviction that had seen her pack at lightning speed, cancel work, persuade her family, hissed out of her like the air in a balloon when the party was over. And it *was* over, Matilda realised.

If ever she'd wanted a sign, this was it—and it wasn't a subtle one. Neon lights flashing over the ground steward's head couldn't have spelt it out clearer.

She'd been stupid to think she could do it, could convince Dante what she felt in her heart was wrong with Alex. Her family, her friends had all poured scorn on the idea, even she herself had when she'd attempted to write down what was screaming so clearly in her mind. That was the reason she had to see Dante face to face, *had* to tell him now, couldn't put it in a letter, couldn't wait for tomorrow, because only now could she really believe it—only now, before her argument was swayed, before she attempted to rationalise what she was sure was true.

Was true because she'd felt it herself.

Had felt it.

"We can offer a refund."

"I don't want a refund." Matilda shook her head. "I have to get this flight." She heard the words, knew it was her own voice, but even she couldn't believe the strength behind it. "I have to get this flight because if I don't get on this plane tonight, I know that I'm never going to…"

And she'd watched the airport shows, had watched passengers pleading their cases, shouting their rage, and had winced from the comfort of her sofa, knowing that no matter how loud they shouted, if the flight was full, if the gate was closed, then they might as well just give up now.

"Gate 10."

"Sorry?" Matilda started, watching as a tag was swiftly clipped around a rather shabby suitcase before it bumped out of view, watching as those manicured fingers caught the boarding pass from the printer and offered it to her.

"Gate 10," came the clipped voice. "Business and first class are boarding now—you'd better step on it."

And the most infrequent of frequent flyers Matilda might have been, but she wasn't a complete novice either. Her overwrought mind worked overtime as she made it through passport control then dashed along the carpeted floors of Melbourne airport, walked along the long passageway, knowing that the comfort level of the next twenty-four hours was entirely dependent on a single gesture.

Right for Economy.

Left for Business.

"Good evening, Miss Hamilton." Blond, gorgeous and delightfully gay, the flight attendant greeted her and Matilda held her breath, playing a perverse game of he loves me, he loves me not. He checked her ticket and gestured her to her seat.

"Straight through to your left, first row behind the curtain."

And it didn't matter if he loved her or he loved her not, Matilda decided, slipping into her huge seat and declining an orange juice but accepting champagne in a glass. It didn't matter that she couldn't really afford the air fare and that if she lived to be a thousand she'd never be able to justify flying to the other side of the world on a hunch. If she'd wanted a sign then she had one. She really was doing the right thing, not for herself, not even for Dante... but for Alex.

Rome, Matilda decided, had to be the most beautiful city in the world, because jet-lagged, at six a.m. on a cold grey morning and nursing a broken heart, nothing in the world should have been able to lift her spirits, but hurtling through the streets of the Eternal City in a taxi, Matilda was captivated. So captivated that when the hotel receptionist informed her in no uncertain terms that her room wouldn't be ready for a couple more hours, Matilda was happy to leave her rather small suitcase at the hotel and wander the streets, plunged from the boskiness of a late Australian spring to a crisp Italian autumn.

A fascinated bystander, Matilda watched as the Eternal City awoke, the roads noisily filling up, cars, scooters, cycles, the pavements spilling over with beautiful, elegant people, chattering loudly in their lyrical language as they raced confidently past or halted a moment for an impossibly strong coffee. Everyone, except for her, seemed to know their place, know where they were going. Matilda, in contrast, meandered along cobbled streets which were rich with history, yet welcomed the modern—buildings that had stood for centuries housing a treasure trove of modern fashion, glimpsing a part of Dante's world and knowing that he was near. Wondering how to face him, how to approach him, how to let him know that she was there.

Message Sent

Matilda stared at the screen of her much-hated phone and for the first time was actually grateful to have it. Grateful for the ease of rapid contact without speech. Well, not that rapid, Matilda thought ordering another latté to replace her long since cold one, watching as some fabulous, twenty-first-century Sophia Loren managed to drink, smoke, read and text at the same time. After a few failed attempts she'd managed to get her message across, had told Dante where she was now and where she would be staying later and asking if they could meet for a discussion—snappy, direct and impersonal.

Everything she'd tried and failed to be.

But when her message brought no response, when, looking at her watch, Matilda realised her room would be ready and she pulled out her purse and unpeeled the unfamiliar money, only then did the magnitude of what she had done actually catch up with her. Nerves truly hit as she realised that for all she knew, Dante might not even be in Italy—he could have stopped in Bangkok or Singapore for a break. It had seemed so important to see him at the time, it had never actually dawned on her that Dante might not want to see her, that she could have come all this way only to find out that he didn't even care what she had to say. Maybe she should have made it clear that she'd come to talk about Alex. Perhaps if she texted him again...

"Matilda."

Thankful that her fingers were still in her purse and not creeping towards her phone, Matilda took the longest time to look up—truly unsure how she felt when she finally stared into the face whose loss she had been mourning. He looked older somehow, his skin a touch paler, the shadows under his eyes like bruises now, as if all the trouble of the past eighteen months had finally caught up with him— nothing like the dashing young barrister who'd walked out of a Melbourne courtroom a few days ago. Clearly he hadn't shaved since then, but instead of looking scruffy it gave him a slightly tortured, artistic look. Matilda decided, as he slid into the seat next to her and consumed her all over again, there was still more than a dash of the old Dante, still that irrefutable sex appeal.

Odd that when there was so much to say, when it was so outlandish that she was actually here, that the silence they sat in for a few moments wasn't particularly uncomfortable. Matilda gathered the images that fluttered in her mind, knowing she would take them out and explore them later. Dante accepted the coffee and plate of *biscotti* from the waiter and pushed them towards her.

"No, thanks." Matilda shook her head and Dante obviously wasn't hungry either because he pushed the plate away untouched.

"Seems I was wrong about you," he said finally. "You're not afraid of confrontation after all."

"Actually, you were right." Matilda gave a pale smile. "I'm not here to confront you, Dante." She watched as his eyes narrowed. "Whatever your opinion of me, please, know that I've got a better one of myself, and chasing after a man who clearly doesn't want me has never been my style."

She watched his face harden, watched his jaw crease as if swallowing some vile taste down before speaking, his voice almost derisive because clearly he thought he knew better than her, clearly he assumed that she was lying. "So why are you here, then, Matilda? If not about us, why are you here in Rome?"

"I'm here about Alex." It was obviously the last thing he'd expected her to say because his face flickered in confusion, his eyes frowning as she continued. "I think I know what's wrong with her. I think I've worked out what causes her to get upset, why she continues…"

"Matilda." In a supremely Latin gesture he flicked her words away with his hands. "I have consulted with the top specialists, I have had my daughter examined from head to toe and you, after one week of knowing her, after barely spending—"

"It's jasmine." The two words stopped him in mid-sentence. His mouth opened to continue, to no doubt tell her she had no idea what she was talking about, but her urgent voice overrode him, her frantic eyes pinning him. Matilda knew if he would only listen to her for a single minute then it had to be a valuable one, that even if he didn't believe her now then maybe tonight, next week, next month, when they were both out of each other's lives for ever, when the pain of this moment had passed, he would recall her words objectively and maybe, maybe they'd make sense.

"The *scent* of jasmine," Matilda specified, as Dante shook his head. "That first day she lost her temper, the first day you called for a doctor, you told me you were on your way to the cemetery."

"So?"

"Did you take flowers?" When he didn't respond she pushed harder, her heart hammering in her chest, because if she'd got this bit mistaken then her whole theory fell apart. But as she spoke Dante blinked a couple of times, his scathing face swinging around in alarm as she asked her next question. "Did you take some jasmine from the garden?"

"Of course. But—"

"You sent flowers the day Jasmine died, Dante," she said softly. "And Katrina told me you'd had every florist in Melbourne trying to find some jasmine. Alex was trapped in a car for two hours with her mother, calling out for her, desperate for reassurance, trapped with that smell…"

"But a scent cannot trigger such a reaction." Dante shook his head in firm denial, absolutely refusing to believe it could be so simple. But at least he was listening, Matilda consoled herself as she carried on talking, her own conviction growing with each word she uttered, the hunch that had brought her to this point a matter of fact now.

"Alex's trouble started in spring, Dante, when the jasmine was flowering, and when it became too much, when all she got was worse, you took her back to Italy…"

"Things were better for a while," Dante argued. "She was fine until…" His hand was over his mouth, his eyes widening as Matilda said it for him.

"Until spring came again. Dante, she didn't run away because she saw us in bed. Alex ran away because you opened the window. It was humid, the scent would have filled the room…"

"She was trying to get away from it?"

"I don't know," Matilda whispered. "I don't know what she's thinking. I just know that I'm right, Dante."

"Suppose that you are." His eyes were almost defiant. "What am I supposed to do? I can hardly rid the world of jasmine, ensure she never inhales that scent again…"

"Why do you always have to go to such extremes, Dante? Why does it always have to be black and white to you? Oh, this isn't working so I'll leave the country. She seems nice, so I'll just be mean. Alex reacts to jasmine, so I'd better get rid of it. Just acknowledge it, Dante, and then find out how to work through it. Tell the experts, the doctors…" She gave a helpless shrug, then picked up her purse and put it firmly in her bag—hell, he could buy her a coffee at least.

"You're going?" Dante frowned as she stood.

"That's all I came here to say."

"That's all?" Dante scorned, clearly not believing a word. "You could have put that in a letter, rung me."

"Would you have read it?" Matilda checked. "Would you have picked up the phone? And even if you had, would you really have believed it without seeing me?"

"Probably not," Dante admitted.

"Well, there you go," Matilda said, heading for the door and out into the cool morning. She stilled as he called out to her, his skeptical voice reaching her ears.

"You're asking me to believe you flew to the other side of the world for a child you have seen four maybe five times."

"I'm not *asking* you to believe anything, Dante." The lid was off now, rivers of lava spewing over the edges as she turned round and walked smartly back to where he was standing, her pale face livid as she looked angrily up to him. "I'm *telling* you that I didn't come here to discuss us. Get it into your head, I don't need a grand closing speech from you, there's no jury you have to sum up for here. You walked out without so much as a goodbye and that's a clear enough message even for me. I'm certainly not going to hover on the edges of your emotions, either waiting for permission to enter or to be told again to leave."

"I told you from the start that there could be no relationship," Dante said through gritted teeth.

"Well, you were right." Matilda nodded. "Because a relationship is about trusting and sharing and giving, and you're incapable of all three."

"Matilda, I have a child who is sick and getting worse by the day. I was doing you a favour by holding back. How could I ask you to turn your life around for us? It's better this way…"

"Don't you dare!" Matilda roared, startling Dante and everyone in earshot. Even if the Italians were used to uncensored passion, clearly eight-thirty on a weekday morning was a little early for them. But Matilda was operating on a different time clock. It was the middle of the night in her mind as her emotions finally erupted, oblivious of the gathering crowd as finally she let him have it. "Don't you dare decide what's best for me when you didn't even have the manners to ask. I loved you and you didn't want it. Well, fine, walk away, get on a plane and leave the country, walk out of my life without a goodbye, but don't you dare tell me it's for the best, don't you dare stand there and tell me that you're doing me a favour—when I never asked for one. I flew to the other side of the world because I care about your daughter and in time I'd have loved Alex, too. I'd have loved Alex because she was a part of you, and you *know* that, you *know* that, Dante." She jabbed a finger into his chest, jabbed the words at him over and over, ramming the truth home to the motionless, rigid man. "You didn't want my love—that's the bottom line so don't dress it up with excuses. You love Jasmine and you always will."

"I loved Jasmine—" He started but she turned to walk away because she couldn't bear to look at him. She pushed her way through the little gathered crowd and started to run because she couldn't bear to be close to him and not have him, couldn't be strong for even a second longer. She'd said all she had come to and way, way more, had told him her truth. There was nothing left to give and certainly nothing more to take. She didn't want his crumbs of comfort, didn't want to hear how in another place, another time, maybe they could have made it.

"Matilda." He caught her wrist but she couldn't take the contact, the shooting awareness that had propelled them on that first day even more acute, even more torturous. She tried to wrench it away, but he gripped it tighter, forced her to turn around and face him. *"Senti,"* he demanded. "Listen to me!" But she shook her head.

"No, because there's nothing else to say."

"Please?"

That one word stilled her, the one word she'd never heard him say, because he'd never had to ask politely for anything. Dante had never had to ask anyone for anything because it had all been there for the taking.

Till now.

"Please," he said again, and she nodded tentatively. She felt his fingers loosen a touch round her wrist, grateful now for the contact as he led her away from the crowded streets and to the Villa Borghese, a green haven in the middle of the city. He led her through the park to a bench where they sat. Silent tears streaming down her face from her outpouring of emotion, she braced herself for the next onslaught of pain, biting on her lip as Dante implored her to listen, no doubt to tell her as he had in the first place why it could never, ever have worked.

"I loved Jasmine..." he said slowly, letting his hands warm hers. She was touching him for the last time, staring down at his long, manicured fingers entwined in hers and even managing a wan smile at the contrast, her hands certainly not her best feature. But it wasn't her short nails or her prolonged misuse of moisturiser that had Matilda frowning. Eyes that were swimming with tears struggled to focus on a gold band that was missing, a wedding band that to this day had always been there. Her confusion grew as Dante continued talking. "But not like this."

"Like what?" Matilda croaked, still staring at his naked ring finger.

"Like *this*." Dante's voice was a hoarse whisper, but she could hear the passion and emotion behind it and something else that drew her eyes to his, recognition greeting her as Dante continued. *"This* love."

He didn't have to elaborate because she knew exactly what he meant—*this* love that was all-consuming, *this* love that was so overwhelming and intense it could surely only be experienced once in a lifetime. And she glimpsed his hellish guilt then, guessed a little of what was coming next as he pulled her into his arms as if he needed to feel her to go on.

"We were arguing the day she died—we were always arguing." He paused but she didn't fill it, knew Dante had to tell her his story himself. "When I met Jasmine she was a career-woman and had absolutely no intention of settling down or starting a family, and that suited me fine. We were good together. I didn't have to explain the hours I put into my work and neither did she. It worked, Matilda, it really worked, until..." She felt him stiffen in her arms, felt him falter and held him just a touch tighter. "Jasmine found out she was pregnant. We were both stunned. We'd taken precautions, it just wasn't part of the plan, wasn't what either of us wanted, and yet…" He pulled her chin up and she stared up at him, stared as that pain-ravaged face broke into a ghost of a smile. "I was pleased, too, excited. I loved her and she was having my baby, and I thought that would be enough."

"But it wasn't?" Her voice was muffled by his embrace but Matilda already knew the answer.

"No."

Or part of it.

"It wasn't enough for Jasmine. We got married quickly and bought this house and for a few months things were OK, but as Jasmine got bigger as the birth came closer, she seemed to resent the impact her pregnancy was having on her career. She was determined to go straight back to work afterwards, to carry on as if nothing had happened, and that is when the arguments started, because our baby was coming, like it or not, and things had to change. I tried to stay quiet, hoped that once the baby came she'd see things differently, but she didn't. She hired a top nanny and was back at work within six weeks, full time. She hardly saw Alex. I understand women work, I understand that, but not to the exclusion of their child, not when you don't need the money. That is when the arguments escalated."

"People argue Dante…" Matilda tried to comfort him, tried to say the right thing, but knew it was useless. Despite their closeness, she could feel the wall around him, knew the pain behind it and ached to reach him, *ached* for him.

"She felt trapped, I know that," Dante said, his voice utterly bleak. "I know that, because so did I. Not that we ever said it, not that either of us had the courage to admit it. The morning of the accident, *again* she was going into the office. It was a Saturday and the nanny was off and *again* she wanted me to have Alex, only this time I said no. No. No. No…" He repeated the word like a torturous mantra. "No. You are her mother. No, for once you have her. No, I'm going out. I told her it was wrong, that Alex deserved a better mother. I told her so many things terrible things…" She heard the break in his voice and moved to help him.

"Dante, people say terrible things in an argument. You just didn't get the chance to take them back."

"I tried to—even as I was saying them I wanted it to stop, to put the genie back in the bottle and retract the things I had said. I did not want it to be over, I did not want Alex to come from a broken home. I rang the housekeeper and was told Jasmine had taken Alex to work with her. She wouldn't pick up when I called and I had the florist send flowers over to her office. I told them to write that all I wanted was for her to come home… She never did."

"Oh, God, Dante…" Matilda knew she was supposed to be strong now, to somehow magic up the right words, but all she could do was cry—for him, for Jasmine and for the stupid mess that was no one's fault, for the pain, for both of them.

"She *was* coming home, Dante," Matilda said finally, pressing her cheek against his, trying to instil warmth where there was none, her tears mingling with his. "She got the flowers, she knew you were sorry…"

"Not sorry enough, though." He closed his eyes in bitter regret, self-loathing distorting his beautiful features. "Not sorry enough, because I was still angry. The problems were all still there and even if she hadn't died, I know deep down that sooner or later our marriage would have."

"You don't know that, Dante, because you never got the chance to find out," Matilda said softly. "Who knows what would have happened if Jasmine had come home that day? Maybe you would have talked, would have sorted things out…"

"Maybe…" Dante said, but she could tell he didn't believe it, tell that he'd tried and failed to convince himself of the same thing. "You know what I hate the most? I hate the sympathy, I hate that people think I deserve it."

"You do deserve it," Matilda said. "Just because the two of you were having troubles, it doesn't mean you were bad people."

"Perhaps," Dante sighed. "But I cannot burst Katrina and Hugh's bubble, cannot tell them that their daughter's last months were not happy ones…"

"You don't have to tell them anything." Matilda shook her head. "Tell them if you must that Jasmine made you so happy you want to do it all over again." She cupped his proud face in her hand and forced him to look at her, smiled, not because it was funny but because it was so incredibly easy to help him, so incredibly *right* to lead him away from his pain. "You did nothing wrong.

"Nothing," she reiterated.

"But suppose that you'd walked into that lift two years ago, Matilda?" Dante asked. "Suppose, after yet another row, the love of my life had appeared then? I punish Edward for what he did to you and yet…"

"Never." Matilda shook her head, blew away his self-doubt with her utter conviction. "You'd never have done that to Jasmine and you know that as much as I do, Dante, because even if the feelings had been there, you'd never have acted on them. My God, you're barely acting on them now, so surely you know that much about yourself."

And he must have, because finally he nodded.

"Don't beat yourself up with questions you can never answer," Matilda said softly. "You and Jasmine did your best—just hold onto the fact that there was enough love to stop either of you walking away. You sent her flowers and asked her to come home and that's exactly what she was doing. The truth is enough to hold onto."

And she watched as the pain that had been there since she'd first met him literally melted away, dark, troubled eyes glimmering with new-found hope. But it faded into a frown as Matilda's voice suddenly changed from understanding to angry, pulling back her hands and folding her arms, resting her chin on her chest and staring fixedly ahead. "You're so bloody arrogant, Dante!"

"What the hell did I do now?" Dante asked, stunned at the sudden change in her.

"Sitting there and wondering whether or not you'd have had an affair with me! As if I had absolutely no say in the matter! Well, for your information, Dante Costello, I'd have slapped your damned cheek if you'd so much as laid a finger on me. I'd never get involved with a married man!"

"Unless he was your husband!" Dante said, uncoiling her rigid arms, kissing her face all over in such a heavenly Italian way. "That was actually a proposal—just in case you were wondering."

Matilda kissed him back with such passion and depth that if they had been in any city other than Rome, they'd no doubt have been arrested. It was Dante who pulled away, demanding a response from a grumbling Matilda, who wanted his kiss to go on for ever.

"That was actually a yes." Matilda smiled, happy to go back to being ravished, to being kissed by the most difficult, complicated, beautiful man in the world. "Just in case you were wondering!"

Epilogue

"Are you OK?"

Standing in the garden—in *Alex's* garden—Matilda hastily wiped the tears from her cheeks as Dante approached, determined that he wouldn't see her cry. Today was surely hard enough for him without her tears making things worse.

"I'm fine," Matilda answered, forcing a bright smile as she turned around. But watching him walk over, Alex running alongside him, Dante's hand shielding their newborn son's tiny face from the early morning sun with such tenderness, her reserve melted, the tears resuming as he joined her.

"It's OK to be sad," Dante said softly. "And you can't argue, because you said it yourself."

"I did," Matilda gulped, but as the sound of the removal trucks pulling into the drive reached her, she gave in, letting him hold her as she wept. "I feel guilty for being upset

t leaving when I know how much harder this is for you.
know this is your house..."

"Our house," Dante corrected, but Matilda shook her
head.

"It was yours and Jasmine's first so, please, don't try
nd tell me that you're not hurting, too."

"A bit," Dante admitted, gazing down at Joe, tracing
is cheek with his finger, "but I was giving Joe his bot-
le, thinking about our new home and Alex was running
round, checking her dolls were all in her bag, laughing
nd talking, and I promise you, Matilda, all I felt was
eace. I knew in my heart of hearts that Jasmine was happy
or me, was finally able to admit..." He didn't finish but
ave a tiny wry smile and attempted to change the subject,
ut Matilda was having none of it.

"Tell me, Dante," she urged, because despite all the
rogress, despite their closeness, sometimes with Dante
he had to. "Please, tell me what you were thinking."

"That I loved her." He was watching her closely for her
eaction, an apology on the tip of his tongue, but he held it
ack as she smiled. "Is it OK to say that to you?"

"It's more than OK, Dante," came Matilda's heartfelt
nswer. "It's exactly how it should be."

"I know we had our faults, I know that it probably
vouldn't have worked, but sometimes when I see Alex
aughing now, sometimes when she is being cheeky or
unny, I can actually see Jasmine in her and finally I am
ble to remember the good bits. Finally I know that she is
n a peaceful place. I know that she is proud of the choices
have made, and it's all because of you."

She didn't even attempt to hide her tears, just leant on
im as he spoke on.

"It's right to move on, right that we make a new start,
vith our little family."

"But just because we're looking to the future, it doesn mean we have to shut out the past," Matilda assured him "Even Katrina seems to have come around."

She had. In the tumultuous weeks that had followe their revelation, it would have been so easy to hate her, bu in the end Matilda had seen Katrina for what she was, mother that was grieving, a mother terrified of the worl moving on and leaving her daughter's memories behind And slowly the tide had turned. Alex's stunning progress Dante's respect, coupled with Matilda's patience, had wo the coldest heart around.

"We need to do this," Dante affirmed. "We need t make new memories, build new gardens and look to th future..." He didn't finish, the words knocked from hir as a very jealous young lady flung her arms around bot of them, eyeing her new brother with blatant disapprov as she demanded to join in the cuddle.

"Together." Matilda laughed, scooping up Alex, clos ing her eyes in bliss as the little girl rained kisses on he face. "We'll do it together."

* * * * *

We hope you enjoyed reading
the bonus story

MISTRESS AND MOTHER

by *USA TODAY* bestselling author

CAROL MARINELLI

This story was originally from our
Harlequin® Presents® series.

Look for six compelling new romances every
month from Harlequin Presents!

Glamorous international settings…
unforgettable men…passionate romances—
Harlequin Presents promises you the world!

Available wherever books are sold.

www.Harlequin.com

*If you enjoyed this story from Carol Marinelli,
read on for a sneak-peek excerpt from her upcoming
Harlequin Presents® story, BANISHED TO THE HAREM*

***

It felt as if Natasha had been sleeping forever. The plan
was darker when she awoke, the shutters down, and sh
stretched luxuriously, a little surprised when she looke
over to see that Rakhal was on his computer. He was no
dressed in the suit she was used to; instead he'd change
into robes and placed a kaffiyeh on his head. Natasha's firs
thought was, to her shame, a little bit of embarrassment a
the thought of walking around Paris with him dressed lik
that. He looked so royal, so imposing. But even before tha
thought had fully processed, before Rakhal turned aroun
the truth was dawning. He wasn't taking her to Paris....

"How long till we land?" Still she tried to deny th
obvious, because things like this surely couldn't happen.

"A couple of hours." Rakhal didn't even attempt to lie.

"And how long have I been asleep?"

"For a while."

She tried to keep calm, but fear was coursing in, pani
had her racing from the bed to him, to confront him wher
he sat.

"You can't do this...."

"This is about protecting what is mine." Rakhal wa
completely unmoved by her dramatics, for she was startin
to beat him with her hands, but he captured her wrists.

"Why are you doing this to me?"

"Because I could not leave you at your home...if yo
are pregnant with my child then I need to be certain you ar

aking care of yourself and will do nothing to jeopardize the aby's existence. You will stay in the palace, where you'll e well looked after."

"Where will you be?"

"In the desert. Soon I am to take a wife. It is right that I o there for contemplation and meditation, whilst we await o see the outcome with you. You will be very well taken are of and if you are not pregnant, of course you can come ack home."

She could feel hysteria rising, wanted to slap him, vanted to run for the emergency exit, but still he held her vrists; there was nothing, but nothing she could do.

"And if I am?" she begged, but already she knew the nswer.

"If you are pregnant—" so matter-of-fact was his voice s he said it, as her heart hammered in her chest "—then here is no question that we will marry."

***

Look for BANISHED TO THE HAREM,
available October 16, 2012, wherever books are sold.

HARLEQUIN *Presents*

Save $1.00 on the purchase of
BANISHED TO THE HAREM
by **Carol Marinelli**,

available October 16, 2012,
or on any other Harlequin® Presents® book.

Available wherever books are sold, including most bookstores,
supermarkets, drugstores and discount stores.

- -

Save $1.00

**on the purchase of
BANISHED TO THE HAREM
by Carol Marinelli,**
available October 16, 2012,
or on any other Harlequin® Presents® book.

Coupon valid until January 23, 2013. Redeemable at participating retail outlets
in the U.S. and Canada only. Limit one coupon per customer.

52610413

Canadian Retailers: Harlequin Enterprises Limited will pay the face v
of this coupon plus 10.25¢ if submitted by customer for this product only.
other use constitutes fraud. Coupon is nonassignable. Void if taxed, prohib
or restricted by law. Consumer must pay any government taxes. Void if cop
Nielsen Clearing House ("NCH") customers submit coupons and proof of sale
Harlequin Enterprises Limited, P.O. Box 3000, Saint John, NB E2L 4L3, Can
Non-NCH retailer—for reimbursement submit coupons and proof of sales dire
to Harlequin Enterprises Limited, Retail Marketing Department, 225 Duncan
Rd., Don Mills, ON M3B 3K9, Canada.

U.S. Retailers: Harlequin Enterpri
Limited will pay the face value of this cou
plus 8¢ if submitted by customer for
product only. Any other use constitutes fr
Coupon is nonassignable. Void if ta
prohibited or restricted by law. Consumer r
pay any government taxes. Void if copied.
reimbursement submit coupons and proo
sales directly to Harlequin Enterprises Lim
P.O. Box 880478, El Paso, TX 88588-0
U.S.A. Cash value 1/100 cents.

5 65373 00076 2   (8100)0 11803

NYTCOUP081.

REQUEST YOUR
FREE BOOKS!

2 FREE NOVELS
FROM THE ROMANCE COLLECTION
PLUS 2 FREE GIFTS!

YES! Please send me 2 FREE novels from the Romance Collection and my 2 FREE gifts (gifts are worth about $10). After receiving them, if I don't wish to receive any more books, I can return the shipping statement marked "cancel." If I don't cancel, I will receive 4 brand-new novels every month and be billed just $5.99 per book in the U.S. or $6.49 per book in Canada. That's a saving of at least 25% off the cover price. It's quite a bargain! Shipping and handling is just 50¢ per book in the U.S. and 75¢ per book in Canada.* I understand that accepting the 2 free books and gifts places me under no obligation to buy anything. I can always return a shipment and cancel at any time. Even if I never buy another book, the two free books and gifts are mine to keep forever.

194/394 MDN FELQ

Name	(PLEASE PRINT)	
Address		Apt. #
City	State/Prov.	Zip/Postal Code

Signature (if under 18, a parent or guardian must sign)

Mail to the **Reader Service:**
IN U.S.A.: P.O. Box 1867, Buffalo, NY 14240-1867
IN CANADA: P.O. Box 609, Fort Erie, Ontario L2A 5X3

Not valid for current subscribers to the Romance Collection
or the Romance/Suspense Collection.

Want to try two free books from another line?
Call 1-800-873-8635 or visit www.ReaderService.com.

* Terms and prices subject to change without notice. Prices do not include applicable taxes. Sales tax applicable in N.Y. Canadian residents will be charged applicable taxes. Offer not valid in Quebec. This offer is limited to one order per household. All orders subject to credit approval. Credit or debit balances in a customer's account(s) may be offset by any other outstanding balance owed by or to the customer. Please allow 4 to 6 weeks for delivery. Offer available while quantities last.

Your Privacy—The Reader Service is committed to protecting your privacy. Our Privacy Policy is available online at www.ReaderService.com or upon request from the Reader Service.

We make a portion of our mailing list available to reputable third parties that offer products we believe may interest you. If you prefer we not exchange your name with third parties, or if you wish to clarify or modify your communication preferences, please visit us at www.ReaderService.com/consumerschoice or write to us at Reader Service Preference Service, P.O. Box 9062, Buffalo, NY 14269. Include your complete name and address.

He's the last man on earth she should want....

A red-hot new romance from
New York Times **bestselling author**

Susan Andersen

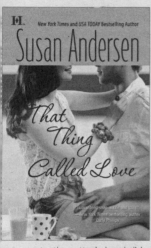

For a guy she's fantasized about throttling, Jake Bradshaw sure is easy on the eyes. In fact, he seriously tempts inn manager Jenny Salazar to put her hands to better use. Except this is the guy who left Razor Bay—and his young son, Austin, whom Jenny adores like her own—to become a globe-trotting photojournalist. He can't just waltz back and claim Austin now.

But Jake has come home, and he wants—no, needs—to make up for his mistake. He intends to stay in Razor Bay only until he can convince Austin to return with him to New York. Trouble is, with sexy, protective, utterly irresistible Jenny in his life, and his bed, he may never want to leave....

That Thing Called Love

Available now!